DOUBTFUL RELATIONS

THE SEAMUS MCCREE SERIES
BY JAMES M. JACKSON

Ant Farm
Bad Policy
Cabin Fever
Doubtful Relations

NON-FICTION
BY JIM JACKSON

One Trick at a Time:
How to Start Winning at Bridge

DOUBTFUL RELATIONS

A SEAMUS MCCREE NOVEL

James M. Jackson

First Edition
Trade Paperback Edition: August 2016

Cover Design by Karen Phillips

Wolf's Echo Press
PO Box 54
Amasa, MI 49903
www.WolfsEchoPress.com

This is a work of fiction. Any references to real places, real people, real organizations, or historical events are used fictitiously. Other names, characters, organizations, places, or events are the product of the author's imagination.

ISBN-13 Trade Paperback: 978-1-943166-04-6
Library of Congress Control Number: 2016909968

Printed in the United States of America
10987654321

Dedication

To my mother, Suzanne Montgomery Jackson

One

MOMENTUM, OBLIGATION, AND A SPECK of hope pulled me down the Masonic Hall stairwell and out the door. On the back stoop, I reread the text message. *Good News. Call ASAP Urgent.* The more I considered it, the more I was not reassured at nine thirty on a Friday night by the juxtaposition of "good news" with "urgent."

"Happy June first," Karen Miller, my real estate agent, said once we connected. "We've received a full-price offer on your house. It comes with a few conditions. Naturally. Inspection, which we know will be fine."

Her tone struck me as overly cheery. I caught myself chewing my inner cheek. "You're telling me the good stuff. What's urgent?"

"That's the Seamus McCree I appreciate. Always to the point. The buyer insists on meeting you face-to-face. I have absolutely no clue why, and I don't think her broker does either. Makes me nervous."

I wasn't nervous; the worst that could happen was I didn't sell my house to this buyer, which wasn't a change from the current situation. The unusual request made me suspicious. I had never heard of such a thing. Why did the buyer need to see me? What could she want to talk about that only I could answer? Was she someone looking for the inside skinny on the shootings that had occurred there? My son's partner, an investigative journalist, might pull such a stunt to get access to a story—but the shootings were three years ago.

Thinking about that night still gave me the willies. "Aha!" I said and chuckled. "This has all the earmarks of a surprise party. Paddy hinted he was contemplating doing something special for my birthday, but it's a month and a half past. Did he put you up to this?"

"I've never met your son."

"He knows our schedule, so he knows we're in Ohio, only a half day from Cincy. It would be just like him to cook up something like this. You didn't answer my question. He could arrange something without you two actually meeting."

She laughed. "Sounds like fun, but no, I'm not part of some master family conspiracy. Buyer's name is Beth Cunningham from the East Coast. Seems motivated. Wants closing in thirty days. I pretended to object and let them persuade me."

Something about the name tweaked a nerve. I tried to chase it down focusing on my East Coast days, but came up empty. "She's in town?"

"Leaves midday Sunday, which is not much of a window, but if you're only a half day away Lady Luck is on our side. Can you do it?"

"We were planning a leisurely drive down to Mom's next gig in Nashville. That's not until next weekend." All I'd need to do was change some motel reservations. "Tomorrow afternoon?"

"Saturday is perfect. I've already notified the two previous prospects—"

"I need to get back upstairs for Mom's finale. Tell me a time and we'll be there."

"Four thirty. By then I'll know how serious the other prospects are, which will determine our negotiating strategy."

"Tomorrow then." Maybe Lady Luck *was* going my way. This trip with Mom would be complete in another month. She was doing well enough that I could get her permanently situated in Boston and begin getting my own life in order. With Mom settled and shucking the millstone of the Cincinnati house, I could decide where I wanted to live when I didn't want to be at my camp in Michigan's Upper Peninsula. I squeaked open the outside door and, feeling energized, hustled up the concrete steps, my footsteps echoing from the plaster walls and ceiling. I muscled the fire door open and heard chanting.

"Tru-dy. Tru-dy. Tru-dy."

I eyed the scene from the far corner of the auditorium. The chanting reverberated in the spacious room with its fifteen-foot ceiling and hardwood floor. To my left, the bar area was doing a brisk business. Most of the cheering crowd sat in folding chairs ordered to provide access from right, left, and center aisles. Mom beamed from her position on the low stage at the front.

Standing next to her was her most recent victim, a mid-thirties guy with more ink on him than *The Sunday Times Magazine*. A chalkboard stage right indicated she had polished the guy off with her third dart of the throw, a double seventeen, reaching the required 501 score on the dot.

I do not understand how a woman in her seventies can inspire largely male audiences to love her even as she beats the stuffing out of the local darts players. Wherever we went, and in the last three months we had traveled all around New England, upstate New York, Pennsylvania, and now Ohio, the same thing happened. Excusing my way through the chanting crowd, trying not to interfere with the exchange of crumpled bills settling side bets, I parked myself against the center of the back wall and waited for my mother to call me to the stage.

She quieted the crowd and, as was her routine, challenged the last player to a match in which she'd throw lefty. She neglected to mention that she's ambidextrous. After winning with her left hand, she beat the guy a third time employing unusual techniques: hiking her darts, throwing them over her shoulder, standing on one leg, sitting, or doing whatever came into her mind.

We were set for her finale. She introduced the blindfolded challenge with a speech. Alone on the stage, she spoke into the microphone so softly people leaned forward to hear her. She told the story of my father's death—a cop killed on duty when I was young. She spoke of her struggles to get her children through college, and how once I had graduated she had retreated to silence for more than two decades. Two years ago she resumed limited verbal communications and now you couldn't shut her up—the crowd always laughed at the line.

I was unprepared the first time she made her speech, and bawled. Partly because she spoke of my father's death. Partly because she exposed her vulnerabilities to a crowd of strangers, something I could no more do than don a cape and fly like Superman. It had taken me a while, but I could now listen to her story without getting teary.

That night, no one talked, no one moved, no one even drank their beer while she spoke of loss and redemption. Applause pulled me from woolgathering about what tomorrow would bring. I should have been focusing on the task at hand, steadying myself instead of worrying myself into what was quickly becoming a throbbing headache. Not good, and no time for a pain reliever. Mom waited for the applause to die down before she spoke.

"I have one final proposition for you tonight. A small wager, should you choose to participate. But first, I need to accessorize."

On cue, the emcee came on stage and tied a bandanna across Mom's eyes. She tapped the microphone with her finger and at the sound the audience settled. "Give me five darts and I'll bet I can hit the bull's eye."

The crowd's murmur swelled. Mom raised her hand and they quieted. "I'll throw an exploratory dart. My son, Seamus—oh, Shay-mus, where are you?"

Her singsong calling of my name was my cue. I ambled down the middle aisle to polite applause. Once on stage, I gave her a hug.

"This is my son, Seamus. He's available and a good catch if anyone's interested. He has all his own teeth, his hair is natural, although I don't like seeing the gray—makes me feel old. He's six foot two, weighs one eighty-five. He's nearsighted, which accounts for the specs, but ladies, he has the nicest baby blues you have ever seen."

Knowing this was coming, I held my hands up in a "why me?" expression that got a laugh.

"I'll throw a practice dart and Seamus will tell me where it lands. Then I have five more darts to hit the bull's eye. Wouldn't you say the probabilities are against me? Despite that, I'll give you even odds. That's fair, right? Should I be fortunate enough to win, I'll donate my winnings to a charity Seamus helped set up to assist victims of violent crimes and their families. Because of its nonprofit status—and Seamus warns me to say this is in no way tax advice—you should endorse your checks directly to the charity to qualify for a tax deduction. If you don't have a check, we're high tech and have a smartphone credit card reader. If I lose, I hope you will be generous in donating my money to tonight's local charity. The most I ever lost was five thousand bucks. I hope you'll do me proud. Questions?"

A guy with a flushed face and prodigious beer belly yelled, "How do we know you're not cheating?"

Mom put her hands at the sides of her face and mimed a shocked expression. "My goodness. What a world we live in when people don't trust a little old gray-haired widow of a policeman. Sir, why don't you come up and check the blindfold? While he's doing that, could someone record the bets?"

The emcee hopped off the stage and noted wagers on a pad. To a mixture of hoots and claps, the doubting Thomas worked his way forward. He tried to boost himself onto the stage, but his protruding belly struck the edge. Failing a second time, and accompanied by cheers and jeers, he mounted by the side steps.

He made a big show of checking the blindfold, the darts, the dartboard, and frisking me. The audience got into his act and applauded his final bow.

The emcee gave me the thumbs up indicating he had finished collecting the bets. I took the microphone from Mom, led her to the oche—the shooting line—where I stood behind her and aligned her in front of the board exactly parallel to the line. I stepped away and she rearranged herself into her throwing stance, stepping back with her left foot, bringing in her right heel and placing most of her weight over her right foot.

This first dart was a reflection of how well I had pointed her. I held my breath, each heartbeat tapping behind my eyes. A big miss was on me. Once she settled her stance, she wasted no time and zipped a dart that thunked into the board outside the scoring circle between the one and four of the fourteen and a bit higher than halfway up the numbers. My shoulders dropped, relaxing on my exhale. Holding the microphone near my mouth so the audience could hear, I reported the dart's position to her.

She and I, (because I found myself mirroring her breathing), inhaled deeply and let it out. During the exhale she released the next dart. It stuck in the thirteen pie slice, two-thirds of the way between the outer double circle and the inner triple circle. Mom nodded understanding of my description of the dart's location. She made a minor adjustment in her feet placement, breathed in and out, and fired again.

"Nine spot, one-quarter inch out," I said and retrieved her three darts. "Two down and three to go. No pressure, Mom." The spectators, who had moved from their seats to stand close to the stage, nervously giggled at my remark.

"Easy for you to say," Mom retorted, "It's not your money on the line."

The remark received a big laugh, despite the reality that it *was* my money. Why should facts get in the way of theater?

She inhaled and released her breath, apparently did not feel centered, and repeated the process. The dart struck the outer green bull's eye. The audience exclaimed a collective shout of glee. She had picked their pockets and they cheered her.

"Green" I announced into the microphone.

Mom held out her hand, and I gave her the mic. Keeping her back to the audience she raised the mic high over her head to request quiet and, as if they were well-trained first graders, they stopped talking. "Wait. Wait," Mom said. "I didn't mean the *green*. I meant the *red* bull's eye."

The crowd shouted their disagreement. Some restarted the "Tru-dy" chant. Mom handed me the microphone and held up a hand for silence.

After a longer time, she got it. She'd made them believers. They wanted Mom to win their money, and now she was refusing them that privilege.

Part of me was proud of her uncompromising spirit. The headache part of me wanted her to declare victory so I could crash at the hotel.

She made a big show of settling in while I described exactly where in the green the dart had landed. Her movement was all upper body; Mom's feet had not shifted a micrometer from where she had thrown the last dart. A number of Catholics in the crowd now grasped the crosses hung around their necks for good luck. The beer-belly guy was actually kissing his silver crucifix. Mom took a clearing breath before she launched the fourth dart into the center red bull's eye.

The crowd roared its approval. Those close enough slapped their hands on the stage. Others rhythmically stomped their feet on the hardwood floor. "Tru-dy. Tru-dy. Tru-dy."

While I helped Mom remove the bandanna, I wished tomorrow would go as well as tonight, and I'd have my house sold.

Two

"SUCH A LOVELY OLD BRICK house," my mother said as I pulled into my Cincinnati driveway. "It looks even nicer than your pictures. Tell me again why you want to sell?"

Workmen had sandblasted the brick, removing more than a century of accumulated city soot along with the recent fire damage. The wood trim was resplendent in its painted-lady colors. Good-looking wasn't the issue. "Because Abigail was shot here. Because I ended up killing a guy here. Because the bad guys tried to burn down the place." My stomach roiled at the recitation.

"You should smudge the house and get rid of the bad vibes."

"Been there. Done that. Didn't work. Come on, Mom, let me introduce you to my agent."

We exited my ancient Infiniti G-20 and met Karen Miller at her Lexus. She brought a finger to her lips and motioned for us to walk with her. Three city lots down, she stopped. "Sorry for the skulduggery, but I didn't want the competition to overhear us." She offered an aristocratic hand to Mom. "You must be Seamus's mother."

Mom pulled Karen into a big hug. "My son's told me so many nice things about you. Thank you so much for helping him."

Karen's eyes became all pupil, but she hugged Mom right back. My agent's unflappability was a quality I appreciated. Hug over, she faced me. "The couple I told you had an appointment earlier today? I'll eat my hat if we don't get an offer from them. The wife really gave the husband the what for because he hadn't let her make an offer last month. I finally had to push them from the house so they didn't bump into your prospective buyer. We might be able to play the couple off against the offer in hand."

"No," I said. "This Beth Cunningham person made a good-faith, full-priced offer. Let's try to get the couple to make a contingent offer in case this falls through." I inclined my head toward the house. "Anything I should know before I talk with Ms. Cunningham?"

"Be your normal charming self. Are you feeling okay? You look a little . . ."

Shaky, I thought. I said, "I'll be fine." With the likelihood of a second offer, my concerns about screwing up this one lessened. I attributed my parched mouth to the challenges of the house itself. The sooner this was over, the better. "Showtime. Shall we?"

Before I could enter the house Mrs. Keenan yelled, "Alice! Alice, come back here." I turned in time to catch Alice, my next-door neighbor's pampered golden retriever, before she barreled into me. She buried her nose in my crotch while I rubbed her ears. "Belly rub?"

She flopped on her back, her tail sweeping the sidewalk. I squatted down and rubbed her chest and belly. "Okay, Alice." I gave her a couple of solid pats. "I have something I need to do. Go to your mother before you get me in trouble." Alice rose to her feet, gave herself a good shake, and trotted off, grinning as only goldens can do.

Mom: "Friend of yours?"

Karen: "I love golden retrievers, but their hair . . ." She checked her clothes for offending Alice hair.

Me: "I owe Alice and Mrs. Keenan a lot."

Mom: "It won't bother anything if I walk around, will it?"

Karen steered us by the elbow to encourage us toward the house. "You've never been here before, Mrs. McCree?"

I wondered how Mom would spin her decades-long institutionalization at Sugarbush that had prevented her from ever visiting me.

"Trudy—please. I'm embarrassed to say this is my first trip west of the Appalachians. I'm so glad Seamus thought of this idea to combine my passion for darts with seeing the country."

Karen's sales smile appeared. "Darts is such a . . . unique game."

"I grew up living above a bar and it impressed the boys when I beat them."

Karen was still shooing us toward the house. I delayed one final time, pointed at the plantings in front of the house. "Don't those lilies of the valley look nice? Usually they're squashed from the newspaper guy's bad tosses."

The buyer's agent met us in the entryway. Whereas Karen was tailored suits, leather attachés, and heels made for comfort, this guy needed his mother to dress him. His getup included scuffed shoes, mismatched socks, a bulge where his wallet stuck out of his back pants pocket. His top half combined a short-sleeved checked shirt whose buttons strained to control his stomach with a too-wide paisley tie. No briefcase for him, he carried a sheaf of papers in one hand and cheater glasses in the other. He reeked of incompetence and I wondered if the buyer wanted a private chat because she didn't trust her agent to represent her interests.

Karen made introductions. Mom commented on the ten-foot high ceilings and the bold colors I had chosen for the first floor. She decided to start her tour on the third floor and work her way down. Watching her climb the main staircase, I recalled the beautifully carved newels and balusters the fire had eaten. My heart sank. Such old-world craftsmanship was irreplaceable.

The artisans I'd hired had done a nice job rebuilding the house while maintaining its Victorian character, but it wasn't the house I had bought, the house I had once loved. My possessions had either burned in the fire or been ruined by water damage. To make the house more presentable I had rented furniture. A whiff of sawdust and paint still hung in the air underlying the fragrance of the fresh-cut flowers Karen had placed in vases around the house. With a will of its own, my gaze slid from yellow tea roses to the foyer floor where I had killed a man.

As though it had just happened instead of occurring over three years ago, I had a vision of Lt. Hastings, the head of Cincinnati's homicide unit and a personal friend, pointing to the head of the outlined body on the floor. "Seamus stood over him and fired shot after shot after shot while Abbott lay helpless on his back. Ka-pow. Ka-pow. Ka-pow. Ka-pow. Ka-pow. KA-POW."

I shivered remembering the percussive way she had pronounced those ka-pows. Hard as I tried, I could not remember the actual incident, but the memory of Hastings' demonstration accosted me in nightmares and now daymares. Already feeling wobbly, I didn't dare look into the dining room, afraid it would produce visions of Abigail lying nearly dead in a pool of blood. I had replaced all the oak flooring to eliminate any physical sign of the event. Unfortunately, I had found no way to refurbish the floorboards of my memory.

Could I ask the buyer to meet me outside on the porch? Beads of sweat formed on my forehead. With luck this was the last time I had to walk into this house.

"Mr. McCree?"

The question mark in the other realtor's voice broke through my reflection.

"I know this is unusual, and I appreciate your flexibility. Beth is waiting for you in the kitchen."

I edged past the agents, who headed for neutral corners. Approaching the dark passageway between the pantry and the back staircase, I realized this Beth person had closed the kitchen door. Even though it was my house, it didn't feel right to burst in unannounced on the soon-to-be-owner. I hesitated and put my ear to the door. Nothing.

I gave the new solid six-panel door a quick double tap, realized it was insufficient, and knocked loudly. Still nothing. I opened the door and peered in.

She was looking out the window over the sink into the backyard. Her shoulders hunched in on themselves. She held her legs stiffly, as though they would collapse if she gave them permission to relax. Her clothes exuded wealth, but hung limply off her thin frame. My impression was of great sadness, but I might have been projecting my feelings about the house onto her.

Not sure how to proceed, I entered the room and said, "Um, you wanted to see me?"

Twirling fast as a shot-putter, she faced me. "I need your help, Seamus."

It was Lizzie. My ex-wife.

Three

In times of great shock my mouth either babbles without input from my brain or refuses to produce words. I gaped like a country boy dropped into Times Square.

Lizzie, now Mrs. Albert Cunningham III, had never gone by Beth. She had been Lizzie to her old friends and Elisabeth to everyone else, which explained why hearing the name Beth Cunningham had triggered a reaction, but not rung alarm bells. We had been divorced more than twice as long as we were married, and I hadn't seen her since our son's high school graduation nearly eight years ago. A pixie cut replaced the ponytail she had once used as a lure. She was thinner than I remembered and looked younger.

As the silence grew, her smile crumbled. "Surprised, I suspect." She lifted and dropped her shoulders in a movement that often preceded tears. "Maybe you should shut the door."

Fear gripped me. The only thing we now had in common was our son. "Is Paddy okay?"

"He's fine. It's—"

"Why this subterfuge, Lizzie?" Remembering we were not alone in the house, I turned the doorknob to retract the latch bolt and closed the door with a soft click. "What the hell is going on? Why are you here?"

She tucked her chin to her chest, blinking away tears. Fisting her hands, she rapped them into each other a half dozen times. "Patrick's fine," she choked out.

Before I knew how it happened she was wrapped in my arms. She sucked in sobbing gasps, and her breasts rose and fell against my chest. Her pelvis pressed against mine, and I physically responded in a way that embarrassed my logical self. That part of our marriage had never been a problem. I hoped she didn't notice. I pushed aside being peeved at the great lengths of her deception and tried for an interested but detached voice. "What's going on?"

She pulled away from me. "Tissue?"

I hadn't been in the house since the shootings and the fire over three years ago except for a number of quick inspections. "Toilet paper's the best I can do."

She shrugged, grabbed the bottom edge of my flannel shirt, and brought it up to blot her eyes. I pretended not to notice the intimacy.

"Al's disappeared." Her upper lip trembled.

A gazillion questions fought to get to my tongue first. The road jam was fortunate since I was able to say something only moderately inane, "Disappeared where?" Before she answered I added, "Better start from the beginning."

She faced the window. Speaking with a heavy voice she said, "Al went on a business trip a week ago yesterday. He was supposed to return that Friday evening late, so the first time I became worried was Saturday morning. I called his cell phone. No answer. I called his assistant, who said all he knew was Al had asked him to arrange a trip to Savannah. I called his partners. They claimed they didn't know of any trip to Savannah."

She pushed the last tears from her eyes with her fingertips. "I didn't know what else to do, so I called the airline. After hours of runarounds, someone confirmed he had flown to Savannah but had not boarded his return flight, nor had he changed the reservation. I called one of his partners again. He insisted they did not have a potential buyer in Savannah. I could hear in his voice that he figured Al had hooked up with someone and would show up when he was ready. I called my stepson to find out if by any chance he had heard anything. Chad hadn't spoken to his father in a week. He didn't think his dad knew anyone in Savannah."

"Potential buyer?" I interjected to give her a chance to breathe and me to think.

"Despite my better judgment, I followed their advice and waited until Monday to call the police. I was so out of it, I forgot it was Memorial Day. The police officer I spoke with was very polite but suggested that, given the long weekend, Al might show up that day. Perhaps I should wait until Tuesday before filing a report. I spent the day embarrassing myself by calling everyone we knew. No one had had any contact with him. I was so worried, I even asked Chad to talk to his mother and see if anything like this had happened during their marriage. Can you imagine how humiliating that is?"

I mumbled encouraging sounds.

"Someone suggested I check our credit cards, so I went online. No charges. Nothing. You have anything I can drink?"

"Water?

"A bottle would be good."

"I don't live here, Lizzie. Tap water is all I have."

Her mouth puckered briefly in a moue of distaste.

Tough. I grabbed a glass from the cupboard and let the water run awhile since I had no idea the last time anyone had used the faucet.

She took three careful sips. "That Tuesday, an ATM charge came through for $500. I showed that to the cops. I wanted them to put out an APB for him in Pooler where the ATM was. They had me file a missing person report and said they'd get back to me."

With deliberate motions, she dumped the rest of the water into the sink and left the glass on the counter. She screeched a chair away from the table and plopped down. "The police have nothing to tell me. His partners aren't taking my calls anymore, and I'm picking up some kind of vibe from Al's assistant that they think Al screwed them. Did you know they're selling their business?"

I shook my head. "You mentioned a buyer."

"I thought maybe Patrick had told you. I thought—" She gulped a room's worth of air and snorted. "Patrick told me about your work with the Criminal Investigations Group. I thought maybe they could help. Can they? Will you talk to them?"

"Why didn't you just call me?"

"Don't stand over me, Seamus. It makes me nervous."

I circled the table, spun around the chair opposite her, and straddled it.

She waited until I was seated. "I know you're all about honesty, Seamus. And speaking the truth no matter the cost. Well, the truth is, I'm scared. I am really scared. Something has happened to my husband and no one wants to help me find out where he is. I can't sleep. I can't eat."

She folded her hands on the table in front of her and leaned heavily on her forearms. "The truth is if I weren't sitting here in front of you, I knew you'd refuse me. Why wouldn't you? You don't owe me anything. I knew you and your mother were in Ohio doing her darts thing. And I figured you were desperate to sell your house since it's been on the market for so long. The plan came together. It's a lovely house, Seamus. You should stay."

She waved away what I supposed was a stray thought. "Anyway, this was the only way I'd be sure you'd see me. That's the truth, the whole truth, and nothing but the truth. Will you call them? Now? Please?"

Lizzie hadn't gone to law school, but she had a lawyer's craft at leading you down a path to unexpected agreements. I needed to tread carefully if I did not want to be trapped by some obscure logic I had not suspected. "I'm sorry, Lizzie. CIG works only with police departments and never makes unsolicited offers of assistance. The request has to come from the department. If you could get your local police to contact them, that's one thing, but they'll never do private work."

She stared grim-faced. "Maybe *you* can help convince the police to call CIG?"

"Like that's going to work. Some schmo the cops don't know calls them up from Ohio and suggests they're incompetent and should call in the resources of Criminal Investigations Group to solve a missing person report."

"So come with me to New Jersey and talk to them in person."

Missed that logic trap. "Al still hasn't used any credit cards?"

"I haven't checked today."

I squinched my eyes shut in frustration. Under control, I opened them. "Through last night he hasn't used his credit cards, correct?" She nodded. "And he only used the ATM once—on Tuesday?"

She pulled back from the table. "No. No! He uses it every day. Five hundred dollars. Every day. He must have lost his credit cards and he's using cash, and—"

"And he hasn't called you or texted or emailed or Tweeted or used Facebook or anything? I know you don't want to hear this Lizzie, but are you sure he hasn't dumped you? Have you been fighting? Like over their selling the business?"

I was constructing a paint-by-numbers picture: Lizzie had wrapped her self-worth in my position while we were married. Assuming she hadn't changed, Lizzie would be against selling the partnership because she needed to be able to say her husband has this muckety-muck position or does that muckety-muck job. Present tense. Lizzie was never interested in the money per se. She was keen about its implied status. After I quit Wall Street and forfeited a sizable bonus, she was not a happy camper regarding the money I had given up.

She was even more ticked that by quitting I had caused her to lose status. Chances were her husband was fed up hearing this crap night after night and found a sympathetic ear. The partners knew of it and covered for him, which was why they weren't talking to her. He should show up any time now.

Lizzie insisted everything was fine. I was all wrong. Her eyes were doing a rumba to avoid contact with mine. The more she talked, the more I was sure she was lying about something . . . or everything.

"Look, Lizzie. The man is living off the ATM machine so he doesn't need to leave his name anywhere. Where the heck is Pooler, anyway?"

"Outside Savannah. In Georgia. But the ATM withdrawals have been from several different machines. In the city, in the suburbs, one was even across the state line in South Carolina. Something's wrong, Seamus. I just know it is. It's not another woman. I'd know. He's in trouble. Somebody's preventing him from using his phone."

"Have you checked his cell phone records to see if he's made any calls?"

Footsteps clunked down the back stairway intended for servants when the house was built in 1895. We stopped talking and listened as the footsteps reached the bottom and the kitchen door opened. My mother entered the room.

Her gaze swiveled between us. Through drawn lips she said to me, "Go with the second offer." Mom slammed the solid-paneled door behind her, rattling dishes in both the pantry and kitchen.

"What does she mean, 'Go with the second offer'?" Lizzie's voice was shrill with anger. "Wait! When did *she* start talking?"

"Paddy didn't tell you?"

"Patrick does not talk about your side of the family. What did that woman mean?"

The parallel was true. Paddy told me little of his mother's life. He had let me know she married Albert Cunningham III, who ran a hedge fund in the City, and Paddy didn't like him. "When it comes to her children," I said, "my mother is not one to forgive and forget. She thinks you screwed me over." I held up my hands. "I am not trying to get into a fight. Back to your problem." I thought I caught a lie I could call her on. "If Paddy doesn't talk to you, how did you learn of Mom's darts exhibitions and my house not selling?"

She looked abashed and spoke through a hand covering her mouth. "I follow your mother on Facebook."

I wasn't on any social media sites, but Mom had developed a huge following because of her darts. I throttled my desire to get into a knockdown brouhaha about her stalking us. I wanted Lizzie out of my life and the fastest way to accomplish that was to focus her attention somewhere else. "Did you check his cell phone records?"

"It's a business phone. They won't talk with me."

Another incongruity worked past my anger into my thinking. "Why didn't you hire a private investigator? They must do this kind of thing all the time."

"I talked to a firm one of my girlfriends used. They just didn't get it, Seamus. Even if your mother hates me, you're my last hope." She dropped her chin to her chest. "My last hope."

"Then you're hopeless." As soon as the words were out of my mouth I regretted them. Mean, small words. I knew better. I had let the molten lava of my unresolved anger at Lizzie bubble up and erupt in a hurtful way. She burst into deep sobbing.

I stood, feeling disgusted with myself. "I'm sorry, Lizzie."

"Just let me be," she said through her crying.

"Maybe I can think of something." She did not respond. "I'll be outside."

I passed Lizzie's agent in the front hall and told him "Ms. Cunningham" was making a personal phone call and would be out shortly. Mom and Karen were engaged in an animated discussion on the porch. I opened the door and the conversation stopped.

Karen recovered first. "Trudy tells me she doesn't think this buyer's serious."

I peered down my nose at Mom, "You think? How perceptive you are today." I ran both hands through my shaggy hair. "I'm sorry, Mom. That was snarky. I'm ticked at Lizzie and especially at myself—not you. Karen, can you please call up the couple's agent and tell them I'd prefer to sell to them if they match the first offer? See what happens." I read confusion on Karen's face. "Mom's right. This deal is toast. Beth Cunningham is my ex-wife."

"Oh." The surprise formed her lips into a frozen 'O.' "I'll make the call."

Once Karen was beyond whisper-hearing range, Mom patted the seat next to her and leaned in. "*What* is she doing here? Hasn't that woman caused you enough trouble?"

During the years Lizzie and I had been together, Mom was not communicating with anyone, so I had no idea how she felt about my marriage or my divorce. We had talked of lots of things during this trip, but Lizzie had not come up. If the slammed kitchen door had not provided a sufficient clue, the venom in her voice did. By the time I finished relating the kitchen conversation, including my bad behavior, the flame in Mom's eyes had banked. "That's terrible. No wonder she looks hollowed out."

The front door opened and the other agent emerged from the house. "My client has retracted her offer." He focused an angry gaze down on me. "What kind of a man are you to make her cry?" He stomped down the steps to his car. Over his shoulder he said, "I assume *you'll* lock up."

I chose not to flip him the bird. He had a right to be mad, even if I wasn't the one he should be angry with. "Mom, do me a favor. Check on Lizzie while Karen and I talk?"

Mom muttered under her breath as she passed me, "I don't do tears."

You're right, Mom, I thought. *Maybe if you had you wouldn't have needed more than two decades of silence to heal.*

Four

Patrick McCree's reaction to his cell phone announcing "That One is My Dad" by Keni Thomas was to feel the lead weight of guilt press upon his shoulders. He considered letting the call go to voicemail, but punched the speaker button. "Hey, Dad, how are you and Grandma?"

"Has your mother told you anything about your stepfather?"

Tension slid off Patrick's shoulders because he could needle his dad about his phone technique, "I'm fine. Thanks for asking. Cindy's fine too, as are Cheech and Chong. Business is going well." His shoulders pulled in tighter at the half truth. He hastily added, "I'm glad you called. I need to talk to you. There've been changes." There, finally out. "I have a meeting with your favorite bankers at All-American tomorrow." True, but not the issue, not the issue at all.

His father chuckled. "Point taken. I'm glad Cindy and the cats and your business are all fine. Your grandmother is fine. I'm fine. I saw Abigail since we last talked and she is fine as well, although she's in California and I'm not sure when we'll next see each other. And now that we're done with the touchy-feely crap, your stepfather—"

"Mom has a new husband. I do not have a stepfather. They both know I think he's a jerk. Mom and I don't bother talking about him anymore. He—"

"He's disappeared."

"See. He *is* a jerk." Patrick wanted to shove the words back in his mouth. Not that he didn't mean them. He did. His first reaction should have been concern for his mother, not some junior-high fist pump because he was right about Albert Cunningham III.

"I won't argue the point." After filling Patrick in on the details of the disappearance, he concluded, "I know I'm catching you cold, but how hard would it be to convince one of your bank clients to let you look at the video from their ATMs?"

His father so rarely asked for his help, and the one big time he had,

Patrick had screwed up. Patrick crossed his fingers to remember to discuss that before they ended the call. Why, oh why, had he not sucked it up and called his old man months ago?

"You there?" his father asked.

"Not legitimately." He pulled at the side of his face, realized he'd uncrossed his fingers and crossed them again. "Probably not illegitimately, either. ATMs come with their own security, and Diebold, or whoever, is responsible, not the bank. Banks keep some stuff local, but they automatically transmit most to an off-site security company. When we test a financial institution's cybersecurity, we might look at ATM accounting interfaces, but we don't touch that aspect of the ATMs. I know TMI." *Listen to Mr. Negativity.* "Why are you asking?"

"Your mother is at my house." He released an exasperated sigh. "She wanted me to get CIG to help her. That'll never happen, but if she proved someone other than your step—her husband was extracting the ATM money, the cops might get interested. And if it is him, well, at least she knows he's alive."

The alarm on his phone rang. He jabbed it silent. Fifteen minutes to get a salad prepared before Cindy came home for an early dinner. He pulled carrots from the crisper and began peeling them over the sink. "Sorry. Which bank?"

"Don't know. I was fishing to see if it would work. Apparently it won't. My other idea hinged on checking his cell phone usage, but your mother can't because it's a corporate account. I'm not sure what operating system it uses, but—"

"Have Mom give his assistant at Antimatter Investments a call. They often work on Saturdays, although after five is late, even for them. Lots of companies use security backup software on their phones. Not only can they check usage, they can locate the phone if it's on and even delete its memory. That's your best bet."

"Unfortunately, they got sick of your mother's pestering them and won't answer her calls anymore. What's that sound?"

"Me chopping carrots. I met Laurence Kleindeinst—the assistant—at their wedding. Maybe I can talk him into it. If that doesn't work, I know some people at the phone companies."

"You know my feelings about that. Can you try the assistant now? I guess I need to take your mother and grandmother to dinner."

Patrick sprinkled the carrots on the salads forming in front of him. "That Indian restaurant on Clifton still there?"

"I have no clue, Paddy. The last time I was actually in Cincinnati was eighteen months ago to put the house on the market. Since then, I've either been traveling or up taking care of your grandmother in Boston. Driving into Cincinnati today, everything seems familiar, but under the surface, nothing's the same. Give the assistant a call and let me know. Oh, and give Cindy a kiss for me."

"Will do. And if that doesn't work, I've got the Jerk's cell number. I can always—"

"I'd rather you didn't if we can avoid it. Thanks, Paddy. I love you."

"Love you too, Dad."

Patrick pressed the end call button and stared at his crossed fingers.

FIVE

MENTIONING ABIGAIL'S NAME TO PADDY stoked my desire to press her to set a date for our next long weekend together. The only real problem I had traveling with Mom was losing my flexibility to visit Abigail wherever she was bodyguarding, which meant I was seeing her only when she could get free—not as often as I wished. That call would need to wait until I had privacy.

I didn't want to reenter the house with its specters, so I opened the door and yelled. "Hey you two, I'll be on the porch when you're ready." I flopped onto the Adirondack rocker. During the second lean back, a brainstorm hit. Earlier, I had been thinking of Lt. Hastings as a homicide cop, but she was also a friend. I could ask her how the police would act if we got them motivated and what we could do on our own.

Strike while the iron is hot. Four rings later, my call went to voicemail. "Lieutenant. Tanya. It's Seamus McCree. I'm in town and need to pick your brain on a personal matter. I know this is . . . uh . . . zero notice, but could we get together for a drink or dinner or . . . anyway, please call."

Lizzie and Mom joined me on the front porch. Neither one sat.

"What's up?" I said.

Mom: "I was telling Elisabeth about the night your father went missing. How it was the worst night of my life because I didn't know where he was. I knew something had happened, I just didn't know what."

Lizzie's head bobbed in agreement. "That's the worst."

Me: "I still think you should try a PI. I spoke with Paddy. He'll call the assistant, Kleindeinst, and try to get the cell phone records from him. If the guy blows Paddy off, Paddy can try to access its cell tower history to determine where and when it was last used."

Mom touched my elbow. "Don't you need a warrant?" She asked so low, I doubted Lizzie heard.

I gave Mom a look to say, "butt out." She rolled her eyes. "Lizzie," I said, "if he's been making calls, we can call those numbers and maybe determine what's going on."

Lizzie: "I don't understand why Kleindeinst won't help us. Nobody believes me."

Her whine and inability to focus on the possible was becoming annoying. Do all divorced people wonder what they saw in their former mate? "You're flying back tomorrow?"

Before she could answer, my cell phone rang. I grabbed it from my pocket as though it were a lifeline. The display read, "Hastings."

To my hello she said, "You think a girl has nothing better to do on a Saturday night than wait for your call?"

The warm flush of embarrassment crept up my neck and covered my face. I hadn't been thinking at all.

"Well it's your lucky day," she continued. "I'll let you buy me dinner at Myra's. On Calhoun? Early's good. Would you like to give me a hint what this is about?"

Now that I didn't want it, I had Lizzie's full attention. "I'm at my house with my mother and my ex-wife." I did some quick calculations. "I can get there in a half hour."

"Therein lies a tale. I can't wait to hear the scoop, but make it an hour. I need to soak off the smell of our latest victim, who we pulled from a dumpster."

We disconnected and Lizzie pounced. "What was that?"

"Me trying to help you," I snapped. "I have to meet someone for dinner. Mom, why don't you and Lizzie go to one of the restaurants on Ludlow. There are some excellent places only a few blocks away. You can walk if you'd like to stretch your legs. Use Yelp and pick one. Maybe we can stay in Cincy for a couple of days before we head down to Tennessee for your exhibition next weekend? There's plenty to do around here."

Mom: "Lovely. We'll use your house as home base. I'll take the back bedroom."

Her words slammed me like a steel-toed shoe to the chest. I had no desire to aggravate my demons by actually staying in the house. "I have no food or tissues or anything," I babbled.

We negotiated. I'd walk to my dinner with Tanya Hastings. After their dinner, Mom would take my car with its GPS and grocery shop using the credit card I had given her. She was tired of staying in hotels and it would save me money. She threw Ben Franklin's "A penny saved is a penny earned" at me.

Mom needed to understand that even the thought of staying in the house made me nauseous, but I'd deal with it when we could talk without Lizzie around.

I told them to have a good dinner and if Paddy called me, I'd call Lizzie.

Tears—of anger or sorrow, I wasn't sure—welled in the corners of Lizzie's eyes. "You haven't told me what you're doing."

"Trying to help. Pick a restaurant and eat something. My treat. Mom will pick up the check."

I rose and Lizzie snagged my arm. "When will I hear from you?"

I stared down at her hand and silently counted to ten.

When I got to six, Mom snapped, "When he knows something. Weren't you listening?" Mom held out her hand. "Keys to the car and house? I'll leave the light on and the door unlocked." She laughed at my expression. "Just like when you were in high school."

Six

MYRA'S DIONYSUS PERCHED AT THE southern edge of the University of Cincinnati. The restaurant was an institution and with the expansion of the university, I wondered how long it would last. I checked the rooms to see if Tanya had already arrived. She hadn't, but it gave me time to look at the local artists' work adorning the walls and, new to me, a bunch of colorful hats decorating another wall. Each was handmade and designed to reflect one of Myra's soups.

A click from the front door and a brush of cool air on my neck suggested someone had entered. Authoritative heels clicked toward me. I peeked from the back room and was shocked to see Tanya's now closely cropped hair was mostly gray. Her chocolaty eyes looked tired. Was this the stress of being Cincinnati's top homicide cop manifesting itself? An observer would have said she was older than I, even though she was a decade younger.

I hustled out front, and she pulled me into an embrace. I smiled at the cartoon picture I envisioned of myself: a character whose heart was hammering in his chest. Her bones had no padding; or did she feel thinner because, despite Mom's "Eat, you look like a scarecrow," I hadn't regained my own weight? After a moment I realized she was not wearing her signature lilac perfume.

She disengaged by giving my back a swift rub and two pats. "I am absolutely starved," she said. "With the new case today, all I've had since four this morning is a stale bagel and an ocean of coffee."

Holding hands, we followed the waitress to a table near the rear, a good spot for quiet conversation. The waitress placed the menus so we would sit opposite each other. Tanya shifted one so we sat at adjacent sides of the table. The waitress took our drink orders, raspberry lemonade for me and "Corinthian Cooler" consisting of hibiscus tea and grape juice for Tanya, and melted away. Tanya leaned in and pecked my cheek.

"I've missed you, Seamus. Your house looked lonely the last time I drove by it."

I waited for an explanation that didn't happen. She plucked the menu from the table and smacked her lips. I used the time to observe her closely. Her cheekbones were indeed sharper than I remembered, her eyes sunken. She had definitely lost weight. "You've been well?"

"Fine." She flicked from her pale yellow slacks a piece of lint I couldn't see. "With your mother and your ex-wife? Last I knew, your mother wasn't talking to anyone, and your ex wasn't talking to you."

I gushed about Mom's darts exhibitions and the road trip. "She's raised tens of thousands of dollars for charities. People love her and she blossoms on the stage—a natural showman. Showperson."

Tanya lowered her menu. "What a good son you are. I'd kill my mother if I had to be with her for months on end—if she didn't kill me first. How are you doing?"

"I'm delighted with her progress."

She stopped me with a shake of her head, and a wry wisp of a smile curved her lips. "I know with you I sometimes need to ask a question multiple times before you answer. How are *you* doing after all *your* trauma?"

This was a good opportunity to embrace my resolution to be more open, even though she was clearly hiding something. "I am betwixt and between. Mom's recovery is a godsend, not just because she's better, but because our time together is making up for the years of her silence. I'm fortunate I don't have to earn a living and can take the time off. Frankly, I was getting tired at the CIG job, so everything's good." I paused to consider how to continue. I was not scoring full marks on the honesty front. "The other trauma stuff? I still wake up in cold sweats."

"Is that why you're selling your house? The guy you killed?"

"Don't think so. I'm okay with killing him—well, not okay-okay, but he invaded my house. He would have killed me." I heard my voice getting louder and tamped it down. "I do shy away from the one spot. I have trouble with the dining room too."

"Because that's where Abigail was hit?"

"Truth is, I get the willies in the house."

"Still with Abigail?"

"It's complicated."

She tilted her head and gave me a one-eyed squint.

Open up, Seamus. "When we're together, we're together. But her job takes her all over, and I've been taking care of Mom for . . . a long time. We don't see each other very often. We talk some on the phone, but—"

The waitress slid our drinks onto the table and recorded our orders. Tanya and I agreed on two sampler plates that gave us six different dishes to share. The waitress bustled away with a squeak of tennies on the floor.

"So," Tanya said, "your sex life sucks. Are you abandoning Cincinnati and your friends and returning home to Beantown with your mother?"

"No! Well, maybe. I don't know." My fingers scrunched the napkin in my lap. I stopped and smoothed it out. "After we finish this swing through Tennessee, my plan is to return with Mom to Boston and get her set up for independent living. I've been telling myself that I don't have to stay nearby. Boston is only a flight away from wherever I am."

I sipped the lemonade, using the time to consider my words. "You've lived here all your life, right?"

"Always and forever."

"Boston's not the same place I left, and I don't know anyone there. I'm ready to settle, grow some real roots. But if I do something new, it might take me to a different location. That suggests I should stay here. Then again, Cincinnati is changing so fast, it doesn't much feel like home either."

She cocked her head at me. "You have lots of friends here."

"Acquaintances. I have no real friends."

"What am I, chopped liver?"

"You *are* a good friend, but how well do you really know me? Really good friends are people you can pick up the phone and say anything, and they'll accept you for who you are."

"You mean the kind of person who gets a call out of the blue on a Saturday night and drops everything to have dinner with you? You've convinced yourself. Far be it from me to try to dissuade you. Here's my amateur psychiatrist's analysis—although if I were a real one, I'd make you figure this out all by yourself. But because I'm your friend, I'll spit it out very plainly. You listening?"

"Yes, ma'am. I am all ears."

"You can't run away from yourself, Seamus. You need to face your fears. Do you still get those dreams where you're being chased?"

"I forgot I'd told you about my chase dreams. They started when I was a kid. But until recently, they involved only faceless people chasing me. Sometimes dogs tracked me. I always woke up before they got to me. Now they sometimes have faces."

The corners of her mouth lifted and the hint of dimples appeared. "The dogs have faces? You mean, the guy—?"

"Not the guy I killed—but everyone else in that case."

"Even me? I know I've chased you some. Still would . . ." She gave my knee a quick squeeze.

I smiled with my mouth, but I knew the smile didn't reach my eyes. I wasn't sure about her expression because I was talking to the tabletop. "Trust me: you don't want me right now . . . and not those kinds of dreams, Tanya. I wish. It's not the good guys. It's the scum. Alive and dead. It's like I used to have unattached fears, but now they have faces and names."

She took my hand. Hers was cool. Her next question arrived as a whisper. "Do you know what you're afraid of?"

I raised my gaze to her. "Being caught. They'll kill me if they catch me." Her eyes narrowed with what I judged to be skepticism. "I know that's crazy talk, but I believed it as a child, and I believe it today. You have your religion. I have my dream belief. It's a matter of faith."

"But they're all dead or in jail."

"I didn't say it was rational. Oh, crap, I should have just told you I was fine and skipped the third degree. So, when did you stop wearing your lilac perfume?"

She bobbed her head several times and shrugged. "Captain developed allergies to perfume. I don't even think about it anymore." She squeezed my hand and placed hers on my forearm. "It really is good to see you, Seamus. I . . ."

She flinched as though stabbed by a splinter. I waited for her to continue and prompted her with "It really is good to see you, Seamus. I—what?"

She blinked and gave a barely perceptible shrug. "No clue. What's up with CIG? You're looking to do something different? I thought you loved that finance stuff."

"We were ahead of the times when I set up the whole financial crimes network for them. Now every police department in the world has a financial crimes taskforce or two or three. Some of the people I hired are being sucked up by international corporations for big bucks. Police departments think they can do it themselves and are using my part of CIG less frequently. And when they do invite CIG in to help, it's mostly impossible stuff where people are covering their butts."

"You jealous?"

"Oh, God no. I've received some outrageous offers. A couple weeks ago an international bank discussed a job with me paying a half million a year plus bonus to run their financial crimes prevention department. I'm done with corporate bosses. I still enjoy a little merger and acquisition work, and that's certainly corporate. I have to shit or get off the pot with CIG. I've been using this trip with Mom to put them off. I'm too young for a life of checkers, so I'd better figure out something."

"Sounds like a perfectly good midlife crisis to me. Some days, I think checkers might be just my speed. Enough of our pity party. You wanted help?"

I related how Lizzie had used my house to lure me to a meeting. "The way I see it, there are two possibilities. Everyone thinks her husband has a dish on the side. Or . . ." I waggled my hand.

She placed both forearms on the table and leaned toward me. Quietly, "So you're talking with a homicide chick because you think he's dead?"

I snorted at homicide chick. "I hope not, but why isn't he using his credit cards? Although I guess you could do fine on five hundred bucks a day."

"If he's hiding someone on the side, he may have a credit card the wife doesn't know about. Could be a personal card or even a business card. This guy has money, right? And there hasn't been any ransom note, so door number two is not a kidnapping. But if his body is stuffed behind door number two, why would someone use his ATM card, but not his credit cards? Usually they order stuff online or go on a mall shopping spree until the credit card companies cancel the cards."

"On my walk here, Paddy called and reported there have been no calls or texts on Cunningham's cell phone. I thought criminals liked stolen phones for their drug deals or whatever."

Her grin broadened into a smile. "Old-school thinking. With the tracking devices on smart phones, most intelligent crooks now stick with burner prepaids. I'm not even going to ask what possessed your ex-wife to travel from New Jersey to Ohio. It's obvious she knew exactly how to suck you right in. Shay-mus Maaa-Cree," she drew it out, long, slow, sensual, and patted my leg. "Always the warrior knight in shining armor. Have you ever passed a damsel in distress without stopping? Never you mind. Knowing you, you have a plan. So, spill it."

I leaned away from her words. "No way am I the world's savior. At first,

I was pissed she tried to use me. But with time to reflect, I keep returning to something my mother said. The night my father went missing was the worst night of her life. She maintains she felt more distraught not knowing where he was than knowing he'd been killed. Everyone deserves to know where their spouse is. Plus, Lizzie is Paddy's mother. Whatever affects her affects him. That does not mean I want to spend forever in Lizzie's company." Leaning in, I continued. "Assuming we can access the withdrawal records to determine exactly which ATMs he used to get the money, is there a way to convince the banks to let me look through their digital video records to see who's making the withdrawals? How would you do it?"

She leaned back and linked her hands behind her head. Was she aware of the effect that posture had on her attractiveness, lengthening her spine, thrusting her breasts out, emphasizing her long neck and toned arms? She settled her chair to the floor with a heavy clunk and leaned in. A full smile painted her face, erasing the worry lines she had walked in with. "Have you considered having her drain the account so he can't make any more withdrawals?"

"That would smoke him out, wouldn't it? We'd know he had online access if he transferred money to replenish the account."

"If I were your ex, I'd clean out all the joint accounts and set up a new account with a new password. I'd cancel all his credit cards. I still suspect he's hiding at least one card from her, so if she knows his Social, have her run one of those credit check things to see if there's a personal card she doesn't recognize. She has cards of her own?"

"I made sure she maintained her own credit rating in case anything happened to me, including two cards solely in her name. I like your thinking. Eliminate the oxygen of easy money and make the whale surface."

Food arrived. Between bites I continued our conversation. "I had been so focused on tracking him using his phone and in looking for a way to access the bank ATM video, I hadn't considered cutting off his funding. I'm still stuck on the video, though. Can you think of any way for me to get the police interested or prevail upon the banks to help out?"

She waved at the waitress for a refill of her drink. "Unless your ex lives in Mayberry and knows the Sheriff or she's got political pull, I can't see cops doing anything with her missing person report. She sort of shot herself in her foot telling them about the ATM withdrawals. Police departments have too many real crimes for them to do much on this type of missing person." She held up her hands to forestall my objection. "Poorly stated, but you know what I mean. And, I can't imagine why banks would open themselves up to all kinds of trouble by cooperating with a private citizen. For all they know, she could be spying on hubby, and they'll find themselves sued."

She clapped her hands together; her eyes widened. "If your ex wants to do some legwork, here's a thought: Everyone and their uncle has security cameras these days. Hell, some dude robs a bank, we not only get the bank's recordings, we canvass the neighborhood businesses. Often we pick up the crooks' car on the way in or out and sometimes get great shots of the occupants. They may cover their faces around the bank, but not while they're driving. Sometimes we can even read plate numbers."

"So we find an ATM in a shopping center."

"Try mom-and-pop stores. Chain stores hire out their security. Just like with the banks, you'd need a judge to pry stuff loose. Small guys are often willing to help 'cause they figure they could be next. You need a friendly owner who your ex can convince—you know, woman to woman—to bend the rules a little and let her check the vids."

She shoveled in a forkful of baba ganouj and washed it down with tea. "If she's desperate enough to come all the way to Cincinnati to scam you, she shouldn't have any problem knocking on doors in Savannah. Hear it's a lovely city."

A warm feeling spread over me. This needle-in-the-haystack search could work. I was fairly certain my bank statement showed the addresses of ATM withdrawals. If that was standard practice, I could have Lizzie go online and get the locations. We could use Google Earth to check the neighborhood and nearby businesses. Then we—

"Knock, knock." She rapped her knuckles on the table next to my plate. "I asked a question, but you disappeared." A mile-wide smile split her face. "It's one of your charms and one of your most exasperating qualities. At the wisp of an idea you're off in your own little world, thinking great big Seamus thoughts. Makes a girl feel you only want her for her mind."

"Sorry, I was thinking how to pull this off. What did you ask?"

She interlaced her fingers with mine and batted her eyelashes. "Forget what I asked. What I really want to know is if you're interested in dessert."

Seven

It had been years since I had been in the Cincinnatian Hotel. My cell phone said 8:25 a.m., but I figured even though Lizzie was not a morning person, she'd be up.

The receptionist connected me to her room. "Where the hell have you been?" Lizzie screeched. "I've been up all night trying to get you. He's got control of everything."

I told her I was in the lobby, and she ordered me to her room. I paused at the threshold of the open door to her room on the top floor. Lizzie wore a Cincinnatian bathrobe. The portion of the room I could see behind her consisted of an unmade bed, two settees—her clothes decorated one—and a bathroom larger than the house I grew up in. "I'll wait outside until you're dressed."

"Don't be absurd. Al locked me out of our brokerage account."

She led the way to the settees, picked up her clothes, and tossed them into a pile on top of the dresser next to the flat-screen television. Sitting down, her bathrobe gaped, showing more cleavage than I needed to see. I didn't want a repeat of yesterday and find her wrapped around me again—especially if she was naked under the bathrobe.

"We'll talk once you've dressed. Ten minutes won't change anything."

"Fine," she huffed. She heaved out of the sofa's embrace, grabbed a bra from the pile of clothes, pulled slacks and a top from her suitcase. I expected her to take everything to the bathroom. Instead, she stepped before the mirror and shrugged the bathrobe to the ground.

I suppose Sir Galahad would have averted his eyes. I watched. It's not like I had never seen her naked. Although it had been years, I had once known her body as well as my own. Under the bathrobe she wore black lace tangas. She had consistently exercised and been thin, but now her skin stretched tight over her ribs.

She checked the mirror, noticed I was paying attention, and the grim line of her mouth relaxed into the hint of a smile. She cupped her breasts and gave them a bounce. "Not bad for an old broad." Leaning forward, she slipped on her bra. She still favored a nearly sheer front-hooking model. She spun around and pinched her sides and slapped her stomach. "You know anyone our age who looks this good?"

"You've kept yourself in wonderful shape." And she had, but she reminded me of an athlete past her prime, struggling to maintain her edge against younger players. She was too thin. She colored her hair with more red highlights than I remembered. Covering a fair amount of gray, I supposed. Her eyes looked slightly bugged, and I realized she didn't have the kinds of lines around her eyes I did. Now that I considered it, she didn't even have the lines she had when we were together. Her cheeks were smooth. The only signs of life's wear and tear were two shallow lines at the corner of her mouth and in her world-weary eyes.

How sad. Lizzie had been naturally good looking when we were together. Now she was a walking Botox exhibit. "Finish getting dressed, please. I've enjoyed the show, but we need to talk."

She stamped her foot. "Everyone believes Al dumped me for some bimbo." She smacked her fist on the flat of her thigh. "It's in their shifty little eyes, darting away because they want to hide their thoughts. Like he's not getting everything he needs at home."

"Lizzie, please."

"You never had anything to complain about that and neither does he. You think maybe he's been seeing someone all along and the acquisition is simply a cover-up. I assure you that's not it."

Was she falling into the trap of stating as an absolute negative the thing she most feared? Did fears of losing him to another woman cause her to blurt thoughts to me she probably didn't tell her best girlfriend?

Angry tears leaked down her cheeks. "Something's happened to him, Seamus. I know it." She shimmied on the top and stepped into and zipped up her slacks. "Satisfied?"

"Relieved you're dressed and we've stopped talking about your sex life. You said he locked you out of your brokerage account. Describe exactly what you did."

She returned to the settee opposite mine and curled her feet under her, cleared the tear trails with the backs of her hands. "As you suggested when you called last evening, I tried to log into the account to change the password. But our password didn't work. I was so anxious the next time I used one finger and checked each letter as I typed. That's when I tried to call you. Why didn't you answer? I couldn't get back to sleep, I was so worried."

She finger-combed her hair. "I can't believe he did that. What's he hiding?"

"Before you jump to conclusions, have you tried resetting the password?"

"How the hell can I do that if I can't get into the account?" She grabbed a mug of coffee off the dresser. "You want any?"

"No thanks." I didn't bother reminding her I never drank coffee. "Usually you can reset the password if you jump through three-question purgatory—you know, where you have to remember your childhood best friend's dog's middle name. Sometimes all you need is your username or email address. Let me watch what happens when you try to sign in."

"Try for yourself." She pointed toward the desk. "The password is the letter e, number three, pound symbol, r, four, dollar sign, t, five, percentage."

I raised the desk chair to a comfortable height and sat. She shifted to the couch I had been on so she could watch. The tablet came alive at the touch of my finger. The brokerage firm app was open with the username "A&E4ever" already completed. "Give me the password one letter at a time, please."

That generated the response, *Incorrect username or password.* Listed below was an 800 telephone number: probably a service desk staffed 24/7. "Do you know your account number or who your broker is?"

Five minutes later they had reset the password to her account. Six minutes later Lizzie's fears met reality. Her husband had drained the account.

While she sat in shocked silence, I scrolled through the accounting ledger. In a series of transactions the day of his disappearance, he had converted all their stocks, bonds, and mutual funds into cash. The mutual funds transactions cleared that evening. The securities cleared the following week. On the Thursday following his disappearance, $23,842,377 was wired from the account. He left exactly one dollar, enough to keep the account open. I glanced at Lizzie to see how she was taking this disastrous news.

Her face had drained of color. Her eyes scrunched shut as though to avoid seeing the facts in front of her. Her breathing had become shallow and rapid. Her hands shook until she sat on them.

"Lizzie?" I said quietly.

"I'm having a hard time with this, Seamus. Getting dumped . . ."

To my knowledge, Lizzie had always been the dumper, never the dumpee. "You have other assets?"

"That's our joint account. Most of Al's earnings go into the business or his fund. We have overseas real estate—condos and the like. I have the money from . . ." She had the grace to look down at the floor. "From our settlement. Al has his own money from before we married. I insisted on a prenuptial to show I wanted him, not his money." She yanked her hands from beneath her and slammed them onto the arms of the settee. "That was stupid, stupid, stupid. Now I don't have either him or our money. This really sucks, Seamus. What will I do?"

"First, limit the damage. Then you can start repairing your life. Is your personal money safe?"

She rose, crossed her arms, trapping her hands beneath her elbows, and walked to my side, bringing with her the scent of her fruity Joy perfume. I hadn't seen her apply it.

"That's not what I meant. I've got plenty of money sitting in Al's fund. It's grown rather nicely." She jutted her chin in a gesture of defiance and petulance I'd often seen as our marriage crashed. "You know, he is really very good at what he does. Last year he earned seventy-five million before taxes."

Holy shit. During my time on Wall Street a great year was a low seven-figure payout. I refocused my attention on Lizzie. She was cycling through the stages of grief in nanoseconds: first shock and denial, then anger and bargaining, with pain and guilt providing the padding in between. I was not invested in my ex-wife's emotions. I had exhausted those resources during our own divorce. Regardless, I didn't want to see her financially screwed by "the Jerk," as Paddy called Al. "Did you change the password to that account?"

She closed her eyes and bowed her head. "Al showed me statements every quarter. I don't know anything about online access. I trusted him. How could I have been so wrong? I always knew you had that Boy Scout in you, so when you quit your job in a huff, I wasn't totally surprised. I thought you would grow out of it because of Patrick and me. But damn you, you didn't and you left me."

Quick as a cat she backhanded me, and before I could even react to the pain or the metallic taste of blood in my mouth from biting my cheek, she grabbed both my hands in hers.

"Oh Seamus, I am *so* sorry. I didn't mean to hit you. If you hadn't left me I wouldn't have met Al and none of this would have happened."

So now this was all my fault? I pried my hands apart and got up. When I spread my arms to disengage, she slid inside them and grabbed me tightly. Her body shook with huge sobs.

"What should I do, Seamus? Oh god, I don't know what to do."

All I wanted was to be anywhere else. I was extremely glad I had insisted she get dressed. Despite her recent recasting of who left whom, I remembered with embarrassment my angry feelings toward her after she ended our marriage. I had fervently wished someone would do to her what she had done to me so she'd know how it felt. Now she did, and I knew I had been small and petty.

Let the past be past and focus on the now. Secure her money and then find his. If he was pulling in seventy-five million a year, there should be a ton of assets somewhere.

Lizzie broke her grasp of me and stepped toward the mirror. "Look at the mess I've made of myself. This will never do." She brushed her cheeks with the heels of her hands and slicked back an errant strand of hair with her tears. "Don't tell Patrick anything. I don't want his pity or his 'I told you so.' I'll need a lawyer, and I'll need to have the house appraised—no I won't. That's in the trust along with those damn cars of his."

She stamped her foot. "Damn you, Albert Cunningham the Third, I wish I had never met you." Collapsing to the settee she sobbed into her hands, "That's not true at all. I still love the asshole. Tell me what to do next, Seamus. You were always the logical one."

"First, lock down whatever you have. Tomorrow, go to the bank and close your joint account so he can't overdraw it. Open one in your name only. Call your husband's firm and withdraw your money from the hedge fund—better yet, have your lawyer do it. Is there someone who manages your international real estate? No? We'll worry about that later. Call a locksmith and change all the locks on your doors. Do you have a joint safe-deposit box?"

"The door locks are electronic. I can change the code. We have separate safety deposit boxes, but we each can sign into the other's."

"Fine. While you're at the bank, take everything from his and put it in yours and eliminate his name from the ability to sign in to yours. Maybe his box will contain deeds or some clue to the international real estate."

She paced in tight circles, shaking her hands over her head. "Too much. I'll never remember all this. You need to write it all down."

"I'll put a list together. You call the credit card companies and cancel all your joint cards. Just because he hasn't used them so far doesn't mean he won't and stick you with the bills." She had continued to walk tight loops near the sofas. I caught her by her shoulders. "You can fret and get angry later. Time to act."

She hauled her purse to the desk, extracted a violet Hermes leather card case, and dumped a half dozen credit cards onto the desk. Her voice was shaky on the first phone call, but she managed to cancel the card and have the helpful agent send her a personal application. I opened a notetaking app on her tablet and listed all the things she needed to do to financially wall herself off from her husband.

Clearly, she would need a ready source of funds in the near future. If nothing else, all those brokerage account sales would trigger a sizable tax liability. My fingers stopped typing at "tax." I scrolled through the brokerage account records and found what I had previously skimmed but not absorbed. Before he withdrew the rest of the money, he sent electronic payments to both the federal and New Jersey tax authorities.

If he stole their joint money and skedaddled, why pay the taxes? It only made sense if he was worried the feds would come after him for tax evasion. Nothing illegal in taking money from a joint account, but not paying taxes could generate legal heat in a New York minute. If I were hightailing it, would I have thought that far ahead? Doubtful. But this guy had.

But if he expected to disappear, probably overseas to where he owned a pile of real estate, why not drain the checking account too? He might consider it chump change compared to the twenty-three million. But if so, why withdraw five hundred bucks a day? Maybe he had forgotten a checkbook, and ATM withdrawals were the only way to get at the money. Or maybe his plan had been to escape to some tax haven and for whatever reason he couldn't leave the U.S. I waited until Lizzie ended her current phone call. "Where does he keep his passport?"

"One time he was in San Francisco and needed to make a quick trip to Japan but had to wait for me to express his passport to him. Since then, he's carried it on his trips."

"So he could be long gone," I mused loudly to myself.

"But he hasn't used our credit cards, and he's taking money from those

Savannah ATMs. The last one was . . ." She went to the desk and checked a note. "At 3:52 p.m. from Ogeechee Road Highway 17 in Savannah."

"That reminds me. I forgot to tell you, Paddy's friend looked at cell-tower records. Your husband's phone went silent at the Savannah/Hilton Head airport that Friday morning. What time's your flight today?"

"You used to be able to fly directly from Cincinnati to Newark. Now they make me connect. It's something like one thirty. I should leave here by noon."

"Better leave earlier. The Reds have an afternoon game and the traffic will be terrible."

"I have one credit card to go." She finished and walked behind me, ruffling my hair and sending a tingle up my spine. "What's her name?"

"Huh?"

"Her name. The woman you were with last night. You're wearing the same clothes you had on yesterday. You're yawning because you didn't get enough sleep, and unlike yesterday when we hugged and you got a hard-on, today, nothing."

I shook my head to grab some thinking time. "For starters, it's none of your damn business. I did not want to sleep in my house, so I stayed with a friend. One of the people I talked to last night suggested a way to determine if the person making the ATM withdrawals is Al, but it involves traveling to Savannah."

"You're right. Sorry. Just my way of trying to cope with all of this." She indicated the credit cards with a wave of her hand. Are you suggesting that I should change my flights?"

"It's more important for you to protect your stuff in New Jersey. If you think the idea has merit, fly down to Savannah later in the day."

"And meet you there?"

Aw crud, why hadn't I anticipated that? Lizzie was proving to be my own personal tar baby.

EIGHT

PATRICK MARKED TIME UNTIL CINDY got home. They'd planned a long walk along Lake Michigan, ending at a downtown restaurant for an early dinner. With the volume of the baseball game on the TV barely audible, he traded Twitter jabs with other Cubs fans. Cheech slept curled on his lap. Chong, tucked in next to his hip, kept rearranging herself, trying for the perfect position.

From his phone the tune "Mommas, Don't Let Your Babies Grow Up to Be Cowboys" announced a call from his mother. "Everything all right?" he asked before realizing how stupid the question was. "I mean with the trip home."

"Your father asked me to check our credit reports. I can't remember why, and I wouldn't know what to look at because Al was paranoid someone would steal our identity and he used a monitoring service."

Patrick clicked off the TV. "Dad didn't say what he was looking for?"

"He gets so impatient with me. I didn't want to ask him again. You think like he does, and I feel like stress is making me stupid. Besides, he already had me cancel all our credit cards, so I really don't know what good the credit reports will do."

"They'll show information on all the debts you and . . . your husband have." He needed to be careful; he had almost called him the Jerk. "It'll show the last balance and whether the account has been paid on time. Maybe Dad wanted you to find out if there were any other cards?"

"That's it! And he wanted to know if Al had used any email accounts since—while he's been gone. I don't know how to do that either."

"That's not from the credit reports, Mom. One thing at a time. For the credit reports, you'll have to answer security questions. Do you remember how to let me remotely control your computer?"

He talked her through it for the umpteenth time. Using the website for free credit reports, he clicked on his mother's resident state, New Jersey, and filled in the required information including her Social Security number.

Patrick scanned the credit report summary: no negative items. "Take your time, Mom. Go through the list one at a time. Any accounts you don't recognize?" While his mother talked her way down the list, he perused the details. Of course, if the Jerk had an individual card, it would show only on his report.

"The cards I canceled still show as active."

"It takes time for the credit card companies to report changes to the rating agencies and for the agencies to post the changes. Take a look at the balances. Do they all look okay? They look consistent in the last few months."

"Oh, my goodness," his mother said. "I forgot I had a Nordstrom's card. I must remember to go there more often."

Patrick counted to five. "Anything else?"

"This isn't right," his mother said. "We don't have a mortgage. Al bought the house from his mother with cash and put it and all those antique cars he collects into a trust. How could they screw up something like that?"

The mortgage originated less than a month ago. Because it showed on her credit record, did that mean her name was on the loan? He did a quick calculation. Even at the current low rates, the monthly repayment on a ten-year loan of six million bucks was something north of sixty grand a month. The first payment was due soon.

"The house is in a trust?"

"Yes. Al's way of making sure no future owner tore it down. His cars also belong to the trust. He plans to convert most of the house and grounds into a museum dedicated to early twentieth-century autos. The trust was for tax purposes. I don't know the details. Last month a bunch of new cars—not new-new—you know, new-to-him cars arrived. That's his hobby, not mine, although it is fun to drive them occasionally."

Should he tell his mother her loving husband had not only wiped out their joint accounts, but had taken out a substantial mortgage in both their names on their home, possibly to pay for a bunch more antiques? With each heartbeat, his closed eyes ached with a dull jab of pain. This was not a conversation a child should have to have with a parent.

"Everything else on here looks okay to me," she said.

"If he ordered a new joint card before he disappeared, it would have shown up. Do you know his Social Security number so we can check one of his reports?"

"Where would I find it?"

He suppressed his first thought, *From the mortgage application.* Instead he said, "Tax return?"

"Oh Patrick, our accountant does all that. I wouldn't have the faintest idea where to look."

And besides, Patrick thought, you wouldn't know the three security questions. Out loud: "You want me to look at his emails?"

Once she accepted Patrick's electronic request to take over Al's laptop, she said she really should get a bite to eat. Could Patrick call her if she needed to see or do something?

He would, and hoped to finish before Cindy arrived home. He found no outgoing email messages since the Jerk had left. None of the many incoming messages provided a clue where he was or what he was doing. Patrick's stomach rumbled and he checked his watch. Cindy was late—again. Might as well see if he could find anything useful on either his mother's or the Jerk's computers.

Patrick ran a series of adware, malware, and spyware-checking programs on both computers. The Jerk's was essentially clean. His mother's laptop had enough tracking cookies to make the NSA jealous of the data she released every time she turned it on. Patrick deleted them all and made a note to tell her she needed to change her passwords to ones her husband could not guess.

Patrick found no additional email accounts, chat logs, or any other forms of electronic communication. He checked their recycle bins (clean) and the folders containing deleted emails not yet erased. Nothing for the Jerk. His mother, evidently, did not automatically erase her deleted emails because she had thousands dating back two years to when Patrick had bought and set up the computer for her.

His custom programs found no hidden files on the hard drives other than standard system files. He did discover one encrypted file on his mother's laptop—interesting because his mother understood encryption as well as she did Boolean algebra, which is to say not at all. He scrolled through their browser histories. Hers had a lot of shopping and redecorating websites mixed in with news and NPR podcasts. His ran more to world news and business stories and a number of financial institutions, each requiring secure logins.

Patrick next explored all the "recent documents" recorded by the various

Office programs. Buried in an Excel spreadsheet labeled "vacation-ideas.xlxs" was an alphabetized list of two hundred websites with userIDs and passwords.

Yes, the keys to the kingdom are in my hands.

Cindy startled him when she kissed the top of his head. "Sorry I'm late," she said. "Ready to go?"

"Too late now," Patrick said. "Want to be Maid Marian to my Robin Hood?"

NINE

MOM AND I SPENT THE day playing Cincinnati tourists. I drove her around the city and was amazed at how much had changed while I had been away. The streets at the south end of the University of Cincinnati had all been redone. Parts of Over-the-Rhine were becoming gentrified; the Banks development was in place along the Ohio River. Mt. Adams looked much the same as I remembered, but I had never known that neighborhood well. The day had warmed up nicely and I knew if I didn't want to fall asleep, I had to keep moving, so after we visited the National Underground Railroad Freedom Center, we strolled through Spring Grove Cemetery and read headstones for a couple of hours.

Now with Mom reading herself to sleep in "her" bedroom in my house, I struggled to keep my eyes open, but I didn't want to miss Abigail's promised Skype call, which was to be "after dinner." Since she was on the West Coast, my computer didn't ring until ten o'clock.

I accepted the call and Abigail appeared on my screen. Her white tank top displayed a recently acquired tan, although untanned skin rimmed her eyes: the opposite of a raccoon-eye look. The offending aviator glasses sat on the table next to her. "I can see you've been spending time on the beach."

"This guy I'm guarding is not exactly an intellectual heavyweight, so please throw in a couple of multisyllabic words, okay? Am I right that you're in your Cincinnati library?"

I related my dealings with Lizzie. Abigail made sympathetic noises in all the right places. "It's been a long time since we've seen each other. Any chance you can meet Mom and me in Memphis? She has a couple of gigs down there next weekend, and it's a town I haven't explored."

She dropped her smile and scrunched her face in what looked like distaste. "I wish I could, but this job is taking longer than we initially thought. It'll probably be another two weeks, maybe three. Where will you two be then? Are you still concluding your trip at the end of the month?"

What caught me by surprise was not her answer, but the depth of my despair at her answer. "I'm really missing you. You can't get time off for bad behavior? Even three or four days?" *Boy, does that ever sound needy.*

She threw her head back, temporarily moving out of the camera's view. Her bubbly laugh arrived with her smiling face returning to focus. "Oh, Seamus, I miss you too, but extreme horniness is not sufficient reason for breaking my commitments. I'd need a real major crisis. Once this job is done, I can visit wherever you and your mother are."

"I thought before we returned to Boston, Mom would like to see where Paddy and Cindy and her grandcats live. If this house sale—rather, deacquisition—multisyllabic enough for you?—had gone through, I thought maybe I'd look for a place in the Chicago area. That way when you aren't away on business, it'll be much easier for us to be together. I'd also be nearer to Paddy."

She shook a finger, as though I were a naughty boy. "I'm not sure chasing your child is such a good idea. Kids tend not to stay put, and then where are you?"

In the following silence, I focused on her expression to gain clues as to why she responded to the part about being near Paddy and ignored the part that had to do with being close to her. She chose that moment to turn away from the camera and drink from a glass.

"I wasn't thinking so much of chasing after Paddy as it being—"

"You know," she interrupted, "even though one bad thing happened at your house, I still have fond memories of our times together there. Do you remember that time I got Mrs. Keenan to help sneak me in?"

I did indeed, and I was glad my mother was behind closed doors far away from the library. The rest of our call lasted twenty minutes and was definitely not mom-rated.

The release I experienced while talking with Abigail dissipated with my first step toward my bedroom. By the time I reached the first landing on the staircase, my feet weighed a hundred pounds each. Standing at the threshold, I realized I had made a mistake arranging the rented furniture in the same configuration I'd had before the fire ruined my bedroom set. A flood of memories burst over me: I hear breaking glass downstairs. Abigail grabs her trusty Sig Sauer. Abigail is shot. I kill the guy.

I shook my head to get rid of the visions. I held out my normally rock-solid hands in front of me and observed them trembling. My corded neck radiated pain up my skull and around into my eyes. "Get a grip," I said out loud. With immense relief, I remembered I still needed to brush my teeth and floss. I tossed my computer on the chair and retreated to that routine.

When I returned to the bedroom and bent down to unlace my shoes, a flash of pain exploded behind my eyes. *That's it.* I grabbed a pillow from the bed and rushed from the room.

THE CELL PHONE'S RING WOKE me. I found the phone on the Infiniti's passenger seat and croaked, "Hello?"

"He withdrew another five hundred dollars yesterday. The ATM was in Thunderbolt, just outside Savannah. Last night after I got home—you know, Seamus, traveling used to be a real pleasure. Now even in first class it's nothing special. The wet towel they gave me before the meal wasn't even hot and the caterers forgot the linen placemats. They had to set the tray directly on the plastic table."

I cranked the seat up and tried to bring the dashboard clock into focus. *Where are my glasses?* My thinking seemed as fuzzy as my vision. The eastern sky was lightening in predawn promise of a new day. "Lizzie, what time is it?"

"You're always up by five thirty."

I found my glasses in a cup holder. The clock reported thirty-two minutes past five. "You got home okay, right?"

"I got home, but we were an hour late." She paused to swallow. *Coffee, OJ, or something stronger?* "I had Patrick do his remote takeover thing on Al's computer. Mine too. He was to look for whatever he looks for and call last night if he found anything or first thing this morning, at the latest. And I haven't heard a thing. I—"

"For heaven's sake, Lizzie. It's only four thirty his time. Anything on the credit reports?"

"Can you believe our bank thinks we took out a mortgage last month? That will take forever and a day to straighten out. One more thing to take care of once the bank opens."

"And you'll close your checking account and empty his safe-deposit box?"

"Oh yes, right. That's why I was going to the bank in the first place."

Good grief, Lizzie. Pull it together. "You called for a reason?"

"To give you my flight information. I get in—"

God, give me the serenity to accept the things I cannot change. "Lizzie, did you send me the email with all the ATM locations? I said I'd help you figure out who was taking money from the account, and I will. I'll use Google Earth to pinpoint your best prospects. As my friend Lt. Hastings suggested, you're the one most likely to elicit sympathy from a local shop owner. Having me around might even hurt."

"I don't know Google Earth, and I've never been to Savannah, and I thought you were coming to support me."

"I'm taking care of Mom. I can't just fly to Savannah. Besides, I can't do anything in Savannah that you can't do as well, if not better."

"Can't you—"

"Email me a list of the ATM locations. By the time you finish at the bank, I'll scout the most likely areas for you to find a shop that might have their own surveillance." Her muffled sobs threatened to derail my train of thought. "Call me once you've inventoried the safe-deposit box, okay?"

Her sobs became a full-throated crying jag

"You know, Lizzie, it still wouldn't surprise me if he shows up at your house now that the money spigot's shut off. Was there anything else?"

Thankfully there wasn't. I really needed to pee.

PATRICK COULD SWEAR SOMEONE HAD removed his eyeballs, scraped them with coarse sandpaper, and shoved them back in his head. When Cindy went to bed, he had intended to look at "just one more thing." Instead, he had spent the night pawing through computer files on both his mother's and the Jerk's computers and crawled into bed only minutes before Cindy's alarm sounded. He'd convinced Cheech and Chong to desert her side of the bed and curl onto his chest. He kept his eyes closed, his breathing steady all through her shower, hair drying, dressing, and applying makeup.

At the click of the front door, he pushed aside the covers and sent the cats scurrying with a scrabbling of sharp toenails on the comforter. He checked his cell phone: four more messages, surely all from his mother. He wasn't ready to talk to her. His first meeting wasn't until early afternoon. He could spend a few more hours sorting through the remaining computer files and—

"What's going on, Patrick?"

Cindy stood at the bedroom threshold, her shoes in one hand, her other hand upraised in question. His tired brain took an extra beat to realize he, not Cindy, was the one fooled.

"At three in the morning with no you to spoon with, I got worried and found you working in the study. And then you tiptoed into the bedroom like a teenager trying not to wake up his parents after partying all night."

Heat burned Patrick's face as it became clear his ploy had not only failed, it had ignited Cindy's investigative reporter instincts. No stopping her now. Why was it so hard to share his concerns?

"You'll be late for work." *That was lame.* Here he was a drowning man, who should be grateful for the tossed life-saving ring; instead he felt aggravated. At himself. At Cindy. At the whole damn world.

She dropped her heels to the floor and slipped them on. "I'm not leaving until we talk." She spread her feet and blocked the door using her "Wonder Woman" pose. She glowered, but couldn't hold it and broke into a deep-throated chuckle. She dropped her hands, put on that crooked smile of hers he so loved, and beckoned for him to come and give her a hug. "Don't mess the paint job."

Her arms wrapped around him and he relaxed, burying his nose in the rosemary overtones of her freshly shampooed hair. "I need to sort it out."

"I'm a smart girl, maybe I can help. If nothing else, talking it through will help clarify whatever's bothering you. And . . ." She rose to her tiptoes and kissed his forehead. "And, I am not leaving until you tell all."

"In that case." Patrick undid her top button.

She flicked his hand away. "You're trying to change the subject."

Nailed again. He noticed she hadn't redone the button and parts of him stirred, suggesting not all of him was as exhausted as his brain. Although she was smiling now, the Wonder Woman pose meant she was serious. Not telling her what was going on was not worth getting into a great big fight, especially when she was right. Open the flood gates and let it all out.

"It's about my dad."

"What's your father done now?"

"It's not him. It's me. You know he asked me to take care of his assets, right?"

"After the whole . . . the situation at his camp. I was worried for him, but it's been two years. I had the impression he's doing fine. No?"

"That's what I said. It's me. I screwed up his investments. I made a couple of large investments. I figured he'd have sold his house by now, so his cash flow didn't concern me. And LT2P should've sold too, so he could cash out his stake. But LT2P's sale is delayed and he hasn't sold his Cincinnati place, which means he's about to run out of money and I haven't told him."

"So sell something to raise cash. I don't understand what the big deal is. And I don't understand why you're still managing his assets. I thought it was a temporary thing."

"One temporary thing turned into another. Now he's traveling with Grandma. And . . ."

Cindy spun her hands to encourage him to get to the point.

"I can't sell anything. He owns the house in Cincinnati, the property in the U.P., his stake in LT2P. I already sold his other assets to buy a position in another startup that I'm sure will do well. All that's left is his IRA. Breaking into an IRA comes with a huge penalty."

"It's a temporary problem. LT2P is selling soon. In the meantime, he can borrow from his credit cards like a normal person. What's the big deal? Give him a call."

Patrick's stomach clenched. There was a difference between knowing what he should do and actually wanting to do it. Besides, now wasn't a good time, what with the shit going down with his mom.

"It's also about my mom."

Cindy chuckled. "Freud says it's all about the mother for you boys. Do I need to warn your father to watch his back?"

"Not funny. Mom might be responsible for her husband's disappearance."

Ten

UPON OPENING THE BATHROOM DOOR after completing my shower, I was surprised to hear NPR's "Morning Edition" coming up from the kitchen. I double-timed it down the back stairway and found Mom sitting at the kitchen table in the same seat Lizzie had chosen. She held a steaming cup of coffee from a shop on Ludlow. A newspaper lay open on the table with the Sudoku, Cryptogram, and Jumble completed; only a few squares on the crossword puzzle remained blank.

"This is early for you," I said. "I didn't wake you, did I?"

"I didn't sleep well last night, so I figured I'd see if there's anything to Franklin's "Early to bed, early to rise" crap. What's an island in Japan with six letters ending with 'shu'?"

I had accused Paddy of being Mr. Nonsequitur. After this trip with my mother, I concluded it might be a generation-skipping trait. "No clue. Do you ever look things up? Google them?"

She gave me a look that could fry bacon crispy.

I flushed at her reaction and dismissed my ignorance with a double wave of my hands. "Forget I suggested it, oh ye mistress of purity in puzzle completion. I jogged an early eight-miler this morning and missed you going out for your morning fix. Have you eaten?"

My phone rang before she could answer. Distracted by mother's unexpected behavior, I forgot to look at the display to tell me who was calling. I answered with a tentative, "Hello?"

"Hey, Dad. Not too early I hope?"

"Your mother already told me about the mortgage, which I assume was no mistake. Find anything else?"

"No. I mean, yes. Well, sort of. Where to start?"

Paddy was not a mumble-mouth. My parental antennae extended fully.

Mom whispered, "Who is it?"

I waved her off and stuck a finger in one ear so I could hear him better.

"I wish I still had access to NSA software to scan the Jerk's emails," he said. "Instead, I stayed up all night reading. No hot-and-bothered paramour emails. Nothing about selling the business. I did discover keylogger software."

"English, please."

"That was English, Dad. I wasn't geeking you." He exhaled a puff of air and in the background I could hear Cindy say, "Just tell him, Patrick."

"In a nutshell, every keystroke the Jerk typed on his computer was sent over their internal wireless network."

"Their network, not outside?"

"Inside—although if someone had their encryption key and was nearby, they could still grab it. Good thing I had control of Mom's computer because I discovered typing something on his computer caused an encrypted file on her computer to grow larger. The program sends stuff to Mom's computer."

"You're saying your mother put spyware on his computer?"

My mother yanked my free arm. "Put it on speaker so I can hear."

"Sorry, Paddy, interruption here. I'm with your grandmother and putting you on speaker, okay?" I couldn't hear his answer as I set the phone down on the table next to the newspaper and punched on the speaker. "Repeat, please?"

"I thought the same thing, but Cindy pointed out the Jerk could have done it."

"You lost me."

Another puff of air came down the line. "What if you wanted a record of everything you did, but didn't want it on your computer? The Jerk could install the sending software on his machine and the receiving software on Mom's, transmit over their home network, and delete things from his computer. He had a shredder program installed, so they'd be securely destroyed, but he'd still have a record available on hers."

"That makes no sense to me. If he planned to skip out on your mother, why use her machine, which he probably can't access? He could have copied his stuff into the cloud in a safe, secure manner."

"Online's not so safe and not so secure. With a court order, any police department could access it. Hackers don't need the court order."

"With a court order, they can get it from your mother's computer. So what are you saying? And if he wanted to copy files to her machine, why not use a memory stick. What good are the keystrokes?"

"Maybe he needed to remember how to do something or prove he had done something. I don't know. The file's encrypted. I'll research the program to understand its security and figure out what kind of key to look for. There wasn't much on his computer, but Mom said he routinely did backups to a hard drive. He carted files to and from work on flash drives. I'm not sure what's going on."

My mother grabbed my head and pulled it down to her mouth and whispered. "He's worried his mother's involved, but he doesn't want to believe it."

"You think an external drive might have information not on his computer?"

"I had Mom look around his office, but she couldn't find anything."

"Can you get to New Jersey and see the whole setup for yourself? Your Mom leaves this afternoon for Savannah." Leaving unsaid that she wouldn't be around to interfere.

"I have an eleven o'clock tomorrow with All-American. I could leave from there."

"Can't you push the meeting back a day or two? No? Maybe he has handwritten notes or an explanatory file on an external hard drive. Understanding that could be the key."

"It's not that easy, Dad. They're a crit—Hold on Cindy's saying something to me." Patrick must have muted the phone because the line, though still connected, went silent. "Cindy says she agrees with you. I'll try to change the meeting. Cindy wants to talk with you, Dad."

"Hello, Seamus. I told Patrick I sense a ticking clock. We haven't found it yet, so we don't know how much time we have left, but every second we delay could be crucial."

"I hear you. During my run this morning I changed my mind. I'll join Paddy's mother in Savannah. My past history with her clouded the issue for me. If it had been anyone else, I know I'd feel guilty if I didn't help any way I could."

"Seamus," my mother said, "you and I need to talk."

I waved her away, popped the phone off speaker, and wrapped up the conversation, ending by trading "I love yous" with Paddy.

Mom hunched over her crossword puzzle, pretending not to know I was ready to talk. Maybe using a neutral spot with other people around would help dissipate the steams of anger I sensed rising from her. I suggested we walk to Ludlow and grab breakfast.

She eased her coffee onto a coaster composed of a folded piece of toilet paper. "You sure you don't know that Japanese island. The second letter could be either an 'i' or a 'y'?"

"Mother."

"I am no longer hungry." She tossed her pencil on the table. "You want breakfast, go get it. I'll be here." She picked up her pencil and scowled at the paper.

I tried to recall our rules of engagement. Our last serious argument had been while I was in college and ended in me slamming out of the house all because my mother wouldn't let me go to the Cape for the weekend with a mixed group of friends.

"You don't have any exhibitions scheduled until the weekend. We have plenty of time to drive to Savannah and help Lizzie figure out who's using the ATMs before we go to Memphis. We can catch Atlanta on the return if you want or hang in Savannah for a few days. It's a lovely city."

"Whatever."

"That's a teenager's response, Mom. Talk to me."

"She's got you wrapped around her little finger. We had plans, and now I'm just baggage. How would you feel if I dumped you and stayed out all night with my ex? And now, rather than spend several days wandering around Kentucky and Tennessee as we planned, she twitches her finger and you run after her to God knows where."

"That's not—"

"You've already decided, Seamus. Go get your breakfast. I'll be resigned to your plan when you return." She shifted in her chair and showed me her back.

I clapped my hands and held my arms up and wide in a supplication to heaven. "You think I spent the last two nights with Lizzie?" Of their own accord my hands dropped and slapped my thighs.

Without facing me she said, "You never came home the first night and last night you slipped out of the house."

"That is so rich. I don't need to explain myself to you, Mom, but I'll try anyway. I had a lot of catching up to do with Lieutenant Hastings, and we ended up at her house killing a bottle of wine. Actually, two. I was not in condition to drive home, so I slept on her couch. She's had breast cancer. Her hair is beginning to grow out, and she really needed to talk with someone not in the department. And she got me talking about the stuff that happened at my place in the Upper Peninsula, which was good for me."

I stopped to take a deep breath. "That was the first night. Last night I tried to sleep here. I couldn't. I got physically sick. I ended up in the car. Now you know how screwed up your son is. Happy?"

"Of course not."

"As for chasing Lizzie, you have no one to blame but yourself. You've said how terrible you felt when Dad didn't get home from second shift when he was supposed to and you couldn't get a hold of him. He always called if he was going to be late, and when he didn't, you were certain something terrible had happened. Your words were 'no one—' and no one includes, Lizzie, does it not? 'No one should have to wonder where her husband is.' *I* am finished being angry at Lizzie for setting me up. Lizzie is Lizzie. Neither one of us might like her tactics or that she wasted the time of two real estate agents, but you have to agree she went to a lot of trouble to try to enlist my help. Why? Because she needs to know what happened to Al. And if you weren't so pissed off at her, you'd agree Lizzie has a right to know. I can help. Paddy can help. We both owe her that."

"I agree she has a right to know. One hundred percent—assuming she doesn't already. Maybe you think I'm selfish, but I am only thinking of you. She can do everything in Savannah by herself. She does not need you. She needs to learn to stand on her own two feet."

"You're probably right, Mom. But she doesn't seem to have any friends to help, does she? Don't make me choose between you or doing what I know inside is right. Can't we just adopt a change in plans?"

"Maybe you think I've forgotten how to be a good mother. Maybe you think I never was one. All I am trying to do is look out for you, Seamus. Maybe you should put me on a flight to Boston and be shut of me."

And stay where? "Come on, Mom. Let's get something to eat. We can continue our conversation once we've calmed down." *Once I've calmed down.*

In a move reminiscent of her days in Sugarbush, she said nothing and returned to her crossword puzzle.

Eleven

PATRICK BEAT A MUFFLED RAT-A-TAT-TAT on the entrance to Lisa Latoya's cubicle. She was in the middle of coding and held up a finger to acknowledge his presence. He plunked down in her visitor's chair to wait. Lisa was the only one in the company who was a one-thing-on-the-desk-at-a-time person. At night, she put away even that one thing. Everyone else's cubicle walls were covered with to-do lists, family pictures, jokes, and whatnot; Lisa had one piece of art mounted: a wood-framed poster of a woman running across a natural stone arch with the inscription: "The race goes not always to the swift but to those who keep on running."

"I heard a big sigh." Lisa turned off her monitor and opened a notepad. "Did we lose a prospect?"

"I need to get to Jersey. Can you take tomorrow's meeting with All-American by yourself?"

Lisa swiveled her chair to face him. "Is your mother okay?"

"Fine. Well, not fine, but it's not her. Well, it is because of her, but—"

Lisa rose and motioned for Patrick to do the same. She opened her arms and steered him into a hug. He bent his knees and stooped to match his six two to her tiptoed five foot two. With the hug, his shoulders dropped an inch, maybe two.

"Remember Lisa's rule number one: Nothing is so bad a hug won't help. Now, from the beginning." She released him and they sat. "Slowly."

With a few prompts from Lisa, Patrick poured out the entire story. He tried to read her expression, but she was a most infuriating boss that way because no one could tell what she was really thinking. He concluded with, "If you don't want to do it alone, I'm sure they'll let us reschedule."

She raised one eyebrow. "Patrick, it is critical for you to be at the meeting. I may be LT2P's president, but they are our client because of you—before you correct me—because of you and your dad. We know their auditor wants to push us out. You agree we cannot afford to lose them?"

The lump in Patrick's throat choked off his air for a reply. He gave a micro-nod.

"Look, Behemoth, Inc.—I've come to appreciate the wisdom in your suggesting that code name—anyway, they already invoked their right to postpone the sale until the end of next quarter. Someone must have cold feet on their side. Unless our revenue declines, deferring the closing will cost them more. But losing All-American could trigger a snowball effect."

A blast of anger at being in this position freed his constricted throat. "You think I don't know?"

She touched his clenched hand with a fingertip. "Of course you know. I'm sorry. I'm feeling the pressure, too. I need you at that meeting, Patrick. No ifs, ands, or buts. Can you fly out, do what you need to do, and fly back early morning? Grab some sleep on the plane?"

"Some of us need more than four hours a night, Lisa."

"If you had help? Like someone to do the electronics while you search for the hard drive and check paper. Ever hear of a dude goes by Sherlock?"

He knew *of* Sherlock, a legendary hacker who for three or four years had been spectacularly active, but gone silent for the last several years. Word was the government was still offering a hefty reward for information leading to his capture. "If I could do the electronics remotely I would. I need to be there."

"I meant to help at your mother's. Two sets of eyes and all that."

Patrick channeled his father *You catching flies?* and snapped his mouth shut. "You know Sherlock? He lives in Jersey?"

"If I get Sherlock, we keep the meeting with All-American. Deal?"

"Awesome." *Sherlock in a real, live quest.* Excitement and relief quickly turned into trepidation. Would the guy think his skills were lacking? What was the cost to Lisa to call in what must be a ginormous favor? Somehow he knew he would pay for this.

TWELVE

WE COMPROMISED. I AGREED TO travel blue highways through the mountains, visit the Revolutionary War battlefield at Cowpens, and spend the night in Columbia, South Carolina. Mom agreed to rise early the second morning so we could arrive in Savannah at the start of business. We traveled I-75 through the rolling hills of Kentucky in silence. I switched to local roads at the Tennessee border where the topography changed from rolling hills into Appalachian mountain remnants.

I wanted to thaw the frost in our relationship. Her insistence on visiting Cowpens—"It's right on the way"—provided what I hoped might be an opener. "Mom, with your interest in colonial history, how come you never traveled?"

She didn't answer. I drove through a series of curves before I could risk glancing her way. Her jaw was clenched, but at my look she said, "Don't you remember the trips we took during the summers?"

"Let's see . . . Old Sturbridge Village. And before Dad died, the four of us spent a few days in Vermont. You bought me a book on Ethan Allen, and I pretended for months to be the last of the 'Green Mountain boys.' You remember? And we went to Saratoga on that trip, didn't we?"

Mom was staring out the window. I wasn't even sure she heard. It's a bit ironic that I had no problem with silences with anyone except Mom. Maybe I was overly sensitive because of her history of retreating to muteness. Her clenched jaw worried me. I had hoped my agreeing to her route to Savannah would make us copacetic. Something was going on in her head, and I needed to drag it into the light.

"Penny for your thoughts?"

"I was thinking back to . . . back before your father died." Her hands waved, conducting an orchestra with loopy gestures. "I know it does no good to dwell on the past or to wonder what might have been. I know we can only live our life in the present, but sometimes I can't help myself. You know, you children were the most important thing for me—and look how that turned out."

At my sharp inhale she laid a heavy hand on my forearm. "Seamus McCree, you've turned out fine. I was thinking of myself. Khalil Gibran said 'you may give your children your love but not your thoughts; for they have their own thoughts.' The same can be said of your doddering old mother. I have my own thoughts and I am responsible for them. Where was I?"

"Trips? Vacations?"

"We didn't have much money while you were growing up. Honest cops don't make a lot and a widow's pension is even less. Your father, bless his soul," she made the sign of the cross, "was a homebody. If something wasn't within a hundred miles of Boston, it wasn't worth the drive. Oh heck, who am I kidding? If it wasn't inside the one-twenty-eight belt, it wasn't worth the drive. It took me two years to convince him to take the Vermont trip. You got your bullheadedness from him."

I smiled. "You say so, Mom."

She showed her best shark grin. "Of course it's true. I'm your mother. Would I ever lie to you?"

I downshifted and floored it to get around a slow-moving truck. I sensed more than saw Mom tense at my maneuver, so I figured I'd lighten it up. "Easter Bunny? Santa Claus?"

She waved those off. "Fiddlesticks. Those aren't lies. Not telling you and your sister how your father really died—that was a lie. Have you forgiven me?"

"I never thought you needed forgiveness. I admit I was miffed at Uncle Mike, but you did what you had to do. I'm surprised you even need to ask."

"Your sister certainly never forgave me."

I faced her, wondering what had brought this twist to our conversation. Her lips puckered as though she would perform an air kiss. Her jaw had relaxed; I was the one grinding my teeth. I opened wide to—

"Watch out!"

I jerked the car from the shoulder onto the road. That got my heart going. I needed to pay attention to driving, but I couldn't let this go. "Didn't you just tell me 'you may give them your love but not your thoughts'? Fiona never told me what caused her to leave, and I have no idea what goes on between my sister's ears."

During the next short straightaway between curves ascending the mountainside, I glanced at Mom. Her image in the side window tapped pursed lips with a pointer finger. "Mom? Did Fiona ever tell *you* why she stopped communicating with me?"

"It took everything I had to keep us together after your father died. I faked it pretty well until both of you were out of the house. The last conversation I had with your sister was a knock-down drag-out about how she treated you. Then . . . then I withdrew. She never gave me a reason why she treated you like shit. Or what she's doing or where she is. I assume she hates me for some reason, but she's truly a cypher to me."

I shot her another quick glance, making sure not to follow my tendency and steer toward her. Tears leaked from the corners of her eyes, followed creases to her chin, and fell onto her lap. Again, I considered abandoning this discussion, but for the first time on the trip, Mom had introduced my sister into the conversation. Mom's doctor had suggested I should encourage her to discuss things that upset her. "She legally changed her name years ago, but if you want to know, I can tell you where she is and what she's doing."

She lowered her window, allowing the humid mountain air to swirl around us. It smelled like rain was soon coming. I hoped we'd be through the mountains before it started. With the heavy air came a light overtone of what . . . dogwood? I wished I knew flowering-tree smells better. I wondered if someone had published a scratch-and-sniff book for trees and shrubs, it would—

"How could you know that, Seamus?"

I snapped to the conversation.

"One time at Sugarbush you sat with me—before you knew whether or not I could even hear you—and you told me she hasn't talked to you since the day she graduated from college. I know she returned all your letters unopened. The way she treated you broke my heart. I can think of no justification for her behavior."

She faced me. No tears now. Her face was all hard angles. "I thought I taught the two of you better. I thought you knew nothing was more sacred than family, except God, maybe. Whatever I have done in this life, I did with that in mind. Maybe that's wrong, but that's the way I was brought up, and that's the way your father was brought up. Did you hire someone to find her?"

"Paddy did it on his own."

"My word! Isn't he something?"

"Yes he is, Mom. Your grandson really is something."

With an electronic zip, she closed the window. "Since we're onto taboo subjects, let me ask you this: Your father died and you end up joining a gang. Why a gang?"

"I didn't realize we had taboo subjects."

"Every family has elephants in the living room. We're special. We have a fucking herd."

If her intention was to lighten the mood, she had succeeded and had me laughing. "The traditional rationale is I was searching for a father figure."

Mom snorted. "You traditional? There's a joke. Besides, sports would have done as well—which is what you eventually discovered with your soccer. How old were you before the gang made you their treasurer? Twelve? Thirteen? You kept track of the money. You made sure there were funds to bail out gang members when they got caught. Granted, you may have joined the gang because you needed male bonding, but in short order you were taking care of them. And did you ever rat one of them out? I don't think you did. They were family, but that's not my point. Why did you marry Elisabeth?"

I was still processing her analysis of my gang years, and took a moment to switch gears. "Because she was smart, she made me laugh, she had a soft spot for people society doesn't much care for." *And she had a great body, and the sex was spectacular.*

"Oh sure, she's intelligent and good-looking, and has a master's, so she understands your fifty-cent words. Did she do anything with her education? No, she did not. You married her because she needed you to take care of her. She produced one grandchild for me, and you mostly raised him. She's a galaxy away from being your equal, yet she dumped you like last week's garbage instead of backing your principled stand against Wall Street. She's weak. She knows nothing about what family means."

So much for the light mood. "I'm not sure that's fair to Lizzie."

"You're right. I'm probably overstating her positive attributes. The next few women you dated were all losers you met at church. Y'know, social workers tell people to go to Unitarian churches because they're so welcoming?"

With a sideways glance, I checked to see if she was kidding. She was not wearing her smiley face. "That's ridiculous, and you never met the women

I dated. I just told you about them. They weren't right for me, or I didn't see them as being good for Paddy. They were not losers."

"If you say so. I know for a fact that social workers do recommend Unitarian churches. Half the people at Sugarbush ended up attending the one nearby. So you finally meet someone who has her head screwed on straight, who has her own job and doesn't care a whit how much money you have or what kind of lifestyle she could enjoy, and you can't deal with it."

Fine, if she wanted to hash this out, we'd autopsy one of those elephants right now. "I assume you mean Abigail?"

"Who else? Are you afraid of strong women? Think about it. You ended up marrying Elisabeth, who you'll have to admit can't stand on her own. You can't get your act together with Abigail, who is definitely strong."

I figured muddying the situation by mentioning Lt. Tanya Hastings was another strong woman with whom I had a conflicted relationship was not in my interest. Somehow this discussion had progressed from the importance of family to this. "Just because Abigail and I are not married doesn't mean it's because I can't deal with her being an independent person. One, who according to your theory, I can't gel with because she wouldn't have to rely on me."

"Didn't Abigail tell you that you need to get over your guilt?"

"Yeah. Sort of."

Mom clapped her hands and spread her arms wide, barely stopping short of whacking me. "And do you not agree that you feel guilty because you think you should have protected her? That's why you can't sleep in your own house?"

I pictured Abigail bleeding on my dining room rug while I gave her mouth-to-mouth. I drew out a "Probably."

"And has not everyone who knows Abigail told you she did not ask to be taken care of? She's a fully qualified bodyguard who put herself in jeopardy? Of course they have. But because you need—catch the word, Seamus—you *need* to be in control, you feel guilty. Everyone knows this, except you."

"So now I'm a control freak?"

"Your mouth to God's ear."

I had to think about that for a moment. "I don't think that's the right expression."

"Whatever." She waved away the objection. "You said it, God agrees."

"Seriously, now. Do you feel I'm too controlling? Overall. Not just this change to our plans to help take care of Lizzie's problem." There was that phrase—"take care of"—I guess I needed to think on that.

"I worry," Mom said. "What happens when this trip is over? We've danced around where I'll live. It's been so long since I managed my own place, I'm sure you worry whether I can do it. I wonder too. Maybe I should have a roommate or even live in some kind of a group home. But I'm happy you'll let me stay in the Boston area and not be like some children who force their parents to move to where they live."

Not a problem since I wasn't sure where I wanted to live. For several miles we each dealt with our own thoughts. Sometime later I realized the clouds had thickened into a gray, fast-moving mass. "Looks like rain, Mom. You didn't have breakfast. Should we stop for lunch or try to beat the weather and push to the battlefield?"

"I won't starve if I miss a meal. When will I get back here? If it pours, we'll leave, but I'm not the Wicked Witch. A little rain won't kill me."

I looked up at the still-darkening sky. "A deal's a deal and I wouldn't want to be accused of being controlling or anything. At least we won't have to worry about sunburn."

Seventeen miles away from Cowpens, the skies opened up. A disappointed Mom agreed Cowpens would have to fend for itself. Rain continued all the way down I-26. Even with new tires, the Infiniti G-20 had never been great on slick roads. Rather than maintain my usual seven miles above the speed limit, I pulled into the right-hand lane and slowed down to sixty-five, five miles below the speed limit. I was the only one worried about the visibility and slick roads. Traffic whizzed by and I received a number of angry looks and extended fingers letting me know I was number one in their books.

Outside Columbia, South Carolina, where the road widens to six lanes, I was relieved to see the speed limit drop to sixty. I eased off the accelerator and the guy behind me ran up my ass. To avoid being a traffic hazard, I was forced to match their speed and white-knuckled my approach to the Y split of I-26 and the spur heading into Columbia itself. Brake lights flashed on the car in front of me. The Chevy to my immediate left also braked. It began fishtailing. With a quick check in the side mirror, I removed my foot from the accelerator and eased right to give him room to recover. He signaled to enter my lane. I tapped my brakes and checked my rearview mirror to make sure the folks following us were paying attention.

The car behind me had also slowed, but an SUV in the left lane ran up on the Chevy. I had nowhere to go and my stomach clenched as the SUV swerved straight for me. I punched the accelerator, but before the Infiniti responded, the SUV crunched my rear panel throwing my car into a spin.

In my hyper-sensitized state, the action became slow motion. My new tires maintained contact with the pavement. The accelerator kicked in and we jerked forward. Forward was no longer straight down the highway. I plowed into the Chevy and sent him in a lazy spin toward the grassy berm protecting the bridge abutment over I-126. My airbag exploded, smashing my glasses into the bridge of my nose and slamming me back in my seat. Something nailed my car hard on the driver's side and, with the stench of tires pushed sideways, we ground into a guardrail on Mom's side of the I-26 curve.

The car screeched to a halt. It stank of acrid chemicals. A fine powder covered everything. A tiny corner of my brain put a tick mark next to the box "How does it feel to have an airbag go off?"

I blinked and blinked, but powder remained in my eyes and my vision wouldn't clear. My heart remained in hummingbird mode. I tried to move my head to look at my mother, and a fierce pain erupted in the rear of my skull. "Mom?"

From behind us came the screech of brakes, the crunch of car hitting car, a horn's blare followed by another crunch. I tightened my shoulders, bracing for a hit that never came. The pain was blinding. "Mom?" I yelled as if she needed hearing aids.

I panted my pain to tolerable and released my seatbelt. Slowly rotating my whole body, I faced my mother. She was obscured by a sea of white. I eased aside her deployed airbag. "Mom?"

Held upright by the seatbelt, she slumped forward. Eyes closed. Head bowed. Blood rushed from underneath her hair. An iron ore basketball of dread filled my stomach. I lightly rested my finger on my mother's neck and felt only my own pulse.

THIRTEEN

THE TAXI DROPPED PATRICK AT the front gate of the Jerk's mansion. A wisp of a person carrying two duffels and dressed like Sherlock Holmes, including an unlit curved pipe dangling from his lips, clambered from behind the forsythia bushes fronting the wall surrounding the estate.

"Glad you could make it, Sherlock," Patrick said. Under his breath he added, "God, I hope this still works and Dad didn't have her change this code, too."

"Hey, dude," Sherlock said in a falsetto. "We're not breaking and entering, are we?"

With a beep of electronic confirmation, the gate swung open. "Mother gave permission. Hey, wait a minute. You're a girl?"

"Last I checked. Does it matter?"

"Lisa? You're Sherlock!?"

"I was. Sherlock is a creature of the past."

"I'm shocked. I would never have . . . Why the masquerade?"

"Patrick, if I had offered to fly here and help you out, would you have accepted? No, you would not have accepted. It's family business. It shouldn't affect LT2P. You'd have a thousand reasons. But you jumped on meeting Sherlock, and I need . . . we all need you in the office at full capacity. This seemed like the best way to do it. I caught an earlier flight and picked up a few things from a friend. Be useful." She handed him one of the heavy bags.

At the front door, Patrick punched numbers for the electronic lock. Once inside, he keyed another set to disable the alarm. Their footsteps echoed in the marbled entranceway.

"Why," Lisa asked, "would anybody want to live in a museum? Look at that staircase. I expect Queen Elizabeth and her entire retinue to descend any minute. And the furniture—it's all antique."

"Women wear jewelry. Men wear houses and automobiles. You should see his old car collection. I know, I know. No time. Get to work. Study's on the second floor." Patrick led her up the marble steps of the grand staircase and down the east wing past a number of open rooms to a closed mahogany door. The door opened into an office appointed with a massive desk fronted by two wingback chairs, their blue leather studded with brass buttons. Behind the desk was a matching chair. Only a laptop and a navy string-tie folder decorated the glass-covered top of the desk. Both squared to the edges.

One side of the room contained an enormous burl coffee table with several stuffed chairs huddled around it; on the other side two loveseats kept their distance from a glass coffee table. Formal fox-hunting scenes decorated the walls. *Lisa's right. This place is more sterile than a silicon disk factory.*

Lisa pointed to the laptop. "That one?"

"His. Mom's is in her study in the opposite wing. You start with this one, and I'll check my mother's stuff. We'll switch when you're done. Text me if you need anything."

His mother's study not only retained her scent, it presented at least some personality. Several pictures in standing frames decorated the desk. Among pictures of her husband, he spotted one of himself with his mother. Taken after the U.S. nationals quad scull race, he had the bronze medal hanging around his neck. She'd skipped out of an important charity gala just to be there. Her smile was genuinely broad. He had painted his on because they should have won. *Enough reminiscing of the simple college days. Get to work, Patrick.*

He ignored his mother's computer—Lisa would examine it—and concentrated on the paper files. The top desk drawer provided nothing interesting. The first file in the bottom drawer was labeled "Death Benefits." Inside was a copy of a ten-million-dollar life insurance application with his mother the sole beneficiary upon Albert Cunningham III's death. Double indemnity upon accidental death. He sped through the provisions and stopped at the effective date. The policy was executed four days before the Jerk disappeared.

That Monday? A coincidence? He supposed so, but his gut roiled with excess acid. Clipped to the policy were documents printed from the internet relating to death benefits payable from all their joint credit cards, a couple of the Jerk's alumni associations and AAA. Nothing in this folder related to her death. The last document in the file was a copy of the key-person life policy; the three partners had twenty million bucks on each other.

Dead, the Jerk was worth a lot of money. A lot of money.

Patrick replaced the folder, wondered if the next one would be her life insurance. He extracted the file. Reading the label, "Divorce," an involuntary shiver rippled over his skin accompanied by the recollection of his parents sitting him down in their living room and telling him his family was broken. With adult eyes and a couple of failed college relationships, he understood how love could wither away. Nonetheless, sitting in his mother's chair, in the Jerk's mansion, the adult part of him was struggling to take charge of the kid who wondered what he had done wrong, what he could have done differently so his parents would have stayed together.

He gazed toward the twelve-foot ceiling and released a cleansing breath. His eyes ached—he hoped from lack of sleep, but more likely the pain related to the recent light flashes in the back of his eyes. What possible good would it do to look through this file of his parents' failed marriage? He pushed the folder aside and stopped his hand midway toward grabbing the last file in the drawer. *Patrick, not your fault.*

Pulling the "Divorce" folder in front of him, he took another deep breath, and opened it. His hand froze midair. The top document was a draft divorce decree between his mother and Albert Cunningham III. Dated a week before the Jerk's disappearance, the red-lined version indicated insertions and deletions from an earlier document.

Patrick had never liked the Jerk, not since the day they met; even so, he did not wish another divorce for his mother. *Time's wasting. Read first. React later.* The original document before changes totally benefited the Jerk. After the modifications, his mother was only slightly less screwed.

He rolled his shoulders to release the tension crawling up his neck, reaching over the top of his head, and pulling his forehead tight. He tried pressing his eye sockets with both hands to push away the pain, but it only brought more. This didn't make sense. Why would the Jerk want a divorce less than two years after getting married? Unless—had his mother lied about who wanted to marry whom? Was it her idea and not his? Had she thought he was slipping away and hoped a golden ring around his finger would fix their problems? Patrick had nearly made the same mistake as a college sophomore. Fortunately, his friends had talked him out of that disaster. People surely did stupid things for love and sex.

Setting the file aside, he removed the final folder from the drawer. Computer printouts bulged the seams. He checked the top page. Header information, which might or might not be of any value, filled the top third of the first page. Patrick skimmed the code following the header, his finger inching down the page a line at a time to keep his place. Unless he missed the boat, he had found a printout from the keylogger program on the Jerk's computer.

So his mother had been involved with the keylogger program, but what was it capturing? Did this have something to do with the divorce?

This particular program did not have the ability to indicate mouse clicks, nor did it provide periodic screen shots, as some programs did. Those missing markers made it challenging to understand what was going on. Fortunately, this program started a new line each time the enter key was pressed.

Many fruitless minutes later, Patrick gave up trying to decipher what had been keyed in from the beginning of the recording. He switched tactics and speed-read the pages, looking for something, anything, useful. On the seventh page he spotted the username and password for their joint bank account.

Patrick's headache eased a titch. Using his tablet, he signed into the account with the new password his mother had given him and duplicated keystrokes from the printout. He followed the screen to guess at the intervening mouse clicks and determined the Jerk had set up a new electronic bill payee—a florist in Manhattan—and paid a ninety-dollar invoice. Big whoop.

Lisa entered the room with a polite cough. "Making progress?" She looked as pleased with herself as Paddy remembered being at sixteen when he cracked the DoD's computer and downloaded expense reports for the top Pentagon brass.

"What did you find on the Jer—on his computer?" He glanced at the tablet's clock. Where had the time gone?

"You were right about the keylogger. It was hidden—"

"Save the details for later, Lisa. We're short on time. I've got a splitting headache, so just the facts, please." The glow drained from Lisa's face. Patrick made a mental note to ask her for every little detail later to make it up to her. Tonight he needed to suck this place dry of information and get home. "You figure out the transmission process?"

"Uses the local network. Password protected. Encrypted. Pretty much what you suggested. The dude does securely erase files, but he doesn't defrag his computer, which means files he downloaded may still be there.

I captured a mirror image of the entire drive so we can look at everything at our leisure." She pointed to the computer paper spread across the desk. "What's that?"

"Hard copy of the keylogger . . . I think. It would nail things down if you match this to a file on her computer. No extra hardware on his system, right?"

"No physical transmitters or interrupters. I'll do another image of your Mom's computer. Unless the file is securely erased, I'll find signs of it. Okay, Patrick, my time at the desk. Never fear, Sherlock is here."

At least someone is enjoying tonight.

Patrick stuffed the life insurance, divorce, and keylogger material into his backpack. Lisa took the warm chair and booted up the computer. Once Patrick made sure she was logged in, he trudged to the Jerk's study to rifle through those files and try to find the external hard drive.

Everything pointed to his mother spying on the Jerk and going to some lengths to financially protect herself. Well, protecting herself against the Jerk made sense. Maybe she was looking for dirt to fight back in a divorce case? Was she a gold digger, divorcing husbands once they no longer earned big bucks? She had divorced his dad after (because?) he quit Wall Street. Was she instigating the divorce because the Jerk was selling his business?

On the next pound of his headache came an ugly thought. If the Jerk were dead, his mother had ten million reasons to find him. Without proof of death, she wouldn't get a cent of insurance proceeds, at least not until a court declared him legally dead. That, he assumed, took years.

A pitch-black idea nearly knocked the support from his knees. *Did Mom order a hit on her husband?* His stomach spasmed. He held down the airport grub, but the upwelling burned his throat and left an acid taste in his mouth. He collapsed onto the chair, digging the heels of his hands into his eyes to try to stop the stabbing pain. The Jerk's partners each received ten million too, so why hadn't he thought of them first? *What does it say about you when you don't automatically rule out your mother?*

As long as he was sitting, Patrick decided to go through the Jerk's desk drawers first. No hard drive, just some USB cables. The only thing of interest was an undated note from his assistant, Laurence Kleindeinst.

Friday flights made per instructions—print boarding pass at kiosk. First class only on return. Sorry. Potential buyer providing limo to their offices. Today's research reports attached so you won't get bored on plane. ☺—LK

Temporarily stymied, he opened the portfolio lying on the desk. Inside was another note from LK, this one dated the previous Friday. It asked Al to contact him to schedule a meeting for the coming week with the other two partners. Attached with a large binder clip were documents from Antimatter Investments, LLC needing signatures: expense reports, overtime approval for several people, a calendar of internal events for the week—no external events were listed—and a number of reports on companies Patrick assumed were either in Cunningham's hedge fund or candidates for inclusion.

Patrick replaced the papers and tied up the folder. He rose from the desk with the intention of checking the closet for the missing hard drive. He walked past one of the windows overlooking the front. Clouds scudded past a rocking-chair moon. In the intermittent light, a movement below caught his eye. Creeping up the driveway were three police cars with their lights off.

Patrick texted Lisa, *Cops here. Leave from back. I'll delay.*

He glanced once more out the window. The cars would reach the house in fifteen or twenty seconds. He had to make sure they all stayed in the front so Lisa could escape.

He raced from the room, down the hallway, and took the stairs three at a time, nearly losing it on the slick marble. Regaining his balance, he sprinted to the front, turned on all the outside lights, and walked onto the front porch.

At his appearance the cop cars split right, left and center. Doors opened and three officers, using the doors as shields, pointed shotguns at him.

Patrick raised his open hands high over his head, knelt down, and carefully slid into a spread-eagle position.

Two of the cops approached the porch. "Sir," one of them yelled, "do not move. Understand?"

"Got it." Patrick tried a cheerful voice. "This is my mother's house. She gave me permission to be here."

"Anyone else in the house?"

"Just me." *I hope.*

The porch floor vibrated from two sets of footsteps: one to the side, the other approaching him. From close by one cop said, "Do not move. For everyone's safety, I'll take your wrists behind you and cuff them. Do you understand?"

Patrick began to move his hands to the side to get them to his back. The cop screamed at him to remain still. Patrick stopped. The cop secured both wrists in handcuffs.

The third cop reappeared with two individuals, who Patrick recognized as Mr. and Mrs. Truvert. He called greetings to them.

"Mr. McCree?" Mrs. Truvert said. "Is that you?"

"Didn't my mother tell you I was spending the night?" Patrick said. To the police, he added, "We can call her if you want."

The Truverts fell all over themselves apologizing for calling the police on the mistress's son, but they had seen lights on in the house. Patrick assured them they'd done the right thing; he should have knocked on their door to let them know. The cops wanted proof Patrick was who he said he was, and one of them followed him inside to retrieve his wallet from his pack.

Patrick sent the Truverts to their lodgings away from the main house. The police wrote their notes and eventually departed. When he was alone, Patrick had a good laugh. Lisa had escaped and if nothing else, he had a good story to tell his grandchildren.

FOURTEEN

PATRICK AWOKE BEFORE HIS PHONE'S alarm went off. It took a moment for him to recall that the strange bed he was in belonged to a guest room of his mother's house. He grabbed the phone from the nightstand and checked the time. There was no reason he should be awake at 5:07 after sleeping only two hours.

Through the open bedroom door came the sound of footsteps slapping up the marble staircase. Much too early for the Truverts. Had his mother returned? No, if she were coming home, the Truverts would surely have mentioned it last night.

He threw off the bedclothes and was surprised by how cold the wood floor was to his feet. The footsteps had reached the landing and were headed away from him. What to do? In last night's excitement had he set the house alarm? He couldn't remember.

It must be the Jerk sneaking home. A flash of anger warmed Patrick. He rapidly donned his clothes. Once in the hallway, he could see light spilling from a room the same side of the far corridor as the Jerk's office. No other lights were on, which was strange, but the Jerk certainly knew his house well enough to wander around in the dark.

Patrick strode down the hall, mentally preparing to verbally flay the Jerk six ways from Sunday, whatever the hell that meant. He looked into the room and found the intruder bent low, opening and closing desk drawers. Patrick cleared his throat to announce his presence.

The Jerk stood—except—not the Jerk. Following a moment's confusion, Patrick placed the face—a face expressing surprise and fear. Laurence Kleindeinst, the Jerk's assistant, was dressed in full business regalia: suit with coat unbuttoned and handkerchief complementing his striped tie, bold colors showing on the field of a starched white shirt.

They said simultaneously, "What the hell are you doing here?"

Kleindeinst puffed up in apparent indignation.

Patrick had seen enough power play moves in his brief time in business to recognize this one. In response, he stuck his hands on his hips. He had home ground and was blocking the exit. "Well? Do I need to call the cops?"

Kleindeinst gave a little head shake. "Patrick, right? Patrick McCree? I'm here to retrieve the material I left for Al—Mr. Cunningham. Since he didn't return to the office—"

"How did you get in?"

"I have the codes. When Mr. Cunningham needs something from the office, I often bring it to him. I don't live far away, so I do it on the way to or from the station. I need to catch the 5:18. Do you know where the folder is?"

Patrick flashed back to his discovery of the police creeping up on the house and recalled he had been holding the folder when he spotted them. What had he done with it?

Kleindeinst checked his watch—*Who wears watches anymore?*—and reached down and closed a drawer. "I've gotta catch that train. I'll have to come back tonight, which sucks."

He moved toward the door and Patrick stepped out of the way. "Did your mother take it? Let me do a quick check of her office." He picked up his pace, Patrick following, and walking directly to Patrick's mother's office, flicked on the overhead light. "Not on the desk. Okay, gotta go."

He brushed past Patrick, quick-stepped down the stairs. Over his shoulder he said, "You'll turn the alarm back on? Thanks. I sure as hell wish your stepfather would show up. This is really a hassle."

Kleindeinst was gone before Patrick spotted the folder lying on a white elephant beside the staircase. He must have dropped it there in his rush to prevent the police from discovering Lisa. Patrick returned the file to the Jerk's room and tossed it on the desk so Kleindeinst would find it when he returned.

Knowing he was too wired to sleep the twenty minutes before his alarm would go off, he hopped into the shower and, relaxing under the warm spray, rehashed the recent encounter. *No way I'd ever let someone wander around my house this early in the morning. No way.*

I AWOKE IN THE HILTON Columbia Center Hotel feeling like I had spent the night in a cement mixer instead of a king-sized bed. I put on glasses, which the state patrolman had found under the passenger seat, and stumbled toward the shower. The digital clock read 9:48. I cranked the shower to hot and, having removed my glasses, stepped under the pounding water and let the heat tenderize my sore shoulders and neck.

How the heck had I slept so late? Had the Percocet the emergency room doctor prescribed knocked me out? My eyes shot open wide. How was Mom? I toweled sufficiently well to avoid leaving pools of water in my wake. With glasses on and a towel around my waist, I searched for my cell phone. Wasn't on the nightstand. Wasn't on the desk. Wasn't in a pants pocket.

Wasn't anywhere. My brain kicked in and reminded me the cell phone was in the wrecked car, which had been towed somewhere.

My distracted and fuzzy thinking was not a good sign. The night before, the Lexington Medical Center ER docs said I had not suffered a concussion, but the accident must have scrambled my thinking. I shut my eyes and concentrated on developing a coherent thought.

Use the hotel phone. When had I last used one for anything more than an internal call? I pulled the hotel services guide from the desk drawer and followed its instructions to obtain an outside line. Hilton promised to automatically charge the room. I was sure they would, along with putting a lien on my firstborn.

I searched my pants pockets for the piece of paper on which I had scribbled the fifth floor nursing station's phone number. Thank goodness I had put myself down as a HIPAA-authorized person when I completed Mom's admittance papers; otherwise the nurses wouldn't have talked to me.

"She's doing as well as can be expected," the nurse reported. "She picked at her breakfast. Poor dear, her mouth will be sore for a few days. And she's still a little foggy. That's most likely a leftover result of the anesthesia. It really takes it out of older folks. You may notice her forgetting things for several days or even weeks. That's pretty typical."

"But she'll fully recover from surgery?"

"I'll be honest, Mr. McCree. It's hard to predict with someone your mother's age. It takes time, and she needs to be patient. Though I'm not sure that's her strong suit. She's already angry as a hornet that we won't let her leave."

Sounded like a good sign to me. "Is there a reason she shouldn't?"

"The doctor wants to make sure she doesn't have any problems digesting food. Breakfast has stayed down. I think he wants her to have lunch and then reevaluate."

An insistent beeping came down the line. "I'm wanted," she said. "Was there anything else?"

"Her arm?"

"We'll discuss her therapy options with both of you before she's released. I understand you aren't from around here, but that's not a problem. She won't be doing the therapy until the cast is removed—six, maybe eight weeks out. She's been asking for you. I'm sure it would relieve her to see you. You can call us with any further questions, Mr. McCree."

The longer I was up, the more I ached. Before calling Paddy, I returned to the bathroom and wiped off the mirror. A wide welt ran from my left shoulder to my right hip—seatbelt bruise. A red notch marked where the air bag had pounded my glasses into the bridge of my nose. I was surprised my eyes weren't the two shiners I had anticipated.

Our luggage was trapped in the car trunk, sitting in a wrecker's lot, which meant putting on yesterday's clothes. Using the hotel's pen and notepaper, I constructed a list for the day:

1. Determine the car's location and retrieve anything salvageable.
2. Call insurance agent. Should have done it last night.
3. Call state cops to get accident report?
4. Visit Mom. Get her released?
5. Rent or buy car.

I tapped the pen on my head. Buying a car meant researching what kind of car to buy. If I knew what I wanted, I could buy one immediately and not have to rent. *Wait, how do you register a car in Ohio if you buy it in South Carolina? Seamus, you're getting ahead of yourself. It's not like you're the first person to buy a car out of state.* Besides, I had no clue what kind of car I wanted, so it didn't matter anyway.

Earth to brain, please stay focused.

6. Call Paddy—tell about accident—find out how trip to his mother's went.
7. Call Lizzie—*dicey since she expected me to be in Savannah already.*

8. Cell phone—if not in car, kill phone and get a replacement.

Calling Paddy came first when I prioritized the list.

"Now I understand," Paddy said after I told him of the accident, "why you didn't respond to my phone calls. Will Grandma be okay?"

"The nurse says she wants to leave the hospital, so I suspect she'll be fine. I haven't been to see her yet or talked to the doctor today, so I don't know. Look, Paddy, I have a ton of things to do. I want to hear what you found at your mother's, but unless something is critical, I need to put it on a back burner until this afternoon."

"We found several worrisome things, but they can wait. And I have some exciting news to share."

FIFTEEN

EVERYTHING TAKES LONGER IN A strange city, particularly if you don't have your own transportation. As a result, I arrived at Lexington Medical Center outside Columbia later than planned. I had cabbed to the bone yard where I removed the contents of my car's glove compartment and various storage areas and dumped them into the dry-cleaning bag I appropriated from the hotel. Using my Swiss army knife, I detached the license plate. The driver helped wheel the luggage to the cab. My cell phone and Swarovski binoculars had grown legs. The binoculars were fairly new, replacements for those destroyed in my house fire. Someone would enjoy them.

Storing everything in the hotel room, I hoofed it a half a mile to buy a new phone and kill the old one—although no one had used it. Despite the salesman's best efforts, I didn't add a texting plan. I told the guy my theory: if people want to tell me something, they can pick up the phone. If they must exercise their thumbs, they can send me an email. Kids have forgotten how to talk face-to-face. I could envision the guy translating the expression into text—f2f.

The conversation was a draw: no texting plan for me; he was texting as I left, probably sharing his story about the Luddite in his store.

My insurance agent assured me the policy paid for the tow and, based on my description, he was sure I had totaled the car. Could I send him the police report?

"It was so old," I said, "I didn't have any collision coverage."

"But you can sue."

"Let's say this was the universe's way of saying I need a new car. When I get one, I'll call you with its VIN."

During the cab ride to the hospital, I ran out of excuses for not calling Lizzie.

"Where are you?" She moved from a whine into a prolonged rant.

My teeth clenched so hard pain ran up my jaw and into my ears. I did a silent primal scream to relieve the tension and, once she drew a breath, I interrupted and related the setback in our plans.

"Oh my gosh, Seamus. That's terrible. But everyone is all right, right?"

"I'm heading to see Mom now. I have no clue when they'll release her, so I don't know when we'll get there, or if we will ever get there. You need to check the areas around the ATM machines I found on Google Earth."

"But—"

"I'm at the hospital. I'll let you know what I find out. Bye."

Two friendly southern women, dressed to the nines and drawling hello to everyone who came in the front door, sat at an information desk. The receptionist gave me directions to Mom's room. I followed the signs to the orthopedic ward on the fifth floor and found her room with the door partially open. Voices from inside suggested my timing was perfect to catch the doctor. I squared my shoulders, anticipating meeting an alpha male surgeon. I rapped twice and entered to find Mom sitting up in bed and Boston crime boss Tommy Kennedy sprawled in a chair, laughing.

Kennedy grunted his way out of the chair. He hadn't lost any of his three hundred pounds since I last saw him.

"Seamus, me boy. Good to see you again." We shook hands. "Take a seat. I was cheering up your ma like old fogies do, bringing her up to date on mutual acquaintances who beat us to the obits. Her doc's supposed to be here sometime in the next hour to make sure she can follow the finger he waves in front of her eyes. Then she breaks out of jail." They both broke into laughter. "So to speak."

I was having trouble with this scene. Mom's entire arm, from shoulder to wrist, was casted in shocking pink. Her color was good—too good. I'd swear she was blushing. She had applied makeup borrowed from an understanding nurse, which I'm sure covered some of the accident damage, and she had recently put on lipstick in a kissing cousin shade to the cast's color. Kennedy looked like a mobster in geezer clothing: brightly colored print shirt, khaki shorts, long black socks—the kind people wear to prevent blood clots—and leather sandals.

"Tommy's the friend I called in Savannah. He retired there . . . what, four or five months ago? When I couldn't get ahold of you this morning, I called Tommy."

One does not retire from heading the Irish mob. You either die of natural causes or unnatural ones or you go on the lam like Whitey Bulger.

"You're right to look skeptical, Seamus," Kennedy said. "Truth be told, I thought I'd leave the job in a pine box." He laughed again. "Fact is, after I cleaned up the aftermath of the affair youse were involved in, some other individuals thought I was weakened and made a play for me business. I considered my options and chose to sell everything, the only stipulation being I cannot return to New England except for funerals and weddings."

Kennedy's use of "youse" brought me right back to growing up in Boston, where in Irish circles the usage is common and one my father had often used for the plural of you. "Chose to sell everything?" I parroted.

"Cheap, but worth it. An immediate lump sum, so there'll be no financial incentive for them to try to avoid future payments by putting a bullet in me head. Enough about me, your mum's been bending me ear with the wee problem your ex-wife's having keeping her man in tow. Anything new?"

"How long have you two known each other?"

Mom sipped water. Her glance ricocheted between Kennedy and me. Kennedy answered. "Probably been sixty years, hasn't it Trudy? You see, she was at a dance with—"

"A long time. Tommy used to visit me at Sugarbush. He and Uncle Mike were my only regular visitors."

"How come I never heard—?"

A loud knock sounded at the door and a doctor and nurse entered the room. "How are we feeling?" The doctor glanced at his chart. "Mrs. McCree."

"*This* part of the *we* is feeling ornery. Can I bust out of here yet?"

"On a scale of one to ten," the doctor asked, "what is your pain level?"

"I have no pain, except for having to stay tethered to this bed. Look, I ate my meals left-handed, so I won't starve." She pointed to me. "My son will see to my sustenance." She pointed to Kennedy. "I've got a ride. We have things to do in Savannah. There's no earthly reason for me to stay here except for you and your hospital to make money."

"Check on the ornery." The doc gave Mom a smile Hollywood would appreciate. "My biggest concern is to make sure your arm heals, Mrs. McCree. As we grow older, the process takes longer, and you have two nasty breaks that required surgery. I know we discussed this before your operation, but everyone was in a bit of shock at the time, so I want to review it again."

He put his finger to his lips to stay another outburst from my mother. "I'll sign your release, the nurse can complete the paperwork, and you and I will be nothing but distant memories. Okay?"

I traded glances with Kennedy. It looked like he was having as much trouble not laughing at Mom as I was.

"So talk," Mom said. "I'm all ears."

The doctor confirmed how long Mom would need a cast. He wanted it checked in a week's time. To whom should he send the X-rays?

"I don't have an orthopedist," Mom said. "I have strong bones—despite the evidence of this cast."

"That you do," the doctor said. "I can make a referral. Are you close to Boston? There are a number of excellent surgeons there."

Mom shot a glance at Kennedy, looked briefly in my direction before focusing on the doctor. "I'm not going home yet. My son and I have some business in Savannah to clear up before we resume our trip. We'll have to take the X-rays with us and find someone wherever we are."

The doctor shook his head. "Mrs. McCree, this isn't a walk-in. You'll need an appointment. You'll—"

"You can't see Savannah in less than a week anyway," Kennedy said. "You don't know how long this . . . this thing Seamus is looking into is gonna take. Plan to stay a week or ten days. I'd very much like for youse two to be guests for the duration. Savannah has a good teaching hospital. I'm sure we can get you an appointment."

The doctor was all over that like a Canada goose on a piece of white bread. While the doctor rattled off names of several Savannah colleagues, I wondered what was going on between my mother and Tommy Kennedy to explain her newfound motivation to get to Savannah.

I had twice begged help from Tommy Kennedy. The first time repaid a debt he owed my family, or so he said. The second put me into his debt. I figured exposing some rot in his organization had made us even again. His proposal would put me into his debt again. Not something I wanted to do.

"We can't—"

"I accept," Mom said. She focused her sparkling blue eyes on the doctor. "I'm sure you could call one of your contacts to get me an appointment in a week's time."

The proverbial horse was out of the proverbial barn, and I suspected Kennedy had pinched the doors even if I did attempt to lock them. Mom had nailed it when she called me a control freak, and I did not like slipping from a position of being the guy with the keys to the car to the guy whose opinion obviously did not matter. Mom must have sensed my lack of enthusiasm.

To Kennedy she said, "If work, or," she squinched her mouth as though she had tasted something sour, "his ex-wife, takes Seamus elsewhere, I'm sure you can arrange to get me to the appointment?"

"I can even lend you my spare car, assuming you can drive single-handed. You'll love it. It's all-electric. I bought it for puttering around town."

"Perfect. Seamus won't have to worry about me at all. He can do what he needs to do, send his ex on her way, and we can still make it to Tennessee for my next exhibition."

How Mom planned to be in Memphis for the weekend and in Savannah for a week or ten days was not clear to me. I had the feeling her brain was as rattled as mine. Once we got to Savannah, I'd have to address the issue with her. Not exactly a conversation I was looking forward to.

THE NURSE STAYED LONG ENOUGH to remove Mom's IV line. Next to arrive was the hospital social worker or patient advocate or some such title—I never did get it straight—who gave Mom a gazillion forms to sign, including notification of what medicine she should take for pain, timing of her appointment with an orthopedist in Savannah, and—the one that made Tommy Kennedy and me laugh—Mom's Medicare patient rights in the event she believed the hospital was discharging her too early.

The guy from patient transport thrummed his fingers on the waiting wheelchair while the social worker double-checked her forms.

"How do I get my X-rays?" Mom asked.

"We'll email them directly to . . ." the social worked ruffled through her papers twice, "to the doctor's office in Savannah. They'll be there before your appointment."

Based on the expressions that flitted across Mom's face, she didn't trust email, but decided to avoid a fight.

"Is there anything else?" Mom asked.

"I believe that will do." She glanced toward the door. "Oh, transport is here. You two can pick her up by the front door. Now, ma'am, sit right there until transport helps you into the wheelchair."

"Oh, for pity's sake." Mom slapped her good hand on the chair arm. "I can walk to the door." She pushed out of the chair, did a quick inhale, and crumpled.

I dove from my chair, knocking it to the floor in an awful racket, and managed to catch Mom's head before it hit the floor. The social worker pressed the red call button for the nurses. The transport guy boomed out, "Nurse! STAT!"

Face is red, raise the head. Face is pale, raise the tail. The only color in Mom's face besides her painted pink lips was the blue of veins showing through alabaster skin.

SIXTEEN

PATRICK AWOKE TO HIS CELL phone playing "That One is My Dad." After he and Lisa returned from the meeting with All-American Bancorp, he'd fallen asleep in his cubicle while drafting follow-up notes. He wiped the crust from the corners of his eyes—the phone indicated it was late afternoon. He swished his tongue across his teeth to combat the dry mouth before pressing the on button. "Hey, Dad, how's Grandma?"

"I don't know, Paddy. I just don't know. Right before the hospital released her she had a fainting spell. The doctor says it might be caused by a temporary drop in blood pressure when she got up. Or it could be an aftereffect of the anesthesia. They're running a gazillion tests to make sure it's nothing more serious." His father proceeded to tell him about Tommy Kennedy being there. "Did you know he used to visit your grandmother at Sugarbush?"

"How would I?" Patrick jotted four notes on a pad: Grandma; keylogger; divorce, cash flow; and put a tick next to Grandma.

"I can't believe I didn't know. You'd think the administrators at Sugarbush would have told me. I suppose that's neither here nor there. With your grandmother's setback, I don't know when or if I'll get to Savannah to help your mother. It's only a two-and-a-half-hour drive, so if your grandmother is stuck in the hospital for a while, maybe I can slip down there for part of a day. Have you heard from her? Your mother that is."

Patrick related a redacted version of the events the previous night. "After the cops left, I figured I'd better call her before the Truverts did. I told her I was looking for the Jerk's hard drive, which I did not find.

The conversation became a debriefing as Patrick explained what he and Lisa had discovered concerning the keylogger program. "She set up each of their computers with software so I can monitor them on my laptop."

"Doesn't it strike you as weird that neither one travels with their computer?"

"Mom uses a tablet I bought her. Lisa hacked that, too, so we're covered.

The Jerk uses his phone to stay connected." Patrick put a tick next to keylogger and another next to divorce. "But that's not all I found." He pulled the life insurance and divorce files from his backpack and told his father everything they contained. "What's your gut reaction, Dad?"

"Could be the possible sale of his firm caused Cunningham to reevaluate his estate plan to make sure your Mom was taken care of in case something happened, and he decided he needed more life insurance for her. Lots of wealthy guys have large insurance policies to cover inheritance taxes."

Breaking his dad's habit of assiduously avoiding saying anything negative about his mother—even when she deserved it—would be hard but necessary if he was to get at the truth. Who else could he ask? "Was it maybe part of a divorce settlement?"

"As a way to give her money? You'd use a paid-up policy. This is term life."

"But he'd have to know about the policy, right, since it's on his life?"

In the ensuing silence, long enough to play one of the complete Mahler symphonies his dad was so fond of, Patrick suspected his father was searching for an easy way to let him down.

His father cleared his throat. "State laws vary, but she does have an insurable interest—a good reason for having the policy because he supports her. And they're married. Usually a policy that size would require a medical exam, but if she used the same company that wrote the key man life, maybe they'd waive it. On the signature line?"

"Just her signature."

"Copy of the binder check?"

"Her personal account."

"I don't know what to tell you, Paddy. It could be what I suggested earlier."

"Or Mom wanted him dead and needs a body to collect the insurance." The words were out before he realized he had spoken them. Heat rushed to his face; a tightness gripped his chest. Because of the import of the statement or because he was mortified he had spoken the words aloud? Cindy was wrong. Sharing his suspicions about his mother hadn't provided relief; it had burned a bridge while the river was in flood stage.

Patrick abruptly stood, rolling his chair smack into his cubicle wall, and spotted Lisa in her cube keyboarding furiously. *Great.* What would she think, she who valued the loyalty of the partners above all? Could she ever trust him? Thank goodness the other two partners were gone. Why wasn't his father saying anything? "You there?"

"I am. I am trying desperately to figure out what I should say to you. I wish I were there so I could give you a hug. I admit my kneejerk reaction was to chastise you. Tell you your mother could never do such a thing. But almost everyone is capable of heinous acts. Since I joined CIG, I've learned murder is frequently the result of people feeling trapped and failing to find another alternative. And your mother is sometimes shortsighted. However, I've recently seen her, and I don't think she's such a great liar that I wouldn't sense it if she had tried to have her husband killed. That came out badly, but I hope you know what I mean."

Patrick considered his father's words. They made him feel a little better, but only a little. "It's been a lot of years since you guys were together."

"True enough. Let's do this. Let's proceed assuming your mom's a victim, and it's incumbent upon us to help determine what's going on with her husband. We can still pursue a parallel set of questions to determine the reason why this has happened. Now, a bit of fatherly advice. Go home—you're not getting any work done anyway—and try to catch up on your sleep. You'll feel better and think better. I'll chew on everything and see if I have any brilliant ideas. Maybe your mother will find something in Savannah. I'll let you know when I learn more. Love you, Paddy."

"Love you too, Dad."

Patrick looked down at his notepad. Three check marks. He had let his father go without discussing the cash flow problem. Again. Oh, crap. He hit redial, but the call went to voicemail, and this was not a voicemail message.

WEDNESDAY'S SUN ROSE INTO A crystal blue sky, filling my hotel room with bright light. I felt great, until I moved. I could hear the creaks and feel the groans. Before I could talk myself out of it, I donned running gear and hit Columbia's streets.

After nearly an hour and a half of jogging—actually, my pace was so slow "slogging" was more accurate—I returned to discover my new cell phone had its first message: Mom saying, "Get me out of here. Now." I worried the entire cab ride to the hospital whether I would soon lock horns with the doctor, or my mother, or both. I was all for springing Mom as soon as possible, but not a moment sooner.

Near Mom's room a nurse was cleaning up a spew of vomit. Good thing I hadn't eaten breakfast because I gagged at the fierce smell. I held my breath until I reached Mom's door where I rapped twice and, not waiting for an answer, pushed inside.

Mom sat in a chair, a phone tucked to her chin. She acknowledged my presence with a Queen Mother's wave. "Elisabeth, I'm only saying this one more time. Get off your skinny ass and start fending for yourself. You've wasted one full day. If you haven't done something by the time we get there, Seamus and I are going home."

Oh great, Mom and Elisabeth were deep into it.

"If I *were* your mother, I'd take you over my knee."

With Lizzie clearly riled up, I had an idea. "Let me talk to her, Mom."

Lizzie fumed, "Your mother can pontificate better than the damn pope."

"I don't want to hear it. I have a—"

"Well you're damn well going to. She was—"

"Were you spying on your husband? Because—"

"You weasel! Me? Spying on Al?"

"Because if you weren't spying on him, someone else was."

"You have no right."

"I have every right. You got me involved, and I don't give a flying fuck what you think of me. Just answer the damn question."

"I. Have. Never. Spied. On. Anyone. You really *are* a son of a bitch. And you can tell your damn mother I said so."

I was willing to grant she was telling the truth, but Lizzie danced the edge between the truth and the TRUTH. I used the time until she ran out of breath to steady my breathing. Into the gap I asked in a neutral tone, "Did you have someone else spy on him?"

"Never. Never! What made you think—?"

"Your umbrage is not allowing you to hear the other part of this. I do believe you, Lizzie. Someone is, and we need to figure out who. Right?"

She started laughing. "Umbrage? Did you use the word umbrage? No one uses umbrage. It's so seventeenth century. I'm sorry I was taking offense and didn't listen to your whole question. His partners?"

"Could be. Paddy told me he found Laurence whatshisname in your house at some ungodly hour this morning. His partners have access to the house, too?"

"Laurence Kleindeinst is forever dropping stuff off on his way home when Al's traveling. He even has his own alarm code. Unless he told the partners the codes, it couldn't be them. But Laurence could be acting for them. What was he doing there?"

"Paddy said he was retrieving a folder he had dropped off. Have you made any progress on those ATM machines?"

"You and your mother. Like I told her, I'll do it this morning. She says you're leaving soon. We'll meet for lunch. Call me when you're thirty miles out." She disconnected.

"Elisabeth," Mom asked, "is spying on her husband?"

Three taps on the door and Tommy Kennedy filled the doorway before waddling quickly to a corner to lean against the wall. "Is this a jailbreak or are you legal?"

Mom smiled. "Negotiated settlement." She held up a sheaf of papers from her lap. "Everything I need, and I promise no sudden ups and downs. You boys let me change, and we can get Seamus to Savannah so he can finish playing games with the drama queen, and we can all get on with our lives."

I had burned off a chunk of my fight-or-flight response talking to Lizzie, but I was still all stressed up with nowhere to go. "Do we need to call patient services for a wheelchair?"

Mom answered with a withering look. No shock where I got my snarly attitude.

Seventeen

Tommy Kennedy, my mother, and I found Lizzie pacing the restaurant lobby. I introduced Kennedy as someone we knew from Boston and smiled at myself; his accent would have given that away.

As I walked past the kitchen, the smell of garlic washed over me, and my mouth filled with saliva. I had skipped breakfast; now I was famished. I followed Lizzie into the booth. Mom and Kennedy took the other side.

Lizzie removed a paperclipped sheaf of papers from her purse, which was the size of a small suitcase. "Proof." She handed a sheet to each of us. "They're not great pictures."

I stared at the grainy black and white surveillance camera print of my replacement. He looked of a type I had known well during my Wall Street days—tanned from a salon, toned from a gym, and styled from a hairdresser. In this picture he was missing the required I-have-more-money-than-I-know-what-to-do-with watch and decent clothes. Did his pinched face indicate he was in some pain? Behind him (and with him?) was an African-American woman best described as rumpled.

"I'll be right back." Kennedy's voice had an edge to it not present during our drive from Columbia. He tossed his napkin on the table and, still holding a print from Lizzie, scurried away as quickly as a three-hundred-pound geezer could.

Lizzie had imprecisely repaired her makeup and a smudge of mascara remained at the corner of one eye, signs of earlier tears. Her lips were a tight line. Her eyes gave me the sense she was feeling even more stress than she had in Cincinnati.

Time for a little positive reinforcement. "Good job, Lizzie." I pointed to the pages. "Where did you get these?"

"Thunderbolt—outside Savannah on the way to the beach. I had a hard time admitting my husband was missing, but people were actually very sympathetic. I'm sorry I wasted a day. I was scared." She tapped the picture in front of us with a hard fingernail. "The two of them bought coffee and muffins from a bakery in the same shopping center as the ATM." Tears leaked down her cheeks. "She looks like a floozy, doesn't she? They're both wearing sweatpants. Al doesn't even own sweatpants. He exercises at the gym."

Not that exercising at the gym had anything to do with owning sweatpants. I credited the faulty logic to her stress. To avoid watching her cry, I examined another of the pictures. I'm not sure I could define what a floozy was supposed to look like, but my first impression of rumpled still seemed right to me. She wore generic tennies with her sweats and a floral print blouse with the top button undone. She carried a lot of excess weight, mostly in her hips and stomach. Her hair and clothes looked thrown together rather than put together. Her eyes looked worn. She did not meet my preconception of someone Cunningham would squire around town.

I sorted Lizzie's printouts by date stamp. "Check this out." I placed several pictures on the table so both women could see them. "As they enter the bakery, he's walking in front of her with his head up. On the way out, he's still leading, but he's slumped and holding a hand to his face, like he's trying to hide. He must have seen the camera."

"And did not want to be seen," Mom said. "So he was doing something nefarious. That fits. Look at the bags under his eyes. He certainly hasn't slept much."

Lizzie released a muffled sob, to which my mother mumbled, "I didn't mean it like that."

I'm not sure how else my mother meant it, but I didn't intend to be their referee. The three of us silently traded pictures. For my part, I had no idea what to say. Consoling Lizzie by reminding her she now knew her husband was alive didn't seem appropriate.

Kennedy waddled back holding a newspaper. The wooden seat creaked as he settled in. He folded the newspaper to display the top half of the second page and slid one of Lizzie's prints so it covered the headline. I leaned across the table to observe. Mother followed my example and our three heads nearly touched.

"Both lousy pictures," Mom said. "But you're right, Tommy. It's the same woman."

Kennedy removed his hand from the headline and upside down I read, "Two Dead in Carjacking."

I glanced toward Lizzie. She was engrossed with comparing prints. I flipped the paper so I could speed-read the article. The woman who was with Cunningham in the pictures, a Kaylee Coffin, was a domestic. A convicted felon, she had been a lifelong resident of the Savannah area.

The owner of the hijacked car, a thirtyish Caucasian woman from Savannah, was the other victim. The article provided the make, model, and license plate of the car, and the basics of the car owner's life: where she worked, who survived her—none of which related to Albert Cunningham III. The incident occurred the previous day on Bull Street. Witnesses claimed two males and one female, all Caucasian, left in the stolen vehicle. The article referenced an earlier incident the same day in which Kaylee Coffin's boyfriend had been killed in a shootout at her rented house on Tybee Island. Police called it a suspected drug-related murder but would not comment whether the events were connected.

"Lizzie," I shoved the paper in front of her nose and tapped the headline. "Have you seen this?"

"Oh my God. That's her! And she's dead? Where's Al?"

If Lizzie faked her two-hands-over-the-mouth surprised look, she had improved her acting skills since our marriage. All around us people twisted in their seats and craned their necks to spy on the disturbance. "Quietly," I said *sotto voce*. "Do you recognize this other person?"

Lizzie closed her eyes and shook her head.

Mom spoke in the same quiet voice I had used. "Elisabeth, now you have something to take to the local police. They don't know about these bakery pictures. There's a good chance your husband was one of the two guys leaving the scene." To Kennedy: "Where's the nearest police station?"

I asked Lizzie if her husband had previously traveled to Savannah. She could not recall any trips since they had been together, nor could she recall him ever talking about the city. So, if Cunningham and the Kaylee woman first met here, why? She could be a hooker, but it stretched credulity to think he had tossed everything away for a hooker he had just met. Something else had to be in play.

"Did he use drugs?"

Lizzie looked at me as though I had two heads. "Never. He hated drugs. He wanted to be in control."

From the corner of my eye, I caught my mother cocking her head in my direction and giving me a knowing look, which I ignored. Recreational drugs had been rampant on Wall Street in my time, but there were lots of us who had eschewed them precisely because of wanting to remain in control.

Nothing in the article suggested any connection between Cunningham and the murdered car owner. Nor did the article contain much on the carjackers other than their sex and race. Besides, if Cunningham had been in charge of whatever this was, they'd rent limos, not hijack a Toyota Camry. Nothing made sense.

I picked through the printouts from the bakery again and noticed the woman had a coat draped over her arm. With Savannah's high temperatures running consistently in the nineties and overnight lows in the seventies, no one needed a coat, especially to buy donuts and coffee.

"Mr. Kennedy," I said. "Would you please look at these pictures and tell me if anything funny strikes you?"

He examined the pictures one by one. "The coat?"

I gave a quick thumbs up.

"A chip off your father's block. You would make a good detective."

Lizzie blotted her tears with the heels of her hands and leaned over the table to look at the picture in front of Kennedy. "What about a coat and good detective?"

"Seamus thinks the woman is using the coat to hide a gun pointed at your husband's back."

"See," Lizzie said. "I told you he didn't run away."

I tuned her out. Fact: Cunningham had been alive and at least reasonably well only two days ago. Supposition: he had been held at gunpoint. Fact: Lizzie had not received any ransom notes. Question: What if he had received a ransom demand for a parent or sibling or his son? Maybe he came to Savannah to arrange payment, drained their joint account, and something went wrong. He might well have kept that secret from his wife.

What if he had come up shy? Or he tried to pay them off, but there was a hitch. Or they kidnapped him to try to extract more money from his partners? If his partners wanted to minimize the number of people who knew, it might explain why they were freezing Lizzie out. Clearly no one was working with the police; otherwise the cops would certainly have contacted Lizzie.

Wait a minute. If this were a ransom situation, why the penny-ante

ATM withdrawals with all the risk they entailed? Why the need for a carjacking? The murder at Kaylee's house was unlikely to be a coincidence.

Only one thing was clear: nothing was clear. Paddy had found the keylogger software on Cunningham's computer. It transmitted information by Wi-Fi to Lizzie's computer, where the encrypted file sat. She claimed no knowledge. Assuming she was telling the truth and further assuming Cunningham was held at gunpoint—two leaps of faith for sure—there had to be a connection. Such a connection was more likely to have begun up north than down in Savannah.

Unless the now-dead kidnapper *was* simply a hooker who had decided to take more than the stipulated fee. Cunningham takes money from his wallet to pay; she pulls a gun, takes his wallet, steals his watch, and forces him to use his ATM card to pull the five hundred bucks a day.

And what? That scenario didn't explain the keylogger, the carjacking, or the murder at Kaylee's place, let alone that days had passed between the kidnapping and first ATM withdrawal. I believed in coincidences only after eliminating all other explanations. The carjacking likely related to the shootout at the woman's house. If I were a betting man, I'd place my wager that Cunningham wasn't currently in charge of his own fate. I did not have a clue whether he had started a game that went wrong or whether everything he had done, including draining their financial accounts, was a reaction to some exogenous force.

If, as I increasingly sensed, everything regarding Cunningham stemmed from up north, the Savannah cops wouldn't get anywhere except by luck. They would concentrate on the drug-related murders. The New Jersey cops would see no need to investigate, and that left me—errant knight in tarnished armor, pretty much what Lt. Hastings suggested—but what were the alternatives? Ignoring it? Not I.

From nowhere coherent, I thought of a way to get inside Cunningham's partnership and hedge fund offices. If I could pull this off, I'd actually be able to look at their books. But I'd need help.

My mother tapped me on the shoulder. "You in there?"

"Thinking," I said.

"Fine, but the waitress wants to take your order."

I REFUSED TO GO WITH Lizzie to the police station. Instead I accompanied my mother and Kennedy to his house in the Landings on Skidaway Island. I did not want to be beholden to Kennedy, but my stronger desire was to placate my mother. Could I get away with only one night? I'd need to strategize my escape.

A guardhouse and barrier across the road blocked entrance to the gated community. The barrier automatically lifted at our approach.

"Cars are barcoded," Kennedy said in answer to my question. "Visitors need a pass. So if youse had your own car, I'd need to call it in to the guards beforehand, see?"

"Why'd you pick here?" Mom asked.

"I didn't want to deal with winters, don't you know? I coulda gone to Arizona, but I like green. And I never lived more than ten miles from the ocean me whole life. I wanted privacy and a place where my mug wasn't known so well."

He exited the main drag onto one private road and then another ending in a cul-de-sac. Kennedy's property included the entire cul-de-sac with the nearest house several hundred feet away. His Federalist-style two-story was flanked by two wings: a three-car garage with "bonus" room above on one side and guest suites on the other. Behind the house was salt marsh. The garage door opened before us. "Truth be told," he said, "Boston is home and always will be. This will have to do."

Kennedy insisted on giving us a tour so we would feel at home. In the main Federalist part, the downstairs contained a kitchen, dining room, two living rooms—one formal, the other casual. Across the rear was a patio covered by a deck running the length of the house. The upstairs consisted of two suites separated by another informal gathering room. Kennedy used one of the suites for his master bedroom. Both bedrooms and the informal den had direct access to the covered deck furnished with rocking chairs and tables.

I led us onto the deck. Despite ceiling fans stirring the muggy air, heat and humidity glued my shirt to my back. No one in Savannah needed to worry about dry skin. The beauty of the marsh captivated me and was worth the sweat beading my brow. The tide was out and in the hint of a breeze I caught a whiff of decaying vegetable matter. A harrier, white rump flashing in the sun, shopped for dinner in lazy arcs across the sky. A red-bellied woodpecker called from the stub of a dying live oak. At my mother's tug on my arm, I exited my reverie and dragged myself away to complete the tour.

Kennedy's guest wing consisted of four additional suites, two facing the marsh and two facing the front. Mom and I preferred marsh-view rooms. Each offered a private patio covered by the second-floor deck.

Kennedy saw me eying the patio. "You don't want to use it this time of year. The mosquitoes and sand gnats are something fierce. The afternoon breeze on the upper deck usually keeps them away. Anything I can get youse? No? Settle in and come back up, and we'll talk over the problem that broughtcha here." He gave my mother's good hand a squeeze and held onto it longer than I thought necessary. "And what Trudy wants to see while she's in town. I'm looking forward to having you both here a good long time."

Which might be a problem for me.

EIGHTEEN

PATRICK PATTED HIMSELF ON THE back for gently replacing the phone in its cradle. A mid-sized banking prospect had informed him that they had selected one of the big four accounting firms because they already did their accounting work and would add stress testing their IT security "for free."

He leaned over the cubicle wall and fumed to Lisa that the buyer used to work for the accounting firm and should know that if the accountants were offering something free it meant they were overcharging for the accounting work. "Why would anyone refuse our risk-free offer to test their systems when we charge them only if we find problems?"

"Because," Lisa said, "they have problems and someone wants to cover their ass until they can fix them. You've seen it before. They're worried we'll find so many holes in their security they'll be exposed to upper management disapproval. It's why we're successful when we can talk directly to senior management and bat only two-fifty if we have to talk with the IT guys. You can't win them all."

"One in four isn't good enough. I want to win them all. I expect to."

"Oh, Patrick," Lisa said, "you'll burn out in no time with that kind of attitude."

Maybe he was burning out, but work wasn't his biggest worry. He was having trouble sleeping because of the stuff with his mother and the Jerk. Still hanging over his head was the financial bind he'd caused his dad. What with the Cincinnati house not selling and LT2P's buyer postponing the acquisition by three months, his father would run out of cash soon.

As though the negative thought had psychic power, "That One is My Dad" blared from his cell phone. Patrick answered and was amused to hear his father go through a greeting sequence, including asking how Cindy and the cats were and how work was going. All the more surprising given his next words were, "Cunningham's alive. Or at least he was."

Good thing Patrick was already sitting because hearing about the carjacking death of the woman the Jerk had been with was a stunner.

"Your mother's currently talking to the police. I expect they'll look for him now that he's a probable witness."

"So if the Jerk bought a hooker and she turned on him, you figure he's either dead or her pimp has him?"

"I hadn't considered the carjackers could be her pimps. Might be, but either way, there's nothing much we can do to find him. Because of the keylogger program, I smell New Jersey roots to this mess. Plus, I can't see him throwing in his lot with . . . with people beneath his class. It's not his style. Do we agree your mother couldn't install the keylogger by herself?"

"Mom had to go to the phone store three times before she learned to retrieve her voice messages."

"But Cunningham could have done it?"

"He's plenty smart enough. It doesn't take much to download software and set it up. But why would he?"

"One of the things bothering me is why his partners aren't more concerned about his disappearance. Why aren't they calling every day to learn what's happened to him? What would you and your partners do if one of the four of you went missing?"

"We'd raise bloody hell."

"Exactly. You're aware Cunningham's partnership is looking for buyers? I think I can convince my friends at All-American Bancorp to give me cover by making it legit for me to do some undercover due diligence on the partnership. I'd like a second person to accompany me."

"Can't do it, Dad. I met them at Mom's wedding."

"I figured you were out. Was Cindy also at the wedding?"

"Chad Cunningham, the Jerk's son, and I were the only family there. Everyone else was business related."

"That reminds me. I had an off-the-wall thought that Cunningham—the father, not the son—was paying ransom for some family member and something went wrong. Do you know Chad well enough to call and find out if his grandparents and aunts and uncles are all okay?"

"I don't know him real well, but I can call him. So how would you use Cindy?"

"It's always teams at these things, and her investigative reporter skills are perfect. We might need two days, depending on what material we can review. I could fly her into New York early one morning and have her home by dinner the following night. I don't know how flexible she can be . . ."

"Not very. She's in the final edits of an investigation into hospital costs for the uninsured. I doubt she can do it, but I'll ask."

"Great. Can you get away too? I know you're swamped. You and Lisa already collected all the files on both their computers, but I think you're right to suggest we do a thorough search of the house. There has to be a reason someone set up the keylogger program, and I'm having a hard time convincing myself Cunningham did it. From what you told me, the divorce stuff was all slanted in his favor. Why would he want it to appear that your mom was spying on him?"

"Doesn't make sense to me either. But if mom went to a divorce lawyer, he could have suggested it—maybe even set it up."

"You could be right, but she did a fine job convincing me it wasn't her. Anyway, while Cindy and I investigate his business activities, I thought maybe you could fine-tooth comb their house."

Patrick laughed so hard his ribs ached. How long had it been since that had happened? He'd try to channel that pleasurable feeling in the future. "Listen to you. First, you unilaterally decide Cindy can do this and then you make fine-tooth into an adverb. I've got a text into Cindy. We'll need to know who, besides the two of them, has access to the house. If neither of them installed the keylogger, it had to be someone else with access, right?" Patrick thumbed open his calendar app. "The only window I have is the end of this week . . . and you walk on water. Cindy's editor is down with the flu and won't return until Monday. She's free, but needs to be back for the weekend."

"Terrific!" His father's enthusiasm petered out in a sigh. "But now your grandmother will think I've abandoned her again. Let me call All-American and see if the timing works. It's been a while since I've seen you and Cindy. This will be great."

MY RINGING PHONE WOKE ME from the nap I hadn't realized I was taking. The ID indicated Vince D'Alessandro, the CEO of All-American, was returning my phone call. As often happened, Vince opened our conversation with a joke.

"How does an Italian get into an honest business?"

"He works in the prison laundry?"

An appreciative chuckle came down the line. "Good try. That's step two. The answer is 'usually through the skylight.'"

I groaned theatrically. "Do you have a joke list, and you're nearing the bottom?"

"Aren't you the one asking for a favor?" His voice became serious. "Here's the problem with using All-American as your cover to check out this hedge fund. We have a long history of disposing of any investment banking, brokerage, hedge fund, and the like that we pick up as part of a bank acquisition. Looking at this firm would send the wrong message to the investment community."

"Good point. Too bad. Sorry I wasted—"

"Don't be a quitter. You wanted to do this tomorrow and Friday right? I found a legitimate buyer for your talents. Buddy of mine's looking to expand his business. He already had some guys take a look at Antimatter, but he'd love another opinion—'specially once I told him it wouldn't cost him much. He'll cover your expenses and a few bucks extra. You'll need to get your report to him by Monday morning."

The timing was perfect. Both Cindy and Paddy could get away for the rest of the week. I wrote down the contact information. "Thanks, Vince. I owe you one."

"Yes, you do."

I made the call and discovered Vince had greased the wheels. We quickly set up a meeting with Antimatter Investments, LLC's due diligence lawyers for ten tomorrow morning. Friday I'd meet with the principals. Time to touch base with Lizzie.

"The cops wouldn't tell me anything." Lizzie said it loudly enough to make me decrease the volume on my phone. "They made copies of the printouts and the records of which ATMs Al got money from. They want me to call them if I hear from him. And, like you, they kept asking again and again about drugs."

"That's because some of the people involved down here are dealing drugs." I told her my arrangements to look under the hood of the partnership and asked if we could stay at her place.

"Well done, Seamus. I really do appreciate how much you've helped. I'm afraid I've seemed self-centered. I'm sorry. I've been so worried, it's affecting everything. Can you ask the partners how I can withdraw my money from the fund? They still aren't taking my calls. I'll let our housekeeper know to expect you so she doesn't call the cops again. I think the police down here want me to stay until they find Al."

"You do know it's only in movies that cops tell you not to leave town. It's not like you're a material witness or anything."

"I know I don't *have to*, but someone kidnapped Al, and I'm staying here until we know what happened."

I breathed a sigh of relief because it gave Paddy full access to search the house. Soon another worry popped into my head. "Lizzie, if someone kidnapped him and finds out you're in Savannah, it's possible they might want to grab you too."

"Don't be ridiculous, why would someone want to kidnap me?"

"More leverage? I don't know. I've also asked Paddy to check with Chad to make sure everyone on his side of the family is okay. I do think this whole thing probably started in New Jersey. I'm still running down ideas on the keylogger stuff on the computers. It doesn't make a lot of sense for your husband to have done it, given he leaves his computer at home. Logic dictates someone with access to the house installed it. Who all has keys—I mean the access codes to your house?"

"Our housekeeper, Jolene, also cooks. Her husband, Torr, is the handyman. The gardeners have the gate code, but there's no reason for them to be in the house. Chad and Patrick." She blew a breath down the line. "This would be before I changed the code. Let's see who else. Oh, we had a painter and plaster guy in to do some repairs. I can't think of anyone else."

"So, a lot of people. Neighbors or friends check on the place when you're gone?"

That spurred her to cough up two more names and realize she needed to give them the new house code.

"Oh wait," she said. "Laurence Kleindeinst—Al's assistant—he's been so unhelpful in this, you know. He's got his own code so if we're not there, he can leave stuff for Al."

"Does everyone know the alarm codes?"

"Each has his own code, or at least I think they do. Al's cell phone would occasionally beep and he'd say something like, 'Laurence left me another care package,' or 'The Truverts opened up the house.' "

I asked for the password to talk with the alarm company and jotted a note to tell Paddy to check with them to try to access the alarm logs. With those we'd learn who had been in the house and what time they entered. "No one else from work? Just the assistant?"

"I don't know what happens if Laurence isn't available. You know the place has been in Al's family for years. I have no idea who else may have codes. If you're right and this started in New Jersey, it pretty much has to be related to the firm doesn't it? Al didn't want to sell, but the other two partners forced him. Maybe he found a way to stop the sale, and they wanted him out of the way. Remember, don't you leave their offices Friday until you make sure I can get my money."

"It would blow our cover if we asked them about your money."

She laughed. "Well, it would, wouldn't it? There I go again, thinking only about my needs. I'll try calling them one more time."

After signing off with Lizzie, I made the travel arrangements for Patrick and Cindy and scheduled a cab to take me to the airport the next morning. Everything was falling nicely into place. It meant leaving my mother with Tommy Kennedy for a couple of days, but she was set on staying in Savannah anyway, so I didn't anticipate a problem. Unless Mom got on her high horse about me dumping her for Lizzie again. Oh, and I needed to make sure Mom had canceled her darts exhibitions for the weekend. I girded myself and went to find her.

Nineteen

Mom and Tommy Kennedy sipped sweet iced teas on the veranda, sharing convivial conversation in the rocking chairs. I relaxed at the railing overlooking the marsh. The breeze had picked up and, combined with the overhead fans, cooled me down. At a pause in their chitchat, I turned away from the view and related the details of my recent conversations. My recitation complete, Mom tilted her head toward Tommy Kennedy in what I assumed was some kind of signal.

Kennedy cleared his throat. "I made me a couple calls regarding the shootout at the woman's place. Her brother was a soldier in a drug gang in town. It's a splinter from the Norte del Valle cartel after they went crappers. These are not nice people, Seamus." He picked up his sweating iced tea and took a long pull. "I called up my daughter. Made lieutenant last year and heads Boston's drug taskforce. She knows people who know people and the word is this group tends to solve problems with bullets. Lots of bullets."

I had forgotten Tommy's only child worked for the Boston Police. The whirring fans pushing air filled the silence. I again considered ways Albert Cunningham III could be linked with drugs. An investor? Using his antique cars to transport product? The cartel cleaning money through his hedge funds? That struck me as most plausible.

Mom broke my train of thought. "What Tommy is saying is we think you should drop this."

"You done good work to get proof your ex-wife's husband is alive. But now the coppers got that stuff. Let them do their work, take the risks. Like I said, these people don't know from rules." Kennedy drained his iced tea, set the glass on the damp doily, and wiped his hand on his pants. "If these wackos get wind that you're interested in their affairs . . . that might not be such a good thing. Trudy is staying to see the sights. You can stay long as you like or go to Cincinnati and get yourself a car and whatnot."

I noticed Kennedy never said he'd walk away in a similar situation. "Ever hear of these drug guys doing kidnappings in the U.S.? In Savannah?"

"Only south o' the border. Most crime organizations don't want to invite the FBI to pay attention to them."

Mother's face hardened, her posture grew rigid. "That girl's making you stupid."

"Thanks for sharing, Mom. First of all, *that* girl is your grandson's mother and also happens to be a human being whose husband has disappeared in unknown circumstances. You said yourself that everyone deserved to know where their husband is, which should in itself be enough. Plus, my son wants me to help. Nuff said, okay?" Her expression indicated none of this sounded familiar. Was this the forgetfulness the doctor suggested would happen?

"You're being stupid," she said. "And it's dangerous. And I worry about you."

"Secondly, I am traveling to New York to kick those tires. Do you really think the police will do that? There has to be a reason why the partners are stonewalling Lizzie. If they are laundering drug money, you'd think they would want her out of their hair and rush to cash her out. That's not happening."

"Tommy, do something. Convince Seamus he's wrong."

"Fools rush in," Kennedy said. "I've learned you can trust only one thing: people look out for number one. That's it. Even do-gooders like Seamus. They're not doing it for some greater good. They're doing it 'cause it makes them feel better. Simple as that. You can make your case, but in the end a man's gonna do what's right for him."

He released a long sigh. "I hope this is what's right for you. But, I gotta say, it worries me, and not just 'cause it worries your ma."

PATRICK FOUND MRS. TRUVERT IN his mother's kitchen. "I thought this time I'd make sure you knew I was here, Mrs. Truvert."

She finished emptying a grocery bag onto the counter and flipped an errant strand of salt-and-pepper hair behind her ear. "Hello, Mr. McCree. You don't want the police—"

"Patrick, please. If you need to call someone Mr. McCree, you can stick that on my father, although he'd prefer Seamus."

"Jolene, then?" She tilted her head to ask for agreement.

"Oh! Like the Dolly Parton song. Mom tells me she asked you to cook dinner for my father, Cindy and me. Did she remind you I'm vegetarian?"

She smiled and nodded. "I remembered. Spinach lasagna? Anything new on Mr. Cunningham?"

She asked the question in a friendly manner, but given Patrick was there to snoop, it made him uncomfortable. He provided a noncommittal response and mentioned that he was hoping to find a clue on Mr. Cunningham's computer. They chatted amiably enough about this and that while she finished putting the groceries away. Her plan, which suited Patrick well, was to return in the afternoon to cook.

He walked her to the door and once he was confident she was heading for the carriage house, he commenced searching the first floor to have it complete before her return. He found nothing.

Upstairs, he chose to explore the rooms in the Jerk's wing next. He spent three hours looking everywhere and found nothing more interesting than a single wiped flash drive tucked in with a bunch of loose paperclips at the bottom of a drawer. Time for a break and to grab a bite before he tackled the wing containing his mother's study.

Passing through the kitchen, he cut a wedge from a small wheel of artisan cheddar he found in the refrigerator, grabbed an apple from a hanging basket, and wandered into the manicured yard. He couldn't imagine bringing up children in such a sterile place with not a blade of grass out of place, not a twig on the ground. He considered stretching his legs by walking the quarter-mile driveway to the Jerk's massive showroom to look at the antique cars. Growing up, while other guys were fixing junkers, he'd been into building computers from spare parts and still didn't care much about cars.

For late June, the heat and humidity were already uncomfortable and prickled his skin. What little breeze there was died, and soon he was swatting mosquitoes. In a minor act of rebellion, he chucked the apple core onto the lawn, thought better of it since the only person it would inconvenience was the gardener, and retrieved it. Back inside, he followed sounds from the kitchen and discovered Jolene had arrived. They discussed what to have in addition to the lasagna, chatted about her family, and Patrick excused himself and headed up the stairs.

The first few rooms of the other wing held nothing of interest. Opening his mother's study door and taking it in, he had the impression this room was wider than the Jerk's study. That didn't make sense. The architecture was faux Palladian, so everything should be exactly mirrored, one wing to the other.

With eager step, Patrick returned to the Jerk's study. It did look smaller. He paced off the dimensions of this study, returned to his mother's and measured her room. Hers was six feet wider than his. Patrick paced the distance from the study door to the adjacent bedroom door in both wings. Exactly the same. The hallways were the same length. He paced the dimensions of the adjacent bedroom and returned to the other wing. Opening the door, he stopped.

He recognized his mother's canopied bed. The dressing table top was crowded with supplies. *Huh.* His mother was using a separate bedroom. He shoved his questions to the back of his mind and concentrated on the immediate task, measuring the room. Exactly the same as the one in the Jerk's wing. Everything measured the same between the two wings except the interior width of the two studies.

There had to be a hidden closet, or alcove, or something between the Jerk's study and the next bedroom. He examined his study wall, but found no hinges, extra spaces between paneling, mismatched paneling or any other indication of an entry. A dull reverberation from solid wood resulted when he rapped the paneling with his knuckles. He methodically checked the entire wall, listening for changing sounds, and found nothing more than the slightly higher pitch marking framing studs.

He walked away from the wall and studied its color but found no differences. With a flash of inspiration, he rushed to the desk to find the hidden electrical switch he was sure must be there. Nothing.

If not from this room, then from the adjacent bedroom? His middle right knuckle throbbed from testing the walls, so he switched to his left hand and obtained the same dismal results.

He called his mother to find out what she knew. The police, she said, wasted her time, asking the same questions as the day before, not telling her anything new. His dad had been right; she was wasting her time in Savannah. She expected to be home tomorrow. Yes, she knew a hidden room had once existed, but it had been sealed years ago.

Why seal it off? Why not restore the study to its original size?

Patrick tried to picture the exact downstairs room layout. A coatroom might conceal an entrance through its ceiling. He galloped downstairs, raced to the coat closet, and realized the distance to the hidden room was too far to work. A parlor with a mammoth fireplace occupied the space underneath the hidden room.

Jolene must have heard him because she came out of the kitchen. "What time do they arrive?"

Patrick checked his cell phone. "Oh gosh, I've got to pick them up at the station. Mom said to take the Mercedes. Where do they keep the keys?"

"By the back door." Jolene pointed at the scrimshaw whalebone someone had ruined by screwing in hooks to hold keys.

He grabbed the fob. "Should I call you if they're late?"

"Thank you. That is very thoughtful."

Following his phone's directions to the station, he wondered if they had found anything useful. His day had certainly been frustrating, but with luck, one of them would figure out the key to breaking into the hidden room. First, they'd have dinner and, as he and Cindy had agreed on the flight out, they'd spring their news on his dad.

I HELD THE PASSENGER DOOR for Cindy. The quality-sounding thump of the Mercedes' door closing left me with a growing feeling of regret. I climbed into the back, buckled my seatbelt, closed my eyes, and leaned my head against the cool leather interior. The scent of automobile leather made me think of money. "Home, Patrick," I said in my best imitation of an upper crust magnate.

Cunningham's car purred like a puma, taking the winding roads to his estate in Far Hills in a lope. Had I stayed in the Wall Street game, I could have had the multimillion-dollar New Jersey house and chauffeur for the commute to and from the city. Although, knowing me, I'd stick with less expensive cars, and if I were to sink a gazillion bucks into real estate, I'd be more likely to buy thousands of acres in the U.P. than an estate in Far Hills.

I should not have been surprised by the timing of these feelings about what might have been. Cindy and I had spent the better part of the day in the lair of the beast, perusing the due diligence material on Antimatter Investments, LLC. What hubris in their name and motto, "We give a positive charge to your investments." The Bible had it that "Pride goeth before destruction." Unfortunately, with Wall Street, the perpetrators weren't the ones who suffered the most from the fall.

TWENTY

PADDY BACKED THE CAR INTO the garage, and we followed him into the dining room, where I was surprised to find the table set for three, garden salads and crystal water glasses at the ready.

"I hope it's okay if we eat before I give you a tour," Paddy said. "I don't want to keep Jolene any longer than we have to."

"Jolene?" Cindy and I said together.

"Jinx!" Cindy yelled.

I formed my face into a confused look. "What?"

Cindy's smile blossomed. "You never played that game? If two people say the same thing at the same time, the first one to yell 'jinx' freezes the other from talking until someone says that person's name."

I mimed a "who knew" expression.

Paddy: "I hadn't heard of it either, but Cindy has me trained. I think in grade school we used to link pinkies or something. I'll let Jolene know we're ready." He pointed us to our seats. "Mom insisted Jolene cook for us. I couldn't talk her out of it. You want wine, Dad?"

"Oh pooh." Cindy gave Paddy's hand a playful swat. "You unjinxed him. I wanted to know how long we could keep him quiet."

Paddy: "Dad can do silence like the Sphinx." To me, "Cabernet good?"

"Sure, if everyone else is having some."

Paddy reached under the end of the table, pressed something, and a bell sounded in the kitchen. A woman entered.

"Jolene Truvert," Paddy said, "in addition to taking care of the house, is an excellent cook. This is my father, Seamus McCree, and my life partner, Cindy Nelson."

Jolene inclined her head to each of us.

"Dad and I would like a glass of the cabernet to go with dinner. Cindy will stick with water. And we'll have the main course with our salads."

Jolene departed. I asked Cindy, "Holding out for those 'Cowgirl' margaritas?"

"Oh gosh, The Dakota Roadhouse in Hillsboro, Ohio." She smiled.

"A lot of water under the bridge since you and I first met up there. I've given up drinking for a while." She glanced at Paddy, whose face shone with excitement.

"We're pregnant," Paddy said. "Let's sit. We've got lots to discuss."

I gave Cindy a big hug and shook hands with Paddy. "Congratulations. When's the baby due?"

Cindy: "End of January."

Jolene placed a silver tray on the buffet. From it she distributed the two wines and three steaming dishes of spinach lasagna smelling of an interesting combination of spices that I couldn't identify, but couldn't wait to eat.

Paddy: "You're sure you and Torr won't eat with us?"

She shook her head. "Absolutely not. I appreciate your offer, but I'm afraid your mother would look askance at—" she fingerquoted, "'the help' mingling with the guests. Please ring when you're finished." She backed from the room.

Paddy and I clinked wine glasses with Cindy's water, all three saying "Cheers."

"Jinx," I said.

Paddy mimed zipping his mouth shut, but Cindy couldn't hold her giggles. "Not fair," she said.

Me: "You cheated. But since I want to hear your plans, I'm releasing both of you, Cindy and Paddy."

Cindy: "Fast learner. I should have remembered."

While we tucked into the food, which tasted as scrumptious as it smelled, I learned they were about six weeks pregnant. Yes, they had been trying to get pregnant. No, I was not the first to know. Cindy had told her parents this week; they had wanted to wait a month after the pregnancy test just to be sure. No, they had not told Lizzie. If she didn't return before we left, they'd call her. They planned to tell their friends once they got home, but it wasn't a big rush. It was too early to tell if their child was a boy or a girl. They wanted the surprise and didn't plan to find out.

Paddy: "We haven't decided whether the baby's last name will be McCree or Nelson or hyphenated. We have agreed on one thing though." He looked at Cindy and got a confirming nod. "If the baby is a boy, we'll continue the McCree tradition to the fifth generation and give him the first name Seamus."

Which meant, unlike Paddy and my father, who went by their middle names, this child—if he were a boy—would go by Seamus. My reverie was interrupted by Cindy's proclamation that, "We'll probably use a nickname like Shay or Moose. I can tell you for sure we won't call him 'wee baby Seamus.' "

At my confusion Paddy tried to clarify. "From *Archer*? FX series? Never mind" While they gazed at each other, I excused myself to the bathroom to blow my nose and wipe away my tears.

Upon my return to the dining room Paddy said, "We'll see what Dad thinks."

Cindy: "Patrick says he should be the one to stay home with the baby. He says I'll kill my career if I do it, but he could do IT contract work from home. Have I got that right, hon?"

"From a practical standpoint, once LT2P's sale to Behemoth goes through at the end of September, I'll probably be out of a job. They'll pay me for a couple of years, but I'll have a noncompete. I've been trying to talk to Dad about the implication of Behemoth delaying the sale date three months, but we haven't had time."

Cindy: "And now he's a captive audience, so you can talk. Or doesn't the mother of your child get to hear this conversation?" Cindy put down her fork and crossed her arms.

Paddy carefully laid his fork on the plate, tines down. "Why would you say that?"

"You know perfectly well why."

I cleared my throat. "Time out, please. I do not believe parents, or faux-parents-in-law, should arbitrate arguments." I hoped my crack about being Cindy's faux-parent-in-law would ease the tension. It didn't. "Shall I leave while you two hash this out?"

"No," they said simultaneously.

Cindy: "Jinx!" She clapped her hands with delight. "My say." She pointed at Paddy. "Quiet. Here's the problem, Seamus. He's the computer guru, right?"

He and I both nodded.

"And you're the financial guru."

"Not really—"

Paddy nodded and Cindy talked over my objection. "And I'm the English maven. Want to diagram a William Faulkner sentence, I'm your woman. According to Patrick McCree's *weltanschauung*, this produces a perfect division of labor, which means—"

"You said my name. I don't have to keep quiet any longer."

"But you will." She shot him the do-not-mess-with-me-on-pain-of-death stare. "So according to his worldview, he doesn't need to keep me in the loop when it comes to LT2P because it's computers and numbers and the secret code word Behemoth for the buyer. The world would end if anyone heard boo about the sale before its official announcement. I'm to stick within my realm of words and feelings.

"But when this maven of the finer points of English language usage observes Patrick's choice of code words for their buyer—Behemoth, something oppressive or monstrous in size—suggests he is conflicted over the sale, he doesn't want to talk about feelings either. Right, dear?"

An overlong silence met her question. She gave him a stage smile. "You may speak now."

He downed the last of the wine, picked up his fork, twirled it around, and set it down again. "I can see how you might have developed your perspective. It's not my intention to block you from the discussion. Nor is it my belief numbers and finance are beyond you, and you can only deal with words and feelings. Several Cook County politicos are awaiting sentencing because you figured out their dirty deals. I do take the business secrecy issue seriously. Maybe too seriously? Dad, did you ever tell Mom anything secret?"

I swished around the sip of wine I had in my mouth. This cabernet probably cost way more than anything I would buy for myself. I noted it had a hint of pepper that I thought paired well with the lasagna. Had Paddy picked? Or Jolene? Or plain luck? I swallowed. "No work secrets—but using me as a model for ideal couples' communication might not be the best idea."

Paddy reached for his fork, but stopped midway. "Maybe so, but I need your advice on what's happening at work for two reasons. You've had experience changing jobs mid-career. More immediately, although I still have your financial power of attorney I want—I need your advice since decisions we make might affect our sales price, and you own the largest block of shares. And I created a problem we need to discuss."

Cindy and Paddy shared a significant look that I could not interpret. The lasagna was getting cold, so while I waited for Paddy to explain the issues, I attacked the meal. After two excellent forkfuls, Paddy still had not continued. Maybe I needed to prime the pump.

"You have me confused, Paddy. You said I own the largest block of LT2P stock. How did my eight percent become the largest amount? Did the partners sell some of their shares?"

Paddy: "On a fully diluted basis, you own 24.7% of the shares. I own 12.3%, as do the other partners. The . . ."

With Cindy occasionally interrupting to ask clarifying questions about what terms like "fully diluted basis" meant, Paddy described the sequence of events that concluded with him using his power of attorney to have me buy another $2.75 million dollars of LT2P stock in a private sale. Listening to his analysis, I was roiled with competing thoughts: a bit steamed that he hadn't asked me about the purchase given its magnitude, since I had been in Boston looking after my mother and available for easy consultation; and swelled with parental pride that he had made the kind of investment I made for myself. Because the sale was private, he had bought the stock at a discounted price—good for me—and it had saved LT2P all the underwriting, investment banker, and legal fees of selling to a venture capitalist—good for the partners.

"The investment makes sense," I said, "but why didn't you ask me before committing such a large amount of my portfolio?"

Paddy finished his water and set the glass in the same sweat ring, rotating it until the raised crest on the outside of the glass pointed directly toward Cindy across the table. "Because . . ." He reached for his glass and retracted his hand when he realized the glass was empty. "Because I thought you weren't taking back management of your assets as some kind of test. You didn't give me any guidance when you thrust the powers of attorney in my hand. You just left. You know . . . Like you were trying to figure out if I had learned the investment lessons you taught me. Could I make good investment decisions without consulting the master? I studied several years of your brokerage statements to make sure I understood exactly what you were doing, and this fit your criteria for taking oversized positions."

As he spoke, a gnawing dread came over me. "Oh Paddy, I am so sorry. I've been thinking of my own stuff and not at all thinking about the burden I placed on you. I . . . I don't even know how to apologize. That you could even think I was somehow testing you—"

"It's my fault—"

"No, Paddy. It is not your fault. I had blinders on. At the time I first asked you, I was shaken by what happened at camp and wasn't necessarily thinking straight. I wanted to save my relationship with Abigail. I had—*have* full confidence in you. But, it has just now occurred to me that I took advantage of you, Paddy. I'm very sorry. I should never have put this burden on you without making sure—let me finish here—to make sure you were completely fine with what I was asking. Under those circumstances, any child would find it difficult to refuse his parent. I shouldn't have even asked."

I held up my finger to forestall his interruption. "But I did and compounded the crime by not relieving you of the burden once I was able to take it back. I'm sorry for all the concern and worry I've obviously caused you. And I especially regret that my actions made you think I was testing you, as though you don't have my unconditional love."

Cindy spoke, and I'm embarrassed to say I talked right over her. "Cindy, I'm sorry for what this has done to you as well." I shook my head in dismay at a recollection. "Minutes ago, I said I didn't believe in parents being arbiters. What I did was so much worse. I hope you two can forgive me."

Cindy folded her napkin and got up from the table. I made to rise as she walked toward me, but she motioned me to stay seated. She leaned in and kissed my cheek. "Seamus, I couldn't think of anyone I would rather have be my child's grandfather. But you will kill yourself if you don't stop taking responsibility for everything that goes wrong in the world."

She continued around the table, put her arms around Paddy, and snuggled into his lap. "You two McCrees are so screwed up, you're lovable. You should know that Patrick's first words to me the day you signed over the power of attorney were, 'You won't believe what my father did today.' His feet did not touch the ground for days. He simply glowed, Seamus. I wasn't there when you two talked. I have no idea what you did or did not say. But I can tell you without any reservation that he took your trust as the biggest compliment you could ever give him. He knew without any shadow of a doubt that you love him and trust him and think he's the best. Aren't I right? The only mistake the two of you made was not talking enough to each other."

Paddy said she was correct, although he thought "without any reservation" and "shadow of a doubt" were shop worn, overused, and probably overdoing it a titch. Cindy gave Paddy a deep kiss.

I had tears in my eyes again and looked away in double embarrassment of my tears and their kiss.

Cindy came up for air. "Seamus, you may not want to stick your nose in our arguments, but I have no such compunction. In so many ways you two are alike. An old wives' tale says to know how the boy will turn out, look to the father. So if I want Patrick to turn out well, I need to fix you first, right?"

She did not wait for my assent. "You have to stop seeing yourself as a screw-up. Everyone else marvels at your accomplishments. They appreciate that you care deeply for people and causes. Sometimes you're a crusader and go over the top. Hell, I'm an investigative reporter, I know crusading and over-the-top behavior. I think it's a good thing. Lots of women must agree with me because I notice they keep throwing themselves in your path.

"And Patrick, you need to remember a shared burden is a lighter burden. You and I, we're in this together, you big dope." She gave him another good long kiss. "And I hate it when you won't tell me what's worrying you. Don't you feel better for getting your concerns into the open?"

His lips formed a weak smile. "Yes."

"Good, but be forewarned. If women throw themselves at you, big guy, I'll kill 'em . . . or you."

That got everyone laughing, but Paddy still looked worried. "Out with it," I said to him. "Something still bothers you."

"Yeah," he said, "there's more bad news. You're about to run out of cash." The words tumbled from his mouth. "Behemoth agreed to buy LT2P with a June close, and I kicked up another great investment: a convertible bond for a startup I know. I thought the timing would work, so I went all in. Then Behemoth pushed the closing until the end of September, and your house hasn't sold, and . . ." Paddy grabbed Cindy's water and drained it.

He looked miserable. I needed to understand this convertible bond, but more important was to start repairing the damage I had done to my relationship with Paddy. I tried to lighten the mood with, "I guess it's a good thing I didn't write a check for the red Lamborghini I was lusting after."

My chuckle died when neither of them joined in.

Try two. "Look, Paddy, you still believe the convertible bond is a great investment, right?" He did. "Then time will fix everything. I have excellent credit. Interest rates are lower than they have ever been in my lifetime. With my contacts and credit rating, I can easily get a mortgage on the house, which will solve any cash-flow problems until the sale goes through. Sounds to me this is a no harm, no foul-type situation. In fact, it sounds like you made me something north of a half million bucks after tax. Good job!"

Paddy: "Only if LT2P doesn't lose any clients and the sale still goes through."

Me: "I hereby formally release you from all obligations of managing my money. If you want to worry, worry about LT2P or the new addition to your family. Not this. Besides, we need to discuss what you found here while Cindy and I were sniffing around Antimatter Investments. But not now. I hereby declare all that out of bounds until we finish this delicious dinner. Let's discuss raising children in an age of electronics or what color you'll paint the kid's room. Agreed?"

I raised my glass. Cindy grabbed her empty water glass from Paddy and chinked my wine glass. Paddy still looked skeptical, but added his wine glass to the mix.

"Agreed," they both said.

"Jinx!"

Twenty-One

Despite Jolene's objections, we insisted on helping her clear the table and do the dishes. We promised we would not tell the Cunninghams of our lapse in good judgment, and we insisted she put her normal hours on her time card. Jolene left muttering under her breath, but smiling.

Kitchen duties done, we regrouped on the patio. Although past eight o'clock, temperatures were still in the seventies: not bad for northern New Jersey on a mid-June day. The chemical-green lawn stretched past the outbuildings to a fence lined with trimmed bushes. The land sloped away to a pond, I surmised based on the group of willow treetops I could spot in the distance. Give me my wild Michigan woods any day. I couldn't stand to live in such a sterile environment.

I waved a mosquito away and spoke first. "The long and short of it is we found nothing strange in all the due diligence files. The firm's hedge funds have done exceptionally well. Tomorrow should be interesting. Cindy and I are scheduled to tour Antimatter's offices. Presumably, we'll meet the partners and learn how they explain Cunningham's absence."

Cindy: "Don't forget, you want to contact the accountants."

Me: "That was curious. Each partner uses a different accounting firm to audit the funds they run, and a fourth accountant audits the partnership's books. All small firms I haven't heard of. Was your day productive?"

Paddy: "Yes and no. I've searched every room except for two and the attic. I thought someone else should do my mother's study since I had already spent some time in there. And she has a separate bedroom. I honestly got queasy in there and kinda hoped one of you would search it while I did the attic. I still need to figure out how to get into the hidden room—if it's even there."

"Hidden room?" Cindy and I said together.

Me: "Jinx!"

Paddy and Cindy shared a look of annoyance.

Embarrassment flushed my face. Never was a game I didn't want to win. "It was self-protection so I wouldn't be silenced. You're released, Cindy."

Paddy: "No more of the jinx game. I'm adding it to slap hands."

Cindy: "Slap hands?"

Me: "We'll explain later. Spill on the hidden room."

Paddy gave us his thinking process and what he had done so far.

Cindy popped up from her chair. "What are we waiting for?"

Me: "Did you check with your mother?"

Paddy's eyes did a quick look toward heaven. "According to her, the house was part of the Underground Railroad. There had been a hidden room, but she understood it had been sealed years ago. She could have misunderstood or the Jerk could have lied to her."

I suggested Paddy take the attic, Cindy take Lizzie's bedroom, and I'd do the study.

Cindy's mouth scrunched to one side, as if she'd tasted a bitter lemon. "Seamus, you should take her bedroom. You lived with her. You'd know if something didn't seem right. I'd bring fresh eyes to the study."

The thought of rifling through Lizzie's underwear stopped me in my tracks. A protest rose in my throat, but I throttled it; Cindy had a point.

The two of them climbed the main staircase hand in hand, and I had another bout of envy. This staircase was three times the width of mine in Cincinnati, with wood carving as intricate as mine had been before it burned. Paddy waited at the top and directed me to Lizzie's bedroom. I stopped before the closed door, gathering fortitude to invade Lizzie's space. Pouring over legal documents and financial statements all day had left me with a sore back and tight neck. I cranked my head right and left to the crackling sounds of bone grinding bone. I was stalling and needed to cross the threshold.

As I entered the room, Lizzie's scent assaulted me. Our bedroom hadn't been small, but this was the size of a middle-class living room. With an attached bathroom on one end and a walk-in closet at the other, you could live your whole life in this space, provided servants delivered meals and removed the dirty dishes. The canopied bed needed a step stool to climb into. The area proximate to the bed held a pair of end tables, two bureaus, and a make-up table sized for a Hollywood diva.

While we were together, Lizzie had decorated our refrigerator, our living room, and our bedroom with family pictures. Most were of Paddy, but there was a scattering of the rest of us, singly or in pairs. Nothing in this room suggested either her husband or Paddy existed—or even Lizzie herself. With nary a picture in the room, it could belong to any generic rich lady.

In an alcove formed by the bathroom and lit by one of the three oversized windows, a recliner sat sandwiched between a table overflowing with hardcover books and an old-fashioned magazine rack with newspapers and magazines hung from horizontal dowels. The rest of the room contained two groupings of living room furniture: sofa, love seat, stuffed chairs, coffee tables, end tables with Tiffany lamps and the like.

I was still dawdling.

I marched to the sleeping area, opened the double doors of the nearest end table, and sifted through the contents. Top shelf: portable reading lamp, e-reader—I set it aside to have Paddy explore in case she was using it instead of her computer for email or saving files or whatever—bottle of Aleve. Bottom shelf: a thin patina of dust.

I neatly removed the duvet and stripped the bed, punched the pillow—soft, checked under the mattress—nothing but the go-to-jail-if-you-rip-this-off tag. Nothing under the bed. Nothing under the step stool. The cedar chest at the foot of the bed held only a down comforter and a cashmere robe.

The end table on the other side of the bed contained only air.

The top drawer of the cherry bureau had the underwear I dreaded, each pair neatly folded cheek to cheek, and a small jewelry box with several rings and earrings. Nothing hid amidst the underthings. The next drawer housed her bras. Socks, pairs folded in on each other, filled the third drawer. Lower drawers contained, in order, shirts, sweaters, shorts, and workout clothes.

The walk-in closet contained clothes, lots of clothes. I patted each outfit for hidden somethings and didn't even find a dust mote. I removed shoetrees from each shoe to check the toe box. Wasted time. The hatbox contained a hat.

And inside the hat were a Burberry passport wallet and a Salvatore Ferragamo card case and money clip. The money clip held ten crisp hundred dollar bills. Inside the card case was a platinum card in the name of Elizabeth Browning. The "s" in Elisabeth's name had been replaced with a "z." I didn't recall Browning in her family tree. All that came to mind were the name of an automatic weapon in World War Two and the Victorian poet I'd been forced to endure in high school.

I fumbled open the passport to the page with Lizzie's picture. The name on the passport was also Elizabeth Browning. It had been issued earlier this year, but the picture dated from a few years earlier. Perhaps the same one as on her real passport? And where might that passport be? I examined the document page by page. It contained no entry stamps, but I knew it could have been used to get in and out of Canada. Did Mexico use entry stamps?

A thousand bucks in cash, a fake passport, and a platinum card in Elizabeth Browning's name. Take the jewelry with her and she had everything a girl could want for a quick escape to foreign lands. I rocked on my heels, ineffectually deciding what to do. She didn't have this stuff with her, so at least for the moment she wasn't planning on splitting the country. I replaced the items in the hat, and hat in the box, and continued my search.

I discovered nothing else interesting in the closet. Back in the main room, I found nothing taped to the bottom of furniture or stuffed in the cushions.

The makeup area had more bottles of moisturizer, skin firmer, eye shadow, and the like than I had realized existed in the world. I switched on the lights and blinked at their brightness. No wonder she needed all the chemical crap. In this light, every flaw showed, which is one reason romantic restaurants use dimmed lighting.

Focus, Seamus. Hold it together. Almost done.

The two sitting areas appeared unused. The alcove with the recliner must be where Lizzie spent her time. Tuesday's, Wednesday's, and today's newspapers decorated the rack, ordered from oldest to newest—presumably Jolene put them there. The magazines included *The Economist*, *The New Yorker*, and to my surprise, *Rolling Stone.* No pages torn out, nothing added.

After checking in and under her recliner, I eased onto it and raised my legs. *Comfy.* I snagged the top book, the latest by Jane Smiley, and flipped it open. A folded piece of paper fluttered to the floor.

When we lived together, Lizzie had absentmindedly stuck whatever was at hand into whatever she was reading to mark her spot. With some frequency, I had had to search through piles of books to find a bill I knew nothing about until I received notice it had become overdue.

I unfolded the paper.

Do NOt cAll the cOPs
If yOu WAnT to see
yOuR hUsBanD aLiVe
i want 25 miLLion
I will cONtact yoU

I grabbed tissues to hold the message and prevent more of my fingerprints from blotting those already there. I reread the message three or four times before my brain kick-started. Clearly a ransom note. When had she received it?

I could understand Lizzie not mentioning a fake passport and credit card, but a ransom note? With all the stress she was under, I found it hard to believe she hadn't let something slip.

How did it relate to the missing money? Had kidnappers sent the note, but before Lizzie could do anything, Cunningham convinced them he could ransom himself and withdrew the twenty-three million? That might explain why he had made a special effort to pay the quarterly taxes. Or was the ransom note an elaborate ruse by him to forestall everyone until he had time to leave the country with the money?

What if Lizzie, not her husband, had removed the money from joint accounts to pay kidnappers and something went wrong? Had she tried to get CIG involved because she was afraid to go to the police? When CIG didn't pan out, she latched onto me, a poor substitute?

My brain ached from the concentrated thought.

Kidnappers bury their victims, sometimes literally. But the woman, Kaylee Whatshername, not only had Cunningham pull money from an ATM, she marched him in and out of a bakery. Which made no sense. And the carjacking?

A new thought shocked me. Had Lizzie created the ransom letter herself? Did she plan to "find" it upon her return? And do what, try to establish an alibi?

Cops always look at family when it comes to murder.

PATRICK FLICKED THE ATTIC LIGHT switch and left the door open. Even the attic was finished with rough-plastered walls, eight-foot ceilings, and hardwood floors. Leaning against one wall were a couple dozen pictures, each gilt frame kept dust-free and separated from one another by oilcloth. Patrick carefully unwrapped the first three paintings: more hunting scenes. He could check the rest later.

He gave a collection of cane-seated chairs stacked in one corner of the room a once-over and pricked his hand on a protruding hair from a nearby horsehair couch. That sucker hurt. He sucked the salty blood off his finger until it stopped. *And to think, people used to sit on those things.*

A trunk with brass fittings blocked a door into the rest of the attic. The trunk latch was locked, and Patrick could not recall seeing any small keys. He made a mental note to ask the others if they had spotted any in their searches.

He braced his feet against a wall and gave the trunk a tentative shove to gauge how difficult it would be to move it away from the door. The piece moved on sliders so easily, Patrick needed to catch himself before he fell. The exposed door opened on oiled hinges. His flashlight revealed an unfinished attic with batt insulation between bare joists and the smooth stone of fireplace chimneys. He stepped into the room on a wide beam and kicked up enough dust particles to trigger a sneezing fit. No one had been in there for a long time.

Patrick backed from the unfinished area and closed the door. He knelt to examine the trunk lock more carefully. It was more complicated than the childhood diary he'd had when he was ten or eleven, but with the right tools, he could probably pick it. Thinking about that diary triggered a memory of his mother's advice to "tape the key to something nearby."

Attached to the underside of the trunk was a key. *Thank you, Mom.*

The trunk was two-thirds full. The pull-out tray on top contained his mother's designer wedding gown from her marriage to the Jerk packed in plastic, veil wrapped separately. He removed the tray and laid it on the horsehair couch. Underneath were boxes of various sizes. He removed the lid from the first box and uncovered his baby book.

His mother's precise writing had recorded his length and weight at birth, the presents he had received. His first word: "da-da." He set the box aside on the floor.

From the next box, he extracted two bundles of letters tied with brown string. The first were addressed to Miss Elisabeth Long in care of the Girl Scout camp she attended. The return address indicated they were from her parents. The second, much smaller group, were the letters and postcards his mother had written home. He read the one on the bottom of the stack and smiled. His mother had never been much on letters. This postcard was a case in point:

Having a wonderful time when it's not raining. See you Saturday.
Love, Lizzie
XXXOOO

Maybe his mother would let him read them sometime. She had kept them, so they must mean something to her.

Next came a heavy shoebox filled with letters bundled with what Patrick thought were white and black hair ribbons. He removed a packet and was stunned to see his father's chicken scratch. "Lizzie Lou Lane," was how he addressed the top letter. He must have hand-delivered it because the envelope had no address or stamp.

Patrick had never heard his dad call his mother Lizzie Lou. He had called her "Triple L" from time to time, and Patrick had wondered at the reference. What was the Lou all about?

He poured the packets onto his lap. All the letters were from his father. He wasn't sure if he was more surprised that there were so many or that his mother had kept them.

Patrick remembered some of the stuff he had written Cindy between the zap of their mutual attraction and their living together. Most of his letters consisted of day-to-day trivial stuff: what was happening at LT2P during their first days, the triumphs of signing new clients, the despair when big banks recognized they had a security problem but considered LT2P too small or too new to be trusted.

He undid one of the ribbons and slid four sheets of paper from the top envelope.

Oh, *The Letter*—the one Cindy claimed should have been sent in a plain brown envelope. He knew his parents had sex; he was the proof of at least one coupling. At the thought of his father writing a letter like the one he had written Cindy, his face heated up, probably to Ohio State red.

Note to self, make sure if it still exists to have Cindy destroy that letter before our kid is old enough to read. Well, if he didn't want his kid to read his letters to Cindy, he shouldn't be reading his parents'.

He slid the unread pages into the envelope, retied the bundle, and set the shoebox aside. Underneath another dress—*prom*?—the trunk was filled with photographs. Many were in frames he remembered scattered around her house. He flipped through several: his mom growing up, his parents together, his early years before they went digital. He knew he looked a lot like his father, but seeing his dad at the same age he was now was a shock. He shook his head to clear his thoughts.

Did his mother still hold a torch for his dad? Did the Jerk know what was in the trunk?

His father bellowed from the floor below, "Cindy. Patrick. Come here. I found a ransom note!"

Twenty-Two

Patrick followed the smell of morning coffee downstairs and found his dad seated in the dining room reading the *Wall Street Journal*. "You made coffee?"

His father chuckled. "It's safe. Jolene made it. She's concocting omelets, although I think I might have insulted her by saying we didn't want sausage and bacon. Where's Cindy?"

"Shower. She'll be right down. While I wasn't sleeping last night, I thought of something I should have thought of earlier. Chad would know of the secret room, so I sent him a text. I haven't heard anything back, but it's early."

"Sorry to hear you didn't sleep well. My head hit the pillow and I was gone. You weren't worrying about my finances were you?"

"No. I was solving world hunger. When I started tossing and turning, I wanted to get up and finish searching the attic because it's the one thing I have left to do. Cindy put her foot down and wouldn't let me out of the bed. Instead, I suffered busy brain."

"Paddy, I'm telling you, it's not worth losing sleep over. Your old man is still in demand if I need to—or want to—resume working. Several corporations have recently dangled big bucks in front of me to get me to head up their financial crimes groups."

A grin crept over his face. "What? They want you to figure out even better ways to rip people off?"

"Cute. The most recent was a bank. They'd been heavily fined for not uncovering money laundering, so ponying up a big salary and bonus is a no-brainer for them." He folded the paper and put it aside. "Look, Paddy, I'll call my bank. I can get a mortgage and a car loan. Really, it's not a problem. Worse comes to worst, I could head up to camp for the summer and hardly spend any money at all."

"And Grandma?"

"She could come with me." The twinkle left his eye. "Besides, I like both of your investments, their combined timing was a little—"

"Sketchy."

"Aggressive, maybe. Switching topics. I've considered your question whether you should stay on with—what was your code name, Behemoth?—or quit and work from home and take care of bumpkin when the time comes. For someone as smart and dedicated as you, I truly believe you should do what you love and the money will follow. After the freedom you've had with LT2P, it'll be a major adjustment to work for a huge organization."

"And they want me to work on client retention, not sales."

"I'm sure if that's what you decide to do, you'll be good at it. I'm not about to tell you what job you should or shouldn't take. That's for you and Cindy to decide."

Cindy arrived in her navy pin-striped power suit, a frilly handkerchief tucked in the jacket pocket providing the one touch of femininity. "You two talking finance behind my back again?"

Patrick gave her a quick smooch. "Every chance we get. In fact, we're forming a cabal to ensure every woman is barefoot, pregnant, and walks three paces behind her husband while staring adoringly at her husband's heels. I already accomplished the pregnant part, and Dad was telling me how to train you to do the three paces stuff."

Patrick gave her a side-glance, caught a smile starting to crinkle her face, and knew they were good. They wouldn't always agree, no couple did, and they needed to keep talking, especially about life after baby. He needed to keep talking. Lesson learned.

"You know," Cindy said, "it won't be long before women will shop online for their baby's genes. Sperm and a turkey baster will be delivered within the hour by drone, and we won't need men anymore."

His father guffawed. "Yeah? Then who will you blame for all the world's ills?"

"Oh, we'll still blame men. Legacy costs."

PATRICK SAW CINDY AND HIS father off in their limo and retreated to the dining room. Over a second cup of coffee, he willed Chad to call or text him about the hidden room. He skimmed the *Wall Street Journal*, his mind wandering to the recent finance conversations. His father had taken the news about his own finances much better than Patrick had anticipated. He wondered if his dad's reaction would have been different if Cindy hadn't been there or if they hadn't just announced their pregnancy. And was there some bite behind Cindy's laugh when she had mentioned legacy costs?

Touchy, are we? Live and learn.

Patrick brought the paper into the garage to toss into the recycle bin. He laid the paper on the top of the pile, and his brain made a connection between the banner across the paper in his hand and the ransom note. The LL in "WALL STREET JOURNAL" had the same shape found in "miLLion" on the ransom note. In fact, wasn't there a WA in the note too?

He lifted the papers out of the bin and went through them. The *Wall Street Journals* and *Star Ledgers* were in daily order. Each day's paper was complete, except for the first section of one *Wall Street Journal*. Had it been the source of the cutout letters? He raced upstairs with a *Journal* in hand. Exactly the same shape and size.

Patrick returned to the garage and removed all the newspapers from the bin, searching for the missing section. He pawed through the trash in the garbage can. Nothing. Perhaps Jolene knew something? He returned to the house and brought the coffee service into the kitchen. "Jolene, did you or Torr use any newspapers recently? For wrapping up some broken glass, or something like that?"

She wiped her hands on a dish towel. "I haven't, and newsprint is so dirty, I can't imagine Torr using it. Why?"

Patrick hadn't thought that far in advance. He couldn't tell her about the ransom note. "Um, I remembered an article I had meant to read for work and wanted to find it."

"You could check their online edition."

She had just given him a way out from the corner he'd put himself, and he jumped on it. "Good thought." He offered a smile. "What I really came in for was to determine if there's a way to check who might have been in the house. Mother says everyone has their own code for the security system. Do you know if the security company keeps track of that?"

"Security company? I don't know, but it's moot. At one time I think they did assign separate codes for everyone, but now I'm pretty sure everyone uses the same code." A wry smile flitted across her face. "The Cunninghams hated having to punch in a code every time they came in, so

Torr or I—whoever is first here in the morning—shuts down the alarm. We rearm the system each night before we turn in. Not exactly Fort Knox."

"So even if I have access to the records, they won't tell me anything?"

"I suppose you could see if people came in late at night, but otherwise, not so much."

Patrick had considered it a long shot, so he wasn't too disappointed. "In other words, don't waste my time. One last thing, then I promise to stop bothering you. Do you know anything about a secret room in the house? Between Mr. Cunningham's study and the next bedroom? My mom said it was sealed off?"

"Oh, sure. It's where they stored the hooch during Prohibition. The only thing Mr. Cunningham ever uses it for is to hide her Christmas presents so she can't find them. It's ingenious. You want to see it?"

"Prohibition, not Underground Railroad?"

"The wine and liquor racks are still there. I clean the room twice a year, spring and fall."

Jolene led Patrick to the bedroom on the far side of the Jerk's office. "Nothing like a little illegal booze to stimulate creativity. You'd never find the mechanism unless you tore the room apart."

She wriggled underneath the king-sized bed. From the closet came a loud clunk. She squirmed out. "That should do it." She opened the closet door, moved aside a quilt hanging from the bar, and reached in to the rear wall. "Watch this." With both hands she pushed on a panel of the back wall and it popped out. She grasped the panel on both sides and yanked it from the wall, placing it on the floor behind the quilts.

Behind the removed panel was an area framed with two-by-fours and filled with insulation. Attached to the surrounding frame were a couple dozen black rectangles. "I'll bite," Patrick said. "What now?" He could feel the excitement building. Despite Jolene's assurance nothing was hidden, with everything happening, Patrick was certain something had been stored in there since Jolene had last cleaned.

She placed her hands on the left-most two-by-four and pushed. The framing became a door hinged inside the secret room. "It uses electrified magnets." She pointed to the panel behind the quilts. "The interior is constructed so if you tap the wall or, these days, use a stud finder, all you'll find behind here is the same configuration as the rest of the wall. It's actually a door."

"Wait a minute, a wire from under the bed goes to these magnets? How cool is that?" He was sure something was back there.

"The bed's fixed in place. The wire goes down the center of one of the legs, under the floorboards, and comes up through the center of the hinge to the magnets. There's even a battery backup." She reached in and flicked on a light switch. Fluorescent bulbs flush to the walls washed the space in light. "After you."

Patrick pushed the door open and hoisted himself inside. The room looked like Jolene had cleaned it yesterday. A flood of disappointment washed away Patrick's hope for a clear answer to what was happening with the Jerk. He turned around to thank Jolene for showing him the room and caught a flash of colored light at the edges of his vision. It had been years since he last suffered a migraine. Most of his had had no aura component, but when they did, they were humdingers. Did he still carry some naratriptan in his shaving kit? It was long expired, but—

"Are you all right?" Jolene asked. "You don't look quite . . ."

"I think I'm getting a headache. Stress, and I didn't sleep well last night. Maybe I'll lie down and try a compress." Patrick put on his salesman cheery voice. "Thanks for showing me the room, it's a wonderful piece of history."

Jolene flipped off the interior light. "Wouldn't you love to learn the secrets an old house like this could tell? If only it could talk."

Twenty-Three

TO MAKE AN ENTRANCE, IN the Hollywood sense of things, Cindy and I took a limo from Far Hills to the Antimatter Investments offices in Midtown Manhattan. Given the rush hour, we gave ourselves two hours for the forty-five-mile trip. In the limo, I related my conversation with Paddy and assured Cindy I had meant everything I had said to him.

"We'll certainly have some adjustments to make," Cindy said. "So how do you expect today to go?"

"We're winging it. Yesterday's fishing expedition at their lawyers, reviewing those due diligence binders, was partly to see if I sniffed any financial improprieties and partly to make today's meeting appear normal. Our first objective is to learn whether they're up front concerning Cunningham's disappearance. I'll be surprised if they are."

"And if they aren't?"

"We shake them up. We make them nervous. We tell them you're an investigative journalist looking for a reason not to blow the story onto the front pages."

As I said those words, her demeanor changed. Her eyes widened. Her nostrils flared. Her shoulders pulled together bringing extra oxygen to fuel her chase. She'd gone from content cat lazing in the sun to a predator scenting prey.

Using all but five minutes of the allotted time, the limo pulled to the curb at the corner of Forty-fourth and Fifth, which was a curious spot for a hedge fund—not downtown where the big firms were. The building was not A-grade office space either. Its location was consistent with what I had gathered from their financial statements, namely they did not waste money on frivolities. Their earnings went to the partners.

Cindy and I were greeted by the receptionist, who ushered us into Yves Bouvier's office. He and the other partner, Donald Griffin, were sipping coffee at a burlwood table set with silver and five china place settings. While Cindy and I settled in, I tried to guess what subspecies of alpha males the partners were. The building and general areas of the office were nice, but utilitarian and not soundproofed from the honking taxis on Fifth Avenue. Yves' office was a striking contrast of ultramodern steel desk and antique table and sideboard. The carpet was well padded, soft, with pile so deep and thick it needed raking.

Pictures of sailing vessels crossing finish lines decorated the walls, marking Yves a competitive sailor. I guessed he thrilled being on the edge of disaster while maintaining control. He would appreciate working with a well-oiled team, since all the pictures showed the crew in action. Crows' feet etched his tanned face. Beneath the European-cut suit, I suspected, was a body with muscles toned by sailing, not at the club.

Donald was impeccably dressed in a Brooks Brothers or Hart Schaffner Marx or some other boxy suit maker, but his face was fleshy and a roll of loose skin showed above his shirt collar. I figured him for fast cars and a fast temper. He might make an easy mark for Cindy and me to get under his skin, cause him to lose control, and say something he shouldn't. I wanted Cindy's read on these two guys, but we had no opportunity to huddle and compare notes.

Entering on the heels of an extremely attractive woman who brought coffee and danishes was a young fellow I recognized from Lizzie's description as Cunningham's assistant, Laurence Kleindeinst. He looked like a younger version of Yves.

At the doorway his glance grazed me, but lingered on Cindy. His eyes widened and he blurted. "What the hell is she doing here?" He pointed at Cindy. "She's an investigative reporter, Elisabeth Cunningham's son's girlfriend." He squinted at me and added, "And that's her ex-husband."

My first fleeting thought was to brazen it out. We had legitimate business here, even though our primary purpose was sleuthing. My second thought was to take umbrage at being a "that" rather than a "he." My third was to realize his grammar had labeled me as Cindy's ex-husband rather than Lizzie's. My fourth was that our cover was truly blown. I relaxed and smiled at the twerp. *Let the games begin.*

Cindy grew tall in her seat. "Busted. Seamus is legitimately here. His client hired him to advise whether they should make an offer for your firm. He has to make his report Monday. Seamus brought me because it's our understanding your boss, Albert Cunningham, has been missing for three weeks." She made a sweeping arm gesture. "And you gentlemen have been stonewalling Mrs. Cunningham."

Since Cindy had gone on the offensive, I shook off my considerations of English grammar and concentrated on reading body language. The woman who had brought the food quickly fled, forcing Kleindeinst to step forward to allow her to exit. Kleindeinst's neck tendons protruded in hard white slashes. His eyes stared out from a face gone blotchy red. Clenching his fists at his side, he positioned his body at an angle to us, which I read as "fight" mode.

Donald's face had become pasty, his eyes searching for escape routes. He was all "flight." Each man checked Yves for direction, leaving no doubt who held the power.

Yves remained seated, legs and arms relaxed. A smile grew from the corners of his mouth to encompass his entire face, revealing pointy canines. He ignored the other two and gazed fully upon us. "Looks like our partner is playing a deeper game than we suspected. Please, do help yourself to coffee and pastries. They're both excellent. Have you found where he's hidden his money?" He motioned Laurence Kleindeinst to join us at the table.

I poured glasses of water for Cindy and myself and took a sip. *Yuck.* It must be the purified stuff with no taste.

Cindy: "What money is that?"

Yves: "In all honesty, we don't know where Al is. I will tell you two things to pass on to your respective clients. First, any trip he made to Savannah was not on Antimatter business. We have no prospective buyers with a Georgia location, and Laurence can confirm that none of the companies Al was reviewing for stock purchases have facilities in the Savannah area. Second, in a routine internal audit, we discovered Al was engaged in unethical and probably illegal behavior."

I did not have to feign surprise.

Yves: "In addition to the public hedge funds we operate, we each manage several private funds. Al's public hedge fund is the Challenging Opportunities Fund. We discovered Al used his private funds to front-run trades in our hedge funds. Furthermore, the day before his disappearance, he sold highly overvalued securities to his public fund from an offshore private account he employed to manage some of his own money. Our insurance company has informed us any loss above our deductible is covered. Donald and I have already reimbursed the deductible to the Challenging Opportunities Fund. You can see why we have been reluctant to include Al's situation in our due diligence files. It hardly seemed necessary when neither our investors nor prospective buyers will lose anything. We hope Al will return from wherever he is hiding so we can obtain a complete explanation—and perhaps receive restitution."

Me: "And you just discovered this?"

Yves: "Frankly, we assume Al is hiding offshore along with his ill-gotten money. I know Elisabeth tried to obtain information from our employees, but once we discovered this impropriety—and yes, we just discovered it—I ordered everyone to refuse her calls. She could be party to the malfeasance."

The disclosure was a new twist, but was it the truth, carefully constructed lies, or a combination? "Have you contacted the police?"

Yves: "No. Obviously, this is embarrassing to us. However, if investors suffer no losses, there will be no reason to bring in the authorities. Our insurance company says the decision is ours. Our counsel agrees with our approach . . . unless the press gets wind of this." He cleared his throat and raised his eyebrows at Cindy. "Then to protect ourselves, we'd press charges and file a civil suit against the wife. I hope, given the ramifications, you will be a responsible journalist." He granted Cindy a beaming smile.

An interesting possibility occurred to me. "To confirm, this is not a situation where Mr. Cunningham has been kidnapped, and you're feeding me elaborate bullshit to cover up while you work with the FBI to obtain his release?"

Yves's smile disappeared. "I wish that were the case. Boy, do I wish that were the case—and I could see how you might think it—keeping a kidnapping quiet, I mean. I assure you that is not the situation. As embarrassing as it is to admit, Donald and I partnered with a . . . a . . . cheat."

I expected more fire, more anger. If I had been "partnered with a cheat," weeks later I'd still be steamed. Using the fact that I was representing a legitimate potential buyer of their business, I tested whether or not they were conning me. "I assume my client's auditors can verify all investors have been fully compensated, which means there has been no direct loss. The privately managed funds are not part of the proposed transaction, so they are not material. My clients may still be concerned with the lax controls that allowed this malfeasance to occur."

Donald: "As well they should. When we formed the partnership, we retained the existing auditors because they had experience with the three hedge funds. We engaged a separate auditor for the partnership books and the limited liability company that sits between the partnership and the individual funds. As is standard practice, our partnership auditor relied on the statements from the original three. We did *not* realize Al's auditor was his uncle by his first marriage, who we've concluded was either in cahoots with Al or incompetent."

Cindy stopped taking notes on her pad. "Are you reporting him?"

"The uncle?" Yves lifted his shoulders and dramatically dropped them. "He's eighty-seven. We terminated his services."

Cindy leaned in toward Yves. "But he skates."

Yves did not respond, so I jumped in. "Is it your belief this was a one-time occurrence, or could this have been a systematic practice?"

Kleindeinst: "Yves and Don tasked me to search for any similar transactions with any of Al's private funds. I found nothing suspicious. I have also reviewed private sales—no problems—and I compared sales prices of all transactions to other market-based information, and the pricing looks fine. It's been a mammoth task, but it's complete. In the process, I found the front-running, which has been a consistent practice."

Cindy: "Front-running?"

Kleindeinst: "Buying or selling ahead of a known transaction so you can buy a little cheaper or sell a little higher." He peeked at Yves. "Unethical, particularly between partners, but not illegal. The other transaction certainly is illegal."

While I sensed this was all true information, I had the feeling something else was not being voiced. "How," I asked, "have you handled Cunningham's funds in his absence?"

Kleindeinst: "I've treated the Challenging Opportunities Fund like he was on vacation. I don't add anything to the portfolio. I do have sell points for a few securities and buy points for some others. You know, fluffing up the portfolio on dips and trimming after bull runs." He slid a glance at Yves. "We'll have to do more soon, but we haven't decided how to proceed. We have not touched the private funds."

Which meant they had not yet decided if Kleindeinst would take over responsibility for the fund. Interesting.

Me: "You were the last from the firm to speak with him?"

Kleindeinst: "Far as I know. He had me make the reservations to Savannah. I've thought back on that, and it was a little weird, you know?"

I didn't know, so I nodded encouragement. A tip of the head from Yves, which, if I hadn't been looking at him, I would have missed, gave Kleindeinst permission to continue. "Yeah, he didn't sound like himself. And he didn't give me any explanation. Something came up and he needed the reservations."

Cindy: "Did he rent a car?"

Kleindeinst: "He was meeting someone at the airport. Maybe they had a car, or maybe they got a meeting room. I don't know. I was bummed because I was expecting him in to approve our expense reports. I had to schlep out to his place with the papers for him to sign and fax into the office and missed a Yankees game I had tickets for." He gave a little shrug. "Wasted trip, obviously."

Me: "You delivered them when?"

"Friday, late afternoon. Caught rush hour both ways. No one was home so I laid the envelope on his desk."

I laid possible trap number one. "You have keys to the house?"

Kleindeinst shook his head. "Everything is touchpad. Although half the time I show up the door and security systems are off."

Cindy: "Why not use a messenger service?"

"Al was paranoid. He was afraid someone would steal his ideas or front-run him. Ironic, I know. He'd use encrypted flash drives to carry whatever electronic files he was working on back and forth. Like I said, paranoid."

Me: "You did this often?"

"Every couple weeks."

Me: "Are you the only one from the firm with the security codes?"

Kleindeinst looked up at the ceiling. "Of current staff, I think so. But the guy who worked for Al before me gave me the code, so I don't know how many people know it."

Confirming what we suspected: if someone could get past the driveway gate, they could access the house unseen. While I was sitting in front of them and could gauge their reactions, I needed to press them. "May we have a copy of the internal auditor's report?"

All eyes checked Yves, who did an internal think-about-it for fifteen seconds and responded with, "I'll need to discuss that with legal counsel."

Me: "If my client is still interested, they will insist on seeing those documents. You say no further liabilities exist. I'm sure they will ask for an additional warranty provision—and want proof."

Yves made a show of looking at his watch. "We hope they are interested. Otherwise you've wasted a lot of our time. Our lawyers would have apoplexy if they knew how much I have already told you. We really can't say anything more."

I had one more spear to chuck at their armor before they threw us out. "One of the reasons Mrs. Cunningham was contacting your firm was to withdraw her money from the Challenging Opportunities Fund. You'll expedite it for her?"

Donald exploded. "She'll get her money when everyone can get their money."

Yves pursed his lips into an angry red line. I wasn't sure if he objected to my effrontery at suggesting such a thing or to Donald not holding it together. "That," he said, "will also require a conversation with our attorney. I understand Mrs. Cunningham's concern. We'll address her question as soon as possible." He rose and faced Cindy. "I do have your word? You will not be printing this story?"

Everyone else at the table also rose.

Cindy offered her hand. "I will work at verifying your story before I decide what I will do. On that, you have my word."

TWENTY-FOUR

PATRICK BLINKED HIS EYES OPEN to a darkened bedroom and his cell phone playing The Postal Service's "Such Great Heights." *Cindy*.

The migraine was at full throttle. He groped for his phone on the nightstand. Not there. The noise stopped. He slumped back into bed. If he moved much or quickly, he'd throw up. He willed his head to stop hurting, knowing it was hopeless. He had soaked in a hot tub and tried the cold compresses with little effect. He'd figured out his last migraine had been nearly four years earlier and remembered Cindy had suggested he should get the naratriptan prescription renewed a couple years ago when it expired. Sure he'd been done with the migraines, he'd ignored her advice. Wrong again.

The phone chirped notification of a voicemail. Keeping one eye closed and the other squinted, he got out of bed and sat on the floor next to his pants. He fished the phone from a pocket, put it on speaker, and checked the message.

"Hi, honey," Cindy's voice said. "Where are you? Your dad and I are at the airport and expected you'd be here already. Is everything okay?"

Patrick caught the sound and cadence of his father's voice in the background.

"Give me a call. I'm not supposed to tell you this, but I know it will make you laugh. Don't bother calling your dad. He forgot his charger and his phone's dead."

Patrick pressed the return call button and closed his eyes to block light slipping past the curtains. Her voicemail answered, professional and chipper. He told it he was in bed at his mom's with a migraine; he'd catch a plane to Chicago tomorrow. He powered down the phone so it wouldn't disturb him again, crawled into bed, and pulled the covers over his head.

◇◇◇

THE BEDROOM DOOR OPENED ON well-oiled hinges. In socks, I tiptoed to Paddy's bed. He lay on his back, arms and legs spread as though he were being crucified, the covers over his head and the pillow piled on top of the covers. I knew migraines. During my years at the investment bank, I would sometimes get them so bad I closeted myself in a dark room and prayed for quiet. All I could do was wait them out. Lizzie had never suffered a migraine in her life. My migraines had stopped once I quit the investment bank. Too bad Lizzie's genes hadn't prevailed in this case.

I whispered that Cindy sent her love, wanted to be here, but she had to get home for work. "Anything I can do?"

In jagged bursts, he told me about the missing newspaper section.

I used my online subscription to the *Journal* to reproduce on my computer what the front page of the missing section looked like. I agreed with Paddy's assessment that the WA and LL on the note were cut from the WALL of the *Journal's* banner. On the first page, I found all the capital and small letters in the note. Didn't prove anything, but it sure suggested someone had created the ransom note using materials at the house. Unfortunately, given the lax security, a host of people could have created the note.

So, who benefits?

The simple answer: someone who collected a ransom and got away with it. Telling Lizzie we found the note would give her permission to tell us Cunningham had been kidnapped for ransom. But so far, nothing in this damn situation had been simple. So, what twisted reasons made some sense?

Lizzie could have created it to try to get the police involved. "Oh, looky here. See what someone stuck under my door? Help my dear husband, he's been kidnapped." Or maybe Lizzie put it together, later decided the note would help no one, and tucked it into a book and forgot. But why not destroy it? With her shredder it would take seconds. Even a stressed Lizzie wouldn't be that dumb. *Who am I kidding? Stress could make Einstein stupid.*

And then there was Lizzie's fake passport. What was I to think of that? If things continued to point to her possible involvement in Cunningham's disappearance, I'd have to ask. *Oh boy.* And if she lies, do I keep looking into this or walk away? Walking away would be the smart thing, but what would Paddy want me to do?

No reason to cross the minefield yet. Trying to wrap my thoughts around the ransom note, Cunningham's deliberate act to pay quarterly taxes on the stock sales poked me again. Why bother? Was Cunningham on the lam, or in trouble, as Lizzie and Tommy Kennedy thought? And if Kennedy was right and this somehow involved drugs, what was the somehow? Where was he hiding—or being hidden? And what was he doing?

Paddy's condition meant he wasn't going anywhere soon, and as my mother used to say, "idle hands are the devil's workshop." I had time; Cunningham's laptop was in his office; I could read his email.

Booting up his program, I found many new messages. I ignored ones alerting him to changes in corporate ratings, the gobs of economic data, and spam his filters had not caught. I clicked through the remaining emails and came to a pair of notifications from a cloud storage firm:

User ACunIII has logged in.

User ACunIII has logged out.

The email heading information indicated the events had occurred a day and a half ago on Wednesday night. The duration of his connection to the website was a shade less than thirteen minutes. Was this Cunningham or had he given his username and password to someone else? Laurence Kleindeinst came immediately to mind.

I checked the website: for a pretty penny, the firm provided encrypted cloud storage. Was it a standard backup service? I checked the programs Cunningham had downloaded onto his computer. No automatic backup systems, and he wasn't using the operating system for backup either. I checked the history for the two internet browsers Cunningham used, but found no reference to that website or cloud service.

On TV, folks like me sit down at someone's computer, make a few guesses and *voilà*, they have access to everything. In my case, I had an added advantage because I knew Cunningham's basic password scheme. I tried a bunch of stuff without any luck at all and it frustrated me no end. After the eight trillionth attempt, I slapped my hand on the desk and uttered a mild expletive.

Actually, uttered and mild were both gross understatements.

Jolene stuck her head in the doorway, bringing with her a lemony scent of clean. "If I recall correctly, they said personal computers would save us oodles of time. I'm not so sure that prophecy panned out. Not going well?"

"In spades. Forgive me for what may be an intrusive observation, but your English is better than ninety percent of the people I meet."

"And you wonder what a nice girl like me is doing in a place like this?"

Put that way, my curiosity made me sound like an idiot. "Sorry, my middle name is Tactless."

"I am a dissertation short of a Ph.D. in literature with a focus in English fiction from roughly Beowulf to pre-Shakespeare, which means I am fully qualified to wait tables anywhere. Or cook and clean here. Torr's cabinetmaking business fell apart in the last recession, and we wanted to remain in the area so Corgan could stay at the same high school. We lucked into this gig. It leaves me plenty of time to do my research, and Torr has a small workshop in one of the outbuildings and is again doing a brisk business without the pressure of it being our only source of income. I'm afraid with Mr. Cunningham gone, our little piece of paradise will collapse."

"Corgan's an unusual name. A son?"

She laughed high like a piccolo. "Billy Corgan." My expression clued her in that I had no idea who Billy was. "Smashing Pumpkins? Most people call him Corr, but I find it confusing because it sounds so similar to Torr."

"I've at least heard of the band. So you don't think Mr. Cunningham will return. Did you notice any changes before his disappearance?"

"Two, three months ago, he became moody. He and Mrs. Cunningham began arguing pretty often. You know the missus moved to a separate bedroom. She doesn't always use it. You know . . ." She blushed. "This is his family homestead. I think he'd be here if he could. Something bad's happened to him. Torr thinks we need to start looking for new jobs."

"You don't think Mrs. Cunningham would keep you on?"

"I don't want to be telling stories out of school, but Mrs. Cunningham once remarked how she feels like the house owns them. Mr. Cunningham didn't like to leave even to take vacations." She bit her upper lip. "Torr and I don't think he left voluntarily."

Hoping for an honest reaction, I intentionally switched gears. "Are you good with computers?"

She tilted her head back and laughed at the ceiling. "We co-exist. If you have a problem, maybe Corgan could help. He's very good." Her face shone with pride. "He's in the honors computer science B.S.–M.S. program at Rutgers, and he'll be home this weekend. He often helped Mrs. Cunningham."

A series of beeps sounded from downstairs.

"Corgan set the alert to signal whenever someone opens the driveway gate. Are you expecting anyone? No? Then it's probably Mrs. Cunningham."

She hurried from the room and her footsteps clapped down the stairs. I peered through a window. A taxi pulled in front of the house and disgorged Lizzie. My shoulders tightened. I did not feel prepared to talk with her, but doing so would take one thing off Paddy's plate.

From downstairs, Jolene said, "Welcome back, Mrs. Cunningham. How was your trip?"

How should I approach this conversation? The big thing was the ransom note—and I wanted surprise to get an honest reaction. I needed to discover what computer work Corr did for her and figured I could wing it to find out what she knew about Cunningham's cloud storage—probably nothing. Then there was the fake passport.

Footsteps tapped up the staircase. Would she seek me out? The footsteps faded down the other hallway. I'd have to go to her. Waiting wouldn't make anything easier. I hid the Ziploc bag containing the ransom note between my shirt and the back of my pants, ready for the big reveal.

Twenty-Five

I PRODUCED A SMALL COUGH to announce my presence at the door to Lizzie's study. "What news from Savannah?"

She spun from her position staring out the window. "I didn't realize you were still here."

Neither her voice nor her eyes contained an ounce of warmth. Both were pinched in pain or distaste. Her hostess skills needed polishing. Or was she treating me like family?

"The whole blasted time was wasted. You know the nickname for Savannah is 'Slo-vannah'? Dynamite up their asses couldn't get them to hurry."

"Oh?" Best to let her vent before I started my interrogation.

"The cops took my information and have done absolutely nothing. Every time I call them I get this big runaround. Transferred two or three times and some schmo tells me, 'We're looking into it. We have nothing we can report. Have a good day, ma'am.' Don't they get that I won't have a good day until they find my husband?"

"Very frustrating. Unfortunately, police departments are designed to collect information. Keeping families informed is not a major priority. What are you planning from here?" I was pleased I had asked a neutral, open-ended question.

"Why *are* you still here? Did you find something useful? Did you get something from those snakes he works with? Why didn't you call me?" She slumped into her desk chair. "You've got that look. What's going on, Seamus?"

"Paddy's sleeping off a migraine. Cindy had to return to her job, so I stayed with him."

Her face grew sympathetic. "Ouch. I thought he didn't get them anymore. They're from your side of the family. Do you still get them?"

"I'm directly responsible for part of his migraine. I screwed up by asking him to take care of my finances for a while. With everything else happening in his life, it was a bit much. But you iced the cake."

Her head snapped up and her eyes shot daggers. "What's that supposed to mean?"

"It means you're hiding things, and he suspects you aren't telling the truth. Is he right?"

"How dare you accuse me of lying, Seamus McCree!" She pushed away from the desk and rose, fisting her hips. The daggers became white hot. "Here I am, doing everything I can to find my husband, and you're sleeping in my house turning my own son against me. "I thought I knew you. That's why I asked you for help. But to stab me—"

My muscles knotted under the assault. "I have not said one thing against you. Don't project your sins on me. He's—"

"My sins?" Now screeching, "My sins? What right do you have to suggest I have sins? You abandoned me, you bastard. You left me all alone. It—"

"Stop!"

We both stared at Paddy, who leaned against the doorframe, holding one hand over his eyes and the other on top of his head.

"Mother, just stop. You've told that story so many times you believe it. You left him, not the other way around. Have you shown her the note?"

Lizzie's jaw trembled. She reached for the chair, missed the first time, and slowly eased onto the seat. She had the dazed look of someone smacked by a frying pan.

I felt as significant as a mouse turd. My intent had been to spare Paddy pain, and here I was aggravating the situation.

"Have you shown her the ransom note?" Paddy repeated.

I walked the evidence to her. "I found this in your study—in a book." She didn't take it, so I dropped it in her lap.

"And," Paddy said, "the newspaper used to produce it came from this house."

Lizzie squinched her eyes, rubbed them with the heels of her hands, and picked up the note. She mouthed the message as she read. Finished, she looked up. A grim expression contorted her face. Softly, she said, "I have never seen this before. What is it you two think? That I hid this from you?"

Her eyes grew wide and her mouth became a thin line. "That's not it, is it? You said the note was manufactured here. You think I'm the kidnapper. No, no! You think I killed my husband and planned to invent a kidnapping scheme to explain his absence."

Neither Paddy nor I spoke.

"You fucker," she said to me. "Get the hell out of my house. Right now!" Her finger pointed the way. "Leave. Me. A-lone."

"If it wasn't you," I said, "then how—"

The veins and arteries at the side of her neck threatened to break through her skin. "Now, goddamn it." She fried me with her glare. "Or do I need to call the police to remove you?"

She telegraphed a roundhouse punch. I caught her hand six inches in front of my face. Its power rocked me onto my heels. "Get control of yourself, woman!" I released her hand and reached past her to retrieve the evidence. My hands were shaking from adrenaline and anger.

She grabbed the plastic bag and held it behind her with one hand; with the other hand she knocked the receiver off the phone and dialed 911.

I gave a fleeting thought to ripping the bag from her. Instead, my anger collapsed in a pool of regret that we had broken our vow to never fight in front of our son. "Hang up," I said. "I'm leaving."

She disconnected and leaned heavily against the desk. "Patrick, go lie down. I'll bring you some compresses."

"No," he groaned. "I'm leaving with Dad."

PATRICK WOKE TO THE SMELL of pizza and remembered he was in a Newark airport hotel with his father. "Time?" he croaked.

"Eight. I thought maybe eating would help."

At Patrick's request, his dad filled the ice bucket from the machine by the elevators and created two ice packs using dampened hand towels. Patrick placed one behind his neck and the other on his forehead. "I can talk now. Keep it soft. Pretend I have a killer hangover."

In a quiet voice, his dad asked, "Do you know Corgan Truvert? He's a computer science kid and has been helping your mother out. He surely could set up a keylogger program, and both he and his parents have access to the house."

"Is Mom still using him? She gets impatient if I can't drop everything to help her. Once I feel better I can give Corr a call. Talk geek to geek."

"And Cunningham or someone recently logged into a cloud storage account. I tried to guess the password, but couldn't. Can you use the garbage that comes along with an email to figure out the location of whoever signed in?"

Patrick tried to process the question. "Garbage?"

"I don't know what you call it. All the gibberish that shows how the email traveled from its origin to you."

"Gotcha. It only tells us where the email servers for the cloud storage firm are located, not the Jerk's location."

"So we have nothing?"

Patrick tried to perk up his voice to counteract the dejection he heard. "Actually, quite a lot. We know the cloud storage firm. We know the Jerk's username. I copied the Excel file with his accounts and passwords onto my computer. If it's on the list, we're all set. If we get into the user control panel we can probably even see what files he accessed. Boot up my laptop for me."

It hurt like the devil for Patrick to open his eyes and type the long string of numbers, upper and lower case letters and special characters necessary to unlock his computer.

"Gosh, Paddy. How do you remember it?"

"If I told you, I'd have to kill you."

"Groan."

Following Patrick's instructions, his father found the Excel file. But, it didn't include the cloud storage firm or anything else employing the username ACunIII.

Patrick resupplied his ice packs and lay back down. "Okay, hacking zero zero one. Set up an account for yourself and let's see what happens with your username and password."

The username was automatically set to SMcCree. The system emailed a temporary password.

"So," Patrick said, "they're using first initial of first name plus first and last three letters of surname."

His father adjusted the ice pack on Patrick's forehead. "You must be feeling better to think of that so quickly."

"I wish. I've seen the naming routine before. What are the rules for your password?"

"Between eight and sixteen characters. Must include at least one number, one letter, and one special character and cannot include my username. Not much help."

"His spreadsheet showed he used Fluffy followed by a number, and if he needed a special character he added an asterisk. Finish setting up your account and mess up the login. I want to understand what happens."

"In red letters it tells me the ID or password is incorrect and to 'Please try again.' There's a link if I forgot my password. Let me try it." A moment later he reported, "Yep, it sent me an email. Now, if we only had access to Cunningham's account."

"We do. Lisa and I anticipated we might want to access his machine without triggering the keylogger program. We set up an overlord program to control the original keylogger on his computer." They talked through the steps of signing in to the overlord program and temporarily disengaged the keylogger. "The keylogger now thinks his machine is off. Now click the link to send the Jerk a password reset email."

His father found the email, reset the password to the cloud storage, and following Patrick's instructions, eliminated any trace of the email.

"Now," Patrick said, "log in to the storage and let's poke around. Tell me everything you see."

"I see only two files with dates after Cunningham's disappearance. You think those are new files?"

"Not sure. It means he doesn't have automatic backup or the computer with the originals isn't turned on. What are the two files?"

"Blank standard American put and call option agreements between two private parties. Why in heaven's name would Al—or someone who knew his password—want access to those two files and nothing else?"

"Rhetorical question, right? I have no clue what you're talking about."

"A put option gives you the right to force the seller to buy a specified number of shares of the company at a predetermined price. A call gives the option for the buyer to acquire a specified number of shares of the company at a predetermined price. Normally, options trade on stock exchanges, but these are private. Can you learn where the login originated? Assuming this is Cunningham and we can find him, we'd get to the bottom of the whole shebang."

"Sorry, Dad. I understand the theory, but I don't have those kinds of skills. I know some people who might be able to help. Could you warm up the pizza, please? I think maybe I can eat a little something. Let's restart the keylogger program, and we need to discuss Mom."

His father released a long sigh.

Patrick removed the forehead ice pack, carefully sat up, and opened one eye. “What?”

“I don’t really have an interest in talking to your mother.”

“I was only talking about talking *about* her. You know what I mean. But here’s the way I feel: either we discuss the situation and draw straws to see who enters the lion’s den to question her, or I have to call the police and rat her out.”

TWENTY-SIX

I VOLUNTEERED TO GO SEE Lizzie. A guy in his late twenties—floppy brown hair, bloodshot eyes, perfect teeth—opened Lizzie's door at my approach and offered his hand. In a singsong voice, he said, "Hey, I'm Chad. I'll take you to Beth."

"I'm sorry," I said, "for whatever your father is going through. And I appreciate you responding to my son so quickly about whether all your relatives were safe."

"Happy to do it. It could have explained everything if someone were in trouble. I apologize for blowing Patrick off when he left his second message. I thought I had better talk with Beth first."

He led me to Lizzie's bedroom. She was lounging on the sofa by the open window. The night air had replaced the smell of her perfume with the cloying scent of some flowering plant. Cricket chirps and mosquito hums provided background music. The ice cubes in her drink had melted to indistinct blobs; glass sweat had soaked the top of a glazed coaster, sliding over the edge to wet the wood. Chad's drink was half-full. I pulled a chair to the grouping and settled in.

Lizzie downed the rest of her drink. Her first? I tried to make eye contact with her. She played with her hands, watching them flutter away from the glass and eventually settle onto her lap. She was as nervous as a junkie without a fix.

"Seamus, I apologize for my behavior. I haven't been myself, what with Al missing. I know I've said that before, but it's true. I was a real shit. I am sorry for what I said, and I'm especially sorry I said it in front of Patrick. I'll make sure to tell him directly once he's feeling better. He said you had questions . . . things didn't make sense . . . things you needed to ask?"

Her gaze eventually lifted so she was looking at me. Her eyes were hollow pits. The light was dim and her pupils and irises merged into a black you could lose your soul in. Had she lost hers or was there some other explanation?

I inclined my head a titch in Chad's direction, silently asking if she wanted him to stay for protection or leave because of embarrassment.

Lizzie must have caught my signal. "Chad's as concerned about finding his father as I am. Anyone want anything to drink? I've had enough myself."

Chad and I muttered our no thank yous. On the taxi ride, I had decided to plunge in with what had earlier resulted in Lizzie tossing me from the house. "You have no idea how the ransom note ended up tucked in one of your books?" I pointed to the stack on the table in the alcove. She must have already told Chad about the note because he did not appear surprised.

"I have never seen it before in my life—not before you showed it to me, I mean. I have no idea where it came from." She settled her feet on the floor, paused a moment to gather herself, and pushed off the sofa. She walked to the end table by the bed and retrieved the plastic bag holding the note. "Jolene assures me it did not arrive by mail." She opened her eyes wide. "That is the God's honest truth. Really."

I paid attention to how her eyes moved as she spoke. They did not, meaning Lizzie likely had rehearsed this little speech. I needed to push her into uncomfortable territory to get a sense of truth.

"Okay, I believe you." My eyes pulled to the right. Made sense, I was constructing this from whole cloth. "Theoretically, given the house is unlocked most of the day, anyone could get in. But to set this up, they'd need to know their way around. Who fits that description?"

"Only me, Al, and the Truverts. That's it."

"Doesn't his assistant come here when you guys aren't home?"

Chad: "Hey, don't forget me. Lots of people know the house layout. Just to name a few, there's my mother, a bunch of family members on both my parents' sides, the staff before the Truverts."

Lizzie: "Why would you even think of them, Chad?"

Chad shrugged once and made a sweeping gesture with his arms extended. "Since nothing makes sense, I was casting a wide net. If it was delayed revenge or something, those people know their way around. If we're inventing motives, my mom could be pissed that my dad is making super big bucks since they divorced. Maybe she decided her settlement wasn't exactly fair. Or maybe the staff didn't retire voluntarily and want revenge on the new mistress of the house. Not that I think any of them are involved."

Those motives did sound farfetched, but then again *nothing* seemed exactly reasonable. "How about the Truverts and their son, Corgan? They have the run of the house."

Chad's voice dripped with sarcasm. "What? The butler did it?"

Me: "Torr nearly lost his business not that long ago. Jolene's working full-time and getting her Ph.D. on the side. Their son's in college. I don't know what you're paying them, Lizzie, but money might be tight, and Corgan helps you with your computer, right?"

Lizzie plopped into a rocking chair. "I just can't believe that. When I convinced Al to hire them, they were so grateful. Torr would have lost his business without us giving him space to work. Sure, Corr would occasionally help with a computer issue when he was in high school. Since he's been away at school, I've had Patrick take care of my problems remotely. Some kind of software I don't understand."

"Besides," Chad said, "I don't want to be classist or anything, but would they even think to ask for twenty-five million? Two million, even three million, sure. But twenty-five?"

Lizzie raised her eyebrows at me. "Good point."

I'd been paying careful attention to Lizzie throughout our discussion. She showed plenty of eye movement, which suggested she was retrieving facts, not making stuff up. I had learned a bit of the Reid Technique used by police forces all over. I had no idea whether it might work with Lizzie, but even though I was not expert, what did I have to lose?

It would require a change in tactics from my question-and-answer approach. Step one is to confront the subject by indicating the evidence points to them. Step two is to provide them an escape route. While Lizzie was looking at me, I tried again to dart a glance at Chad in hopes she would dismiss him. No luck.

"Look," I said, "for argument's sake, let's say it wasn't the Truverts. The note was in your book in your study. The cutout letters appear to have come from a newspaper in your house. We know you two are having money problems of some sort. He recently transferred most of the money from your joint accounts. We know you guys were having some . . . um . . . marital difficulties." Lizzie started to raise an objection. I held up my hand. "You mostly sleep in separate bedrooms. Maybe in the beginning your husband put you up to this and something went wrong?" *That was sufficiently vague to cover anything and everything.*

Step three is to try to prevent the person from making a denial. It's harder to get a confession once they have already said, "I didn't do it." Unfortunately, I had already let her say that earlier, so I wasn't strictly following the program. Like I said, amateur effort. She shook her head no, but did not voice it.

Step four is for the suspect to provide reasons why it could not be her, and Lizzie was with that program.

"I already told you I've never seen it. If I'm supposedly colluding with Al, did he sneak into the house when I was gone? That doesn't make sense. You told me the newspaper was from right before I traveled to Cincinnati and he was already gone."

I needed to point out her flawed logic. "Nothing says he had to use the most recent newspaper. How do we know he didn't have another set of tickets, a set that brought him back here from Savannah any time after that newspaper was published, and no one knew? Maybe he flew on a fake passport? The evidence that he withdrew money from an ATM is circumstantial. You two could have anyone do it. You—"

"The pictures are the proof. He was in Savannah."

"Granted. But it doesn't prove he stayed in Savannah the whole time."

"No. No. No." She shook her head. "You're making this all up."

The ping-pong referee raised a hand and we both looked at him. "I don't for a minute believe Beth had anything to do with whatever has happened to my father, but I will have to say, as unlikely as it is, nothing proves what Seamus suggests is incorrect. Seamus, you mentioned a fake passport?"

Step five: Reinforce sincerity to make sure the subject is receptive.

Since Lizzie had not picked up on the fake passport, I ignored Chad's question and focused on Lizzie. "I know how much strain you're under. You've lost weight. You haven't been sleeping well. You've said things you wouldn't normally say. You're at your wits' end. This has been terrible for you." All true, but when this false empathy worked and she relaxed into the sofa cushions, I felt like a sleazeball. She wasn't looking at her hands, but she wasn't looking at me either.

Step six: Into this calm, introduce alternatives.

I kept my voice quiet, understanding. "Did you figure out he had stripped away most of your marital assets, and this was your way of providing yourself financial security?"

"No, Seamus. No. It wasn't like that." Tears streamed down her cheeks. According to the Reid Technique, these tears implied guilt.

"What was it like?" I held my breath, waiting for a confession.

Lizzie addressed her answer to Chad, not to me. "Yes, we were having problems. Your father wasn't the same after his partners decided to sell the firm. He wouldn't talk. He became moody. He worked longer hours than ever. I even considered the possibility he was having an affair. I forgot about the fake passport. He was worried the U.S. might become totally unstable and we'd have to flee. I was shocked, but what was I to do, turn my husband in? My real passport is in my safety deposit box. I hid the fake one in the house to humor him. I have no idea where he kept his."

She brushed tears away.

No confession, other than to having a fake passport, so I tried a different approach. "Did one of your friends suggest putting the keylogger program on his computer?"

"I told you, I've never heard of it." She rushed on. "And I didn't know about our finances either. I was shocked to learn the house was mortgaged and our investment accounts drained."

Chad: "The house is mortgaged? I thought it was in the trust Dad set up."

Lizzie: "It is, but it's mortgaged. I don't understand any of this. We were having problems, but we would work them out."

Me: "You were getting divorced."

"What?" Her voice screeched. "You're just saying that because you and I got divorced. You—don't you leave this room, Seamus."

"I'll be right back." I hurried next door to her study, retrieved the file with the divorce papers from the desk drawer where Paddy had returned them. I placed the folder on the coffee table between us and opened it to the document I needed. "You're denying this? It's the second draft of the agreement between you two."

Lizzie's hands grasped her throat, as though she were choking herself. She curled her legs under her, making herself into a ball in a corner of the sofa. Chad slumped in his seat, an expression of surprise painting his face.

"These are all lies, Seamus. Did you plant them? Is this a trick to steal my son's affections?"

I towered over her, using my height to force her to feel diminished. "That's crazy talk, Lizzie. Get a grip here. Paddy found these before I ever stepped into your house. Why don't you drop the façade and tell us what's going on? Whatever it is, we can find a way to make it better."

She slammed the flat of her hand on the coffee table, scattering the papers. "As soon as they open their offices you can call whatever lawyer's name is on this crap and talk with them. I have never seen this. This is all bullshit." She crossed her arms over her chest, thunderclouds decorating her face.

With that declaration, the Reid Technique crashed around me. I had come here three-quarters believing Lizzie's need for security had caused her to slip to the dark side. Only a quarter of me held out hope that someone had done a magnificent job framing the woman who'd given me a son. There was absolutely no way—okay, almost no way—Lizzie could be so angry and so righteous and so truthful about some things, the false passport for one, and still lie about everything else.

But, if not Lizzie, who? And, how to find out?

I pulled my chair closer to her and sat down. In what I hoped was a soothing voice, I said, "I believe you, Lizzie. Someone went to a lot of work to make it appear you were complicit in your husband's disappearance. Motive and opportunity. What would anyone gain, and who could do it?"

From behind me Chad stirred. "Look. I don't believe for a second he did it, but of everyone, Dad has the easiest access to both his and Beth's computers. He could plant stuff in her study. Dad never told me he wanted to divorce Beth. He and I had several conversations before he and my mother divorced. He could have planted the fake divorce papers or even had real ones drawn up that she didn't know about. And if I heard right, he's drained the accounts. Both the joint and personal accounts or only your joint ones?"

"Everything," Lizzie said.

Chad leaned forward in the chair, forearms resting on his knees. "Which is what he would do if he was planning to disappear and for whatever reason wanted suspicion placed on Beth. As I said, I don't believe it. That's not the father I've known all my life, but as some scientist said, when you eliminate all the possibles and are only left with the impossible, then the impossible must be true. Who besides him could have pulled all this off?"

The ransom note bothered me. "How could he have gotten into the house without anyone noticing him? We know for sure your father was in Savannah Sunday. We have a security camera picture."

Chad: "I hadn't heard."

Me: "And the ransom note was constructed from Monday's newspaper. How could your father slip into the house, unseen, between the time Lizzie left for Savannah on Monday and our discovering the note yesterday? Wouldn't the staff have seen him?"

Lizzie: "Not necessarily. The main house blocks the carriage house where Jolene and Torr live. They can't see the driveway or the front of the house."

Me: "The alarms aren't set to ring at their place?"

Lizzie: "Oh sure, but only if someone doesn't disarm the system, which Al did all the time with his cell phone app. He could have allowed anyone in during the night if he gave them the gate and house codes and disabled the alarm."

I threw my hands up in frustration. "So if he has an accomplice, anything is possible regardless of where he actually is. That's damn helpful. Lizzie, what would you have done had you come home tonight—Paddy and I weren't here—you came home alone and found the ransom note tucked into one of your books? Wait. Would you have found it?"

Lizzie: "Which book was it in?"

"Top of the pile."

"Sometime tonight. Don't you remember? I bring a glass of wine or sherry to the room and read for at least a half hour before retiring." She looked down at the remains of her drink. "Probably not tonight."

"So you find it, what do you do?"

Her lips pursed. She rocked in her chair. "I'd probably hide it in my desk. The note said the kidnapper would contact me, and I shouldn't go to the cops, right? I'd be a nervous wreck and wait for them to contact me."

"And if there were no contact?"

She made a big yawn. "I'd wait."

"You wouldn't tell the cops? You wouldn't tell Paddy or me or Chad?"

At her silence I continued. "Maybe its sole purpose was to buy time."

Chad: "For who?"

For whom. "The person who planted the note . . . assuming they knew Lizzie wouldn't go to the police."

Chad: "You said he took all your money. Did he take the gold too?"

"What gold?" Lizzie and I said simultaneously. I stopped myself from saying, "Jinx." Wrong group.

"In the safe in the secret annex. Patrick's message asked how to get in. I didn't want to tell someone over the phone. I came by as soon as I got back into town."

Me: "Jolene showed Paddy the secret room. There's nothing in there."

Chad gave Lizzie a hard look. Challenging her to say something? What? She appeared clueless. He slapped his thighs. "That's the so-called secret room Dad used to hide our presents. There's another room I guess Dad didn't tell you about that was used to hide slaves."

Twenty-Seven

PATRICK WAITED AT THE MOTEL, gulping more pain meds and continuing to apply ice packs to the back of his neck and forehead. He felt like a laundered rag doll put through an old-fashioned wringer, but at least he could function. He gulped a slice of cold pizza. Now odorless, its congealed cheese tasted like the cardboard box. At least it would tide him over. The Italian sausage on his dad's half of the pizza made him lust for something interesting on his half to liven things up. A vegetarian for fifteen years, he'd probably get sick if he actually ate meat. He tossed the dirty napkins into the empty box and carted it outside to the trash barrel.

He checked his phone, subtracted an hour for the time difference in the Chicago area, and tried Lisa at work.

"LT2P, Lisa speaking. How may I help you?"

"It's Patrick. I'm stuck in Jersey with a migraine and I need Sherlock's help if possible."

"Shit, Patrick. Don't even breathe that name. It's dangerous."

Patrick apologized and explained that someone had accessed Cunningham's cloud storage for which Patrick had the account username and password.

"I gather you want to know the location of the computer that accessed these files?"

"Exactly. I'm hoping it didn't go through a phantom proxy."

"What happens when I find him?"

Patrick noted the use of when, not if. He had the feeling this might actually work. "I'll try to make direct contact. But, backtracking—I don't know where to start."

"I need to put on my boss's hat. Your quest is distracting from your work at a time we can't afford it."

The throb behind Patrick's eyes increased. He shut his eyes. "Are you offering another deal?"

"You misunderstand me. I'll get some Red Bull on the way home and work on your problem until I solve it or determine it cannot be solved.

While we speak, I am clearing your calendar for Monday and Tuesday. You are officially on vacation. You have four days including the weekend. Then I need you one hundred percent. Starting Wednesday, your schedule is chock-full of client and prospect meetings. You owe it to me. You owe it to your partners. Most importantly, Patrick, you owe it to yourself."

Patrick did the math: he had a hundred hours, give or take, to track down the Jerk.

CHAD LED LIZZIE AND ME to the garage where he collected flashlights and a ten-foot stepladder. He brought the items to the basement and set the ladder up near the foundation of a large brick chimney in an area shadowed by indirect lighting. "If you didn't know this was here, you'd never find it in a bazillion years."

He climbed the ladder, tilted an eighteen-inch square of ceiling board away from the chimney and angled it up and into a hole. "There's plenty of room for all of us, but duck, the room's only four feet high." He flashed the light inside.

I tried to picture where we were relative to the upstairs rooms. We couldn't be far from the hidden room on the second floor.

Chad clambered inside and, carrying the second flashlight, I followed him up, slowing when the bruises from the accident reminded me I was not yet healed. Lizzie started up the ladder before I reached the top. I stuck my head and shoulders in to survey the room. The main section was maybe twelve feet long and half as wide. A three-foot-wide wooden bench ran the length of one wall. Halfway back from the trapdoor, three chairs with shortened legs huddled around a circular rough-planked table. An empty kerosene lamp sat on the table. Above, soot darkened the ceiling.

"This the place they used in the Underground Railroad?" I asked.

Chad: "Legend has it, but it could be where they hid Jimmy Hoffa before they planted him in the Meadowlands. Who knows?"

I pulled myself into the main room and stayed on hands and knees. Reaching back, I helped Lizzie move from ladder to hidey-hole. Chad duck-walked to the far end and shined the light into a space behind the chimney.

"Gold's gone. It used to be stored on the shelving behind the chimney."

Lizzie: "I never even heard of this room. Or the gold. Was there a lot?"

Chad: "A bunch, but how much?" He shrugged.

I followed Chad and looked past him into the space illuminated by his flashlight. The shelving was empty, but I could see the faint outlines of where ten rectangular somethings had been.

Chad ran his fingers along and behind the shelves. His face expressed surprise as he retrieved a rectangular pouch, which he opened. "Here." He handed me the pouch.

Inside were a receipt for ten 400-troy-ounce gold bars and a U.S. passport. With Lizzie looking on, I flipped open the passport to the picture page. Albert Browning—the same last name as the passport I had found in Lizzie's hat box. "False name. Expired six years ago." I wondered where its replacement was.

Lizzie took the gold receipt from me. "How much was it worth?"

I did a quick mental calculation using sixteen hundred bucks an ounce. "In the neighborhood of six million dollars." I figured his gold stash was the equivalent of normal people stuffing a few bucks under the mattress or in a pickle jar in the refrigerator for a rainy day. Problem with gold is you can't pack the stuff in your suitcase and fly away to your favorite country with no extradition treaties.

Lizzie's bottom lip quivered, but she held it together while staring at proof she did not know all her husband's secrets. Or did she? No, she was not that good an actress.

Chad finished searching the area. "Nothing else here. I'm starting to feel like an old-time coal miner in this cramped space. My back's starting to object. Let's leave." He followed us out and replaced the square hiding the entrance.

Looking around the basement, Lizzie wondered aloud how anyone could move six million in gold.

"Each bar's less than twenty-five pounds," Chad said. "A few trips to the car and you're done."

"Yeah," Lizzie said, "but where do you sell it? It's not like you can put them on eBay."

"With the right connections," I said, "you can take them to New York's diamond district—that's only a couple of blocks from where your husband works—and have cash as soon as they measure and weigh the bars to confirm they're real. Chad, who knew about this room?"

"I stumbled across Dad coming down a ladder when I was a teenager. He swore me to secrecy, but like any kid I had to see what was hidden."

Me: "Last time you were in there?"

Chad looked sheepish. "Shortly before Dad married Beth. I don't even know if my mother knew. I can ask her tomorrow if you want. It's too late tonight."

"It is late," Lizzie said. "I've had a long day, and frankly, all this new information is too hard to digest. I need to take a shower and sleep on this."

Chad offered to drop me at the hotel since it was on his way home. I accepted. Not only did it mean I wouldn't have to wait around for a taxi, it would give me a chance to talk with Chad without Lizzie around.

Twenty-Eight

Paddy burst through the door connecting our hotel rooms, banging the door into the wall and waking me up.

"We got him. We got the Jerk!"

I fumbled eyeglasses onto my face and blinked myself awake. Paddy stood at the foot of the bed. He was shielding his eyes, so I assumed his migraine was still present, but a grin covered his face. I croaked, "Got him where?"

"Well, actually, I don't know for sure it's the Jerk. Maybe. It could be anyone who knows his username and password for the cloud storage."

I motioned with my fingers for him to give me more.

"It was right before our eyes, but we all missed it. Sign into his cloud account and all the prior times accessing the website are available in a log. It's all in a tab. Gives us his ISP, which we've tracked to someplace near Kitty Hawk, North Carolina."

"The Outer Banks?"

"It's like halfway between Savannah and New Jersey. We know who the provider is. We're attempting to figure out the exact location. I asked Lisa to help, but I should have been able to do this myself. Now she's working on narrowing down the location."

"How close can you come to pinpointing where Al—where whoever accessed the cloud storage site actually is?"

"Depends." He grabbed the desk chair and brought it to the side of the bed and sat down. "I'm kind of hopeful because it didn't come up like Nowhere, Texas, which is how lots of the satellite internet providers list their address. If it's by phone or cable, we might—emphasis on the might—be able to pin it down to a single switch. That could still include a bunch of blocks. If we're really lucky, it's a dedicated ISP with an exact address. If it's using a cellular network, depending on the provider, we might determine the tower. With a subpoena it's a snap."

Which was what I feared. Paddy and Lisa were bending—maybe even shattering—laws. "We could give the information to the Savannah police. They want to find him."

Paddy snorted. "Where's that on their priorities?"

"Given they're looking into multiple murders, maybe pretty high."

"You're kidding, right? We're talking about a black prostitute, maybe druggie, in Savannah. No press coverage." Patrick pointed at his eyes with two fingers. "So, Dad, let me picture this. You call them up because Mom could never get it right. And you tell them someone, maybe the Jerk, maybe not, accessed a cloud storage site a couple of days ago from a computer somewhere around Kitty Hawk. Oh yeah, and you're the ex-husband of the wife of the missing person. Which do you think they'll do first, get a subpoena to obtain ISP records or check on you? Like, maybe, you're jealous and you decided to knock off the current husband to get your ex back."

Totally insane. Except that police had already considered me a murder suspect. Twice. They even arrested me—also twice. A few keystrokes on their database, and up I would pop like the Pillsbury Doughboy ready to be poked and prodded to see what I was up to. No, thank you. "Point taken. How long before you'll know if you can pin down the address?"

"Unknown. So, what happened last night?"

"Hold that thought. Now I'm awake, I need to pee." I creaked out of the bed. *Geez, we're a pair of sad sacks.* Bags under my eyes accurately represented how tired and rickety I still was from the car accident. I pulled up my shirt to check the bruises. Still there, with all the colors of an oil sheen on water.

I dressed and informed Paddy of everything I learned in the second secret room. During my recitation, Paddy began frequently rubbing his eyes. "You want to lie down again. Should I soak a towel for you?"

"I'll live. Are you saying either the Jerk framed Mom or she's scamming us and screwed up?"

"Or something else. The ransom note bothers the hell out of me. I do not see Cunningham getting from Savannah to Jersey and back to create and leave the note without being seen. How did he even know Lizzie wouldn't be there? He'd have to have an accomplice."

"Who, besides Mom, benefits from helping him?" Paddy answered his own question. "Following the money leads to Mom—if she's in it with him—or the partners—if they can get rid of him without costing themselves any money. If he's dead, they collect on the life insurance and buy his third with the proceeds. But doesn't Mom have enough of her own money—well, you know, the money from your divorce settlement?"

"She does," I said. "Laurence Kleindeinst has access to the house and could be a proxy for the partners. With their money, they could buy any kind of forged documents, and they have the smarts to frame your mother to look like she had a part in it."

Paddy poured a glass of water and downed half of it. "But they'd need the Jerk dead to collect, right?"

"And you think he's alive. I suppose they might want to find him to do him in. I also considered the Truverts. They see the marriage falling apart. Cunningham disappears and they think they're about to be unemployed. They're either just making it or still financially shaky and losing their jobs would be a disaster. They've got a kid in college—a kid with computer skills—so they plant a ransom note to try for a big payoff, not realizing Cunningham has already taken the money. Chad didn't think they'd ask for so much money."

"Plus . . . Paddy grimaced. He was sounding just like his father. "They'd be too smart to use Mom's newspaper." He cranked his head from side to side. "How did Mom take last night?"

"She apologized to both of us, and I got the feeling the ransom note was a surprise. An actress she's not. Shock her—doesn't matter how—she comes out with her first reaction. She didn't know about the Underground Railroad room or the gold, but she fessed right up to her husband's providing a fake passport."

"We better hope Lisa comes through because from what I hear you saying, we know exactly zero."

"Not zero. Not knowing drove your mother to see me in Cincinnati. I agree we don't have a clue what Cunningham originally planned, what your mom knew or didn't know about those plans, who else might be involved, or what has or has not happened to Cunningham. But I'm certain your mother doesn't know where her husband is and she needs to. I have two objectives. If I can find him, I can look myself in the mirror and feel good. She can call the police if she chooses. Not my issue. Not my problem."

Paddy scrunched his face into what could either be a reflection of migraine pain or rejection of my statement. "Second objective?"

"If you tell me you need to know whether or not your mother is involved, I'll do whatever I can to help you find out."

He rubbed his chin. "Let's take care of your first objective, and then we'll see."

"Okay, here's my plan. I need to go to Savannah to pick up my clothes and your grandmother. I have to write a report on why my client should definitely avoid Antimatter. After that, I'll start wading through the material in Cunningham's online backup. You go home. We'll see what Lisa kicks up. A little break will do us good. If we decide I should talk with the police, at least I'll be right there."

So arresting me will be easy. Brilliant thinking. "If Lisa comes up with an address, I can drive or fly up, knock on a door, and see who answers."

I ARRIVED IN SAVANNAH TO find a triple H day: hazy, hot, and humid. My mother and Tommy Kennedy picked me up at the Savannah/Hilton Head airport. New Jersey's heat was nothing compared to Savannah's, where the humidity smothered me like a baking sauna. Fortunately, Kennedy had snagged a nearby parking space and the walk to the car was short.

"New outfit, Mom?" She sported white shorts and a light blue linen blouse that contrasted nicely with her pink cast. Kennedy helped Mom into the rear seat of the Audi A8, behind the driver so the seatbelt would cross her good left shoulder.

"Tommy took me shopping for summer clothes. You should get some shorts and sandals. You'll feel much cooler. You'll love Savannah, Seamus. It is so charming. The people are so polite. And it's small, but it's so lively with all the kids from SCAD, and . . ."

From the passenger seat, I listened closely enough to say "yes," "no," and "uh-huh" in the right places while she gabbed about trolley rides, and Forrest Gump's bench, and Johnny Mercer's grave, and a host of other attractions I must see. I had no clue where we were driving, but it wasn't the way I remembered to Kennedy's house.

Mom temporarily ran out of things to say; I asked her to hold on while I checked voicemail. My real estate agent had called while I was in the air. "Bad news. The husband kept dragging his feet because he planned to get divorced but wanted to wait until he'd qualified for spousal benefits under her Social Security. I'll tell you, Seamus, when I heard that, I wanted to help the wife qualify for survivor benefits. Keep faith, the right buyer is out there and the market is getting stronger."

At least I knew for sure the Cincinnati house would not save me from my cash flow problems. I opened my calendar app and entered a reminder to start a mortgage application Monday morning.

"What's with all these nail salons?" I said. "We must have passed three thousand already."

"They're wonderful." Mom held her fingers over the front seat. "See? Southern women take such good care of their nails."

Each nail was a miniature seashore scene with waves and gulls and sunrises. God only knew how much that cost.

Tommy cleared his throat. "I think they're Southern smoke shops."

I didn't get it and said so.

"Money laundering. Up north you ever notice most of them smoke shops never had customers. Same thing. The price for cleaning the money is to pay taxes on the cash you cycle through, which shows up as profits."

I had never given it a thought, but I figured Kennedy would know.

Mom defended *her* nail salon, "It was filled with customers," and recommenced her travelogue. She eventually ran down and Kennedy said, "I've done a mite of sleuthing for youse guys."

I glanced his way. Nothing on his face revealed his thoughts, and he appeared to be paying attention to the road. Since he didn't continue, I figured he wanted a prompt. Or maybe he had noticed I was not paying attention to my mother. "And what did your sleuthing uncover?"

"Seems the head of that crazy drug group spin-off is still after your Albert Cunningham guy. Put a twenty-five large bounty on his head, which, believe me, is enough to get a lot of guys' attention. And by guys, I don't mean just guys, youse understand?"

I said I did, remembering he had once employed a female hitter. "Any idea why?"

"No. Alls I'm saying is being around the guy may not be healthy. Assuming he *is* still alive—and this guy apparently believes he is—he better go into deep hiding 'cause he's wearing a bullseye."

Mom pulled the seatbelt away from her chest, leaned in between us, and touched my shoulder. "I don't want something to happen to you because of Elisabeth."

"But she still doesn't know where her husband is, and that's just not right. Plus, I think Paddy needs to know why it happened."

I resumed looking out the side window and noticed a US-80 sign, which didn't mean anything to me until we passed under the Truman Highway. "Where are we going?"

"Tybee Island," my mother replied. "Tommy brought me there yesterday, and I found something unbelievable. You'll love it."

I tried wheedling the information from her, but she insisted I wait for the surprise. An idea popped.

"Tybee's where that Kaylee person lived, right? Is it something about her?"

"Not hardly," my mother said.

Oh goody, another surprise. She was all smiles; the third degree wouldn't work. Resigning myself to being a prisoner of their conspiracy, I sat back and enjoyed the scenery. Not much else I could do until we got to Kennedy's where I could email my due diligence report on Antimatter Investments, LLC and start looking at Cunningham's online files.

We crossed several islands—one contained Fort Pulaski, one of the last castle-type forts built in the U.S.—before reaching Tybee. If I had time, I'd return and tour the Civil War relic whose eleven-foot-thick walls proved no match for the Union's rifled cannon. Driving down Tybee's main street, the kitsch reminded me of parts of the Jersey shore.

We veered left from the main drag before we got to the beach area and followed signs toward the Tybee lighthouse. No longer in use, the lighthouse—the symbol chosen by locals to declare their attachment to the island—towered above us with its horizontal stripes of black over white over black. We drove past it and another piece of history dropped into place. Across the road from the lighthouse was Fort Screven, abandoned after World War II.

Tomorrow was Sunday. I could use some down time. Maybe we could tour the forts and lighthouse and spend a bit of time walking the beach. My mother's words slammed through my daydreaming.

"This place needs a little work, but it's a steal, Seamus."

"I think she's right," Kennedy said.

Kennedy pulled to the curb in a residential neighborhood.

"Of course I am. I've worked it all out. You get it fixed up and rent it during the summer. A house like this with private beach access has no problem renting. I'd like to stay at the beach during the winter. Maybe I can even run a little B&B. Gives me a place to stay away from Boston winters and generates some income for you. They aren't making any more shoreline, Seamus. Wait until you see the view. You can see Hilton Head from here, and the container ships heading to Savannah, and sailboats, and they tell me it's great for birding. You'd love that." She pointed to a silver Jag pulling up. "There's the agent."

Often I use silence as a tactic to get other people talking. This time was not an act. I considered asking how much this fixer-upper cost, but I hardly had enough ready cash for a down payment on a new vehicle, let alone a house. Mom was already out of the car and shaking hands with the agent.

A light breeze through the open car door brought with it the ocean's salty scent. I inhaled deeply. *Nice. I wonder what low tide smells like.* Laughing gulls called from beyond the house. Looking up, I caught the distinctive shape of a brown pelican gliding above the water.

Kennedy extricated himself from the Audi. "Actually, it is a good deal. Fixed up and a decent market, this could probably sell for a couple million. The market hasn't fully recovered, and most people aren't interested in something they need to rehab. This baby has good bones, but it does need updating. It's listed for only eight hundred thousand. Probably cost you a couple hundred to get it in top shape, and in a few years you've doubled your money. You'll make your mother happy, and the rent will more than pay taxes and upkeep, even with the new higher flood insurance premiums."

My stomach gurgled its distress. I wasn't discussing my finances with someone who used to run loan shark operations. "Let's take a look."

"Fair warning," he said, "you don't buy it for your ma, I just might do it."

Twenty-Nine

Patrick drove directly from Chicago's O'Hare to Lisa's condo since Cindy wouldn't be home until dinnertime.

"Any progress?" he asked through the screened door.

"You look like shit. Patrick, go home. Go to bed. I'll let you know if I learn something."

Three low buzzes sounded behind her. Patrick checked his phone: three forty-seven. The triplets sounded again.

"I wonder if this is another false alarm. You might as well come in and we'll see what this is."

Patrick latched the door and followed Lisa into a dining room converted to an office. A single sheet of paper and a ballpoint pen sat on the table next to her laptop. Her clean surface work habits applied to home.

"Hot diggity, dog," she said. "He's signed in to one of the chat rooms."

Patrick remained standing and watched her fingers race across the keyboard. "That's him? StonedGoss? Think he's a fan of Stone Gossard?"

"Who?" Lisa muttered as her fingers dished lines of code.

"Pearl Jam guitarist."

"Shh. Let me work."

StonedGoss invited Nif8yrbk to a chat.

Patrick pointed at the screen. "Can you follow them?"

"Does a goose have *foie gras*?"

Patrick chose not to analyze Lisa's line. The conversation scrolled down the screen. StonedGoss was teaching Nif8yrbk how to chat, how to invite others to chat, and various IM shortcut symbols. People often chose monikers with meaning; what was Nif8yrbk's? Ni was the symbol for nickel. f8 could be fate, yr was short for year and bk was back. The phrase "nickel fate year back" made no sense. How about "nickel fate you're back?" With punctuation and imagination that could have something to do with hoping the price of nickel was going up?

He retrieved his laptop, signed into Lisa's LAN, and searched "nickel fate you're back." No direct hits. Without the quotes around the phrase the search engine pulled up a ton of entries, none of which related to what he was looking for. He must have been mumbling because Lisa said, "Knife at your back?"

Patrick shivered at the visual. Knife at whose back? Was it just a tough-guy moniker or a specific threat, reminding the Jerk that there was a knife at his back?

"Can you tell where they are?" Patrick asked. "Anything?"

"Patience, dear heart. Patience. He just showed the other one how to invite someone else and their room recently changed from private to public. And now he's gone."

Nif8yrbk invited ExcellionBull to a chat room.

"And StonedGoss popped into a private room and invited Knife at Your Back. And he, she, it accepted."

"If it's private?"

Lisa snorted. "Privacy is such an overrated concept . . . or practice."

ExcellionBull to Nif8yrbk: Watching the sun shining on the Hudson.

A half minute later StonedGoss to Nif8yrbk: Tell him bullshit and sign off.

Nif8yrbk to StonedGoss: ?

StonedGoss to Nif8yrbk: Skycam showing cats and dogs r pouring from sky.

Nif8yrbk to StonedGoss: k :)

Nif8yrbk to ExcellionBull: Bullshit Excellion.

Nif8yrbk has left room.

"Now what?" Patrick said.

"We wait."

Nif8yrbk has entered room.

ExcellionBull to Nif8yrbk: UR right. How much EXEXP r u long

Thirty seconds later StonedGoss to Nif8yrbk: 250k looking to buy more & U? Got any to sell?

Nif8yrbk to ExcellionBull: 250k looking to buy more & U? Got any to sell?

ExcellionBull to Nif8yrbk: What price?

StonedGoss to Nif8yrbk: Don't answer. Leave him hanging!!!

"This doesn't make sense," Lisa said. "I don't see that StonedGoss hacked their conversation. What am I missing?"

Patrick's bad feeling about Nif8yrbk became stronger. "I don't think he has to hack in. I think they're together. He's typing responses in the one chat room so the other person can copy and paste them into the other. Keep an eye on him. I'll try a direct IM"

PMcCree to StonedGoss: U OK?

StonedGoss to PMcCree: WHO R U

PMcCree to StonedGoss: Beth's son, Patrick. R U OK?

"Crap. He left," Patrick said. "Now what?"

THE OVERHEAD FANS ON TOMMY Kennedy's veranda chirped each time the blades rotated, but I was willing to put up with the annoying metallic cricket to experience the cool breeze it provided while keeping the bugs away. Tommy sipped an after-dinner drink. Mom, who was still taking pain meds, was forbidden alcohol, so she and I had sweetened iced tea. Too sweet for my taste, I didn't want to offend Kennedy and so took neat sips. I still had three-quarters of the glass to go and considered and rejected chug-a-lugging it to be finished.

A squeaking kiss sound caught my attention. I followed it to a bird clinging to the trunk of a nearby tree. "Brown-headed nuthatch?"

"You want binoculars?" Kennedy put his hands on the chair arms, preparing to rise.

My cell phone rang and I waved him down. I remembered to check the caller ID. "Hello, Paddy." I figured he'd be proud of me for my advanced phone behavior.

"We've made contact," Paddy machine-gunned over the connection. "He used one of his IM services. Lisa has been monitoring those and his emails. Anyway, it looks like he was showing someone named 'Knife at your back' how to use instant messaging on the internet. I contacted him and asked if he was okay. He asked who I was. I answered and he logged off. Lisa confirmed he's still in the Outer Banks. She pinned it down to a general area, but not yet an address."

"What's your plan?"

"Lisa is trying to nail an exact location. I booked a flight for first thing tomorrow to Greenville, NC. I can change it to Norfolk, which would make more sense if you were also flying in, but I figured you'd rather drive up, and Greenville's more or less on your way. Once Lisa narrows it down a little more, we can scope out the area and maybe find exactly where he is and what the situation is. We think someone is with him. Once we know for sure, we can either tackle him ourselves or let the police pick him up. I have to be in the office first thing Wednesday for a partners' meeting or Lisa will kill me. Means I've got a narrow window."

"Driving's good. I can leave your grandmother here with Tommy Kennedy and meet you. Do I need to leave tonight? What time's your plane get in? Did you remember to ask your mother if she knows anyone with a place in the Outer Banks?"

"Was I supposed to? I don't remember your asking. It's a good idea, but I didn't do it. I really don't think you asked me. I get in late morning, so there's no reason for you to leave tonight. It's supposedly six hours from Savannah to Greenville."

I copied down Paddy's flight details as he read them off, and he wrapped up the call.

Kennedy asked the obvious question, "Sounds like you have a lead. What's happened?"

I quickly explained how someone accessed Cunningham's accounts from a computer located on North Carolina's Outer Banks—maybe.

My mother assured me she was having a wonderful time. "In fact, we've scheduled a darts exhibition for tomorrow evening at one of the clubs. The people in this community are for the most part well off. We should raise a ton of money."

"Mom, you need to make sure you don't hurt your arm. Are you sure you want to do this left-handed?"

She gave me a withering look. "Seamus Anselm McCree." The way she drew out all three names reminded me of her scoldings when I was young.

I was delighted my mother was doing things and making plans. It showed how far her mental recovery had come from her years of self-imposed silence. "Fine, but I can't be here, so you'll have to modify your finale."

"I've already planned the show. Why don't you borrow one of Tommy's cars? He's offered."

I didn't want to be in any more debt to Tommy Kennedy and insisted I'd prefer using a rental. I even rationalized that it allowed me to leave the car at any airport if I had to fly somewhere.

Mom gave me one of her "You are so full of it" looks. "How long will you be gone? I'd hate for someone to buy that wonderful Tybee beach house while you're away."

Kennedy was watching us with a wry smile on his face. I had not wanted to have this discussion in his presence. I could pull my mother aside—rude. Or duck the question—dishonest. Or embarrass everyone with the truth.

"Mom, I don't have the money to buy a house right now."

"Oh." She deflated in front of me. "I must have misunderstood. I thought you said the half million dollars you gave to the charity for the victims of violence represented less than ten percent of your money. And I'm not at Sugarbush, so I'm not costing you that anymore. And . . ."

"Everything is locked up either in retirement plans or property or Paddy's company." Her face changed from confused to concerned. "It's a short-term situation, Mom. I couldn't do it now even if I wanted to, and even if I were in a position to buy, I wouldn't want to without considerable thought. Didn't you see the pole we passed down by the pier? A category two hurricane floods the first floor, and a category five puts the whole house underwater."

"But Seamus," Mom said, "the agent told me they haven't had even a category three hurricane in more than a hundred years."

"Just means they're overdue." I waved my hands. "We're arguing about something that right now does not matter. I don't have time to check the house further. I don't have enough cash to buy it right now. And frankly, before you set your eyes on it, I had never considered buying property this far south."

My mother crossed her arms over her chest. "Fine." To Kennedy: "Can I have another of these?"

"You'll be fine here while I drive Seamus to the airport to get a rental?"

"Have him call a cab. Why drive an hour and a half when he could have borrowed one of your cars?"

"You've already done the airport trip once today, and I appreciate your picking me up. I'll call a cab to the airport and get a rental."

Kennedy looked between the two of us. I could sense the wheels turning. He produced what I figured was a neutral pronouncement. "You know your mother is welcome to stay here for as long as she likes." With a pause that made me wonder about its truth, he added, "She's safe here. I'll call in a pass at the gate so when you return, they'll let you in."

◇◇◇

I AWOKE TO AN ALARM, but not the one I had set for four thirty so I could drive to Greenville and meet Paddy. This was the whoop-whoop-whoop of a house security siren. I groped for eyeglasses and switched on the nightstand lamp. It didn't work. In my grogginess, I decided the house had lost electricity and triggered the alarm. I activated my cell phone's flashlight app, catching the time: 2:17 a.m. I struggled into yesterday's pants, and touched the door with the back of my left hand in case the alarm was signaling a fire. Cool and a little moist because I had left the windows open to the night air.

The alarm's whoop became painful once I opened the door. Battery-powered backup lights, so unobtrusive I had not previously noticed them, illuminated the hall. The air smelled fresh, no smoke. I poked my head into my mother's room through the open door. Her room was empty and the bathroom door closed.

I tapped on the bathroom door. "You in there, Mom?"

The alarm might have drowned out my question. I rapped harder and yelled the second time. Still no response. I pushed open the door, accidentally slamming it into the wall.

The bathroom was empty.

From the other wing of the house came several short, deep brrrps. Automatic gunfire. Without thinking, I dropped to the floor and punched 911 on my cell phone. Realizing I had no clue what number Kennedy's house was, I tried to picture the mailbox without success. Screw it. The cops would know. His was the only house on the cul-de-sac.

More gunfire erupted in the other wing. *Where the hell is Mom*?

I thought I gave the emergency operator a detailed description of what was happening. Much later, I heard the tape. I was nearly incoherent. The operator's drawl was calm and reasonable. She managed to get my name, the street name of Kennedy's house—I still could not come up with the number—that shots had been fired, and the electricity was off.

She ordered me to leave the house and stay on the line; officers were on their way.

Screw that. I unlocked Mom's patio door and ran to the marsh edge, where I stopped and looked back. Soft light flowed from the windows. No one on the verandas. No shadows in the windows. Accompanied by the siren's whoops and a horde of biting insects, I circled the house at a gallop, hoping to come across Mom. No one else was outside. Parked in the driveway next to my rental sat the type of van electricians or plumbers might use. The back and two front doors were wide open.

Mom must still be inside. And Kennedy. And who else?

I loped up the steps to the open front door. The battering ram used to shatter the doorframe lay in the entryway. Keeping close to the walls, I eased around the corner and sensed no movement. "Mom?" I yelled up the stairs.

Only the alarm's whoop answered.

My head ached from the tension and the siren, each heartbeat bringing a fresh stab of pain. I looked outside. Still no cops. Over the alarm, I wouldn't hear their sirens until they were near. No reflection of pulsing blue and red lights bouncing off the low clouds. I ran up the stairs, stopped at the landing to listen for voices, for movement, for anything, and continued to the second floor.

I dropped to the floor and slithered to a spot where I could peek down the hallway. Two guys lay in a sea of blood. Beyond them, Kennedy lay halfway out his bedroom door. Again I shouted for my mother.

A feeling of relief tingled into my fingers and toes. Mother had been smarter than I, and at the first alarm she had escaped and run to the nearest house.

I padded down the hall, my bare feet making little sound. I avoided the blood and knelt by the two guys. Both beyond help. Taking no chances, I kicked their army-style rifles aside. Approaching Kennedy, I realized his pajama top was soaked in blood. No bubbles formed in the blood near his mouth. Nevertheless, I leaned down to check his pulse. Past him lay another male body, head toward me, face down on the carpet.

Someone else must be alive because this person had gotten past Kennedy before being killed. Staying low, I moved past Kennedy and into the room. My mother stood in the shadows, partially hidden by the bed. Her left hand held a gun pointed at me, her casted right arm providing a firing platform.

"Mom." I slowly rose. "It's me. Your son, Seamus."

The wail of police cars sounded above the alarm.

Her unblinking eyes followed my progress. I sensed incomprehension and confusion. "Mom! Put. The. Gun. Down."

Thirty

An equipment malfunction delayed Patrick's flight into Charlotte and caused him to miss his connection to Greenville. He had left a message on his dad's phone to let him know of the delay and his new expected arrival time. With no sign of his father and no return message, he now paced the Greenville baggage area, wondering where his old man was.

Worry gnawed Patrick's stomach. He left another message. His dad was prone to letting his battery run down or forgetting to turn on his phone. He shouldn't worry, right? *But even if he can't meet my flight, he'd find a way to leave a message.*

Had his father arrived, gotten distracted, and was around here somewhere? Or had he never arrived? With no place to eat in the airport and feeling starved from missing lunch, Patrick settled for two candy bars from the vending machine—he'd pretend they were vegetarian. Chowing down, he made one more tour of the airport.

Something bad has happened.

He didn't want to worry his grandmother, but if something had delayed his father from leaving Savannah, she would know.

Listening to the phone ring, he had visions of his dad in another accident. He was laid up in a hospital. Or dead. Voicemail picked up. No reason to worry her unnecessarily by leaving a message.

Did his father carry a slip of paper in his wallet: *In case of emergency contact* . . . contact who, or was that whom? Dimes to donuts it would be him. Dimes to donuts was one of his dad's expressions, and he shivered with anxiety just thinking it. No one had contacted him, so either his father didn't carry a note, or someone else was the contact. Abigail?

He scrolled through his phone's address book, found Abigail Hancock, and called her cell. Listening to the brrring of the call, he figured he was out of luck again. She was probably overseas on an assignment.

"Hello, Patrick?"

"Have you heard from my dad today?"

"I have not." In her Secret Service-trained voice she continued, "What's the situation?"

He started with the immediate crisis of his missing parent. Her questions forced him to slow down and, since she already knew of the Jerk's disappearance, he brought her up to date with Lisa tracking Cunningham—or at least someone posing as him—to the northern part of the Outer Banks.

"And the last time you talked with your father was last night?"

"He was staying with a friend of my grandmother, but I can't get her either."

"Let me think a minute."

Interrupting the silence, a bustle of new passengers arrived. He walked to a quiet corner and stuck a finger in one ear. *Something has happened to him; I can feel it. Then again, my gut has been off lately when it comes to my parents.*

Abigail's voice brought him back to the present. "Call your mother. Given the circumstances, she seems like the only other person who might know something. Then call me back. I'll get someone to start checking hospitals between Savannah and Greenville, just in case."

She disconnected before Patrick could suggest he put her on hold and dial his mother. Fortunately, his mother did pick up. She had not talked to his father today; why did he want to know? He stole a page from his dad's playbook: the best defense is a good offense. "Did Dad remember to ask you whether you guys know anyone with a place on the Outer Banks of North Carolina? He forgot before and didn't tell me, so I figured he might have forgotten again."

"Sometimes he'd lose his head if it weren't stapled on. I told him last night I thought somebody from Al's work went down there for duck hunting or something. The town name was Duck, and I remember wondering if the town was named after the bird or maybe Donald Duck. I still can't remember who owned the place, but I'm sure he spent a weekend down there while we were dating."

"Okay, thanks Mom." Patrick disconnected, knowing he would hear about his rudeness.

Abigail didn't answer, so he left a message. He called Cindy and filled her in on his missing father. "I figured since I was sharing a bed with an ace investigative reporter, she could tap her databases and presto-chango up would pop an address for someone who works with the Jerk and owns property around Duck, North Carolina."

Her laughter was great to hear and cheered him up some, since even with all of his sharing, he was feeling more and more anxious about his father. "May I point out you are not sharing my bed at this moment? How do you propose to pay for my services?"

"Take it out in trade, okay?" he snapped. "You met the partners. Look at them first before the other employees."

"Lighten up a little, Patrick. I know you're pressed for time and worried. Just because the world is treating you like shit doesn't mean you have to treat me the same way. I have copies of all your dad's notes from the due diligence meetings, which will give me everyone's name. I'll see what I can do, but don't get your hopes up. The property is probably held in a corporate name, or it's part of a timeshare. We'll need to be lucky."

Patrick admitted he could use some luck. "I'm sorry I'm a grump. I feel like a million pounds of pressure is on my head and shoulders. I'll rent a car and drive to Duck."

"Let me know where you stay. I'm sure Abigail will get to you shortly with news of your father. I have a strong feeling he's okay. And I'll try to get you a name and address."

They said their goodbyes and Patrick made one more tour of the airport, ending at the car rentals.

Patrick's eyes hurt, his head was pounding, and he needed several deep breaths to control his voice before he spoke again to the rental car company clerk.

"You're telling me," Patrick said, "I need to pay an extra twenty-five bucks a day to rent your car because I won't be twenty-five for a few months? Is that only at the airport or everywhere?"

"I'm sorry, Mr. McCree. It's corporate policy everywhere." She tossed her magenta hair. "It's because of the extra cost of insurance."

"That's ludicrous. I have auto insurance and my credit card takes care of anything not covered by my insurance. An extra twenty-five bucks a day is nine grand a year. Because I'm not twenty-five? A total rip off."

"I understand, but I have to follow the rules or they'll fire me." She gave him an apologetic smile. "Does your employer have an account with us? We waive the age restrictions for corporate accounts."

"So you only stick it to the people you can. Corporate customers won't put up with that bull?

She gave an eye roll. "I agree the rules are stupid. You can try one of the other firms."

Patrick exhaled slowly. He shouldn't take the stupid corporate policy out on the girl. If only he had kept the fake driver's license he had in college. It would solve the problem—except it was expired. "I apologize for venting. I'm sure you're right. Your competitors will screw me as well. Let's just—"

His phone rang. Abigail. "I'll be back," he said to the clerk. He walked away from the counter and answered.

"Your father's fine," Abigail said. "Well, not hurt anyway."

Patrick's initial flush of relief that his father wasn't hurt was replaced by a splitting headache once Abigail informed him of the break-in and shootings. He closed his eyes, which were now light sensitive. Switching the phone to his other hand, he popped out his lenses and pressed fingers hard into his eyes. "How did you learn this?"

Abigail laughed, "Like father, like son. You want to determine for yourself how reliable the information is. I got it from your father's sometime boss at CIG, Robert Rand. He knows everyone or at least knows someone who knows someone. CIG's done a lot of work in Savannah. So as I was saying—" Abigail produced a long sigh, "—your relatives are not hurt."

"But Dad didn't call, so what aren't you telling me?"

This time a heavy sigh came down the line, "The police are still questioning them. I assume they aren't allowing him to make calls. There's one more bad thing. Your grandmother has gone silent again. I think—"

Patrick's sphincter contracted and now he needed a bathroom. "Ah, man."

"Yeah, I know. She was doing so well. We should assume your father is out of the picture for the foreseeable future. He'll be tied up with your grandmother. I've arranged backup for my current job—it'll take a couple of hours. Long story short, I can't get to Greenville until morning. I'll call you when I have an exact time."

A wave of relief washed over Patrick. He considered protesting her coming and stifled it.

"Listen carefully, Patrick. Here's something we need to consider. I have no clue if the attack relates to Tommy Kennedy's criminal activity or to Albert Cunningham's disappearance. Odds are someone targeted Kennedy, and your family was in the wrong place at the wrong time. But we need to act as though they're targeting your family. That means two things."

Patrick experienced a profound exhaustion even a week's sleep wouldn't fix. "Two things," he robotically repeated.

"First, do not do anything more until I get there. Whatever McCree genes you've inherited that cause you to want to do something NOW, please don't. People are getting killed and we don't know why. Second, I want you off radar. No contact with your mother. None with Cindy unless you can find a pay phone or can buy a disposable phone somewhere. Are we straight?"

"That's crazy."

"If the attack was not because someone wanted to take out Tommy Kennedy, but because someone did not want your father to find Cunningham, how did they know where your father was?"

"Someone told them. Or followed Dad."

"Or hacked a phone or a computer. The government and people like you aren't the only ones who can do that stuff. Check into one of the hotels near the airport for tonight. We'll make a plan tomorrow after I get there. Keep sending IMs to Cunningham. If you can get him to respond to you, don't be judgmental. Tell him you want to help. If we can open a line of communication, it will give us a big leg up."

"Where are you?"

"San Diego. I'll be catching a red-eye. If I learn anything, I'll let you know. You do the same for me. And please, Patrick—and I know I'm talking to you and not your father, but I'd tell him exactly the same thing, except I hope you might listen—don't do anything stupid."

Well, one good thing: Abigail could rent the car and he wouldn't have to put up with this age discrimination crap. He left the airport, ignored the cab driver's "Taxi?" and walked toward the exit onto Memorial Drive. By the time he got there, he reconsidered his decision not to take a cab. Chicago could easily get as hot, but this heat had fangs, opening every pore so his juices flowed like an overripe peach. His shirt already showed sweat stains from his collar to his waist. Besides, his head hurt something fierce.

He legs slowed, as if he was walking through the deep end of a pool.

Surely he could make it to a hotel, but he'd be a puddle. He trudged back to the cab line and melted into the taxi whose cool air rolled over him, instantly changing his sweat into icicles. His goosebumps had goosebumps. He waved the driver past an expensive chain motel in favor of a cheaper one a few blocks further on.

Yes, they had rooms available. No, he couldn't check in—the cleaning crew was not yet finished. No, he could not use the business center. He had to be registered to have a key to access the business center. No, he couldn't use the internet until he had a room number—

"Is there anything you *can* do for me?"

"Would you like a complimentary bottle of water?"

On principal, Patrick couldn't bring himself to accept the plastic. What would his father do with forty minutes of otherwise wasted down time and a splitting headache? He would make a list to make sure he didn't forget anything he had to do.

Had Patrick fallen so low all he could do was make a list? He should have stayed at the airport where he could access free Wi-Fi, but he was damned if he'd pay for two more taxi rides. What he needed was to exercise and blow off the accumulating tension and steam, and thereby eliminate the headache. Maybe. Or make it worse.

He thanked the desk clerk for his kind offer—the guy didn't get the sarcasm—and followed signs to the pool and fitness center. A mother and three small ones were by the pool. Piercing kid squeals hurt his ears even through the door. How could they make that sound? Plugging into his iPod while hitting the treadmill would take care of the stress and the noise. He knocked on the door, knocked louder when no one responded. Hit the damn door even harder to get their attention. Great, now his knuckles hurt.

One of the kids spotted him, and he motioned for the middle-grader to let him in. The child looked at his mother, who shook her head no, which made him laugh. He wouldn't open the door to someone who looked like him either.

From the ether came the realization he had lost a full day. He'd promised Lisa he'd be at work first thing Wednesday. Once Abigail arrived, he'd only have one and a half days to find the Jerk before he had to return or break his promise to Lisa and destroy their friendship.

For a split second he wished the Jerk would turn up dead so he'd be free of it. But that wouldn't really put an end to anything, would it? He'd still need to know what his mother's role had been. Which meant maybe he needed to return to the airport, rent a car, and start searching in Duck himself.

A hammer's blow of pain behind his eyes squelched that plan. First thing to do tomorrow was schedule a doctor's appointment at home so he could renew his migraine medicine. Now, where was the reset switch for this day?

Thirty-One

THE POLICE RECORDED MY STATEMENT and kept me incommunicado in a Chatham County jail holding cell reeking of sweat, fear, and human misery. I paced the room, splitting my worry between concern over what Paddy would do when I didn't show up at the airport and anxiety from not knowing what was happening with my mother, whom they had removed to the woman's side of the county jail.

I had managed to get Mom to put down the gun before the police stormed into the house, but I had not been able to get her to speak. Worse, I couldn't get a yes or no headshake from her. She had retreated to the state that had kept her institutionalized for more than two decades. She needed medical attention, and I couldn't do squat to mobilize help until the lawyer showed up, which finally happened after lunch. I must have showed my surprise when he called my name because his first words were, "I wasn't what you were expecting?"

"The last time I called Leroy Patterson to find me out-of-state counsel, he coughed up a retired criminal attorney in Michigan who dressed immaculately, had a wicked sense of humor, and wore dreads with colored beads."

"And this time you get a young white dude—name's Josiah Lee. Pleased to meet you." We shook. "So this white guy struts in wearing a bowtie and Chucks and talks with a hick Georgia cracker drawl. Much as I'd like to chitchat and trade some good ol' boy stories, I need to understand what happened—in particular why you insisted I see you before your mother, since from what little the police told me, she's the one they may charge with a crime." He sat down and motioned for me to do the same.

"I don't care if you wear a purple tutu if you represent us well." I explained my mother's medical history. "I'm sure the police are skeptical—if I didn't know her, I would be too—but she needs immediate medical attention."

He pulled a legal pad and cheap ballpoint from his backpack and scribbled notes.

"Dr. Draco at Sugarbush in Leominster, Massachusetts is her physician. Mom needs his immediate attention. And I need to get a message to my son. I was supposed to meet him earlier today at the Greenville, North Carolina airport."

He tapped the table with the end of his pen. "When your mother wasn't talking, could she understand or was she in some kind of catatonic state?" Tap. Tap. Tap.

"She understood everything. Still does, I think. For example, she placed the gun on the bed after I told her the police were coming up the stairs, and if she didn't put the gun down they would shoot her."

Tap. Tap. Tap. "Given the circumstances you described, your mother should be immune from prosecution under Georgia's so-called 'Castle Law.'"

"You're missing my point, Mr. Lee. I want my mother out of Georgia and on a plane to Boston immediately. She doesn't have twenty more years of life to lose to silence."

"They won't like it. She's the one who knows what happened. They won't want to release her until she tells them what she knows."

"I don't give a flying fuck what the police want." I grabbed my ears and pulled hard. The pain helped give emphasis to my point. "The longer she remains mute, the harder it might be for her to talk again. I want my mother under the care of physicians who understand her and her condition. Are we perfectly clear?"

"Yes sir, we are. Except until, and if, your mother is declared incompetent by a judge and you are appointed her guardian, the courts say I have to represent your mother's best interests. You've provided your perspective. Now I have to hear hers."

I could not believe his stupidity. Even a fool would understand Mom needed to receive assistance, and Sugarbush was the place to provide it. If she didn't receive immediate medical attention, the police might never hear her utter one word, and I might not either. "At least talk to Dr. Draco. He'll confirm everything I've said."

"This will take some time. You should have waited for me before you talked to the police. Do not—"

"I talked to them because I hoped they would free me to arrange care for my mother."

He packed his pad in his backpack and shoved the pen in his shirt pocket. "Understandable, but I am here now. Please do not speak further with them except in my presence."

He was gone before I remembered I hadn't given him a way to contact Paddy.

JOSIAH LEE SHUTTLED BETWEEN MY mother and me throughout the afternoon, resulting in my agreement to try to talk with her in an interview room wired for sound and pictures. The police hoped a friendly face might loosen her lips so they could get her insight into what happened. The forensic evidence would make it clear who shot whom. I wanted Mom to break her silence.

The detective led Mom in. I enfolded her in a hug, being careful not to put any pressure on her right arm, which was once again in a sling. Receiving no return hug, I kissed the top of her head with a loud smacking, hoping she would find it funny. Nothing. I ushered her to one of the two chairs I had placed on the side of the table facing the ceiling camera. She looked like she had aged a decade. Her breath was sour—she hadn't had a chance to brush her teeth either. I did a quick check of my own breath.

"You want anything to drink, Mom? Are you hungry? I can have them get you a bite." I waited for a response, but got none.

"So here's the plan, Mom. We'll fly to Boston so I can take you to Sugarbush. Dr. Draco is waiting to talk to you. Sound good?"

Mom stared straight ahead at the wall with the camera. I could not detect a hint of cognition. This was reminiscent of my visits with her at Sugarbush, long before she nodded yeses and shook her head for nos.

"Mom," I said in a pleading voice. "I have to know if you're hurt. Nod once if you have pain." I demonstrated a nod. "And give me a head shake if you're physically okay." I demonstrated.

She blinked, but I did not take it as communication. It gave me the idea. I leaned close and whispered so the audio couldn't pick it up, "Yes, I know they are watching and listening. Here's what we'll do. Blink twice if you did not get hurt and three times if someone hurt you. Please, Mom. This is important."

I leaned back and waited. Fifteen slow seconds later she blinked. Once.

"Okay, Mom, I'll see you in a few." I leaned in, gave her a kiss, and was surprised to feel a warm tear trickling down her cheek. "I'll get you out of here no matter what it takes."

Thirty-Two

THE SOUNDS AND SMELLS OF brewing coffee woke me up, but I did not feel at all rested in a strange, too-soft bed. I found my glasses on the nightstand, put them on and read 6:30 on the clock on the bureau. I twigged to being in Uncle Mike's spare bedroom. He had met Mom and me at the airport the previous night. We settled Mom in at Sugarbush before returning to his townhouse in Waltham, Massachusetts. Donning yesterday's clothes, I padded downstairs in bare feet—a bad decision. Sharp crumbs remaining after Uncle Mike's lick-and-a-promise cleaning jabbed my soles. A nearly filled box of Dunkin' Donuts on the kitchen table indicated he had made a trip for the fat fix before making coffee. Sitting at my place was a twenty-ounce Diet Dr Pepper making a ring on the table.

"You don't drink coffee," he explained at my questioning glance, "and it's gonna be a busy day."

The low buzz of Route 128 traffic a mile away muscled its way past the open sliding-glass door to the deck. I gestured toward the noise, "You ever wonder what Henry David Thoreau would say about today's commuters?"

"Never. Who cares what some tax evader thinks?"

Forgot I was talking to a cop. In honor of my birthplace, I selected a Boston Kreme. I toasted him with "Breakfast of champions." The center oozed out and I licked my lips clean. Three hundred calories of pure bliss.

"With your ma in the car I didn't wanna ask for details. And coming home from Sugarbush you fell asleep before we were out the driveway. What's going on?"

Uncle Mike was not a relation. He was my father's best friend and looked after me in my wayward youth. Most people know him as Captain (Ret.) Mike O'Malley of the Boston Police Department. Not officially an interrogation, but by the time I'd finished the Dr Pepper and another donut, he'd extracted every detail I could remember, starting with the call from my real estate agent in Cincinnati and ending with yesterday's fun at the county hoosegow outside Savannah.

"Uncle Mike, did you know my mother and Tommy Kennedy were close?"

"Didn't take long after she went to Sugarbush before her so-called friends gave up on her. In fairness, it's a long drive to Leominster to sit with someone who doesn't acknowledge you're there. Tommy never stopped. Your ma probably thinks she kept his visits a secret. I didn't think it would do any harm. Hell, I woulda chauffeured him me own self if it woulda helped your ma. You know, Seamus, friends are those people who stand by you when you're at your worst. Tommy Kennedy did that for your mother. Doesn't mean I'd trust him with a plugged nickel, but with your ma's life? Sure I woulda trusted him. So what's today's plan?"

"You didn't think to tell me this when I got involved with Kennedy a while back?"

He slurped his coffee and smacked his lips before scarfing up half a glazed donut. I suppose he was right: the facts had answered the question.

"I'll need to get to Sugarbush to see Mom and take care of paperwork. I haven't heard from Paddy, so I need to make sure he got the message I left on his voicemail."

"You ain't renting a car. I've got nothing major planned. I'll take you where you want to go. Or I got a second car you can drive. I'd like to see your ma, though."

Telling Uncle Mike I needed time alone to recharge would not fly: a gregarious old coot like him would not understand, and I'd hurt his feelings. "And I'd like to borrow your computer. Maybe Paddy left me an email." Which was a smokescreen. I could easily check email with my phone, but for the mortgage application, I preferred using a computer. "And I need Hermione Granger's Time-Turner if you've a spare one."

"Did you get a blow on your head? You ain't making a whole lot of sense."

It had popped out and now was not the time to explain Harry Potter to Uncle Mike. But my unconscious was expressing the building pressure to make a decision either to stay and take care of Mom or go to North Carolina and take care of Paddy. I needed to talk to my son, but didn't want to wake him, so my impatience boiled slightly below steam level.

Paddy called eightish and went on a nonstop tear concerning the unfairness of rental car companies and his frustration with his internet research not pointing a finger at anyone. In particular, the Truverts checked out to be exactly who and what they claimed. He had talked with Corgan Truvert on the phone—the kind of kid he'd love to hire at LT2P—and was convinced if Corgan had installed the keylogger, he would have used a wireless device to capture the data remotely in his family's rooms on the estate. Cunningham, in the form of StonedGoss, hadn't come online again, and he was wasting time waiting for Abigail. He could be searching the area. I verbally nodded in all the right places and wondered what I would find at Sugarbush.

"Oh, hey, I do have one question for you," Paddy said. "Ever hear of a company called Excellion Exploration? I told you StonedGoss was messaging with Knife at Your Back, who was doing the same with ExcellionBull. Those two were talking about shares of EXEXP. I looked it up. It's like some rinky-dink minerals mining exploration company."

A distant chime sounded in my mind, my mental Zen master reminding me to be attentive. I asked him to repeat the conversation if he could. Instead, he read screenshots of the chat room. Smart boy, my Paddy. "I think you're right. StonedGoss could well be Cunningham. It's a penny stock. Not listed on the exchanges, but his hedge fund owned a boatload. My notes are behind police tape at Kennedy's place, but I'll do some research on it. Please send me the screenshots."

"Is Grandma going to be okay? If you think it might help, you can tell her she'll soon be a great-grandmother. You know, like, shock therapy?"

"I don't even know if they'll let me see her. Geez, and I just thought, I need to get your grandmother's clothes from storage, and I need to buy some for myself. Give Abigail a hug from me."

"Maybe the universe wants you to become the new Jack Reacher, Dad. You know: hitchhike around the country, press your shirts under a mattress, and buy a new one when you need it?"

"Way to cheer me up, sport." I did laugh at the absurdity of it, so maybe he was cheering me up.

"Yeah, well consider this. Abigail asked me a question you should ponder. Why did someone invade Tommy Kennedy's house while you and Grandma were there? Bad timing or something else? And if something else, who knew you were there?"

I couldn't breathe, as though someone had punched me in the solar plexus.

Only Lizzie knew.

WHILE I APPRECIATED EVERYTHING THE folks at Sugarbush had done for my mother over the years, I had never been at ease in their facility. Parents are supposed to take care of their children, so when the roles reverse, everyone becomes uncomfortable. I stewed in my discontent while I waited for Dr. Draco to complete his rounds.

Uncle Mike knew I experienced turmoil around visiting Sugarbush. I doubt he understood it. He was more of a General MacArthur type: "Duty. Honor. Country." Although he would probably substitute Boston for Country, or at least consider them synonymous. He followed the Nike commercial slogan to "Just Do It."

I considered and rejected calling Paddy again. I'm sure if Lizzie had heard anything she would have called—and I couldn't think of a thing I wanted to say to her. I should have brought a book to read, but I had forgotten that part of my routine. Uncle Mike was being uncharacteristically quiet, not filling me in on the cancers, heart attacks, and other traumas his and my father's now aged cop friends were enduring.

The more I stewed, the more I experienced a sense of helplessness—which meant I was on the verge of depression; one false step and I'd be down the rabbit hole. The last time I felt like this, I buried myself in the snows of Michigan's Upper Peninsula and became a semi-hermit. I had to be vigilant and fight the beast.

Dr. Draco eventually arrived with a whisper of footsteps and the whiff of hand sanitizer. He sat in the chair kitty-corner from me and crossed his legs, tapping his mustache with two fingers. I waited.

"Your mother has suffered a deep trauma. She presents herself much like she did when I first met her. She gives no apparent sign of hearing what we say, although we believe she does, and she refuses to communicate in any fashion. I'm afraid we are in for a long haul. With your permission, I recommend we readmit her."

I nodded dumbly. The financial portion of my brain spewed reams of calculator tape. The costs of Mom's reinstitution made a mockery of my decision to temporarily fund cash flow with a mortgage. I'd have to do something I'd sworn to myself I would never do: withdraw money from my IRA and pay tax penalties.

Draco ticked items on his fingers. "We're scrambling to make a room available. You do still have your mother's medical power of attorney? Good. You'll need to bring her clothes, sundries, set up a petty cash account for her incidentals."

"May I see her?"

"Briefly. She's very fragile. You mustn't upset her."

Thirty-Three

Patrick and Abigail checked into their rooms at the motel on the beach in Kitty Hawk. While Abigail changed from travel clothes, Patrick booted up his computer and checked emails. Only the two from Lisa were of interest. In the first, she reported no further progress pinning down the address of the person in Duck, but believed the computer was still in place.

His mouth went dry as he read the second, which reminded everyone of the Wednesday 6:30 a.m. breakfast meeting to discuss LT2P's future. In capital red letters she had added I EXPECT YOU THERE!!! He rolled his neck and stretched his shoulders to try to relieve the tension. He had twenty-four hours before he'd need to return to the airport.

While waiting for Abigail to let him know she was ready to visit Duck, he logged on using PMcCree. Neither StonedGoss nor Nif8yrbk was online.

Abigail politely tapped once on the door, came in, and stood next to him. "I've readied the car and looked at some online photos of our target. Tell me if I have anything wrong. Brown hair, collar length, has body, but not curly. Five-ten or five-eleven? Looks the prim and proper sort. Buttoned down. Not heavy, but not lean. Does he wear hats? How does he walk?"

"I've never seen him in a hat. I remember he had a little catch in his right step, like he has a tight hamstring—maybe he pulled it playing racquetball or something and it never fully healed?" He rose and demonstrated the gait. Stopping, he measured the top of Abigail's head against how tall he remembered the Jerk to be. "You're five nine, right? I think he may be closer to five eleven. The rest you nailed pretty well."

She tilted her head a little and squinted at him. "You a good guesser of heights or do you know I'm five nine?"

She'd catch him if he lied. "I looked at your license at the car rental."

She raised a single eyebrow.

"You placed it on the counter. I wanted to know how old you are." She didn't respond, so he continued. "Well, what would you do if your dad got serious about someone?"

"Kick him in the nuts since he's still married to my mother. Look, kid," she said, "I don't think you're cut out for a life of crime. You confess way too easily. From now on, if you have a question, just ask. Let's have a relationship based on trust, okay? Those work better than ones based on suspicion."

"Not all people are trustworthy."

"Truer words were never spoken. If some guy wants to go halvsies with you because you have money and he knows the secret to three-card monte, run. I'm talking relationships here: your family, your friends, your business associates. Some will let you down. I'm not denying it happens, but the philosophy has served me well. A little application of Ronald Reagan's "trust but verify" doesn't hurt either if something doesn't smell right. Which, I gather, is part of the reason we're here?"

He grabbed the proffered lifeline. "In this case I don't trust, but we need to verify. Why don't we drive to Duck and hunt down the turkey?"

"Remember, your turkey is probably wearing different clothes. Down here with the sun, he might wear a hat. He could have dyed his hair or even shaved his head. If he's cautious and he's good, he could have changed his gait. He could use a cane, or stoop, or droop his head. Any of those would make him appear shorter. You see anyone who looks like a possibility, shout out."

I MAY HAVE BEEN READY to see Mom, but Dr. Draco decided she should have lunch and take a nap to make sure she was well rested.

Uncle Mike was not one for sitting around. He'd start pacing, which would drive me nuts. I sent him to pick up Mom's clothes from the storage facility and buy me a couple of changes of clothes. He made lunch plans with the local police chief, a guy who had worked in his division "back in the day."

I found a quiet corner and tapped Sugarbush's public wireless connection with my cell phone. I confirmed my recollection of Excellion Exploration, the stock whose ticker symbol was EXEXP. The thing was a typical penny stock—no revenues, virtually no expenses, but it had assets.

During the previous twelve months it had rarely traded, and when it did, the transactions had settled within a half cent of $0.02 a share.

No longer. Last Thursday someone or ones had begun buying the stock, pushing its price to a high of $0.0975 at Friday's close. I pulled up a free stock chart app (free because it had a delay between transactions and publication). The stock had already sold for $0.20 per share, ten times the price early last week. Something was going on with Excellion.

The Excellion trading commenced the same day Cindy and I had done our undercover due diligence on Cunningham's firm. Excellion had been one of the few stocks in the hedge fund I had never heard of. I confirmed from the due diligence information I had stored in the cloud that Cunningham's hedge fund owned some eighty-seven million shares of Excellion, nearly ninety percent of the authorized stock.

I had initially treated it as a minor curiosity; the total investment worth only $1,750,000—a rounding error compared to the several billion in the hedge fund. Nonetheless, the stake had grown to $17,400,000. Cunningham was missing. StonedGoss had mentioned the stock. These pieces were connected, but how?

And why did the fund own a controlling interest? When did he buy it? What were Excellion's prospects? Why the run up in price?

In less than an hour I reviewed Excellion's SEC filings. The company sat on a bunch of mineral rights in the hopes someone would want to buy them. Excellion had no money to explore, let alone develop any of its territory. Their bets dotted the Iron Range from Minnesota through Wisconsin and into the Upper Peninsula of Michigan. Had they spent the same money buying mineral rights a decade ago in Alberta or the Dakotas, Cunningham's hedge fund would have benefited hugely when the shale oil and gas boom exploded.

What caused this sudden interest in Excellion? In my distant past as a bank stock analyst on Wall Street, I would occasionally check in with the online groups where bears and bulls would try to convince others of their perspective. In those forums, employees would anonymously gripe about management or pump up the company. The chatter was mostly distracting noise, but sometimes I could glean a hint of something real. Careful research often allowed me to ferret out the truth before it became generally known. There was nothing illegal about any of this if there wasn't a coordinated attempt to manipulate the stock. If they were attempting to manipulate the price, their actions could range anywhere from morally repugnant and legally iffy to downright criminal.

The stock chart updated with another sale, twenty minutes ago, at $0.25 a share.

I had won a stock-picking contest in B-school by choosing a bunch of volatile penny stocks. It only needed one big winner to wipe out losses in the rest of the stocks. I figured either I'd win, which would boost my resume, or I'd be last and no one would remember. My wager had panned out. Who was betting on Excellion and why?

On a Yahoo message board I found devoted to penny stocks of mining companies, I initiated a new thread with the question, "What's up with EXEXP?"

As though waiting for the question, ExcellionBull immediately responded, "RIO to announce buy at $2 per."

RIO was the ticker symbol for Rio Tinto, a large, global mining company. I ran a search on them. Their earnings report and conference call were later that week, but I could not sniff any acquisition rumors.

Another person (Dayshorter) hopped into the thread. "Hey Bull—this gonna trigger other offers?"

ExcellionBull: Unlikely. This one is driven by Au, Pt & Pd

Dayshorter: Thought EXEXP was mostly Fe & some Cu & Ni?

ExcellionBull: Correct, but test bore showed Au, Pt & Pd

I had found no press release announcing any test bores on Excellion leases. Gold, platinum, and palladium were byproducts of some copper and nickel mines, like the Eagle Mine outside Marquette in Michigan's Upper Peninsula. The U.P. had been punched full of holes by people looking for gold, but there had never been any big operations—certainly nothing big enough to attract a company Rio Tinto's size.

Dayshorter: Test bore? Where?

ExcellionBull: RIO paid

Dayshorter: Why haven't we heard anything from EXEXP management?

ExcellionBull: They're locked up until Wednesday's announcement

Nif8yrbk: They've already signed?

ExcellionBull: So say my Rio sources

So Nif8yrbk was hanging around Excellion Exploration stock, which meant StonedGoss was maybe nearby? Which meant Albert Cunningham III or someone close to him was also involved in this deal. I did a quick calculation. At two bucks a share, the hedge fund would earn a tidy $175 million.

Another trade had gone through, pushing EXEXP up to $0.375.

I opened a new browser window and did a quick search on Rio Tinto. Their quarterly earnings announcement was scheduled for Wednesday morning, paired with an analyst conference call later that day. They'd be in a news blackout until they released their earnings report. Perfect for someone manipulating a stock. I checked on RIO's ticker. Nothing unusual.

Okay, if I were Cunningham trying to get a bunch of money by manipulating a penny stock, how might I do it? Suppose he used some of the money he had pulled from his and Lizzie's brokerage accounts and made a private trade with his hedge fund. The due diligence material I viewed showed positions at the end of the previous quarter, nothing more recent, so anything could have happened. Say he sold a few million shares from the fund to himself at $0.02 a share. Five million shares would cost $100,000. If he could pump up the price to even a buck a share and sell his shares before the scheme collapsed, he'd earn a quick $4.9 million in a classic pump-and-dump operation—illegal as hell, but only if they catch you.

ExcellionBull: Stockholder approval is a lock, but arbs might buy if they could start a bidding war.

Dayshorter: Feels like BS to me. At $1.00 I'm gonna short.

ExcellionBull: Just bought 100K more at ½

As I followed the conversation between Dayshorter, ExcellionBull, Nif8yrbk, and several other new voices who entered the conversation, I wondered if I was watching an internet version of the old-time stock manipulation game. A pool of "investors" would decide to make a play on XYZ stock. They started buying it, even trading it among themselves at ever-higher prices. The sharp price uptick would attract momentum investors who jumped on the bandwagon.

Once the man on the street was touting how wonderful XYZ was, the syndicate would sell into the enthusiasm. After the crooks sold all the shares they owned, they'd short sell even more by borrowing shares. The pressure of all those sales would drive the stock down, then they would buy the borrowed shares back at a much lower price.

A successful pool made money while the stock rose and made even more as it fell. The manipulative practice was legal before the founding of the SEC. Just because it was illegal now, didn't mean it didn't still happen.

I continued reading messages, hoping StonedGoss would show up—and maybe he had under a different name. While financial sleuthing as a bank stock analyst, I used a variety of Yahoo IDs to make it much more difficult for individuals and corporations to track me from one group to another. I also had a separate identity to play games on Yahoo, another for various Civil War discussion groups, and one for a birding group.

Twelve minutes after Bull's claimed purchase, the delayed price for EXEXP popped up to fifty cents.

Assuming Cunningham was behind this, what was his plan, and had he disappeared to execute it? If not him, it had to be someone who knew Cunningham was out of the picture. Otherwise, by owning 87% of the company, Cunningham's hedge fund could be selling shares at a tidy profit. Or cause the price to crash by offering ten million shares to the market. Unless Rio Tinto actually was making an offer.

Was there any way Paddy or Lisa could legally tell if StonedGoss and ExcellionBull or one of the other players was the same person? I still had industry contacts. Should I alert the SEC to possible manipulation? I had no proof, and SEC computers had presumably already noted the huge stock price increase. In fact, all the penny trader websites probably featured Excellion on their big mover list.

A knock at the door interrupted my contemplation.

Dr. Draco smiled from the doorway. "Ready?"

I doubted it.

Thirty-Four

THE DRIVE TO DUCK WAS uneventful. Patrick used a cell phone app to check the IP address assigned to his phone from the cell towers. Cruising the area, he mapped each point his phone switched from one cell tower to another. No surprise; Lisa had nailed it. The main residential streets ran between Route 12, Duck Road, and the ocean. Some of those connected to a T road near the ocean. Others dead-ended. The area was a flipping maze, even with his cell phone's map.

Having completed two passes of the area, Abigail pulled into a parking lot near a group of condos. "Tell me why we're running up and down these streets. I have the feeling I don't know the whole plan."

"I wanted to make sure Lisa had us in the right area. We are, which means you can relax now because I've confirmed the information without breaking any laws. All she did was save us time."

Abigail looked like she would object so Patrick pressed on. "I know. I know. TMI. This little excursion was to get the lay of the land. It gives us a better feel for the streets than we could get from a map. I'm still hoping I can talk to him in a chat room, but I'm on a short leash. I don't have time to sit around and wait. It's ninety degrees out. Everyone's either inside or at the beach. The only place we can't get close to is the gated community we just passed. Let's walk the beach and check it out from the oceanside. My luck, that's where he's holed up, and if we have to get in there, it's either busting through their gate or going in from the beach."

"I haven't seen any public access."

"We can slip around the side of the building."

"It's private. See the sign?"

He gave a quick shrug. "Loosen up a little, Abigail. You're an ex-Secret Service agent. A tiny misdemeanor won't keep you from heaven. Besides," He pointed to her black, long-sleeved shirt and white pants. "You'd look as out-of-place on the beach as a penguin. I'll do this myself."

She pulled binoculars from her large knapsack. "Pretend you're a birdwatcher and use your cell phone to take pictures of places to get onto the beach—especially around the gated community."

Outside the car, the heat rising from the pavement staggered him like an uppercut to the chops. He stripped off his shirt and threw it onto the backseat. The sun warmed him and brought with it memories of the Jersey shore. He removed his tennies and socks and hopped from one foot to the other on the hot asphalt.

"We forgot sunscreen," Abigail said. "And you should wear a hat." She tried to hand him the floppy one she had picked up from the hotel gift shop.

"Not catching me in that thing. I won't crisp in an hour." He sprinted across the parking lot, around the side of the condo, down a boardwalk over the dunes, and onto the beach. The tide was out maybe three or four feet, so he jogged to the area of hard-packed, wet sand. He could almost hear the sizzle when his feet touched the coolness.

The beach was surprisingly empty even for a weekday. If this were the Jersey shore, bodies would be everywhere. He could see the advantage of private beaches—at least from the perspective of property owners.

He moseyed toward the gated community, making sure to check out everyone on the beach, even though he knew Albert Cunningham III wasn't likely to be wearing a bikini. Two young women played with a Frisbee. One had the ripped muscles of a serious athlete. Tall enough for basketball or volleyball, she had splendid eye-hand coordination and her run for a bad throw caused him to stop and enjoy the view. The other wasn't bad, but not in the same league. While he was checking them out, he was pretty sure they were eyeing him too. The athlete's next Frisbee toss to her friend had a tilt, so the wind caught it and arced it over her head toward him. He judged the distance and broke into a short sprint, catching it before it hit the ocean.

"Nice catch," they said in unison.

"Let's see what you've got," the athlete said.

Patrick smiled at the double entendre. He'd played some Ultimate in college before he got serious about crew. He tucked the binocs around one shoulder, pinned them to his side with his left elbow, and sent the Frisbee on a curling path. He'd accounted for the wind perfectly: without taking a step, the athlete caught it eye high.

"Nice," the athlete said.

"Come on and play with us," said the other.

Patrick mimed looking at his watch and raised his hands wide apart in a "What can you do?" gesture. He didn't let them see his smile, but they had made his day. For a short time, he'd forgotten why he was walking the beach.

The heat was getting to him again. To cool down, he walked to the edge of the ocean. Waves washed over his feet on their inward rush and tugged at his toes on their return to the sea. Up ahead, two ranks of seagulls stood with their beaks to the wind. His father would know the exact species. He checked them in the binocs as he figured a birdwatcher might do. They looked like standard gray and white seagulls, although he realized the grouping consisted of small ones with yellow legs and bigger ones with pink legs.

Having walked past the gated community, he chose to retrace his route closer to the dunes to see the real estate better. The sand was hot, and even with wraparound glasses, the light hurt his eyes. Sweat trickled between his shoulder blades, following his backbone and soaking into his underwear. Because of the dunes, he could see only the upper levels of the houses. Each had its own boardwalk onto the beach. They all had gates, but easily breached. The gated condo community had three beach access routes. If Cunningham was holed up somewhere in there, it would be hard to get him out—assuming they ever found him.

Patrick's steps dragged. The chances of narrowing down exactly where the Jerk was before time ran out were becoming more and more remote. If they hadn't found him by tomorrow, they'd need to tell the police and let them perform a house-to-house search if they felt like it.

He faced the ocean and gazed at the horizon. Nothing made him feel smaller than the ocean, hearing the waves rolling in, feeling their strength as they tugged at his feet, seeing the sun rise from it in the morning, the openness, the power. Why did he think he could change anything? Whatever was going to happen to his mother would happen.

But dammit, he wanted to know who, what, where, why, when, and how. Determination reaffirmed, he jogged back to Abigail. They could return to the hotel, monitor the online chat rooms for StonedGoss, eat dinner and, if nothing had changed, return to try again to spot him.

◇◇◇

MOM LOOKED SALLOW AND EXUDED the energy of a chunk of granite. The room was set up like a psychiatrist's office with a small desk, a couch—black, no less—and a grouping of three chairs. Mom sat slumped in one of the chairs. I moved another so we directly faced each other.

I tried the how questions first. How was she feeling? How did she sleep? How was her arm? No response. In her past silence, she had at least sometimes looked at me. Today she focused on the floor between her splayed feet.

Switching tactics, I told her how much I had enjoyed her company on our trip and asked if she had enjoyed mine. I enthused about how much fun I had at her darts exhibitions; what part did she enjoy the best?

At the mention of darts, she tapped her side and wrinkled her forehead. Normally, she carries a fanny pack in which she stores her darts. Did she remember the police had confiscated it for evidence? A positive flush ran over me. She's listening and paying attention. I needed to keep talking and find more ways to connect. *This will work; I know it.*

I reminded her of funny road trip incidents, of people we had met, of places we had visited. I told her how much this trip had meant to me. My hope generated by her check of the fanny pack slowly drained away. Mom did not react to anything else I said. I became like a small child watching his mother, desperately seeking approval of the finger painting he had just completed.

I tried upping the ante. "By the way, Paddy asked me to give you some really good news. I think you'll like this a lot. Paddy and Cindy are having a baby. You'll be a great-grandmother. Isn't that terrific?"

Thinking how happy and excited Cindy and Paddy had looked brought a genuine smile to my face. When Mom still did not respond, my smile crumbled. I puffed a sigh. This was hopeless, and that pissed me off.

I bolted from the chair and stepped in front of her. She did not lift her head. "Dammit, Mother! You can't do this to me again. You deserted me for more than twenty years. You owe me. You owe me big. I don't mean for the money I spent keeping you here. I mean—" I leaned down into her face and enunciated each word separately. "—you're my mother. I *can not* stand your rejection one more time."

Anger welled from a spot long buried. I pulled away and paced in a tight circle. "For twenty years you had nothing for me. You couldn't give me one smile, one wink, one word. I thought I'd built a wall strong enough you couldn't hurt me again."

I screamed, "But I was wrong!"

I knelt in front of her. Tears poured down my cheeks. I whispered, "I can't do it again, Mom." I pitched forward and leaned my head onto the rug. Crossing my hands behind my neck, I pulled myself into a tight ball. *I lost control. I screwed up and made it all about me.*

God only knew what damage I had done to my mother because I had been selfish and lost control. I was no better than Lizzie when she was self-absorbed. Keening filled my ears.

The wail came from me.

Thirty-Five

I WAS TUCKED INTO A fetal position. Someone patted my shoulder, gently at first before becoming more insistent. I rocked back and forth, scraping my forehead against the industrial carpeting before summoning enough strength to get up and face Dr. Draco, sure he had been monitoring the room and was now offering me comfort. "I'm sorry," I choked out.

"No," my mother said. "I'm sorry, Seamus. I will not let it beat me this time. I need to remember I don't have to be silent to keep my secrets."

A shiver of joy ran through me. *She's talking! Hallelujah!* My grin grew so wide the sides of my face ached. Until I processed her words: Mom had more secrets. I jerked my head at the realization and cracked into her chin, bowling her over. Dr. Draco and Uncle Mike rushed into the room. The next few moments were a confusion of arms and legs and helping hands while they tried to raise Mom and me to our feet. I was rubbing the top of my sore head and babbling apologies like an idiot.

My mother, once they got her settled in a chair, pointed at me and laughed.

Relief poured into me, and I thought I might float away. I hugged her tight. She rubbed my back in little circles. "At least you didn't hit my nose. I don't want one of those crooked McCree beaks."

Uncle Mike jumped on the opportunity to tell Dr. Draco his broken nose stories: how he busted my nose, and because of him I hadn't become a gangbanger, and how I had accidentally broken Paddy's nose. His was intentional, don't youse know.

Dr. Draco looked at us and shook his head. I chose not to wonder why; the possibilities were endless. He shooed Uncle Mike and me out so he could speak privately with Mom.

I used the opportunity to call Paddy and connected. "Patrick McCree's phone, Abigail Hancock speaking." My heart raced from the starting blocks; butterflies filled my chest.

"Mom spoke," I blurted.

Abigail must have put the phone on speaker because she and Paddy both exclaimed, "Excellent!"

"Jinx." I said.

"Dad, it doesn't work that way. You have to be one of the people saying the same thing to call 'jinx.' So Grandma will be all right?"

"I think so. Dr. Draco's with her now. Has anything changed since we last talked?"

Abigail: "We have rooms at the Hilton Garden Inn in Kitty Hawk. The best way to reach us is by cell phone. We've scouted the general area, and Patrick just returned from walking the beach."

Paddy: "We still don't have an exact location. You remember Mom said she thought someone at the hedge firm had a place on the Outer Banks? Cindy tried to correlate hedge fund employees and property owners without success. Much of the property is owned by corporations or partnerships, and she doesn't have the time to track them all down."

Me: "Tell Cindy to send me an email with whatever she's got. Once I get to Uncle Mike's, I'll see if anything clicks for me. Actually, scrap that, I don't have a computer and Uncle Mike still uses dial-up. No, have her send it to me anyway. I can go to a library if I have time. I've been using my cell phone, which is cumbersome. I think Cunningham or someone close to him is running a scam." I explained how a scheme using EXEXP might work. "You guys have a plan?"

Abigail: "I wonder if the timing of this means things are coming to a boil. We're headed to the hotel. Patrick will try to contact Cunningham again by computer. If that doesn't work, we'll try using a door-to-door survey to get people to open their doors. Maybe we'll be lucky. It's better than sitting on our duffs doing nothing. We're here. Look, you're obviously tired. Take care of your mother. Get rest. We'll keep you posted."

She clicked off before I could tell Paddy I loved him.

Or tell Abigail I loved her. Although with Paddy listening in, I was unlikely to express those feelings.

PATRICK WAS DISAPPOINTED TO FIND no relevant emails upon his return to the hotel. He again ignored Abigail's ban on outside contact and called Cindy. "We made no progress today," he said. "I only have tonight and some of tomorrow. Lisa's called a big meeting of the partners on Wednesday. She's been super-stressed. Probably the buyout, and she's worried we'll lose clients."

"Nothing to do but wait and see what Wednesday brings." Changing her tone from serious to light. "What is the most interesting thing that happened to you today?"

He related how the two girls had tried to pick him up.

She let loose a long laugh. "Do I need to write into our contract a prohibition against you going bare-chested in public?"

"This is the same contract that stipulates you shall at all times walk three steps behind me, keeping your eyes down?"

"Right. Wearing a burka. Oh, and I'm moving to Sweden until the baby comes."

"Because burkas are outlawed there?"

"No, that was France or maybe parts of Switzerland? European women have less morning sickness than Americans, and Sweden's rate of C-sections is half the U.S.'s. And their life expectancy is more than two years higher than for the U.S. Only the best for our little *Liebchen.*"

"I don't think life expectancy works that way."

"Of course it doesn't. By the way, did you know many women get hornier when they're pregnant?"

Patrick put on a fake German accent. "And vat else are you planmink to write into our contract?"

"I'll show you . . . at home."

Abigail's knock on the door interrupted their banter.

"Give your belly a pat for me," Patrick said. "I'll be home soon."

"Promises. Promises. Do what you have to do, Patrick. I'll be waiting for you."

PATRICK OPTED FOR A LIGHT salad and seven-bean soup for dinner. Abigail chose fresh fish. Between bites she showed him the "survey questionnaire" she had developed on the ever-contentious topic of restricting beach access for off-road vehicles. Patrick could easily be a graduate student. With a crop top and peasant braids wrapped around her head, Abigail would also pass. The whole purpose was to evaluate the people who answered their doors. With luck, they would get a glimpse of Albert Cunningham. Unfortunately, a few people would waste everyone's time by taking the survey; they hoped most were so tired of the issue they would not.

"I like it," Paddy said. "It's a long shot, but better than waiting for something to happen."

They finished dinner and went to their rooms to prepare for the evening. In his room, Patrick checked email (nothing of import) and, in case StonedGoss was around, issued him an invite for a private.

StonedGoss entered room.

StonedGoss: Saw you on the beach. Who's we?

The cursor blinked, awaiting Patrick's response. The Jerk's acknowledgment pinned his location to houses or condos on the beach within the ten or fifteen blocks he had walked. Patrick tried to reconstruct what he had written during the last brief contact. Didn't matter.

PMcCree: How can we help?

StonedGoss: My son & wife are in danger!!! Get them to safety!!!

StonedGoss: Being followed

PMcCree: U or them?

StonedGoss: Them

StonedGoss left room.

Patrick showed Abigail the screen with the messages when she got to his room.

"Call your mother," Abigail said. "Make sure she's all right."

Patrick's mother reported nothing had changed other than, according to the paper, the cops identifying Tommy Kennedy's invaders as "part of an international drug cartel." Good to know it had nothing to do with his mother or the Jerk. It also meant the cops were unlikely to charge Patrick's grandmother for killing the intruder who had made it past Tommy Kennedy. Answering his question, she reported she hadn't been out of the house, and there had been no visitors over the weekend or today.

At her question, "What's up?" Patrick thanked her and disconnected before she could turn the tables and interrogate him.

"Now the son," Abigail said. "Do you have his number?"

Patrick pulled up the number on his phone's address book. "What do I say?"

In answer, Abigail grabbed the phone, dialed the number, and punched the speakerphone button. On the third ring a male voice answered, "'Lo?"

"I'm calling on behalf of The Stray Cat Neutering Foundation and—"

"Hey, listen lady. I'm on the no-call list."

"So sorry. I was trying to reach one of our donors, Morris Captcha at . . ." She reversed two digits of his number.

"You got the wrong number." He clicked off.

Patrick held his laughter until the disconnect. Between giggles, he said, "Captcha?"

"It popped into my head along with Morris the Cat. That was him? He sounded fine."

"Nice accent. You and Chad have that in common. He's a great mimic. At the wedding he did a funny routine in his father's voice. I asked him if he could do other people, and he did a pretty good job parroting my words back to me, as me. Now what?"

"Some of us have the ear. Whenever Cunningham signs in again, tell him your mother and his son are both fine. If we can assure him they're both safe, and if he really is in trouble, I have a feeling he'll tell us where he is. The other alternative is he spotted you, considers you a threat, and is trying to throw us off."

"I never thought of that."

"My bodyguard clients aren't always good guys. Sometimes I need to keep scum alive so they can testify. I've learned how they think. They can be smart or stupid, but they're all devious. Can you convince your mother to go into hiding?"

"Maybe, but I probably don't know Chad well enough to convince him, and I doubt Mom does either. He had left home before Mom and the Jerk started dating."

"Turn it around. If your father thought you were in danger and needed to hide, how could Chad convince you?"

"We had a secret password. Only if someone outside of the family gave me the secret code word would I know I could safely go with them. No code word, I'd scream my head off and run to the authorities."

"Really? What was it?"

"Asparagus."

◇◇◇

TO MAKE SURE ONE OF them was awake if Cunningham came online, Patrick was to rest first. Abigail was still on West Coast time, so she'd remain awake until 2:00 a.m. They'd switch and each have six hours to sleep.

Patrick had no sooner crawled into bed, Abigail in the chair reading *The Big Book of Women Saints* on her tablet, then someone was shaking his shoulder. He blinked his eyes open. Abigail gave him another shake.

"What?"

"Cunningham's online. You do know how to sleep."

He peeled back the covers and nearly tripped on the bedspread on the way to the computer.

StonedGoss entered room.

StonedGoss: U there?

PMcCree: talked to both—They're OK

StonedGoss: He's watching Chad

PMcCree: we can get him to safety

StonedGoss: Time running out

Abigail said, "For whom?"

Patrick almost typed it and realized it would be a mistake. They needed to get Chad and his mother to safety before attempting to secure Cunningham.

PMcCree: when Chad was a kid, did u have a code word so he knew a message was really from you?

StonedGoss: Big Bird

PMcCree: ok we'll get them safe.

PMcCree: where r u?

StonedGoss: Tell me when they ARE SAFE

StonedGoss: Until then too dangerous

PMcCree: u need ransom?

StonedGoss: Let me know when they r safe

StonedGoss left room.

Patrick set aside his laptop and realized he was dressed only in his skivvies. Oh well, they showed less than a swimsuit. He opened his email program and while it refreshed, he slipped on shorts and collected his phone from the end table.

"Who are you calling?" Abigail asked.

Patrick glanced at the new emails. "Chad."

"Hold on, cowboy. We need a plan. Remember, this is what I do for a living. Until we have a plan, anything you do may expose him to even more danger. And we still aren't sure if Cunningham is on the up and up or if he's wrangling a way to get you alone. After all, he is on a computer. Would you let someone on a computer if you were holding them for ransom or something?"

Patrick barked a laugh. "Hell no. Unless I needed him to run the Excellion scam. But remember, letting me on a computer is different than letting Joe Schmo on a computer."

"Point taken. Assuming it's legit, where will Chad hide? If someone is following him and he visits friends, all you might accomplish is to endanger the friends. See what I'm saying?"

He checked the clock: only 9:22. "You have a plan?"

Thirty-Six

I SAT ON UNCLE MIKE'S deck enjoying the tart taste of a Killian's Red. The low hum of Route 128 traffic added a background meditative drone to my contemplations. Uncle Mike was watching some cop show on TV. My cell phone rang. I swiped the connect doohickey and stuck the phone to my ear. At Patrick's "Hey, Dad, did I wake you?" I settled the bottle on the deck with a shaky hand. "Something happened?"

Paddy and Abigail used the speakerphone and related Paddy's online chat with Cunningham—surely it was him? Their question was how to get Lizzie and Chad to safety.

"From your description, Paddy, it sure sounds like Cunningham is held by parties unknown. And reasons unknown. Look, the cosmos wants me to own my house in Cincinnati. Maybe this is why. It'll be a good place for your mother and Chad to go. Chad's never been there, Lizzie only the one time. Cunningham doesn't know where it is, so he can't . . . um, accidentally give away the location."

"You mean," Patrick said, "if someone tries to torture the information from him, or if the Jerk is using us to get them someplace remote so he can arrange for someone to take them out? How do we get them there?"

"I'll take them. Your grandmother has resumed speaking, but everyone, including her, agrees she should remain for a while at Sugarbush. She feels safe there, and the daily counseling can help make sure she's ready to deal with the world. Point being, I don't have to be here. Uncle Mike's offered me his spare car. I can drive down and pick them up. If I start now, I should arrive fourish, maybe earlier."

"But, Dad. Chad is being followed. Maybe you should all fly to Cincinnati. No one would know where you went until it was too late."

"Good point. Abigail, what do you think?"

"If either Chad or Patrick's mother appears to be running for the airport, it might trigger a violent response by those following them. Cunningham said Chad was being followed, but we don't know if his information is accurate. It could be both of them. My armored car's ideal, except that it's in Chicago. I'm leaning toward your plan, Seamus, because it allows lots of flexibility. You sure you're up for this?"

"Traffic will be light early in the morning, so I should be able to spot a tail. If I do, there are plenty of places to lose them between Jersey and Cincinnati. We could be at my place before dinner. Abigail? Since we don't know what we're dealing with here, do you think it would make sense to call that PI firm? I don't remember their name, but their motto was something like, 'When female intuition isn't enough.' Have them perform perimeter guard duty on the house? Just in case?"

"Shecurity, and I like your thinking. I'll take care of it. But once you collect your passengers, I think we should involve the police with Cunningham. We've narrowed down his location fairly well and could contact the Savannah police. If they believe us, they have the wherewithal to get a subpoena and discover exactly where the computer is."

"I don't like it," Paddy said. "Cops showing up now could endanger the Jerk. He's given us every indication he's being guarded. We still have no clue if he's a victim or guilty as hell. Let's see what tomorrow brings."

"I think," I said, "it's Lizzie's call. I'll sound her out when I see her. Paddy, you're most capable of convincing your mother to go with me. Then, you and she should conference call Chad. I'll pack and head down to the Garden State. Call me if something changes."

"Seamus," Abigail said, "remember once you pick them up to do all the surveillance maneuvers I taught you. You do not want to bring anyone else to your home."

PATRICK SCORED A TWOFER CALLING his mother: she answered and Chad Cunningham was visiting. "Ask him if anyone other than his parents knew his code word was 'Big Bird.'"

"Oh my God," Patrick's mother said. "He's alive! Where is he? Is he okay? What did he say?"

"Mother, stop. Listen to me. I have something important to say. You. Must. Pay. Attention." Her babbling dried up and Patrick continued. "He believes you and Chad are in danger. He told me the Big Bird code word so Chad would know it's him. Until you're safe, he won't tell us where he is or what's happening. He needs to know you are both safe. Tell me you understand."

A muted, "I understand," came down the line.

"We have a plan. Dad is already driving down to you from Boston—Grandma is back at Sugarbush—I'll let him tell you why. He should get there by four tomorrow morning. He'll take you to his house in Cincinnati. No one would expect to find you there. You've never mentioned it, right? Good. I don't know how long this will take to sort out, so pack a bunch of clothes. Can you convince Chad or do I need to talk with him?"

Muffled conversation came over the line, suggesting his mother had covered the microphone. He'd bet a large sum of money she had no clue where the microphone on her cell phone was and had accidentally covered it.

"Patrick, we're having a hard time taking this all in. Why would anyone want to follow us? That doesn't make any sense. But Chad says only his parents and grandparents knew the 'Big Bird' code, so he thinks we should take it seriously. How long do you think this will take? Chad has work and I have a charity auction planning meeting on—"

"Mother!"

"Don't you yell at me, young man."

Abigail massaged Patrick's neck while he performed a silent scream. "Getting mad," she whispered, "won't help anything." Under her strong hands he relaxed into what he wasn't sure was pleasure or pain.

"Sorry, Mom. I know this is stressful for everyone. I don't know any more than you do. Your husband thinks you are at risk. The first priority is to get you both safe. Is Chad coming with you or do I need to talk with him?"

More muffled conversation. "Chad says he'll go, but he'll have to buy some stuff because he has nothing here anymore."

Patrick ended the phone call and Abigail gave him a pat on the shoulder. "You done good today, kid. Give it up for the night and get some rest. Cunningham won't do anything until your father has them safely away from New Jersey. I have a feeling tomorrow will be a big day."

UNCLE MIKE'S TEN-YEAR-OLD CROWN VIC steered like an unwieldy boat and made me nervous. He had tricked out his ride with cop toys: multiple antennae, brush guards in the front, swivel spotlights, and a radio constantly monitoring police channels. One thing it did not have was a decent sound system—everything sounded tinny. I'd look like a cop, he told me, if I acted like one and drove way faster than my usual seven miles over the limit. According to him, I could cut my travel time significantly without worry about being pulled over. I asked if he'd pay for my traffic tickets. Not hardly.

Reaching I-287 in New Jersey, I realized Uncle Mike's car didn't have GPS. I pulled over and punched Lizzie's address into my phone's map, which guided me to her gate. Before entering her estate, I zipped down the power windows so I could listen for anything unusual and cruised the neighboring streets looking for any suspiciously parked cars. If someone had followed Chad, they'd be near Lizzie's place. Nothing caught my attention except the chirping of frogs from the ponds folks had in their front yards. It must have recently rained because the woods smelled damp, which got me wondering what the weather was at my Michigan camp. That would be a fine place to hide, except Lizzie would never go there.

I pushed the call button and the gate opened. No questions; I could be anyone. Talk about lax security.

The front of the house reminded me of a store's grand opening; the only things missing were colored spotlights crisscrossing the sky. So much for an inconspicuous getaway. Lizzie and Chad watched my arrival from the doorway. I dragged two of Lizzie's bags to the car. She had taken me at my word and packed three large suitcases. Chad carted Lizzie's third bag, his leather computer bag, and a small backpack. The luggage went into the trunk; people and laptop into the car. Everyone offered to drive; I said I'd take them up on it later, but for now I was still wired.

I asked Lizzie if she wanted Paddy and Abigail to call in the police. She considered and finally said, "Patrick has made contact with Al. I think we should let it play out."

No reason to press her now. We could revisit the issue once we reached Cincinnati.

Two hours later, I faded. I exited I-81 at the rest stop near Grantville, PA and cozied up to the wrong side of the gas pumps because I didn't know which side of the car the gas cap was on, and this car was so old it didn't have an arrow symbol next to the fuel indicator pointing the direction. Lizzie and Chad needed to use the facilities. While I pumped a mortgage payment's worth of fuel—Uncle Mike swore the beast was tuned for premium gas—I stretched. At our arrival, a Toyota truck had been in the adjacent bay. A nondescript tan Honda Accord driven by a guy wearing a loud Hawaiian shirt soon pulled up to the far pumps. His stretches and eye rubs gave me the impression he was as tired as I was.

Lizzie and Chad returned from the restrooms, Lizzie carrying two containers of coffee with steam pouring into the early morning chill. Chad was thumbing his phone.

"You must be getting tired," Lizzie said. "Want me to drive?"

"Great. There are a bunch of places to eat once we cross into Ohio from West Virginia. Pick one for breakfast. I'll grab a catnap"

"I'll take the passenger seat," Chad said, "and keep Beth company. You can stretch out in the back."

"Good to have a navigator," I said. "Lizzie's been known to mix up her left and right. There was the time—"

"Seamus." Lizzie's voice had an edge to it, but she softened the effect by patting my shoulder. "Go to sleep. Even I can find my way on the interstates. Are we heading east or west?"

I AWOKE TO LIZZIE SHAKING my knee. She had parked close to the restaurant. Rain tapped a steady drumbeat on the car roof, making me regret leaving my raincoat in the closet at Tommy Kennedy's house. The home invasion felt so long ago, but had been just two days.

Sprinting to the building saved me from the rain but running through the puddles soaked my jeans. Lizzie and Chad calmly wove their way around the puddles. Behind them I caught a glimpse of what looked to be the same tan Honda I had seen at the rest stop in Pennsylvania. *Is the driver wearing a Hawaiian shirt?*

Too little sleep, too much stress, and Abigail's caution about checking for tails were making me overly suspicious.

By the time we finished breakfast, the rain had lessened to a drizzle. The Accord was gone, but not my worries. Chad insisted on driving. I claimed the passenger seat, and Lizzie sprawled in the back. We didn't yet need gas; we could fill up when the morning's coffee wanted out. Chad flicked the wipers to variable. The rubber squeaked on too-dry glass. While he messed around adjusting the wiper interval, I used my phone's map to plan a new tail-checking maneuver. We could get off I-70 at exit 215 to National Road, which I thought was the old name for US-40, and hop back on the interstate two miles later.

Approaching the exit, I told Chad to wait until the last minute and make a quick turn. Without signaling, he steamed up the ramp at seventy miles per hour and slammed on the brakes at the stop sign. He swung left too quickly onto the National Road, causing my seatbelt to pull hard against my chest and lap and bring tears to my eyes. Not healed yet.

Using the sideview mirror I confirmed several cars had followed us up the ramp and two made the same left we had.

Chad sped past a couple of factory parking lots, tires swishing on the damp street.

Me: "If you see a lot or a street around a curve, pull over and stop. I'll hop out and see who's behind us."

Chad: "Not looking good."

Lizzie: "It's raining."

Chad earned full credit in my book by not responding. My phone map showed a short curve immediately before the Belmont Hills Country Club entrance on the left. The satellite view indicated the right side of the road was open. Bushes and trees lined the left side and might hide our turn. I told Chad what I had in mind and worried what I would do if the other car stopped.

Chad entered the curve with too much speed. The right tires skidded in the berm, spitting gravel into the guardrail. I grabbed the door to hold on. He tapped the brakes and brought all four tires back to the pavement.

I expected a reprimand from Lizzie and glanced over. She stared straight ahead, her lips pinched into a thin line.

At a slightly slower speed, we passed a house with its green garbage can ready for pickup and came to a flowerbed with a modest white sign proclaiming "Belmont Hills."

I pointed to the sign. "That's it."

He careened into the drive, slammed on the brakes, and came to a skidding halt. I jumped out and ran behind the trees toward the main road. With the whine of high RPMs, the car accelerated down the narrow lane leading toward the clubhouse.

I ran behind a low hedge and knelt. Water wicked up my pants, soaking my legs. The first car, a blue SUV with Ohio plates passed. The second car, a Honda, was hard on its bumper. It flashed by and I had the impression of a younger guy wearing a Hawaiian shirt. The plates featured a palmetto tree: South Carolina.

With a screech of brakes, Chad stopped the car. I raced to it and flung myself inside. "Follow that car. Let's get his license plate number."

Thirty-Seven

Patrick and Abigail parked on the first street within the area Lisa had pinpointed for the Jerk. Patrick tried once more to invite StonedGoss to a private chat and again received no response. It must have been the ten thousandth time he'd tried since his father had picked up his mother and Chad. How could he tell the Jerk his family was safe if the guy didn't go online? Which was precisely why they had no alternative than to try Abigail's survey ploy.

He slapped the dashboard. "Let's get this ball rolling."

"A couple more minutes, Patrick. Nine o'clock. Remember, keep ringing the bell for a minute. Even if their first intention is to ignore you, they'll be so irritated by the time a minute's up, they'll want to tell you off. If you spot him, get away as quickly as you can."

"Are you nervous?"

Abigail did her raise-one-eyebrow thing.

"You're talking more than normal. I got it. I have my spiel down. I have the survey down. I'm wearing an ugly Walmart tie so I look like a dorky college kid. I'm ready to go." He opened the door. "By the time I get to the first building, it'll be nine."

"See you at the end of the block. And remember—"

"I got it!"

I was again in the driver's seat and my skin prickled with the heat of the mid-morning sun pouring into the car. I switched on the air conditioner.

"Don't do that," Lizzie said. "I'll get too cold."

"Close your vents."

She rubbed her upper arms. "That only effects the blowing. This doesn't have dual temperature controls. I'll still be cold. Besides, it smells stale, like it hasn't been used in ten years."

"It probably hasn't."

From the backseat Chad piped up. "Hey, you two sound like a married couple."

Talk about hitting below the belt. I cranked the thermostat up a degree, but left the A/C on.

Lizzie was quiet for a short while. "What were you guys going to do if you caught up to the vehicle you thought was following us? You'd be like the dog finally catching a car. You wouldn't know what to do with it."

I appreciated the line, a line she stole from me. I considered the theft as a compliment. "Chad and I would have chewed his tires until he couldn't drive." I was not about to fess up to feeling extremely pumped doing something active rather than running away. I'd never hear the end of her testosterone cracks.

Chad chuckled and provided directions. "The map wants us to turn and get on the highway, but stay."

Normally, I'd enjoy wending my way home to Cincinnati from northeast Ohio traveling two-lane roads I had never been on. I found no enjoyment in the scenery because my brain was spinning. Once NPR news ran its course, I cleared my throat by way of indicating we should converse. "I have to admit," I said, "the more I learn, the less I understand. Be honest now, 'cause we're all in this together. No one has contacted either of you, have they?"

Lizzie: "Just the ransom note you accused me of creating."

Me: "That's bizarre. If someone was intending to ask for a ransom, why no follow-up? I have to admit I'm having a hard time rationalizing why someone breaks into your house to plant the note and the divorce stuff."

Chad cleared his throat. "It does point a finger at Beth—at least until someone discovers they're not true."

Lizzie said, with heat in her voice, "They aren't true."

"Which," Chad said with a tone sounding to me like controlled exasperation, "was my point."

Me: "At the risk of having you both angry at me, I'll be honest. I keep wondering if he planned to take all the money and live someplace without extradition treaties. Since he didn't take Lizzie along, either he planned to convince her to join him at a later date, or he was dumping her because he had someone else."

Lizzie faced me. Her lips formed a snarl.

"Please let me finish before you tell me what's wrong with the scenario. It's happened before, Lizzie. One partner dumps the other and the dumpee doesn't see it coming. You said you two had a prenup, so would he banish himself from the U.S. to save a few million on a divorce? Maybe, but plenty of rich guys know how to hide assets from ex-wives without fleeing the country. But, if he decided he needed to leave the country and planned to convince you to meet him, it would explain not only stripping the accounts of the money but why he paid the quarterly taxes. It bought time. Still, why all the chicanery? Only one thing comes to mind."

Chad: "Hey, I'll act the straight man. What?"

"He was breaking the law."

Lizzie was shaking her head. "Seamus, Al wouldn't."

Me: "If nothing else, he bought false passports."

Chad: "Dad has always been a little wonky, worrying the U.S will be taken over by pinko, commie liberals who will redistribute wealth. Or ghetto hordes will leave their cities and invade the countryside. Dad's philosophy has been to work hard and follow a plan. But make sure your plan has contingencies. I'm sure the false passports were part of his contingency planning, as were having overseas assets."

Me: "I wasn't really talking about risk diversification. I've seen men, good men, corrupted by insider trading. Someone gives them a tip. They know they should ignore it, but they check it out. And either they convince themselves it really is *their* research that informs *their* decision, or the drive to win overcomes their inhibitions. It's just the once, even if they are caught it will be a slap on the wrist. And nothing happens. The money is easy. It boosts returns. The next time it's a bit easier and down the slippery slope they go."

I stopped at an intersection with a bunch of traffic signs. "Am I turning?"

"Nope. Straight ahead."

"Funny stuff is all over Wall Street in small ways and big. The vast majority of Wall Streeters didn't go there because they wanted to be crooks. But it happens. Ponzi schemes too. A guy has a bad quarter and thinks he can make it up, so he finds a way to hide the loss. He takes more risk and loses even more. Now, either he has to face up and be out of business or he cooks the books and starts paying old accounts with new ones. Or some expense comes up and there isn't enough ready cash. He borrows a little from someone's account and makes an adjustment in the books."

Lizzie snorted. "He was paid millions, Seamus."

"Irrelevant. Does he gamble?"

They both agreed he liked a game of poker and occasionally went to Atlantic City with friends.

"But he always set limits," Lizzie added.

I barked a laugh. "Investment banker types? They're constantly testing who's smarter, has more balls, is willing to take more risk. I know guys who started with a friendly dollar-stakes poker game and ended up addicted to the thrill. It's their cocaine. They have to stay pumped. They have to be on the brink."

Chad: "Hey, I see some of those same characteristics in the import–export business. But the risk addiction thing does not describe my father. As I said, he was all about plans and fallback positions."

Lizzie: "Maybe Al learned something he wasn't supposed to at work."

Chad: "What, like his partners were skimming money or involved with insider trading? Why not report it? No, it's gotta be something worse."

Lizzie: "Maybe Laurence Kleindeinst is mobbed up, and Al was frightened someone would kill him."

Me: "Kleindeinst?"

Lizzie: "He's the one Paddy found in the house in the early hours of the morning."

If you learned something upsetting about the people you worked with, wouldn't you tell your wife? "I suppose you're right, Lizzie. Being scared for his life could explain all the same things as being a bad guy in over his head. Whatever the plan was at the beginning, I get the sense something went wrong. He got involved with people who killed two other people in a carjacking, and now it looks like he's running a classic pump-and-dump scam."

I explained how someone was hyping Excellion Exploration, which I presumed was to sell the now-overpriced stocks to dupes and make a fat profit before the stock tanked. Since I had the two of them trapped in the car, I thought I'd learn more about Albert Cunningham. I asked Chad what growing up had been like.

"Fine. We were never, like, really close. I didn't see him all that much. When I was little, Sunday was our day to do stuff together. He worked like eighty, ninety, a hundred hours a week. Once I started school, I was only home for holidays. Summers, I spent at camp or traveling. He was always practical. He told me to study Spanish, the *de facto* second language of the U.S., and Chinese because of the potential size of their economy."

Lizzie: "I didn't know you spoke Chinese."

"I didn't take that part of my father's advice. Spanish has been great though. I did a junior year abroad, and it's excellent not to need a translator when I do business in Central and South America. Dad isn't big on philosophical discussion. Cash on the barrelhead is his style. I had an allowance at four and had to budget by the time I was eight."

Lizzie: "Seamus insisted our son have an allowance."

Me: "The allowance served Paddy well. He learned to manage his money and has never gotten over his head with debt."

Chad: "Did you charge your son usurious rates? Dad deposited money in my school account on the first of each month. Once, when I was ten or eleven, I ran through the money before the month ended, and there was a new video game coming out. All the kids decided to go into town the day it released and buy their copy. So I called my father and asked him to give me next month's money early. He said I should have planned ahead, and besides, I didn't need the game. If all my friends had it, I could play on their consoles. He totally missed the point that I would be humiliated.

"He agreed to lend me the money, but I had to pay back twenty-five percent more—this for a two-week loan. My first experience with usury. At least once a year he'd ask if I was still playing that computer game. Of course I wasn't. He'd laugh and insist the only reason he gave me the loan was as an object lesson. Fact is, he'd never lend me money unless it was a business proposition."

Me: "But you learned your lesson."

Chad: "Sure. If you need a loan, go to Mom, not Dad. No way would Dad cover a mistake or bad planning. If he is running a scam, he won't lose any sleep over so-called greedy people losing money. He'll consider it as a good object lesson for them."

The mention of the Excellion scam inspired a thought I should have put my finger on earlier: to execute the scheme, he'd still need access to his investment funds. I pulled to the side of the road. "Can one of you drive? I need to make a call."

Chad placed his phone on the center console so he could see the map while driving. I took his place in the backseat and dialed Yves Bouvier at Antimatter Investments.

"News, Mr. McCree?" Yves asked once his secretary connected us. "Where are you calling from?"

"A question. Does Cunningham have remote access to the hedge fund? Can he run trades?"

"Once we understood he was missing, we locked him out. What's going on?"

"Are you aware of Cunningham's investment in Excellion Exploration?"

"Not all investments work out. Its mineral rights have some value, but most likely Al would eventually use the corporate shell for some other purpose. Sell it to someone who wanted to show a long corporate history. You know this. It's done all the time."

"Who's running the trades? His assistant, Kleindeinst? Can you check whether the fund has traded EXEXP in the past week?"

Down the line came tapping on a keyboard. "What the hell is going on, McCree? It closed at a buck fifty-three last night."

"Somebody's pushing a rumor that Rio Tinto will announce an agreement to purchase Excellion at two dollars a share."

"Laurence Kleindeinst is handling the day-to-day activities, but any trades for Cunningham's hedge fund must be approved by me. I have not approved any EXEXP trades. Al may have also owned some personal shares or had them as part of the private portfolios he personally managed. Are you suggesting he's manipulating the stock?"

"If there were a deal with Rio Tinto, given the fund is the majority owner, who would know? Would he share the information with his partners?"

"Of course."

"But assume this was part of Cunningham's shenanigans, whatever they are." Lizzie drew in a big breath. I shook my finger at her so she wouldn't say anything while I tried to extract information from Yves. "Who else," I continued, "would likely know?"

"Kleindeinst—probably. Possibly their administrative assistant. You're not telling me something, McCree. What? You've already destroyed any chance we had to sell ourselves at a reasonable price."

Not my doing, but I understood his anger. "Check on Excellion. Something's up and I suspect it's related to Cunningham's disappearance.

You say you have to approve all transactions before Kleindeinst can make them. How do you know that's happening?"

"You've raised interesting questions, McCree. I'll make sure our compliance folks get to the bottom of this Excellion thing and investigate your suspicions. I expect we will bring this to the SEC's attention to protect ourselves. They'll want to talk with you in person and soon. Where will they find you?"

"Traveling." I disconnected the call.

Lizzie: "Was he threatening you?"

Me: "No, he should report this to the SEC. But did you notice early on he asked where I was. If Antimatter is the reason your husband disappeared, they might have been the ones tracking us."

Thirty-Eight

Abigail waited at the end of the street for Patrick to finish his side and waved him over. "Patrick, muzzle your charm. I had only one person take the survey. You convinced four of them. At this rate, we won't be done for a week."

"Sorry, I guess I got into the role."

"Which is why you're the head of sales and I'm a bodyguard. Keep in mind our only purpose is to find Albert Cunningham, and you have limited time. The next block has the rich folks with ocean views."

"While we walk there, let me try to contact him again." Patrick used his phone and invited StonedGoss to a private chat. No response.

Patrick pressed the ringer on the door of the last townhouse and checked his phone—still no response from StonedGoss. Abigail had already finished her half and was walking to the car to move it to the next street. He pressed the bell for one more rendition of the Westminster chimes' hourly tune in five-four time. He hummed along until the latch of the inside door disengaged. Patrick plastered on his college-student-conducting-survey smile.

Albert Cunningham stood on the other side of the screened door. His eyes widened in astonishment and darted everywhere other than looking directly at Patrick, who could smell the man's fear. A woman remained in the shadows close behind the Jerk.

Patrick forced his smile to remain unchanged. "Good morning."

Cunningham croaked out, "What do you want?" Red splotches dotted his cheeks, his hands trembled.

Act your part, Patrick. Play this thing out. "We're asking local residents to participate in a survey concerning limiting ORVs on—"

"We're renters," the woman said in a southern accent.

"That's okay. We want renters to know their wives and children are safe.

They're out of harm's way. In fact, we want to assure you that *anyone who escapes to the beach will be safe*. Can—"

Cunningham flinched, pulling back his shoulders. Had he been jabbed in the back? "Sorry," he said. "Can't help you." With one hand he prepared to close the door, all the while flicking downward glances.

Patrick followed the glance. Using the hand hidden from the woman, Cunningham made the sign of a gun and pointed at his own stomach.

PATRICK FOUND ABIGAIL AT THE car and related his encounter with Cunningham while she drove to his street.

"Do you think," Abigail asked, "he understood you were telling him his wife and son are safe, and if he got to the beach we could protect him?"

"Unknown. But one of us has to be there in case he does figure it out and makes a break."

"We should contact the police. They can extract him."

Patrick undid the tie and tossed it to the backseat. "We've been down this road. Unless you can guarantee his safety, we should wait."

Abigail pulled the car into a spot from which they could watch the front door of the condo Cunningham was in. She kept the car running so the A/C stayed on. "Guaranteeing anyone's safety's impossible. We've done what we came to do. We've found the guy. You need to leave in two hours to catch your plane. It could take that long to mobilize the police."

Patrick crossed his arms, uncertain what to say, what to do.

"McCree silence won't change my mind. This is not a line I am willing to cross. We contact the police or I leave you here and drive to the airport myself."

Patrick knew she was right. "I suppose I could call nine-one-one. Say I heard screaming inside the house."

"That's probably a felony and would endanger the police because they would misunderstand the situation, maybe rush in when they should be tactical. I suggest a two-pronged approach. You call your mother and give her the address and tell her to call the Savannah police, since they are the ones who want the guy. I'll have more luck than you talking to the local police. My credentials may carry some weight. But in case Cunningham does decode your message, I'll go broil in the sun. The woman saw you, not me. I can hang on the beach without causing suspicion."

"And he would go with you because?"

"I'll use your name and Chad's 'Big Bird' safety phrase. Are we agreed?"

"If Mom thinks it's too risky?"

"This is not her decision, Patrick. It's yours. Right here. Right now. If she won't call Savannah, I will. Same Secret Service handshake crap. The first thing the local people will do is contact Savannah. In fact, I'll call them both. On the slim chance your mother is involved, we should keep this to ourselves until it works out. Are we agreed?"

He nodded once. "Make the calls."

"I'll do it from the beach."

He took her place behind the wheel and cranked the A/C to high while lowering the temperature all the way. The blast of cold caused a shiver but didn't help slow his breathing. Getting into arguments with Abigail triggered an inferiority complex he experienced with no one else. He did not know why and shoved the whole issue into the recesses of his mind.

Abigail had much more confidence in the police than he did. All he could do was will the Jerk to escape to the beach. He agreed with his father and grandmother: his mother had a right to know what happened to her husband. He could at least let her know they had found him and had contacted the police.

Abigail skirted the side of the building and headed toward the beach. He checked his cell phone on the off chance the Jerk had come online. Nothing doing, so he dialed his mother's cell phone to give her the good news.

NO SOONER HAD LIZZIE HUNG up from hearing Paddy's news than she began to lobby for heading straight for North Carolina.

"We're almost to Cincinnati," I argued. "We can all use the rest."

"I wish they had waited on calling the police," Lizzie said. "I'm afraid of what might happen, but I want to make sure he's okay."

"Paddy will call and let you know."

"I want to see him. Don't you get that?"

She was the one under the most stress. I needed to stay calm even if she didn't. "I do understand. I'd want the same thing if it were Abigail. In fact—"

"You *can* see Abigail. She's there."

For the briefest moment, I wavered. But by the time we got there, Abigail might well be on a plane to the West Coast. I steered with my right hand and ironed the wrinkles on my forehead with my left. "I'm sorry I'm not expressing myself well. We don't even know if he'll be in North Carolina. He may end up down in Savannah talking with the police there. We don't know, Lizzie. We're all tired. Once we know where he'll be, we can figure out the best way to get you to see him."

From the backseat Chad piped up. "Hey guys, we still don't know for sure if we were being followed or not. If they did follow us to try to get to Dad, we don't want to do anything to get back on their radar and endanger him before he's rescued."

"Oh," Lizzie said, "I hadn't thought of that."

I tried to catch Chad's eye in the rearview mirror to silently express thanks, but he had already returned to working on his phone.

Lizzie shifted in her seat and rested her head against the car window. "The stress of not knowing is exhausting. I'm taking a nap. Wake me if something happens. And if I haven't told you before, Seamus, I appreciate, really appreciate everything you have done. It's above and beyond."

Just when I thought I had Lizzie pegged, she surprised me again. Or was she manipulating me one more time?

WE ARRIVED AT MY HOUSE to find Mrs. Keenan's golden retriever, Alice, conked out on the porch. Mrs. Keenan must have spotted us from inside. She and a woman I recognized from Shecurity met us on the porch.

"Seamus," Mrs. Keenan said, "I do hope everything is all right? Abigail called and asked me to let the security people in. I've already bought you some staples. I understand you're all grounded for a while. Once you put together a list, I'll do a complete shopping for you."

"Thank you, Mrs. Keenan." I reintroduced myself to the woman from Shecurity. "What arrangements did Abigail make?" With split attention I heard Mrs. Keenan introduce herself to Lizzie (and figure out she was Patrick's mother) and Chad (and sort out he was Lizzie's husband's son).

Alice also introduced herself, sticking her nose into everyone's crotch and not leaving until she had extracted a ransom of ear scratches.

The Shecurity person border-collied everyone inside. "Abigail asked us to sweep the house for bugs—not that she expected any. In any case, you're clear. I'll sweep your car to make sure no one added a tracker. Until the situation is settled, she wants everyone to remain here. We'll have one person with you full time, Mr. McCree. We primarily do electronics and surveillance and such. We've arranged for off-duty Cincinnati policemen to do the actual guarding."

"Lizzie, why don't you and Chad pick your bedrooms? And show him the house? And can you two make a list of groceries—say, two days' worth?"

Chad to Lizzie: "Hey, you've been here before?"

Lizzie gave me a side-glance. "It's a long story."

They trundled off with Alice and Mrs. Keenan in attendance ("I want to make sure you have enough sheets and towels.")

"My apologies for the craziness," I said to the Shecurity person. "I wanted to keep them busy."

She gave me a shrewd look. "And, I gather, not hear the details. We've set up a command post in your front room. Remote cameras on both ends of the block feed monitors. We also operate remote cameras in the back and side yards. Initially, one of us will be here to train each of the off-duty officers on the system."

"Sounds incredibly thorough." *And incredibly stifling.*

"I sent the officer to get coffee supplies since I didn't find any in the house."

From upstairs came the sounds of Alice's toenails trotting down the hallway and the indistinct sounds of Mrs. Keenan and Lizzie's voices. "I'll look over the setup while you check my car?" I motioned toward the room I thought of as a library even though fire and water had destroyed all the books.

They had drawn the curtain in the front window and converted the room into a command center with monitors covering two folding tables shaped into an L. Based on the pictures on the monitor screens, I surmised where they had placed the cameras and wondered what the neighbors thought.

The Shecurity woman was first back and announced my car was clean.

She held open the door to let the rent-an-officer in with the coffee fixings. Lizzie and the gang returned from their tour, requiring an interchange of greetings, handshakes, dog pats, and name trading. I should have handed out little "Hello, my name is" badges. What a zoo.

I ushered Mrs. Keenan and Alice out the door with a promise I'd call with a food list. While the Shecurity woman showed Lizzie and Chad how the monitoring equipment worked, I slipped upstairs to my blessedly quiet bedroom to think. I sat on the bed and exhaustion immediately gnawed at my ambitions. To counteract it, I paced, keeping awake long enough to catch up on a few details that I'd been chewing on during the drive.

I called Abigail to let her know we had arrived and to find out their current status. Went straight to her voicemail. In addition to leaving a message, I texted her the information. I checked the address of the place Cunningham had been staying against the building ownership information Cindy had sent me. A Delaware-based limited liability company owned the condo. In Delaware you can hide an LLC's true owners behind a hired registrant, which in this case was LLC4DEL. Stymied for now, my contemplation about corporate shells moved my thinking to Excellion's stock price.

My app informed me EXEXP had plummeted to a nickel a share. Either the stock manipulation game was finished and the schemers had pocketed their gains, or someone burst the bubble. Everything was either coming together around Albert Cunningham or exploding apart.

Thirty-Nine

PATRICK HAD NOTHING TO DO except watch the clock tick toward the moment he would either have to leave to catch his plane or stay and destroy his relationship with Lisa and everyone at LT2P. The Jerk did not come online. Abigail's phone continued to jump immediately to voicemail. He assumed she was still talking to one police department or the other. How would the police react? How long would it take? He should have asked but hadn't, and now he sat staring at the condo.

He speed-dialed Abigail again. This time it went through.

"Just finished talking to the locals," she said. "I expect—"

Movement from the condo caught his attention. "Hold up. The garage door is opening."

"Tell me what you see." Abigail used her command voice. "Do you see Cunningham?"

Patrick shifted the rental from park to drive. "I can't see anything." He lowered the A/C fan to hear her better.

"Keep talking, Patrick. Paint me the picture."

"The garage door is up, but no one has come out yet. The garbage collectors still haven't come to this street. Maybe they're late with trash? Still no movement. Wait. Brake lights. A car is backing out. Can't tell what kind. The sun's too bright. Two heads."

"Nothing is happening on the beach side of the house."

"Car's out." He pulled off his shades to see better.

"Talk, Patrick. Keep talking. I'm coming."

"Turning around. Two people. It's the Jerk and the woman! He's driving up the street. Real slow. Now speeding up. Where are you?"

He glanced toward where Abigail would appear. Nothing but the shimmer of heat. "Crap." Patrick grabbed his seatbelt and wrenched it across his body. It jammed. He released the tension to try again.

"Patrick. Talk to me."

"They're getting away." He floored the accelerator. The rental roared to life and shot toward the oncoming car. At the last moment, Cunningham pulled left and Patrick slammed the rental into the passenger side front fender. An exploding airbag shoved him hard against his seat.

He sensed rather than knew he needed to get out of the car, but sat for the moment listening to a white-noise hiss. From under his seat a tinny Abigail asked if he was okay. He bent to reach the phone and arcs of pain radiated from his nose and his right shoulder. He hoped his nose wasn't broken again.

Panting to control his pain, he peered through the spiderweb cracks in the windshield at the other car. The crumpled door on the woman's side had her trapped. The Jerk was getting out the driver's side.

He told himself to move, but nothing happened. "Now," he said. "Move now." With a banshee yell, he muscled his door open. Pinning his right arm to his side, he hurried to the Jerk, who jumped out at Patrick's approach and telegraphed a punch at Patrick's head. Without thinking, Patrick kicked the Jerk in the balls. He crumpled to the ground in slow motion and made no move to get up. Peripherally, Patrick caught movement in the car and hipped the door shut.

The cursing woman was crawling over the center console. With a gun.

Patrick dropped on top of the groaning Albert Cunningham, pinning his neck to the ground with a forearm. Patrick tensed against the expected percussive explosion of shots and tried to wriggle himself and Cunningham closer to the car, hoping the car's frame might protect them. He could not move Cunningham's dead weight.

Instead of shots came the creak of an opening metal door. The Jerk squirmed underneath him and Patrick pressed down harder. Where the hell was Abigail? He couldn't take these two by himself. The immediate adrenaline surge passed, leaving him trembling.

Abruptly, the woman's cursing stopped.

"Suspect is secure," Abigail said. "You okay, Patrick?"

"Holding down Cunningham."

"I could use your help. I don't think he's going anywhere. Can you open the driver's door?"

Patrick pressed his forearm hard on the back of Cunningham's neck. "Do not get up until I tell you." He eased off and, on hands and knees, waited for Cunningham to try something. The Jerk stayed curled into a ball, both hands cupped over his crotch.

Patrick attempted to rise, but his once-fluid athletic movements became herky-jerky in his pain. As his eyes reached window level, he realized Abigail had climbed into the backseat and controlled the woman with a rear chokehold.

"Patrick, do exactly as I say. Her gun's in the driver's floor well. Damn good thing she forgot to take off the safety. Pop the trunk. Good. Now to avoid getting your fingerprints on the gun, pick it up with your shirt and carefully place it in the trunk. Remember your weapons training. Don't point it at anyone."

Patrick's shirt was too tight to free enough fabric to grab the gun. He unsuccessfully tried unbuttoning the shirt with his left hand.

Abigail must have seen him struggling. "Never mind the gun now. We need to extract her from the car. Can you put her into a front chokehold while I get around to your side? Grab her right shirt collar—"

"Not sure I can. I hurt a lot."

"Okay, plan two. We need to keep these two separated. Put Cunningham into the rental—backseat. There might be child locks if you can figure it out. Keep him there. I'll get her out. Oh wait, before you do. Where's your cell phone?"

"Somewhere in the car."

"Secure Cunningham, then call nine-one-one in case no neighbors have called in the accident."

From the ground, Cunningham said, "She's got a gravity knife strapped to her right arm. That's what she killed Kaylee with."

"Good to know," Abigail said. "Right now, neither of us can get to it. Mr. Cunningham, would you please accompany Patrick to the car. We need to make sure you're safe until the police arrive. Can you do that for me?"

"Sure."

Patrick warily watched the Jerk struggle to his feet and shuffle to the rental. Patrick opened the backdoor, spotted his Walmart tie and realized he could use it to pick up the gun.

The Jerk collapsed inside. "Can you turn on the A/C? It's boiling in here."

Patrick noticed for the first time the car was no longer running and steam poured from the engine compartment. "Slide into the middle and shut the door. I'll open the windows."

"Why'd you kick me?"

"Because you tried to hit me."

"I did? I guess I was dazed. Your mother? Chad? They're safe?"

"Yes. Now scoot."

Once Cunningham complied, Patrick closed the door and powered down the windows a couple of inches.

Patrick found his cell phone underneath the seat, punched the red emergency button, and reported the accident. He provided the emergency operator the information the police needed to find them. They'd send two tow trucks. "Oh," he said as an afterthought. "I made a citizen's arrest of a woman wanted in Savannah for murder." He disconnected at the operator's direction to, "stay on the line, Mr. McCree."

Cunningham was slumped in the backseat, behaving himself. Patrick wrapped the gun in the tie and shut it in the trunk. Only then did Abigail extract the woman from the car. Maintaining the chokehold, she secured the knife and discovered a set of cuffs in the woman's pocket. Abigail attached those to the woman's ankle and wrist and released the chokehold. A torrent of invective flowed from the woman's mouth.

Patrick returned to the Jerk. "What the hell's going on?"

"You tell me. I flew to Savannah to meet with prospective buyers and the next thing I know, I'm kidnapped by some drug gang. They tell me it's just for a few days, and I figure they're demanding a ransom. The two holding me are dumber than sticks. We're eating this crap food, and I convince them to take me to an ATM so we can get money for something decent. I hoped someone might see me or trace the ATM withdrawals."

"We did." Patrick pointed toward the cursing woman. "Who set you up?"

"I assume my asshole partners. They're the only ones who knew I was traveling to Savannah. You sure Beth and Chad are safe? That Jerome is nasty bad. He killed—"

Patrick was lost. "Jerome?"

Abigail yelled over, "Where is this guy, Jerome?"

Multiple sirens wailed in the near distance.

Cunningham pointed to the woman. "Sally's partner in crime. We left because he called, said you'd found us. Name's Rozelle. He's the one who was keeping an eye on Beth and Chad. That's why I couldn't escape. Sally used Facebook or something to learn where we live and check on Beth . . . the work she did for charities and stuff. I knew they'd kill me, so I tried to make them enough money to leave the country."

"The Excellion Exploration manipulation?"

Cunningham shot Patrick a look of surprise.

"My father guessed you were running a pump and dump."

"I had to stay alive, right?"

"You've skipped ahead," Abigail said. "Why didn't you try to escape from Kaylee on one of your ATM runs or at the bakery?"

"Because she had a gun. And, and, they told me they'd kill my family if I did."

The wail of sirens grew louder and Patrick thought he saw flashing lights at the far end of the street.

"Patrick," Abigail commanded, "stand away from the car with your hands out where the cops can see them."

Abigail had moved away from the trussed Sally and held her hands open and away from her body. Patrick mirrored her behavior, although raising his injured arm brought tears to his eyes.

"And Patrick?" Abigail's voice jerked him away from the pain. "Do not talk to the police without a lawyer present. I have no clue what is and isn't legal in North Carolina."

Two squad cars pulled up and officers exited with their guns drawn.

Sally wailed that she was a victim of kidnapping and thank God they had rescued her.

Forty

I MUST HAVE FALLEN ASLEEP while I was wondering what was happening in Duck, North Carolina because I lost three hours and woke to the ringing of my cell phone. Caller ID announced Cindy Nelson.

"Patrick missed his plane and he's not answering his phone."

Trying to make sense of Cindy's statement, I uttered, "Huh?"

"I'm at O'Hare. To meet him."

Her words drove breath from my lungs and filled the space with dread. I was sufficiently awake to hide my feelings by adopting my business voice. "Last I knew, he and Abigail were waiting for the police to arrive. What time was his flight? Maybe they're held up talking with the police. Or maybe he's in the air?"

Twisting to the right to stretch, my spine realigned with an audible pop. Cindy was rapid-firing flight details and a connection in Charlotte, and I was not tracking it at all. "Wait a minute. Did you try Abigail? Let me call her. Maybe she knows if he caught a later flight. I'll call you right back."

I disconnected before she could reply. My call to Abigail went to voicemail. "It's Seamus. Please call. We—Cindy and I—don't know where Paddy is—and I don't know where you are. We're both worried as hell. Tell me everything is okay." I hung up, shaking my head at such a disjointed message.

Using the phone's browser, I searched on "Duck, NC police" with today's date. Result one was a link to a week-old Duck police blotter. I found nothing newer. A few results down allowed me to search an interactive portion of an Outer Banks news website where readers post breaking news. Nothing there.

Rather than try to figure out the best way of getting information on my own, I explained the situation to the off-duty Cincinnati police officer monitoring the video screens and asked if he had any ideas on how I could check.

"Why not call the Duck police?"

Duh.

I found and dialed their number and explained my concerns to the non-emergency dispatch officer. Did they have information on my son, Seamus Patrick McCree? He put me on hold.

In something of a daze I walked to the kitchen and poured a glass of water, downed it and was working on another before a sergeant whose name I did not catch came on the line.

"Sir, can you verify who you say you are by telling me your son's date of birth?"

I spit out the date. "Is he all right?"

"Yes, sir. We are investigating an incident in which your son was involved. Let me assure you the emergency room doctors indicate he is fine other than some bruises. We are currently discussing the incident with him. That is all I am at liberty to say."

"Emergency room? My God, what happened? He's okay? Is Abigail Hancock okay? Can I talk to either one of them?"

"We are also speaking with her."

My heart raced as I paced the kitchen, burning away the physical need to act. "And Albert Cunningham?"

"How is it you know Mr. Cunningham?"

"He's my ex-wife's current husband." Even as I said the words, they sounded funny to me. "Can you tell me the nature of the incident? I can get his wife on the phone."

They would not release details. He wanted to know where I was and how to get in touch with me. In addition to my phone number, I gave him Lizzie's and Cindy's numbers. In retrospect, I don't think I was operating at full power because I was so worried about what had sent Paddy to the emergency room and whether Abigail was all right.

Conversation complete, I started a list on my phone of things I could do while I waited. Try to learn what caused Excellion's stock price to tumble? Determine who was behind the LLC owner of the place in Duck where Cunningham was staying? My thumbs hovered over the keyboard waiting for my brain to signal another idea.

Holy smokes, Cindy was awaiting my call, and I needed to tell Lizzie to call the Duck police to see if she could get more information on her husband.

Come on brain. Don't fail me now.

◇◇◇

PATRICK HAD NEVER BOUGHT INTO the "if it doesn't kill you, it makes you stronger" theory. However, he now realized his previous time in police custody had made him better prepared for this encounter. He had tried to forget his experiences of the Iron County Michigan sheriff's office incarcerating him and his father a couple of years ago. Now he embraced it. The noise and confusion, inmates catcalling and whistling at the new arrivals. Even the deep clang of security doors closing didn't intimidate him. He knew the police were interviewing each of them separately, checking stories, piecing together what really happened.

He followed Abigail's warning to seek legal counsel, which threw a monkeywrench into their proceedings, turning the police officers against him. He exacerbated their antagonism by insisting they take him to the emergency room to evaluate his injuries from the airbag.

The emergency room doctor went through a concussion protocol and determined no scrambled brain. Patrick had suffered a severely bruised right shoulder from the airbag, but no fractures, cracks, or separations. Even his nose was intact. Good news all around. While waiting for assistance at emergency, Patrick eeny-meenied his choice from the list of defense attorneys. She was at the jail waiting for him. Once through the booking process, the police provided them an interview room. Patrick required more than an hour to bring her up to speed.

"Here's the thing," she said. "You managed to find the one state in the union without a citizen's arrest law. Since you didn't transport anyone after apprehending them, your actions technically aren't an arrest, but a detention. Our laws allow a citizen to detain someone if they are committing a felony. Unfortunately, we don't know this Sally woman was actually committing a felony, do we? This," she checked her notes, "Albert Cunningham may not have been unlawfully restrained. If the two were heading out to get a carton of cream . . ."

Leaving it hanging gave Patrick the idea he was in a world of trouble if the Jerk wasn't a kidnap victim. "What do I tell the police? Or are you suggesting I don't tell them anything?"

The lawyer nervously tugged at her hair. "This Sally had the gun. She had the knife. You have the IM conversations with Mr. Cunningham. If a felony was not in progress, we would still have excellent chances with any jury regardless of what the law says. They'd put themselves in your shoes and be proud of what you've done. I think your best strategy is to be open. Tell them how you learned of Mr. Cunningham's disappearance and skip ahead to your messaging with StonedGoss. Some of the stuff in the middle—you're on pretty shaky ground."

She ruffled her hair with both hands. "Your other choice is to remain silent and rely on the police to piece everything together based on what Ms. Hancock tells them combined with whatever Mr. Cunningham and the Sally woman say. Cunningham and Sally won't say the same things, and both will probably disagree with Ms. Hancock's statement. So, if you don't talk, they'll probably keep you locked up for a good while."

Which he could not be. He owed it to Lisa and his partners to be available and devoted to LT2P. "Why? How?"

"Oh, no doubt you've broken a number of laws. For example, they could charge you with reckless driving, aggravated assault with a motor vehicle, probably stealing the rental, since you weren't authorized to drive it. The list is only limited by their imagination. Doesn't mean they'd win, but they can tie you up for a long, long time. As it is, you're likely to be spending tonight in jail. My guess is they'll find a reason to hold you until the folks from Georgia get a chance to interview you. I suspect the locals will want to involve the state experts. And with your suspicion of stock market manipulation, the feds will want their piece."

Her words pressed down upon him. Abigail had been right; they should have called the police earlier. The past was past; he could not change it. Focus on the now. He closed his eyes and asked himself what he could do to make things better. He couldn't attend the LT2P meeting in the morning, but if he could get out of jail, he could join them using FaceTime. Lisa would be justifiably pissed because he would miss the client meetings scheduled for later that day. Still, out of jail he could do something; in jail he was worthless to his partners.

"I have a make-or-break business phone call the first thing tomorrow morning. Let's fully cooperate so I can get out of here tonight."

She shook her head. "Even if you had started singing like a diva when they first questioned you, it's unlikely they'd release you before the Georgia folks show up tomorrow."

Patrick could feel the anger well up. He closed his eyes and concentrated on his breath. *Do not kill the messenger.* The person he was most pissed off at, most disappointed with, was clearly himself. "I understand their position. This call is super important. If I sing like a canary, do you think we can arrange a FaceTime or even make a conference call tomorrow morning early, like, seven thirty? If not, I have a bunch of people I need you to call."

Her grim mouth told Patrick the conference call was unlikely. "We'll ask. You need to use the facilities before we start?"

I COLLECTED CHAD AND WE found Lizzie in her room. I told her the news; she naturally wanted to drive to North Carolina to see her husband.

"None of us is in any kind of shape to do another all-nighter," I said. "Besides, we don't even know where he'll be. They might extradite him down to Savannah, and we'd be chasing our tails."

"But we'd be closer. He needs me."

I had the good sense to not express my doubt on that subject.

Her eyes took on a calculating appearance. "Our son needs us."

"Lizzie, I had the same first reaction. Getting in a car and driving will not do a single thing to help either one of them. We need to stay by our phones so we can respond to whatever happens, and we need to remain flexible. Maybe you can get more information from the police because you're his wife."

"Remember, guys," Chad said, "we came here because my father thought someone was threatening us. That guy might be out for revenge now. I'm with Seamus. We should wait and let the dust settle."

Chad repaired to his room. To avoid Lizzie, who wanted to continue the discussion, I followed Chad's example. I don't know what the two of them did for dinner; having no appetite, I skipped it altogether.

Paddy's lawyer called in the evening, the upshot being I was relieved to hear Paddy really was fine, and the only thing I could immediately do for him was to front the lawyer's retainer. I maxed out a credit card; I'd worry later where the money was coming from.

At Paddy's request, relayed through his lawyer, I called Lisa and informed her Paddy would not be able to attend or call in to the partner's meeting.

"That is . . . disappointing. I'll leave it there. One of the big accounting firms is targeting LT2P, telling our clients we must have financial problems because we canceled the last round of investor funding. We didn't cancel, we sold that round of stock to you. We need to strategize how to counteract their push, which is starting to gain momentum. Patrick had scheduled a number of meetings with our largest clients for this week. Can you conference in with us tomorrow? With Patrick out of commission, maybe we can find a way to use your contacts?"

I wasn't sure what help I could be, but I was happy to try and agreed to call in at 7:30 a.m. my time.

"Thank you, Seamus. We are close to the summit, but we either scramble past this obstruction and plant our flag—or an avalanche of client defections takes us out, and we are left with nothing but memories."

Yep, and memories don't put food on the table.

THERE IS NOTHING LIKE A new crisis to drive old traumas out of my mind. The nap proved I could sleep in the house in my own bedroom. Exhaustion proved I could sleep the whole night through without ghosts or chase dreams. I awoke early enough to squeeze in a five-mile run after telling the off-duty officer my plans and ignoring his grumbling. I returned in time for a quick shower before calling in to LT2P for the conference call.

The fridge contained no Dr Pepper, diet or regular—I made a note to ask Mrs. Keenan to buy some. Next to the coffee fixings, I found a box of Tetley tea she must have bought. I boiled a mug of water in the microwave and dunked the bag.

To read their body language, such an important component of communication, I videoconferenced into the LT2P meeting using a phone app. Lisa propped her phone against a stack of books on the conference room table.

It had been some time since I had seen Paddy's partners. Lisa and her pixie cut were as cute as I remembered. The first time I had met her she was dressed in cutoffs and a tank top. Now she looked professional in a dove-gray pant suit and silk blouse, although for this internal meeting she had her blazer draped across a spare chair and her feet tucked under her. I had once jokingly said I wanted to buy stock in Lisa. In a sense I had done that with my financial commitment to LT2P, but I'd still bet long on Lisa if she put herself up on one of those online funding platforms. Tom

Nickles, the treasurer, sat to her right and Pete Vermouth, the operations head, sat on her left.

"Last week," Lisa said, "a client told Patrick that one of our esteemed competitors was spreading false rumors about our financial stability. I checked with a number of our other clients. They've received the same spiel. We're being targeted in a blitz, and I'm afraid it will be the excuse some IT heads need to dump us and return to their old cozy relationships. We're in fine shape, and our upcoming sale makes it moot anyway. Unfortunately, we can't tell anyone of the sales agreement because the contract forbids it. And we've purposely not released information concerning our last round of financing because it was a private transaction with Seamus."

"Let me jump in, Lisa." I squeezed the tea bag against the mug with a spoon, fished it out, and cautiously sipped, burning my tongue anyway. "Ouch. That was dumb—not you, me. I tried to scald my mouth. Anyway, you have my permission to reveal anything you want concerning your financing with me. Second, Tom—how quickly can you put together a financial statement showing current cash position and the last couple of months' cash flow? I assume those would indicate LT2P is solid?"

Tom was explaining their current financial position when a loud pounding at their door interrupted him. Pete answered the door and returned with several individuals. The jumbled sound of people noise picked up by the phone's microphone made no sense until one guy came into focus. His jacket read FBI.

He approached Lisa. "Lisa Latoya? You are under arrest. We have a warrant to seize all computers, electronic storage devices, and relevant files." The agent handed a piece of paper to Pete.

The mug slipped from my hand and crashed to the kitchen floor. It had been nearly a decade since the FBI had arrested Paddy, then a high schooler, for hacking the DOD's computers and publishing the top brass's expense reports. All the worries, all the fears I had pushed aside through the years, rushed into my soul, filling me with dread.

Lisa rose and held her hands in front of her. "What charges?"

I could not breathe with a gorilla bouncing on my chest. Was I having a heart attack?

"Let's just say we've been waiting a long time to catch you, Sherlock. Now, where is Patrick McCree?"

Forty-One

THE POLICE IN NORTH CAROLINA released Patrick thirty hours after taking him into custody. His lawyer had racked up a ton of billable hours attending Patrick's "interviews" by local, North Carolina, and Chatham County detectives, as well as both the FBI and DEA. He was to meet with the feds again tomorrow because—or at least he feared—they had suspicions concerning the whole chain of events.

Abigail was waiting for him. "Let's get you a shower and some clean clothes before we eat and strategize."

While Abigail drove to the hotel, where she had rebooked their rooms, Patrick checked voicemail. Nine messages. In strained silence, he listened to the news of Lisa's arrest, LT2P's computers being confiscated, and the FBI specifically wanting to talk with him, maybe arrest him too.

"Are you okay, Patrick? You're ghost-white."

Patrick held up a finger to indicate Abigail should wait until he finished the phone messages. By the ninth, he had the general picture. While the FBI in Illinois were searching for him, he had spent several hours talking to other FBI agents in North Carolina. He'd need to decide whether their lack of communication would hold through tomorrow, or whether he was better off turning himself in to the local folks. He could not ask Abigail; he knew she'd say he should turn himself in.

In his gut, Patrick was certain his mistake on the phone of referring to Lisa as Sherlock had triggered the whole raid. It might be paranoid thinking, but having worked with the NSA, he knew they monitored virtually all communication in the U.S., their computer programs designed to detect key phrases. Because the legendary Sherlock had allegedly hacked government databases, he—well, Patrick knew Sherlock was actually a she—had probably been labeled a domestic terrorist and included in the key phrases some FISA court judge had approved for domestic spying.

His dad's quick thinking had given LT2P at least a chance for survival. While cops were destroying the place and working through the employee list, interviewing each one, his father had found a nearby furnished rent-an-office place and arranged the installation of a bunch of computers on short-term lease. After the police finished with each employee, the person set up shop in the new offices and downloaded backup from the cloud. They had lost a day—but only a day—and were operational.

A quickie internet search found no news of Lisa's arrest. The FBI might or might not make an announcement, but probably some employee had already published it on social media. Clients would soon hear, and everything they had worked for would come crashing down around them. He had, at most, one day to formulate and execute a plan.

MY PHONE CHIRPED A SKYPE invitation from Abigail. Nine p.m. already? Where had the day gone? I clicked accept and thought about answering with something mildly provocative and was glad I stuck with a plain hello.

Paddy's head came into view. "It's your son."

His eyes were hollow black pits, his brows pinched tight with worry. An invisible raptor dug its claws into my back and neck, tightening my muscles and shooting pain up and down my backbone. He quickly assured me he was fine. I collapsed onto a chair, realizing my dinner plate sat untouched on the side table where Lizzie had put it. I had run all day on energy reserves and Diet Dr Pepper Mrs. Keenan had kindly supplied, and I was whipped.

"We don't trust my phone, and I have made it permanently unavailable, okay? And Dad, thanks so much for everything you've done for LT2P today. The shit'll hit the fan tomorrow or maybe Friday once word gets to our clients. I've been thinking. What if we appoint you president to replace Lisa? Gray hair. Respected. You could call our bigger clients and explain we are up and running? If they stay with us, we have a better shot of keeping the smaller clients."

I propped my phone on the dinner plate so I didn't have to hold it as if I were taking a selfie. "Have you talked this over with Tom and Pete? I'm working on another angle."

"Pete suggested it. He and Tom were awed by how quickly you got everyone back working. And the speech you gave everyone a couple of hours ago? The employees are all still working, making up for lost time. Pizza and beer was a good idea. We're thinking gray hair may be a real asset right now. What do you think?"

I had spent my day salvaging LT2P from the wreckage of the FBI raid, but had worried the whole time whether Paddy was in real trouble. From his business-like manner, I sensed I shouldn't ask. The best way I could support him was to back his proposal, even though I didn't think it stood a snowball's chance on its own.

"We can try, but let me zip another thought past you. What if we offered Behemoth a new deal? I had Pete email me your current agreement with them. What if we suggest they close the deal two days hence, on Friday? In return for the expedited closing, we defer all stockholder payments for a year and make the level of the payout contingent on revenues a year out. Getting your clients safely in Behemoth's hands might be more reassuring than whatever I can tell them."

Some would characterize what followed as a pregnant pause. He ducked his head and rubbed it with the heels of both hands. I wanted to reach out and hug him. My focus shifted as Abigail floated past in the background. Where was their hotel? I wondered, but knew better than to ask.

He looked back into the camera and in a soft voice he said, "But Dad, you need the money before then."

"Paddy, listen to me. No clients, no deal. No deal, no money. Ever. You, Tom, Pete, and I have enough votes to approve a new deal. If you guys need to touch base with your other investors, fine, but don't let it slow us down."

"Let me talk with the others. I'd better write up a proxy in case . . . well, you know, you were Skyping when the raid happened. How's Mom doing? Does she know?"

"I made an executive decision not to add more to her worries. To be honest, I alternately want to ring her neck and sing her praises. And if I think about it, I feel guilty because I've abandoned trying to figure out what was up with Cunningham because of . . . this. She thinks she needs to be by his side and is chafing against my insisting she's still at risk while this Jerome guy is still loose. Fortunately, Chad agrees with me and talked her down. I almost forget Chad's around. He stays in his room doing his business on the internet. He's stealing access from Mrs. Keenan, who never encrypted her signal, but she wouldn't care. Anyway, your mom has been very civil, thanks me profusely for going out of my way to help, and has taken care of cooking meals. If you decide to tell her about your situation, please give me a heads up first."

"I can't deal with Mom now. Do you want me to conference in Pete and Tom?"

"No, you guys talk. I'll be up for a while." *What an understatement.* I was too worried to sleep. The only thing keeping me marginally sane was focusing on helping LT2P. "Let me know what you decide. Can you put Abigail on for a sec?"

The picture wobbled as he carried the phone to Abigail, who was lying on a bed. "Seamus, I have to say, you and your family sure do make life interesting."

"Nice. I miss you too. Truly, I sure do wish I were lying there next to you. Do you agree Lizzie and Chad are still in danger?"

"Keep the protection through the weekend, then reevaluate. Being ex-Secret Service carries some weight, so I'm plugged in with the locals. There's a BOLO for Jerome Rozelle and the car. I don't believe the police here will charge Patrick with anything. And the other thing? I've suggested he discuss options with his lawyer. If I hear anything, anything at all, that makes me officially know something, he and I will need to part company before I'm forced to turn him in. I hope you understand."

"Who knew being in love had so many complications?"

She laughed. "Only with McCrees and all your complexity. Look, don't contact us. We'll contact you."

"Why?"

"Right now my phone is safe because the Chicago feds don't have a clue your son and I are together. They'll make that connection soon." With a closing-door sound, her picture faded to black.

It struck me now was a good time to apply the first stanza of the Saint Francis Serenity Prayer. I could not affect what the FBI thought Paddy had done wrong. I could not immediately affect how quickly I was running out of money. It was too late in the day to call and find out how Mom was doing at Sugarbush. I could do nothing to address my concern that Abigail and I were moving apart rather than closer together as I wished. I *could* help LT2P survive.

Forty-Two

If I had ever thought Mom's idea of running a bed and breakfast might be fun, the experience of having Lizzie, Chad, and off-duty cops in the house, even with Lizzie doing all the cooking, convinced me I preferred my privacy.

I spent all Thursday on LT2P business, other than brief breaks to check up on my mother—Sugarbush reported she was doing well—and provide documentation for the mortgage application. I set up three Google Alerts. One for Paddy in case there was news of the FBI searching for him. Another was for Lisa to learn when her arrest became public. The third was for Jerome Rozelle—I didn't expect anything, but it wouldn't hurt. Lisa's alert generated tons of traffic, but nothing of interest. Paddy's and Rozelle's alerts produced nothing.

From the get-go, the LT2P kids had assured me their company had a zero-tolerance policy for hacking. The feds would find nothing illegal relating to the business. Because the FBI had not announced Lisa's arrest, I crafted an offer Behemoth would be stupid to refuse if they wanted to be in the IT security business for financial institutions.

With the kids' approval I made it a no-risk investment for Behemoth: we sold them the clients, retained any and all liabilities, and made the final sales price contingent on revenues a year later. If they didn't snap up LT2P, we promised them we'd sell to the auditors. We agreed on terms quickly, but by four p.m., something within the corporation had put brakes to signing. Given time, the bureaucracy of any large corporation will find hoops to jump through and hurdles to surmount. I needed to eliminate their belief they had time to dillydally.

While on one more conference call with their legal counsel discussing some triviality, I pardoned myself to "take a phone call." There was no call. I left the phone and walked to a corner of the room where I spoke just loudly enough for the folks at Behemoth to "overhear" parts of my faked conversation with one of the large accounting firms. Dropping the accounting firm's name, a reference to a backup deal, and LT2P's name, I hoped to leave the impression LT2P would sign with the accountants tomorrow if Behemoth did not sign in the next few hours.

My tactic bordered on dishonest, but this deal was truly in Behemoth's best interest. They knew it and signed within the hour.

Friday, I snuck out for an easy run. I was still sore from the accident, but improving quickly. I returned to discover Yves Bouvier of Antimatter Investments in my dining room chatting amicably with Lizzie and Chad. He had arrived dressed for yachting: double-breasted blazer, white pants, and boat shoes, no socks.

I blurted, "How the hell did you know we were here?"

"My fault, Seamus," Lizzie said. "I had to sign a withdrawal request to get my money from the hedge fund, and I told him to messenger it here." She waved her hands in surrender. "Don't say it was stupid. The proof is sitting here. I figured we'd be safe with the police guarding us."

"And," Yves said, "I hoped Mrs. Cunningham had power of attorney and could sign the partnership dissolution papers for Al. Alas, since he is back among us, that part of the trip was for naught."

I put on a game face and asked if I could speak with Yves privately. Lizzie gave me an inquisitive look, but escorted Chad from the room. I apologized for sitting on a radiator cover to prevent my sweat from staining the furniture, and asked what he knew about Cunningham's current situation.

He shot his cuffs and looked directly at me. "Hadn't heard a word until Mrs. Cunningham informed me he had been arrested. Any idea when he'll be released? We have some business." He picked up the legal papers.

"Nope. I assume you engineered the Excellion stock price crash?"

"Sure." He hesitated. "With the SEC's knowledge."

Possible, but not how the SEC usually worked. "Cunningham was staying in a condo in Duck, North Carolina owned by a Delaware LLC. His or someone else's at the firm?"

"That explains the squatters. The rental agency Donald—you met my other partner—uses to manage the place in Duck called to tell him someone had used the place. Al's been there hunting several times. He'd know it's empty this time of year and where the spare key is kept."

Certainly possible, but if the partners were behind Cunningham's kidnapping, they could have chosen the unused condo to stash him. I had no clue who had links to someone in Savannah to arrange the original kidnapping. "Why the partnership dissolution?"

Yves scratched the underside of his jaw. "After Al's stunt, we can't sell. Donald and I figure we can retain more value by splitting the pieces. The two of us are still valuable commodities."

Left unsaid was that Cunningham was the rotten apple, and they needed to remove the good apples before the rot spread. Probably true, regardless if Cunningham were villain or victim.

He raised a sheaf of papers. "If you have any influence, it's a fair deal. If they don't take it, we'll have to sue."

"I'm sure you already expressed your feelings to Mrs. Cunningham and Chad. When does Lizzie get her money?"

"We'll liquidate her position today. Three days to clear, so Wednesday."

"Ever used a keylogger program?"

His face curled into a puzzled expression. "What's that?"

Hell, he was a poker player; I was unlikely to read him. He tried to get more information about Cunningham, which I deflected. Likewise, he demurred to provide any information about partnership matters including what would happen with Laurence Kleindeinst.

"I offered to give either of your guests a ride home on the Gulfstream I rented for today. They should pack if they want to go."

I was afraid Lizzie would take him up on his offer, but she surprised me. She had committed to staying through the weekend unless something changed, and she would. Chad said he'd stay with her. Yves called a cab and departed for the airport.

While showering, I replayed our conversation, considered all I knew, and concluded I had no clue what was really going on. Not why Cunningham flew to Savannah. Not who knew someone in Savannah to arrange the kidnapping. Not who drained the accounts nor where the money was. Not, not, not.

Part of me wanted to follow my curiosity; emotionally, I wanted to hibernate. I had helped Lizzie find her man. The police presumably had things under control, meaning I could and should return from a life deferred. Except Jerome was still out there.

I couldn't protect Lizzie forever, nor was it my responsibility. With Lizzie giving away our location to the Antimatter folks, I wanted to get Abigail's thoughts on what we should do. Contacting Abigail might endanger Paddy, so I put the thought out to the universe for Abigail to call me.

Good news arrived early afternoon. A Google Alert informed me Connecticut state troopers had stopped a stolen car and apprehended one Jerome Rozelle of Savannah, Georgia after a high-speed chase on I-84. *What was he doing in Connecticut?*

Lizzie wanted to start driving home immediately. I said we needed time to dismantle the surveillance setup. We could leave first thing in the morning. I'd be able to continue from her place to Uncle Mike's to return the car and see my mother. "All right," she conceded.

Those plans changed with a Skype call from Abigail. The audio connected before the video, and her excited voice said, "Breaking news. Gather the Cunninghams."

Abigail's face appeared on the screen, and my heart kicked up a notch. "So tell me," I said. She insisted I gather Lizzie and Chad so she could say it only once. They came galloping down the stairs at my call.

"Mr. Cunningham's made some kind of deal with federal prosecutors. My source says he'll be released on his own recognizance, but have an ankle monitor. He meets with the feds in New York City Monday morning."

Lizzie became all choked up, tears wreaking havoc with her makeup. Chad asked, "When?"

"I'm told within the hour. And Seamus, your son also has a Monday appointment to meet with the feds in New York. Patrick met with them here on Thursday. Fortunately, the FBI's right and left hand still didn't connect the dots, so they released him. He went off-grid and used his lawyer to negotiate his surrender."

My guts clenched at the word surrender. "That seems really weird."

"He can give you the details when you see him. Mr. Cunningham can't take any kind of public transportation because his ID was stolen in Savannah. Patrick asked if I can take them both to New Jersey and I've agreed. To be honest, Mrs. Cunningham, I think Patrick hopes it's an opportunity to grill your husband for eight hours, although I'm sure the lawyers have told him to keep mum. If you three leave immediately, you should arrive shortly after us."

I told her of my plans. "Why not wait until morning?"

"Because I don't want to be responsible for figuring out where to keep Mr. Cunningham overnight. Once I get him safely home, I can breathe easier. From what you've told me, there's plenty of room at the Cunninghams to put everyone up for a night. Saturday I can dump the rental, and you and I can return Uncle Mike's car. We can visit your mother and take a few days for ourselves. It's been a while." She winked.

I liked the sound of the last part, and I was probably too wired to get much sleep anyway. "We still have a few things to take care of here. We probably won't get there until two or so in the morning."

Everyone agreed to the plan and Lizzie and Chad left me alone on the connection with Abigail. "Do you think Paddy will want me to stick around while he deals with the feds? For support or anything?"

"Ask when you see him." She chuckled and, using her sexy Lauren Bacall voice, said, "It doesn't matter where we are, it's your body I'm after."

A tingle of anticipation ran through me. "Hey, I just had one of my brilliant ideas. What if we set up an Agatha Christie-type thing and invite everyone involved in this fiasco for a Saturday get-together at the Cunninghams. You'll have him there. I'm bringing Lizzie and Chad. Get the Truverts and their kid—I can't remember his name. Invite the Antimatter Investment people: the two principals and Laurence Kleindeinst."

"Why the hell would we want to do that?"

"Christie's Hercule Poirot said if he could get the suspects together, someone would say something to give themselves away. Somebody within that group has the answers."

"Now, Seamus—"

"Hold on, hold on. Better. We set it up as a party to celebrate Cunningham's safe homecoming. Invite all those people and let them know the police have put it all down to a kidnap-for-hire ring that pulled his name from a *Wall Street Journal* article or some such line. Everyone will be there, nice and relaxed, and we spring the trap, put the screws to them, and see what happens. You and your trusty Sig Sauer will be there to protect us."

A tired sigh sounded through the phone's speakers. "Let's get everyone there safely and let the police sort it all out."

"I'll talk to Lizzie and Chad on the way back and see what they think."

"It's a terrible idea. Give it up and spend *your* time thinking of *me*."

Forty-Three

WE HIT THE ROAD ONCE Shecurity finished dismantling the surveillance setup. Everyone was anxious to get there and agreed to limit our stops to pee breaks and fast food takeout. I drove, Lizzie was in the death seat, and Chad relaxed in the back. Once I got us on the highway, I broached my idea of a welcome-home party for Saturday. I didn't tell them my reason was to put all the players into a confined space and hope something boiled over.

Lizzie dramatically slapped the dashboard. "I am not inviting Al's low-life partners into our home. Them, wanting me to sign papers for Al that he would never sign. If I never see them again it will be too soon."

Chad laughed. "Tell us how you really feel, Beth."

So much for my great idea. I consoled myself with the thought that, unlike a Christie novel, in the real world, getting everyone together on such short notice was impossible. Our chitchat died away. Lizzie laid her head back and closed her eyes. Chad appeared to be playing games on his phone. I silently gnawed over what was next with Abigail and me.

Abigail and I had been like two sine waves with different periods. We were rarely at the same point at the same time, either physically or, I worried, emotionally. This year's trip with Mom, seeing my house in Cincinnati again, staying in it and working through my psychological reactions to the traumatic events that had occurred there, made me realize I wanted something different. I wanted our waves to come together. In ten hours our physical waves would join, but would our emotional waves be in sync?

By the time we got to the entrance of Lizzie's property, I was as nervous as I had been before my first real date with a girl. I punched in the security code. The gate swung open. We proceeded up the long driveway in silence, Lizzie and Chad leaning forward in anticipation. Upstairs and down, light poured from all the windows, casting elongated parallelograms onto the front lawn. A wide yellow ribbon now decorated a large oak in the center of the lawn.

I wondered who had put it up. Had Lizzie ordered it done when she called the Truverts and let them know the master was coming home and to expect company? Maybe the Truverts did it themselves in celebration. What had Cunningham thought when he arrived with Abigail and Paddy?

I parked Uncle Mike's Crown Vic between a car with North Carolina plates—Abigail's rental I presumed—and Chad's classic Corvette, sitting where he'd left it earlier in the week.

Lizzie was out of the car before I had it in "park." She raced up the steps. Her husband greeted her at the front door with a powerful hug. With a burst of empathetic wishfulness, I hoped this experience might bring them together. I was pleased to discover my earlier desire to see Lizzie suffer for the pain she had caused me had vanished. I smiled to myself at this successful baby step in my personal growth. Hopefully, my next planned step would be a giant leap.

I unpacked the trunk, setting Lizzie's three bags on the ground next to my single traveling bag and Chad's backpack.

Chad picked it up. "Go ahead, Seamus. I'll throw my stuff into my car and bring in whatever you can't carry."

I pulled up the handles on Lizzie's two largest suitcases, stuck my bag on top of one, and hauled everything toward the house. My heart was doing the pitter-patter thing it does in anticipation of seeing Abigail. A nervous tightness filled my chest. I tried to see past the still-entwined couple to find her. If she had already gone to bed, it would spoil my plan. No, lights were on throughout the house. No one was in bed.

I rattled the wheeled bags up the bricked drive toward the front door. "Okay, you two," I said. "Get a room."

They broke their grasp and shuffled inside with arms still wrapped around each other. All they needed for a three-legged race was to bind together their adjoining legs and a crowd to cheer them on.

I followed them inside. "Lizzie, where do you want these?" I indicated her bags with a tilt of my head.

"Sorry, Seamus. You haven't met Al, have you?"

I let go of the bags and shook hands with Lizzie's husband. His handshake was firm, not typical Wall Street macho-squeeze-until-one-of-us-yells-uncle tough.

"Thanks for keeping her safe," he said. "I'll take her bags."

"And I'll take yours," Abigail said from somewhere above me.

I spun toward her voice. My heart's pitter-patter became a full-fledged gallop. She and Paddy sat partway up the grand staircase, apparently enjoying the show. Standing next to me, Lizzie was saying, "Hello, Patrick. And you must be Abigail. I am so pleased to meet you."

My vision narrowed to include only Abigail. A single strand of her hair had escaped the elastic holding her ponytail and curved in front of her ear. She wore simple gold hoop earrings, a peasant blouse flowing over blue jeans. Her feet were bare.

I left my bag in the entryway and walked toward the staircase, which I now noticed had yellow ribbon decorating the two newel posts at the foot of the stairs. I sensed Lizzie was walking with me, but my attention focused on Abigail's expression: a wide smile decorated her glowing face.

Abigail rose and moved a couple of steps down the stairs before I remembered my plan. "Wait right there." I held my hand in a stop sign. Abigail paused a half dozen steps above me, her left hand on the railing, right foot on the next lower step, left foot flexed to join its partner below. Patrick's expression changed to quizzical. I sensed Lizzie had moved toward me.

"This way," I said, "I don't have to kneel." I steepled my hands in front of my chest. "After so much driving, my knees are creaky. Will you marry me?"

Abigail's smile melted like hot wax.

From the doorway Chad said, "Hey, how touching is that?"

Patrick's expression widened in surprise.

Abigail's eyes narrowed, and she reached behind her back.

A vise gripped my chest and I couldn't breathe.

A loud bang jolted the reptilian part of my brain into action. I dove sideways and drove Lizzie to the floor under my weight. I tried to bring my hands in front of me to break our fall, but in the seemingly infinite space between thought and action, I could not extract them from their earlier prayerful position. My weight pounded Lizzie onto the floor, knocking her breath out in a whoosh. I rolled off her and rose to face the noise. At a second report, pain exploded in my chest.

From above me came two answering shots.

Lizzie screamed "Albert!" into my ear and struggled to get out from under me. I wanted to move. I thought I would move. I could not move.

Through the din of Lizzie's wail came Abigail's calm voice. "Officer, three people have been shot. Send police and ambulances to—Elisabeth, what's your address?"

Forty-Four

I AWOKE IN THE ROBERT Wood Johnson University Hospital in New Brunswick with a tube down my nose, a stinging catheter, wires running every which way, and monitors displaying my vitals in red and green flashes I couldn't read because my glasses were missing. A rhythmic beep provided an annoying background.

The room smelled equal parts of antiseptic and piss. I closed my eyes and concentrated on recalling recent events. Bits and flashes jitterbugged: proposing to Abigail, gunshots, white pain. I found and pressed a call button.

The nurse enthused about me being "back with us" and settled my glasses onto my face.

To my question about what happened, she responded, "People sometimes block out physical trauma." She smoothed an IV line. "Are you up for visitors? Two ladies have been waiting."

"What time is it?"

"Sunday, half past eleven."

I had lost more than a day. "Sure. I feel fine, except for the Foley tube."

"Your morphine drip's talking." She adjusted the bed to raise my head. "I'll get them."

Abigail wore a wonderful smile and carried in a planter with paperwhites. I tried to reach her to get a hug. A jolt of pain dissuaded me. I pursed my lips and made a kissing sound.

Lizzie slumped in, her face gray underneath hastily applied makeup. "I am so sorry, Seamus." Her gaze focused on the floor. "It's all my fault. I should never have gotten you involved."

Abigail put an arm around her. "Look, that's the same bullshit line Seamus tried to use on me after I was wounded in his house. I'm a big girl and make my own decisions, and he's a big boy and makes his own decisions. Right, Seamus?"

I tried to nod, couldn't pull it off. "I'm fuzzy on what happened."

Lizzie choked back a sob.

Abigail pulled her in tight. "Chad fatally shot his father and tried to shoot Elisabeth next, but you took one for your ex. Have they told you the extent of your damages? No? It entered the upper left quadrant of your back." She disengaged from Lizzie and pointed on herself. "You'll have a nice pucker there. It expanded and blew out a fair piece of your chest. They've sewed you up pretty well, but your days of posing for 'body beautiful' posters are done."

"Permanent damage?"

"Scar tissue for sure. They need to evaluate your left arm function. But, you're lucky to be here. By the time I made sure Chad and his weapon were secure and got to you, I was afraid we'd lost you."

"Sorry to disappoint."

"Yeah. Yeah. You owe your life to your son. He applied direct pressure on your spurting artery, which kept you alive long enough for the EMTs and emergency room doctors to save you. Your left lung collapsed. You owe the blood bank forever from nearly bleeding out. The doctors told us your excellent physical condition probably made the difference. You're looking at some serious rehab time."

"Chad?"

"He came in shooting," Lizzie said. "There's nothing Abigail could have done."

"Dead?"

Abigail tipped her head in assent.

"Lizzie," I said, "I don't blame Abigail. I don't blame you. I blame Chad. He acted perfectly normal traveling with us and while you guys were at my house. Do we know why?"

Abigail gave Lizzie a little hug. "My intel. I overheard some conversations I probably wasn't supposed to. A joint task force was meeting in the room next to where they put me in the police station. Chad's import-export business was mainly drugs with a few other things to disguise it. High-level management, not retail."

"Learning that," Lizzie said, "might have killed Al anyway. But it still doesn't answer the why."

From my stupor came another thought. "Paddy's okay?"

"He's in a hotel." Lizzie sighed. "He said he was never setting foot in that house again. I think he's working with his partners at LT2P in case the

FBI arrests him tomorrow like they did Lisa. You know they've denied her bail because they claim she's a flight risk?"

I was having a hard time keeping up with Lizzie's rapid-fire speech. My arms and legs grew heavy, and my eyes closed of their own volition. What could only be Abigail's hand stroked my cheek.

"We'll let you rest," she said. "But Elisabeth needs to ask you a favor."

Lizzie demurred and Abigail talked over her. "If not him, you need someone else, and you need to know now. He's the best. Ask him."

Her hand left my face, and I opened my eyes in time to see Abigail give Lizzie a little shove toward the bed. "Don't apologize, just ask."

Lizzie caught her balance. She looked toward the ceiling, maybe praying for guidance or looking for the right words, I don't know. "To deal with all the crap Al left me, I've secured legal counsel. Based on his recommendation we'll keep the appointment Al had with the FBI to show I'm willing to cooperate. You know my finances are a mess. I've already heard from Al's partners, who, I'm sure, are unaware of my planned meeting. They'll collect *beaucoup* bucks on their key man life. They expressed their deepest condolences and without taking a breath wanted me to know they plan to buy Al's share. I know this is asking too—"

Abigail cleared her throat.

"Right," Lizzie said. "Will you help me understand my finances and help me deal with the former partners and the feds? Please?"

"Sure." Exhaustion weighed down my eyelids. Abigail had not answered my question. I forced my eyes open. "I'd like to talk to Abigail alone. Just for a minute."

I waited until the door closed. "You didn't answer my question."

Her faced tightened. "Priorities changed."

I clamped my eyes shut. "Is that your final answer?"

She put down the side railing and perched a haunch on the bed. She held my near hand with both of hers, one thumb caressing my hand as a metronome caresses time. "I love you more than I've ever loved anyone. I'm not cut out for marriage, Seamus. I can be a one-man woman. I want to be a one-man woman and for you to be that man. But I can't say yes. Saying yes would give away part of who I am. You'd want to tell me I can't do something. Oh, Seamus."

I sucked in a gaspy breath, the kind you take when you are trying hard not to cry, but know it won't work.

"Shh. Don't say you wouldn't tell me what to do, that you'd never ask me to give up being a bodyguard. I know you wouldn't, but I know you'd want to. I love you, you big Irish lug. I wish there were another way."

FORTY-FIVE

ON THE AFTERNOON BEFORE MEETING with the feds in New York, Patrick held tightly to Cindy's hand as they strolled the paths along New Jersey's Palisades. At what Patrick figured was three miles away from their Fort Lee hotel, he suggested they should head back.

Cindy dropped his hand and slid her arm around his waist. "If you don't start talking or pick up the pace, by the time we get to the hotel you'll have been silent longer than your grandmother ever was."

A grin flitted across his face; he knew she hoped it would. "Well, a little hyperbole never killed anyone. I don't even know where to start. I think I do, but by the time I form the words a new thought takes hold. My concentration right now is measured in nanoseconds."

"So do what you accuse me of: talk until you figure out what you want to say."

That brought him to smile. Why not? His way wasn't working and, if he had learned nothing else, he'd learned sharing his thoughts with Cindy made his concerns easier, lighter. "What kind of a person am I? I should be celebrating Abigail's news that Dad's on the road to recovery. But instead, I'm thinking of broken families. What drives a person to kill his father? Was Chad behind the kidnapping or is there something else I don't understand?"

He cinched in his arm and gave hers a squeeze, felt her press against him. "I can't get the images out of my mind. Seeing the spray of blood and tissue when the bullet hit Dad. How cool Abigail was. And how certain. She fired and called nine-one-one. Like it was another day at the office. Even my mother was strong."

Patrick stopped and pointed them toward the Hudson River. He saw, but did not see, the sailboats tacking in the fresh breeze. He gave Cindy another squeeze, wondered what she was thinking, but knew he had to go first—talk out his issues.

"You know what I was thinking right before the gunshots? I was wondering if I'd be the best man and whether they'd get married before or after our little one arrives." He disengaged his hand, patted her belly, and intertwined their fingers again. "How self-centered is that? My only problem with my father and Abigail getting together is that, separately, neither one of them gets shot, but put them together . . ."

Cindy smacked his shoulder. "You're bad, Patrick. And I've been meaning to ask about 'slap hands.' "

A little weight lifted from his shoulders. "Yeah, but I'm 'good' bad. Right? So, slap hands. It's a game of reflexes. Hold your elbows by your sides and hands out in front with your palms up." He placed his hands palms down on top of hers. "Now the object is for you to use one or both of your hands to slap mine before I can pull my hands away."

"And if I slap you?"

"You stay on the bottom. If you miss we trade places, and I try to slap your hands. Dad is all fast twitch muscle. He never loses at this game—not to me, not to anyone. I realized the only way I would beat him was if he became old and feeble—and maybe not even then. So we stopped playing."

"And your father, has he conceded anything to you?"

"Arm wrestling. I took up crew and he was toast. So, why can't I be like my father and decide my mother didn't know anything, wasn't part of the Jerk's plans?"

He picked up the pace. Cindy caught up, matched his stride. "Why do you say that?"

"Abigail said he agreed to help Mom figure out her finances and stuff."

"You think agreeing to help her means he's decided she's blameless? Consider it this way: helping her control her finances means he gets to see them all. He gets to follow the money. Maybe he's not sure either."

Her idea had merit. But why would his father care? He had been married to the woman and she threw him over. Into his fog of questioning he realized Cindy had repeated a question.

"You do realize none of us is perfect. Whatever your mother did or did not do is over and done. My father was a diplomat, for Pete's sake. He lied all the time. I spent my first twenty-two years unsuccessfully parsing whatever he said. Compared to him, your parents are normal. I think you're sittin' pretty, Mr. Patrick McCree. You have a woman who is crazy about you and thinks she's the luckiest person in the world. You're soon to be a father."

"Well, there is this minor little matter of the FBI tomorrow."

"They want you to turn on Lisa. They'll trump up a bunch of charges and tell you they'll all go away if you rat out Lisa. They think you're Sherlock's right-hand man and they want—or maybe need—you to testify against her."

"They're in for some serious disappointment. I haven't done jack to warrant their interest, and I'll tell them everyone knows Sherlock has to be a guy—no girl could be that good!"

"Smile when you say that, mister."

"I'm practicing for tomorrow. You know I consider Lisa and Tom and Pete to be my second family. Families need to stick together."

"They do, which means no more putting yourself in risky positions because soon our *Liebchen* will be counting on you. Here's a secret, Patrick: all families are dysfunctional. All families are filled with doubtful relations. Regardless, we choose to procreate and bring another generation into a screwed-up world. Why? Because we're stupid?"

Patrick stopped and tried to spin her so he could look at her full on, but she wriggled away from his hold, snared his hand, and hauled him down the path.

"No!" She threw her head back and laughed. "Because we're filled with irrational hormones and they make us horny as hell and—"

"And that problem we know how to solve. Speaking of which, do you still have *the* letter I sent you?"

"*The letter?* Oh, yes. I'm saving it for blackmail should I ever need it."

EPILOGUE

(New Year's Eve)

THE END OF ONE YEAR; the beginning of another. I have long preferred to spend New Year's Eve in quiet contemplation of the past and of the future. This year opened full of promise with my mother and me having a great time on our road trip. She was doing fabulously. I was content, although in retrospect I was starting to strain at the bit of an undefined future tied to my mother's care. Lizzie's appearance in my Cincinnati kitchen pumped steam into the well of my discontent, reopening veins of feelings and needs and desires. For that, I suppose, I should thank her.

At year's end, I usually create a balance sheet, so let me start with the easy stuff—the numbers. No, that's the old Seamus McCree, relying on numbers. Let me restart by admitting Abigail found the right medicine to start me recovering. Not until I became fully engaged assisting Lizzie's legal counsel in dealing with the feds did I start healing. Oh sure, physically I got stronger each day. My physical therapy was and still is shockingly painful. I relish that pain because I know it will diminish as I grow stronger. I cannot say the same thing for mental anguish.

Each time Abigail stopped by, all I could see in her eyes was her rejection. On the third day, I suggested, well maybe I told her, she should do what she does best and go be a crackerjack bodyguard for someone who needed it. That's what she's doing this evening, although I plan to Skype her at midnight. She'll take the call. I think.

It did not take me long once I dug into the Cunninghams' finances to confirm all three Antimatter Investments partners had engaged in insider trading. They'd been slick: on any given deal, only one had participated. On a smaller scale, one or both of the others would do something contrary. They kept an accounting of the pluses and minuses in the Excel files Paddy had found, which I had not had time to review while all the drama was going on. Their crimes would probably have gone undetected unless someone involved squealed to the feds.

Lizzie found, or claimed to have found, her husband's fake passport in the glove compartment of his car, along with a couple million dollars of bearer bonds. I don't believe there is any way we'll know what his real plans were. My suspicion is he planned to leave the country and hoped to take Lizzie with him.

Speaking of people with plans to leave the country: neither Sally nor Jerome talked. When he was captured, Jerome's phone contained a picture of Uncle Mike's Crown Vic—the one I had been driving—zeroed in on the license plate. His map app contained directions to the address on the registration—Uncle Mike's place in Waltham. As Abigail said, "They don't know why, but it wasn't to deliver a bouquet of flowers."

Blood on Sally's knife linked her to Kaylee Coffin's murder, and the prosecutors charged her for the carjacking and two murders. Because no one knew for sure what Albert Cunningham III did or didn't do, the prosecutors did not charge her with his kidnapping and its related offenses. Police found the carjacked car in the same lot where Jerome's stolen Honda came from. Apparently the circumstantial evidence was not sufficient to prosecute Jerome for the double homicide. Sally's silence meant the most they could pin on Jerome were a bunch of auto theft charges. He pled out and is serving prison time.

My family was indirectly responsible for Tommy Kennedy's death. Police informants said the local drug lord heard Kennedy had been asking questions about him. Not realizing it had to do with Cunningham's kidnapping, he feared Kennedy planned to take over and made a preemptive strike. I feel terrible that it happened, but to my way of thinking, Kennedy sowed the seeds of his death by the life he chose. I dithered over contacting Kennedy's daughter to tell her how sorry I was at his death, but in the end I wasn't sure what I would say and let the time slip away.

The Behemoth sale went through on the terms I had renegotiated. Unfortunately, with Lisa Latoya languishing in jail awaiting trial and Paddy sidelined facing the possibility of his own charges, the corporation put a guy in charge of their operations with no feel for that business or client relations. The auditing firms are eating their lunch. The kids will be well-compensated for their startup, but they won't be wealthy enough to stop working. I'll get my money back on my investment in LT2P with a small return.

I'm not complaining, though. Paddy's decision to make the other outsize investment was pure genius. Once the IPO lock-up period is over in another couple of months, Paddy will have quadrupled the money I had before I turned my investments over to him.

Did you notice I've slipped into my comfort zone: talking money and finances? Okay, let me finish. Before I ran out of cash, I signed a mortgage on the Cincinnati house, which still hasn't sold. I needed a place to live and recuperate, and with some trepidation, I returned to the house. Being shot had one beneficial effect. The ghosts from the shooting at my house no longer had power over me. Lizzie loaned me the mortgage money on better terms than the bank. More on her in a minute.

First Paddy.

Cindy, using her investigative reporter bully pulpit, launched an attack on the FBI, its presumed use of intelligence from the NSA and the probably illegal information gained through a FISA court-approved monitoring of U.S. citizens while in country. She used a combination of the lack of public charges against Lisa Latoya, the lack of bail, and the government's position that all evidence against her was classified as exhibit one. The crap they put Paddy through was her exhibit number two. The government threatened both her and her employer, neither of whom buckled.

The day after Christmas, the FBI charged Lisa with a list of crimes long enough to go down one of her arms and up the other using fine print. When Paddy visited Lisa a couple of days later, he reported she claimed virtually all the charges were "complete bullshit," and the few with merit would "be damn hard for them to prove." The same day they charged Lisa, the FBI informally told Paddy he was no longer "a party of interest." They did not apologize for the harm they had caused him personally or professionally. They did, however, offer him a job. He politely refused.

The FBI couldn't prove Paddy had broken any federal laws, but he was not pure. While waiting for the EMTs and police to arrive, he had cloned Chad's phone memory. Using that information, we determined Chad's phone had called Laurence Kleindeinst at precisely the time Kleindeinst claimed Cunningham had called to make the Savannah reservations. Paddy reminded us Chad was a good mimic of his father's voice. "He fooled Kleindeinst, and then the note from Kleindeinst that we found at my mom's house fooled the Jerk into thinking one of his partners set up a last-minute meeting in Savannah."

Chad also maintained a text conversation with a burner phone detailing our plans, including turn-by-turn directions of the trip from Lizzie's house to mine in Cincinnati. He sent a final text shortly before Sally and Cunningham's attempted escape in Duck, alerting the receiving party—who had to be Jerome Rozelle—that Paddy and Abigail had discovered them.

Retained historical data from various of Chad's phone apps allowed me to confirm his import-export business was drug related, and he had been laundering their money. Big time. Chad had put the keylogger program on his father's computer to front-run his trades. To safeguard the process from discovery, he sent the information to Lizzie's computer. It had worked well for him until he made one major purchase he didn't realize his father had decided against at the last minute. Cunningham had been correct to reject that disaster, which had cost Chad's fund nearly twenty-five million dollars. He needed to earn it back before the drug bosses found out. I surmised Chad's plan was to contract his father's kidnapping to keep him out of commission long enough to steal the gold and loot the joint investment account. I suspect he acted before he had thought everything through. Once Chad decided on murder to cover up his theft, he spent considerable effort framing Lizzie, probably to give himself time to disappear. Police found the stolen gold at Chad's home, along with preliminary drafts of both the ransom note and fake divorce papers. I'm pretty sure Lizzie never knew of the gold's existence.

My discovery of the money laundering led the feds to confiscate all those monies—a coup they trumpeted nationally. Thankfully, my part remained hidden. I did not need any drug lords pissed at me for their missing millions.

Lizzie's lawyer and I were able to convince the feds that Lizzie's only mistake was marrying the Jerk. They chose not to prosecute her for any of his criminal actions. Realizing what her husband had done, she wanted nothing to do with any of his money. She used the life insurance proceeds to retire the mortgage on the house, so the antique car trust he had set up had no debt. The trust retained the Truverts to maintain the house and grounds. Lizzie sold his foreign investments and repaid the hedge fund investors. Investors in the Challenging Opportunities Fund received full value once the fund liquidated its holdings. She stuck the rest of his money in a fund, which various federal and state agencies will fight over as they determine whose fines will be paid first.

Fortunately for Lizzie, her personal assets—those she received from our divorce settlement all those many years ago—were hers free and clear.

"I had dreams of going back to school," Lizzie told me. "I'm not blaming you, Seamus, but I gave them away by chasing false securities. First your job, then Al's. I want to reboot and pick up those deferred dreams. I've complained for years about how nonprofits are run. Now I'm going to do something about it." She returned full time to our alma mater, Boston University, to get a Public and Nonprofit MBA.

Not long before Mom's release from Sugarbush, I received a call from Lizzie. She was doing well in her first semester at BU and wanted to let me know she had signed a lease for a larger apartment so my mother could move in with her.

"She wants to move in with you?" I blurted.

Lizzie guffawed. "Believe it or not. Feel free to check with her. And Seamus, this is my treat. It'll only be until I get my degree. I don't know what I'll do next, but you'll be on your feet by then. It's the least I can do, so don't argue."

I called Mom and caught her on the road doing her P.T. Barnum of darts thing. She'd hired a manager who arranges for her to fly all over the country putting on charity darts events. I want her vitality when I'm seventy-five. After catching up on news, I broached the subject of living with Lizzie in my characteristically subtle style. "I thought you didn't like her."

"I didn't like *that* Elisabeth. This one is the one you fell in love with. She's different. I like her. She visited Sugarbush two or three times a week to spend time with me. We get along fine, and she knows I need somewhere quiet but don't want to live alone. And no, I am not suggesting you two get back together. You and Abigail deserve each other."

Her comment got me to thinking—something I'm supposed to be excellent at—but I had been focusing on things financial, not things of the heart. Surprise, right? A couple of weeks ago on a ramble with Alice in one of Cincinnati's larger parks where I can let her off lead, I revisited Abigail's words rejecting my marriage proposal and arrived at an actionable idea.

It's two minutes before the next year begins. Now's the time to execute the plan. I decide not to use Skype and instead call her cell phone. My heart beats hard while I listen to it ring. To her hello I respond with, "I still love you, you know. Now use your imagination. I'm on bended knee."

"Seamus," her drawn-out warning comes down the line.

"Please hear me out." When she doesn't object I continue. "Will you, Abigail Hancock, take me, Seamus Anselm McCree, to be your business partner with benefits from this day forward: for richer or poorer, in sickness and in health, to love and to cherish, to share the joys and challenges of the personal protection services business, to participate in wild and abandoned lovemaking when we are together, and to put up with until death do us part? Please say yes.

"If you respond in the affirmative, I have arranged for the country to celebrate with fireworks in ten, nine, eight . . ."

Author's Note

NO NOVEL IS CREATED IN a vacuum. Everything that is screwed up, I've done myself. Things done correctly probably required assistance from others including, but not limited to, Brad Jackson, Carol Baldridge, Dave Stull, Dottie Caster, Elaine Douts, Frank Coyne, Hank Phillippi Ryan, Jan Rubens, Jim Wilson, Julie Spergel, Karla Brandenburg, Kristina Stanley, Maggie Toussaint, Nancy J. Cohen, Paula Gail Benson, Karen Miller, Karen Phillips, Polly Iyer, Ramona DeFelice Long, Rhonda Lane, Rita Stull, Sam Morton (who, sadly, has passed away), Terry Odell, and Tina Whittle.

I enjoy reading stories that use real places, and I have followed that practice in this novel—mostly. This is fiction. Occasionally the story requires a new road or marsh or business that you won't find on any map. Stories are of a time; towns and cities change, real businesses come and go, technologies are created, morph, and disappear. This continual change is a hazard of using reality in fiction, a risk I gladly accept and hope you will also. Other than Karen Miller (who is real, but not in real estate; she won the right to have a character named after her), I've made up everything else.

Seamus, Paddy, and I have not spent so many hours together creating this tale of their family, friends, and enemies because we were bored and had nothing else to do. We did it for you, the readers. Thank you all for spending time with my fictional creations and letting them share their lives with you.

James M. Jackson
Amasa, Michigan

James M. Jackson authors the Seamus McCree series: ANT FARM, BAD POLICY, CABIN FEVER, DOUBTFUL RELATIONS, and EMPTY PROMISES (2017). Jim has also published an acclaimed book on contract bridge, ONE TRICK AT A TIME: *How to start winning at bridge*, as well as numerous short stories and essays. He splits his time between the deep woods of Michigan's Upper Peninsula and the open spaces of Georgia's Lowcountry.

His website is http://jamesmjackson.com.

37303902R00151

Made in the USA
San Bernardino, CA
14 August 2016